ROSIE BEST

Skulk

STRANGE CHEMISTRY
An Angry Robot imprint
and a member of the Osprey Group

Lace Market House
54-56 High Pavement
Nottingham
NG1 1H
UK

Angry Robot/Osprey Publishing
PO Box 3985
New York
NY 10185-3985
USA

www.strangechemistrybooks.com
Strange Chemistry #18

A Strange Chemistry paperback original 2013
1

Cover by Steven Meyer-Rassow
Set in Sabon by EPubServices

Distributed in the United States by Random House, Inc., New York.

ISBN 978 1 90884 470 5
Ebook ISBN 978 1 90884 471 2

Printed in the United States of America

9 8 7 6 5 4 3 2 1

SKULK

Run free amidst the shadows of the dark streets of London

To some, Meg Banks' life might look perfect – she lives in a huge house in West London, goes to a prestigious school, and has famous parents. Only Meg knows the truth: her tyrannical mother rules the house and her shallow friends can talk about nothing but boys and drinking. Meg's only escape is her secret life as a graffiti artist.

While outtagging one night, Meg witnesses the dying moments of a fox... a fox that shapeshifts into a man. As he dies, he gives Meg a beautiful and mysteriousgemstone. It isn't long before Meg realises that she's also inherited his power to shift and finds an incredible new freedom in fox form.

She is plunged into the shadowy underworld of London, the territory of the five warring groups of shapeshifters – the Skulk, the Rabble, the Conspiracy, the Horde, and the Cluster. Someone is after her gemstone, however, someone who can twist nature to his will. Meg must discover the secret of the stone and unite the shapeshifters before her dream of freedom turns into a nightmare.

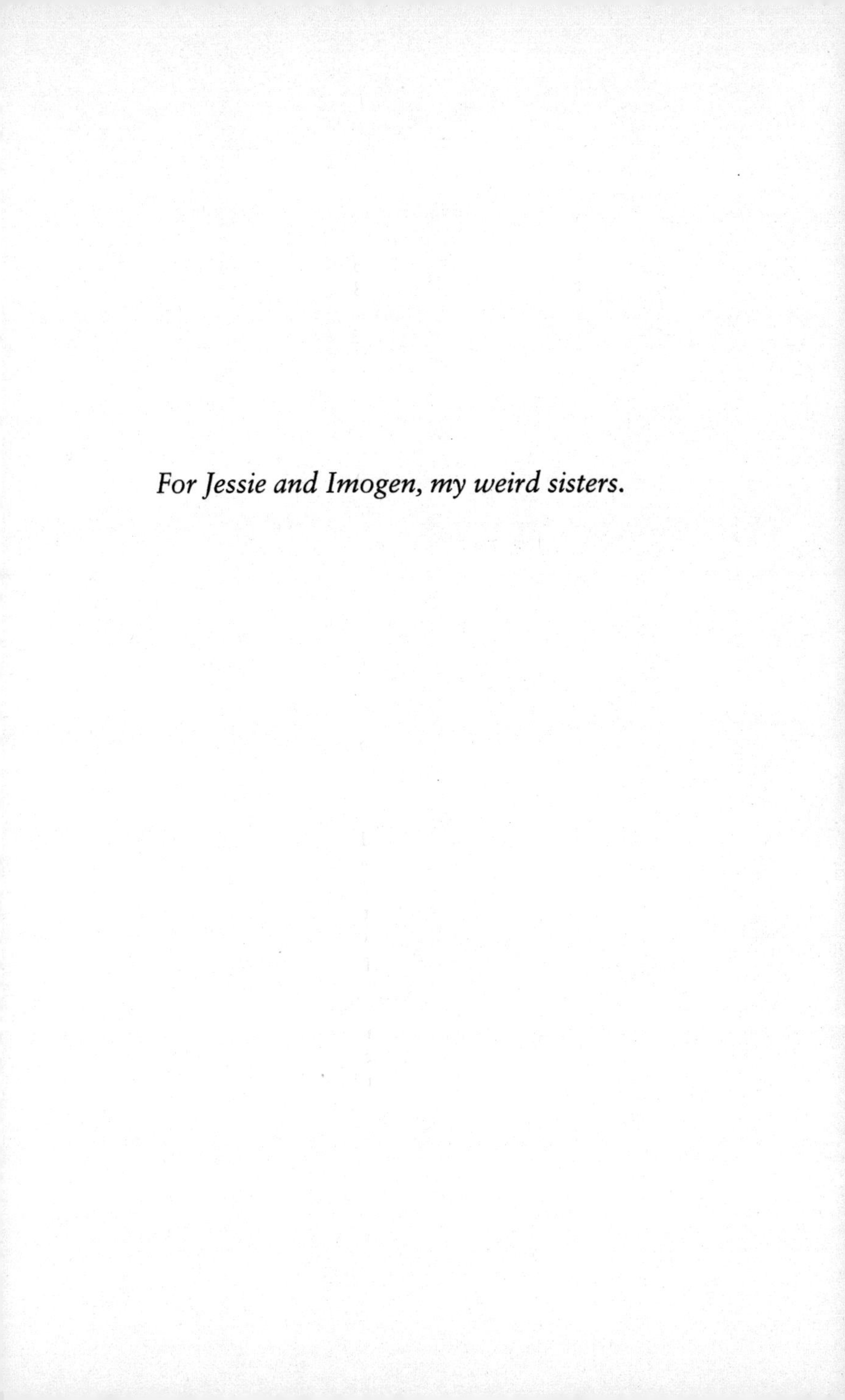

For Jessie and Imogen, my weird sisters.

Chapter One

Sitting half in and half out of my bedroom window, a foot resting on the fire escape, I checked myself over one last time. Phone. Oyster card. Keys. Mace. Paint.

I hoped I wasn't going to need the first four.

I climbed out and the window slid into place behind me with the kind of silence you have to work at. It'd taken a week and four whole cans of WD-40.

The freezing air hit the back of my throat and I shivered. There's something about the night between 2 and 5am that crawls into your bones if you let it, leaves you breathless and shivering. You can do one of two things – stay safe and warm in bed, or get out and keep moving.

I tiptoed down the fire escape and landed with a crunch in the alley round the back of the house, between the big black cars. Their polished bodywork glittered in the moonlight, like the carapaces of giant sleeping beetles. At the security gates I tapped out the code that kept our little bunch of houses locked away from the rest of the city; fortress, madhouse and ghetto in one neat silky package.

Lingering in the shadow by the wall, I zipped up my old grey hoodie, pulled the hood up over my face and shifted the backpack on my shoulders, feeling the reassuring slosh-clank of the aerosol cans against my back. I looked like a troublemaker – but an anonymous one.

A flock of CCTV cameras perched all along the fence, silently judging the passers-by. Even at this time of night the footpath through the park wasn't deserted. A homeless man sat in one of the patches of light beneath a wrought-iron streetlamp with a scabby terrier at his side, and a lone mad jogger bounced past me in skintight Lycra shorts, fluorescent headphones swinging with every stride. I'd seen him before. Was this the middle of the night to him, or the first hours of tomorrow?

I heard a screech of drunken laughter and four girls stumbled onto the path in front of me. Their vintage frocks hung wonkily off their shoulders and one of them was limping along in a single Jimmy Choo.

They wove close enough for me to make out their faces, and my hands flew to my hood, pulling it right down. Cold water seemed to flood through my veins. I stumbled and nearly stopped in my tracks, but forced myself to keep putting one foot in front of the other.

It was Ameera and Jewel, and Mary, and that flautist Mary plays in the orchestra with whose name I can never remember.

I hung my head and swallowed. A hot flush of embarrassment flooded up my neck. I knew they'd be out tonight – they'd talked about nothing else at school that day. They'd invited me to go with them, but...

Well, they were walking home pissed at 2am with one Jimmy Choo on. I'd bet my inheritance that they'd spent the evening in a hot, dark room, jumping up and down to bad music with sexist lyrics, straining to hear horrible pick-up lines from boys whose attention I could not possibly care less about.

I like Jewel and Ameera. I like hanging out with them. I like alcohol, too. But I don't do clubbing. I just don't see what part of it is supposed to be fun.

They were walking right towards me. I fixed my gaze on the floor and tried to keep my pace steady and my heart from pounding right out of my throat and off down the street. A tangled, distinctive ringlet escaped from under my hood and hung right in front of my eyes, glowing dirty blonde in the street light, like a flashing neon sign saying *MEG IS HERE*. It dangled just too close to focus on, taunting me. Should I ignore it, and risk them knowing it was me, or should I move to tuck it back and risk drawing attention to myself?

And then, while I was lost in the indecision, the girls had passed me and were gone into the patchy darkness.

They were drunk. It was dark. And I looked like a tramp. We might as well have been on different continents. I paused to adjust my backpack and suck in a deep sigh of relief. I was invisible, alone on the dark path, and right now that was exactly the way I wanted it.

Sorry, guys, I thought, casting a glance over my shoulder at their disappearing backs. *I can't share this with you. This is just for me.*

I came out of the park and onto the main road, blinking in the glare. The lights here were still bright. The clubs were just starting to chuck out. Packed night buses crawled along the road. Workers in fluorescent jackets carried engineering parts out of a truck and down into the tube station.

I crossed the road and dived into the back streets. The cold air folded over me again and I could see my breath clouding in front of me. I hurried past darkened bistros and glossy converted townhouses – consultancies, dealerships, surgeries, embassies – until finally I found myself in front of a building on the edge of a leafy square. A subtle brass plaque and some finger-paintings in the windows were all that told the world this was the home of Kensington College for Girls.

My heart beat faster as I thought about going to work on the front of the building. It was painted a pristine uniform white, dotted with windows. A massive empty canvas. I could make it beautiful and alive, and *fantastically* embarrassing for the school.

But it was too public. Just loitering on the other side of the square I guessed I was burning onto the hard drives of eight or ten surveillance cameras.

Maybe one day. When I was Banksy. But not this time.

The walls around the back of the school building were just as blank and inviting, and a lot safer. They faced the combined garden/playground/Thunderdome where the

Year Seven to Nine girls, who weren't allowed out on the Square yet, spent their breaks and lunchtimes. They'd play under the big oak tree, gossip in the mud, or try to sneak a stealthy fag behind the Kit Shed.

My first and not-quite-only cigarette was smoked behind that shed. To this day I can't get a lungful of secondhand smoke without flashing back to the leathery wooden polished smell of PE equipment and the way Jewel's hands shook as she tried to light a cigarette from a safety match in the rain.

Tomorrow, if luck was on my side, the girls out in the playground would get an eyeful of searingly insightful political graffiti art. Or the deluded scrawling of a ridiculous poser. It could really go either way.

But first I had to get back there. The gate was around the side of the building, half in the next street. Beyond it there was an alley just wide enough for a car (but not wide enough for a minibus, as Miss Eggersham and Elite Coach Transport's insurance company found out that one time).

A dirty bronze padlock the size of both my fists gleamed on the black metal gate, but the gate itself was only about six feet high. I guess the school thought perverts wouldn't bother with the climb. Actually, they were right – the perverts generally hung out in the Square behind the bushes. They were surprisingly persistent, considering that the Parents' Council had shelled out for a private security firm to police the Square in plain clothes. At least once a term some creep would risk it and we'd all stand around pointing and laughing as he was arrested with nettle stings in humiliating places.

There was a stone statue by the side of the gate, a sort of knee-high roaring lion thing that we all called Henry, with at least fifty years' worth of old chewing gum stuck behind its ears. I hoisted myself up with one foot on Henry's head, one hand clutching for the cold metal spikes on top of the gate. My other foot scrabbled for a toehold on the brickwork as I flexed my arm muscles and pulled myself up.

Suddenly Henry shifted and tipped, as if he was rearing up on his hind legs, and there was a sickening second where I thought I'd lose my grip and fall hard on the spikes and be found next morning strung up on the gate in a tragic mangled mess of blood and spray paint...

I snatched my foot up, wobbled wildly for a second and then pushed up and over, toppling across the spikes. Henry slammed back onto the pavement with a crash, and I hit the ground hard on my side, the cans in the backpack digging into my ribs.

I tried to gasp for air without making a sound. Pain flared all along my side. I stuffed a hand into my mouth, balled in the sleeve of my hoodie. The dark emptiness of the sky overhead seemed to swirl around me and my head rang with the echoes of cracking stone, long after they'd faded from the street.

Nobody came running. Nothing moved in the square.

I managed to peel myself up from the ground and settled into a crouch at the foot of the wall, staying there while five minutes ticked away, just to be certain. A mangy urban fox trotted along the road as if it owned the place, but nothing else happened.

I was going to have massive bruises in the morning – but I'd got away with it. For now.

"Jesus Christ," I breathed, getting to my feet and stumbling down the dark path towards the garden.

When I finally made it I shrugged off the backpack and stretched out my shoulders, taking a second to perch on one of the picnic benches, catching my breath and staring up at my canvas.

I've been doing graffiti since I was ten. I started out mimicking the tags I saw on the street, scrawling a mixed-up form of my name on exercise books and lampposts and my mother's Bentley – she called the police when she saw it, but never suspected the criminal was right under her nose. I've expanded my artistic horizons a little since then.

I opened my backpack and pulled out the aerosol cans, and got to work with a wary glance up at the CCTV cameras that dotted the top floor. Maybe when the caretaker arrived in the morning to find the graffiti on the wall and the security computer mysteriously unplugged, they'd know for certain it was an inside job. Maybe it'd lead them straight to me somehow. I shook up the can of black, placed my finger on the button. If I was going to get expelled for this, I might as well make it worth the trouble.

Once I was into it, I hardly knew how quickly time was passing until my phone buzzed once to let me know it was 3.30. Time to step up the pace. I should be gone by 4.30, because at 5am the cleaners would come in and the street begin to wake up. The light would change from the grimy yellow streetlight-darkness to a weird grey pre-dawn light that seemed to come from everywhere all at once, and by then I ought to be already gone.

I stepped back and looked up at my work, the sketchy lines of colour that formed school desks and unemployment lines, bank statements cascading into thousands of pounds of debt, young faces twisted in despair, withering under the stress as they fought each other to get to the top of the heap. I reached into my bag for the last can, the fluorescent turquoise. Just the right colour to highlight the sickness of it all.

Don't get me wrong – *I'll* never have to claim unemployment benefit. I may never have a single penny of debt. My mother would never allow it. But that's not the point.

Or maybe it is exactly the point.

I stepped up to the wall to scrawl a shadow of stinging turquoise around the head of one of the girls.

A plastic *tunnng* sound rang in the air right behind me, and I yelped and spun around, my heart hammering. For a second I blinked against a painfully bright glare coming from the motion sensitive spotlight by the bins – I'd been careful to avoid it, but something had turned it on. My mind's eye filled the empty garden with ghouls and knife-wielding mask-wearing psychopaths, before a patch of grubby orange and grey fur stirred and my eyes adjusted enough to yank it into focus.

It was just a fox, jumping down from the high wall onto the bins. Maybe even the same one I'd seen earlier. It stood gazing right at me for a second in the piercing beam. There was something dark in its jaws. I wondered if it was a rat, but it seemed too small.

I couldn't hang around wildlife-watching. I could almost taste the dawn, the sharp tangy dip in temperature that happens around 4am. I shivered and wrapped my arms around my chest. Leaping around painting the wall had worked up a sweat, and now it was prickling on my scalp as it cooled, like dew on the grass, but more likely to give me a cold. I had to get moving – even after I was done, I still had to get back over the fence...

As the fox leapt down from the bin to the ground it stumbled, and I realised there was a patch of darkness on its flank, black against the halo of backlit orange fur. Something glistened on the ground.

It was blood.

The fox turned towards me, took a couple of unsteady steps, and collapsed, panting. It turned its black eyes on me, and then closed them and let out a pathetic whine. The thing in its mouth tumbled out onto the grass.

I should have left the fox alone. But I couldn't just let it die where it lay – even though I had no idea what I could do. As I inched towards the animal I could see that there was lots of blood, caked around a deep gash along its side.

Maybe the kind thing to do would be to try to put it out of its misery. But could I kill it in cold blood, even to end its suffering? How would I do it? Bludgeon it with a cricket bat from the Kit Shed?

Tears pricked my eyes and I blinked them away. "Well that's not going to help," I whispered.

I was about six feet away, crouching in the dewy grass, when the fox stirred. I froze, not wanting to scare it, as if it didn't have bigger problems than a paint-splattered human right now.

Its legs spasmed. It hunched down and then threw its head back. Its fur rippled along its length, like the ground during an earthquake. Its eyes opened.

A scream curled up and died in the back of my throat, and I twitched away, falling back onto my elbows.

They were human eyes. Bloodshot, but human, with white whites and grey-green irises. I whimpered, trying to crawl away, but found myself up against the Kit Shed, watching through my hands as the fox writhed and hissed and grew. A paw reached out, and then dirty fingers were clutching at the grass. Hair shrank back into naked skin and sprouted on top of the head. Leg joints popped and clicked as they twisted into elbows. The tail was gone, the ears were gone, the snout was gone; the teeth bared at me were blunt and square.

He was naked. And a man. And blood was streaming from the stretched wound in his side.

He looked at me, with those human eyes, red-rimmed and desperate. He made a deep, rattling, bubbling sound in his throat.

"No," he groaned, and his head drooped, his elbows bent. He toppled to the ground on his good side. Deep red blood trickled across his pale chest like a theatre curtain coming down. *Exeunt Omnes.* "Oh God. Please," he mouthed.

My skin crawled across my flesh like it was trying to run away, whether the rest of me was coming or not –

but I couldn't move. I couldn't think. Naked man. Fox. Blood. Blood, everywhere.

Except then there was a thought, absurd and sudden:

He's human now.

My hands slid into my pockets, numb and slippery fingers grasping. *Keys. Mace. Oyster card.*

Phone.

999.

"Ambulance please." It was someone else's voice, hoarse and squeaky.

The man-fox – the fox-man – his head rose and his eyes widened. Shock? A tear trickled down his face and he suddenly reached around, a trembling hand swishing through the pool of dew and blood. It closed on something and he cradled it to his chest.

"He's… I think he's been stabbed. His side. Kensington College for Girls. Kensington Square. Round the back in the garden." The voice – not mine, surely I'd be stammering – fell silent. My hand fell into my lap. The phone felt heavy as I slipped it back into my pocket.

"Girl," he whispered. "Please."

He held out his hand. There was something lying in the palm, small and softly rounded. It was a stone. That was what the fox had had in its mouth. Not prey, but a stone.

"Please," he said again. "The fog."

There was no fog. The night sky had been cloudy, but the air was clear.

"Take it." His gaze focused and flickered to the stone.

For a moment I still didn't move or speak. Then I think I shook my head, and swallowed.

"I called an ambulance."

"No," he breathed. "You... have to take it away... from here..." The strain of uttering a full sentence looked devastating and his head drooped again, his mouth hanging open. A thin line of pink-tinged saliva dripped from it onto the grass. "Take." He managed to raise his head just enough to look me in the eye. More tears were fighting their way down his face. He said nothing else, but that look did something to me.

I tipped onto my knees and shuffled towards him.

"Do – Do you have–?" the absurdity of choosing whether to say *children* or *cubs* made me stop.

"Nnn... nn..." he couldn't form the word but I think he shook his head.

Blood bubbled at the corner of his mouth as I reached his outstretched hand. The stone was a gem, I thought – a polished black cabochon with a bright white star in its depths. Surely he wanted it to go to someone?

"Take it where?" I asked. Warm tears stung my cheeks.

"...way," he whispered.

As I reached out and touched the stone, he fell back, his eyes half-open and empty.

I should have felt something, when he died – a shiver, *something*. But all I felt was the cold surface of the stone in my blood-slippery palm.

I heard sirens.

Chapter Two

The fire escape creaked under me, sounding a hundred times louder than it had on the way down. I paused under Mum and Dad's window with my heartbeat thumping between my ears. I waited for the sound of the wooden frame pulling up, a voice yelling "MARGARET ELIZABETH BANKS!" as if *she* could be summoned into existence to replace the crushing disappointment lurking under the window.

Nothing.

My head swam. I realised, with a sick twist in my throat, that the journey home was a blur of lights and the thump of concrete against my soles. I wasn't sure when I arrived home. I had no idea how I got back across the gate.

There was a corpse in the school garden. He was lying with his arm stretched out, naked, bleeding. Bled.

I took the rest of the stairs slowly, and only when I'd slipped through my window and locked it behind me did I put my hands into my pockets. Sitting on my bed in the rusty glow of the street lamps outside, bloodstained fingers pulled out keys, mace, phone. A shaky, messy swipe of sticky fingertips, and my recent call log shone through the dim red streaks. 999, Monday, 03.54.

The other thing in my pocket was cold and smooth. I turned it over in my fingers, not pulling it out yet.

I had to wash my hands.

I stumbled into the en suite and jabbed at the light switch with my elbow. In the mirror above the sink I saw my reflection lurch into view. I looked like a zombie. My face was pale and my eyes were bleary.

My hands left more red streaks on the wide white bowl as I leaned over and rested my forehead on the cool mirror. For a hysterical second I thought of leaving the bloody handprints there for Gail the housekeeper to find in the morning. It'd serve her right if they gave her a heart attack.

You love finding things for my mother to freak out about. I'll give you both something to freak out about.

I put my hand in my pocket and my fingers closed on the smooth stone again. I pulled it out and examined it, turning it over in the harsh light. It fitted comfortably into my palm, about the size of an egg and perfectly oval.

It wasn't black. As I washed the film of blood away under the tap, the stone shone a deep blue with a bright white six-pointed star right at the centre. It happens sometimes when a gemstone cracks deep inside, at just the right angle to catch the light.

Did that mean this was a giant sapphire? It was polished up, to show off the star, like a gem would be. I remembered seeing one a bit like it before, years ago. I'd spent a day lurking around the display room at Christie's, waiting for Mum to decide just how much she was willing to spend on a footstool that had once belonged to Oliver Cromwell.

But this was *huge* for a precious stone, and I'd seen some whoppers in my time.

Then again, there wasn't much point getting incredulous over that when it'd been bequeathed to me by a man who was also a fox.

I let the stone slip into the sink with a ringing *clonk*, and staggered back to sit perched on the edge of the bath, my still-pinkish hands clenched on the porcelain. The shock of the cold surface helped a little. The bath was real, my aching soles and the gleaming tiles were real, the Fortnum & Mason handcream and the streaks of blood and the enormous cabochon sapphire in the sink were all real.

I should've known it wasn't a dream. My dreams were never like this.

Although there was one chilling similarity.

I have to clear this up before Mum sees it.

At least in real life I had some chance of managing it.

I had a shower first, leaving my blood-spattered hoodie and jeans in the bath, where they couldn't stain the plush pinkish carpet. I scrubbed myself and then the sink, not bothering to wrap myself in a towel until I was done. I dripped nakedly on the horrible carpet as I padded to and fro, scooping the clothes into a plastic bag and sluicing down the bath, wishing I could persuade Mum to let me redecorate in a colour that didn't make me feel like I was washing in Candyland.

Back in the bedroom I stuffed the plastic bag back into the backpack and dived into the recesses of one of the wardrobes where there was a battered, neglected leather trunk. Pink and yellow flowers dotted its surface in crackling acrylic paint – *Flowers*, by Meg Banks, aged six years and four months. Inside, a layer of ballet programmes and school art projects hid a second layer of old diaries and secret, faintly rebellious cartoons.

Below that there was the real hidden compartment, just big enough for a backpack full of aerosol paint and some old clothes.

A secret within a secret. I was proud of how sneaky it was. I knew it'd worked when Mum confronted me with the contents of one of the diaries – standard stuff about how I hated that Gail went through my things – but never mentioned what was in the bottom of the trunk.

I sat on the floor, cradling the sapphire in my hands like a delicate bird's egg.

And now? I glanced at my watch. It was nearly 5am. I shut my eyes, tiredness sitting heavily across my shoulders, but in the darkness I could still see twisting limbs, fur crawling back inside skin like a thousand microscopic burrowing worms, and the eyes – human eyes in an inhuman face.

And now he was dead.

I had no idea who – no, stranger than that, I had no idea *what* he was. But I didn't want him to be dead. I never managed to ask him if there was anyone in his life, anyone I should be breaking the news to.

After another few silent moments on my knees, turning

the stone over in the shaft of light spilling out from the bathroom, I stood up and went to my laptop, to do what I always do when I don't know something. I googled it.

Obviously, *fox shapeshifter* got me nothing remotely fact-based. I read the Wikipedia entry on shapeshifters four times, in case there was something I'd missed, but couldn't get past the idea of scouring lists of mythical figures for hints about the man I'd just seen fall down and die in my school playground. After that I poked around paranormal research sites for a while, but couldn't escape the distinct whiff of bullshit.

Frustrated, I clicked away. Habit hooked me and I opened a private browser and rattled off the address for graffitilondon.com. The first topic on the board: *New E3 art, Waterloo Bridge*. My heart lifted a little. E3 was my total hero. He had a genius for colour, composition, positioning, *everything*. I clicked through, hoping someone had taken a picture, though I almost didn't have to – I trusted, I *knew*, that it was going to be beautiful. I suppose that's what it's like to be a fan.

The piece was right on the underside of the bridge, where it passed over the Victoria Embankment. It was a figure of a man with wings, falling through cloud. The photo wasn't the greatest quality, but I could make out the clean stencil lines on his dark skin and coppery wings, and the splatters of silver and white dripping all around him as he fell.

Unnamed, as usual, the poster had written underneath the picture. *But E3's definitely using Icarus symbolism here so I'm calling it Icarus ☺.*

I scanned down to the comments, expecting a chorus of agreement… and my heart sank.

Nice. but his tag's not E3. it's two hearts on top of each other.

It's two 3s with one reversed, retard.

your wrong its a flower.

my god how arE YOU ALL SO DUMB IT DOESN'T MATTER WHAT HE'S CALLED I <3 HIM.

omg E3 stans r the worst hes a banksy wannabe raghead.

I loved E3's work, but the mystery over his tag had caused so many flame wars I was surprised the graffitilondon servers hadn't melted. We all knew how this would go – the volunteer mods would lead the forum in a rousing chorus of Don't Feed The Trolls, which wouldn't work, and then they'd spend a couple of hours threatening and then liberally applying the banhammer. They were going to have a busy night and I didn't envy them one bit.

I shut the browser with a weary sigh and lay down on my bed, wrapped in a towel, holding the stone up above my head and turning it slowly in the mingled blue-and-yellow light from the computer screen and the streetlights outside my window.

I might never know who the fox-man was. I might be left with nothing but a story nobody would believe and a stone I could never show anyone. My stomach twisted urgently, selfishly, at the thought. This couldn't be it. I wanted to know more.

How did he get the stone? Why was he carrying it with him?

And how did he get to be a fox, anyway? Could he turn back whenever? Maybe he was cursed... maybe it was something he had touched...

I dropped the stone with a little cry. It dropped onto my chest and lay there, heavy, cold and solid.

Of course, if it was cursed, it would've changed me already, right?

My stomach grumbled, and I rolled over to glance at the clock. 5.27.

I could lie awake for an hour, buzzing with weirdness, waiting for my alarm to go off so I could get up and join my parents for our normal silent breakfast: a bowl of muesli with skimmed milk, and a cup of herbal tea without any sugar, while Dad circled things in the *Financial Times* and Mum scrawled notes in the margins of her Cabinet memos in violent red ink.

I could do that. Or... I could do something else.

A couple of minutes later, clothed and dry, I swung carefully over the creaky step at the top of the stairs and headed down the dark, perfumed staircase.

The lilies on Mum and Dad's landing glowed like alien parasites in the faint dawn light from the staircase window. I held my breath as I passed their door, but nothing stirred.

The shock of the freezing tiles on my bare feet as I stepped into the entrance hall sent adrenaline pumping through me. I stopped by the hall table and leaned there for a second, my palms sticky on the polished oak and my legs suddenly unsteady. A wave of tiredness hit me and I thought about just going back to bed for an hour. Then my stomach rumbled again, sounding like a roll of thunder in the silent hallway, and I willed it quiet, pricking my ears for any sign of movement from upstairs. There was nothing.

The kitchen echoed to the soft slap of my feet on the tiles. Dim steely reflections of myself followed me across the room, like ghosts. The enormous main refrigerator loomed in one corner, next to the walk-in pantry. They were too large for a family of three with just two staff, and locked, of course. I eyed the gleaming padlock, but steered clear. That wasn't my target for today – it was like the Everest of rebellion. If I broke into the Party Fridge I wanted to have plenty of time, equipment, and possibly a Sherpa and a rescue helicopter on standby.

I pulled open a cupboard and rooted around until I found an open, half-used bag of peanuts. Perfect. I poured about half the contents into my palm and put the rest back, then leaned on the central island, surrounded by low-hanging saucepans, chomping on my spoils.

They were gone pretty quickly and I lingered in the kitchen, wondering what else I might find in the cupboards. The brushed steel clock read 5.45. I still had a bit of time...

And that was how I came to be standing by an open cupboard when Hilde turned her key in the back door. She was early. I yelped guiltily at the sound and jumped back as she walked in, her chef's whites slung over one arm, her enormous black handbag swinging beneath them.

"Meg!" Her face flushed and darkened in the dim slanting light coming through the blinds. "You know you are not supposed to be in here."

My face went hot and my heartbeat hammered in my throat. A flash of memory – the fox and the jewel and the blood – did absolutely nothing except to make me selfishly one hundred per cent sure that this situation was worse.

"What are you doing?" Hilde demanded. She threw her whites down across the counter and her handbag thudded down on top of them. "How *dare* you steal like this?"

I didn't bother to point out that this was my kitchen, my home, that they were therefore my nuts.

Nothing in this house is really mine. Except for my paints.

And the stone.

Hilde planted her hands on her hips.

"Sorry," I said, my voice cracking. "I was just hungry." I cringed even as I said it. Her sharply over-plucked eyebrows twitched, but she didn't comment.

I backed away, but she crossed the kitchen, her black heels clacking on the tiles with the precise inevitability of a ticking clock. "Stop," I said. "Please."

Hilde paused, by the door, one hand reaching for the handle. Then she shook her head and walked out of the kitchen.

I turned to stare out of the back door, across the lawn, as the sun rose over the roofs of Kensington, behind the sculpted cherry trees. I could have run away, charged out through the alley and not looked back. But the idea barely flitted through my mind before I brushed it away. I wasn't going to give up everything I had over half a bag of peanuts.

I only wish my mother had such a keen sense of perspective.

She strode into the kitchen with her thin pink dressing gown pulled tight around her shoulders. She looked at me and sighed, her lips pursed.

"Oh, Margaret, how could you?" She looked tired, though her drooping eyelids were the only clue in her pale, smooth post-Botox face. She sighed deeply again and looked away – apparently she couldn't even look at me, such was my *utter betrayal*. "Is this why you didn't lose weight this week? Hilde is so good to you she goes out of her way to make sure your diet is appropriate..."

Oh yeah, *Saint Hilde*. I met her eyes over Mum's bony shoulder. *Sneak*.

"This is how you repay her? And me? We do our best to help you deal with your problem!"

I drew in a deep breath. Breathe with the rage, I told myself. Just breathe, and look away, and in a few seconds you won't need to reach across the room and strangle the word "problem" out of her.

My mother turned red-rimmed, half-tearful eyes to me. "You ungrateful little *bitch*."

...*oh crap*. My eyes snapped back to her face and I fought against the urge to back away. Sudden, unwarranted swearing is like Mum's poker tell. When she breaks out the B word, all bets on reasonable behaviour are off.

"I'm sorry," I said. I felt it, too, under the blowtorch heat of her stare. My palms prickled with sweat. I cringed inside, my stomach squeezing painfully around the handful of peanuts. Bile rose in my throat. I could feel the ghosts of her hands tight on my shoulders, forcing my head down, hot vomit stinging my throat...

It only happened once. On the night of the last general election. I'd gained a few pounds and I couldn't get the zip done up on the size twelve Versace she'd had made for me to wear to her re-election party. Maybe it was election night stress, but she just snapped. I could see it in her eyes, something mad looking out through her, in the seconds before she seized handfuls of my hair and held my head down over the sink until I threw up, retching over and over because her bony fingers were digging into my scalp and I was scared and I just wanted to get her off me...

When I was done she threw a flannel at me and walked out, and neither of us ever mentioned it again.

I never did fit in the stupid dress.

Standing in the kitchen, awaiting sentencing, I twitched my head around, shaking the hair over my face, so that I wouldn't scream at her.

She drew in a big shaky breath, like she was surfacing from a long dive underwater.

"Ungrateful child," she muttered.

Maybe she'd been remembering that night too. I could never tell.

"Go to the wardrobe till it's time for school," she said. "Whatever you took, let that be your breakfast."

I didn't try to argue. That lesson, at least, I'd learned early on.

The wardrobe was a big old oak thing in my mother's study, and she'd been locking me in it as a punishment as long as I could remember.

When I was three, it was terrifying. A huge dark cavern full of witches and monsters and crawly things, and coat hangers that hung down like butchers' hooks.

Then there was a wonderful period of grace when I was about six when I stopped being afraid. I simply imagined my way out. I knew, with perfect six year-old's logic, that either Mum would let me out, or the door would swing open and I'd feel a pine-scented breeze on my face and I'd just walk into Narnia and leave this world behind forever.

Sadly, Mum always got there first.

I knew we probably looked faintly absurd now, as she marched me up the stairs with one bony hand digging into my soft fleshy upper arm. But the wardrobe was just as effective as it had ever been. Now I was sixteen, five foot six and a size sixteen despite her mad, megalomaniacal efforts to get me down to a size zero. I banged my elbows on the solid wood, the hangers tangled painfully in my hair and the shoes dug into my thighs if I tried to sit down.

Mum locked me in and I hunkered there, in the close, shoe-smelling darkness, and lifted my fingers to trace graffiti patterns on the smooth wood.

Chapter Three

A couple of hours later I turned into Kensington Square, running my fingers over and over the cabochon sapphire in my coat pocket. All around me, gangs of girls walked and chattered, laughed, fought, bullied and flirted their way into school. For a few more yards everything seemed normal, but the atmosphere changed as I drew closer to the front door. A murmur of excitement passed through the crowd. The chatter grew louder. My heart started to pound, and I felt sweat prickling behind my ears.

There was police tape across the side gate. It wound around Henry's neck like a bright yellow scarf.

I dropped my gaze to the pavement and kept it there.

The stone was cool against my fingertips.

Miss Kilgarry and Miss Wolfcliff were pulling double duty on the big staircase in the entrance hall, doing their best to keep things moving, waving their arms like they were signalling a plane in to land.

I shuffled up the stairs with everyone else, hugging the banister – until a scuttling patch of blackness shot over the back of my hand. I snatched my hand away with a yelp. Heads turned, someone walked into my back, and the chorus of "What, oh my God what?" rolled over me like a wave. A glimpse of eight thick legs and a furry body streaked up the bannister and vanished.

"Banks?" Miss K demanded from the top landing.

"Spider, Miss," I gasped.

Possibly a bad move. Several girls shrieked and tried to pull away from me, shaking out their arms – except there wasn't room, and I heard cries of "ow!" and "oh my God, watch yourself, yeah?" as I managed to ride the general upwards tide to the top of the stairs. A bony arm dripping with jangling bangles elbowed me in the ribs, and I tripped over a trailing backpack strap. At the top of the stairs I burst from the crowd almost at a run and escaped into the relative calm of our classroom with a relieved gasp.

Most of 10E were already there. They were crowded up to the windows, looking down at the garden.

I was about to join them when I stopped, looking over at our lockers in the corner behind the teacher's desk. I slipped my hand into my pocket again and gripped the stone tight.

It wasn't safe at home. Sure, if Gail found my paints I'd be in the deepest shit since that guy on YouTube with the elephant, but I could always get more paints. I was never going to see another stone like this one. I wanted it safe, and that meant not keeping it in my mother's house.

I crossed to the lockers and slipped my key into number fourteen.

"Hey, Mags," Ameera called over. I spun, my face probably shining with guilt. "Don't you want to see?"

"Yeah, coming," I said. "Just dumping some stuff."

I opened the locker and slipped the stone in between my history homework and my secret sketchbook. I heard the soft *thonk* as stone hit metal, and swung the door shut and locked it.

As I stepped back, something scuttled across the top of the lockers, and I leapt back, flailing stupidly. Another spider.

Great. I bet the building's infested.

I turned, quickly, and crossed to the window.

"So, what's going on?" I asked Ameera.

"Some guy got stabbed or something," she said. I tried to see over her shoulder, but nobody was making room. "Apparently he like, climbed over the wall and did a bunch of graffiti and got stabbed."

"Gang stuff," said Lauren, nodding wisely.

I sighed. Some imaginary ASBO-toting scum was always going to get the credit for my work. I suppose I'd rather it was the Fox Man. It could be like my gift – after all, I had nothing I could give him that would make up to the value of his last gift to me.

And then Ameera finally budged aside and let me get to the window and look down. There was the white tent and loitering policemen, familiar from a thousand episodes of *CSI*, but much less attractive – and there were men in overalls wielding long-handled paint rollers, scrubbing over the back wall with white.

I clenched my fists and tried not to swear out loud.

All that effort, for nothing. Nobody – except the police – even got to see it.

I backed away and sat down on a nearby desk with a huff of frustration. It was just my luck, just my shitty, stupid luck. I'd been planning this one for *months*. It was supposed to inspire people – to wind them up, to make them *think*. Even if they thought "that art is a bit crap" – I didn't care. I'd have put *something* into their ringfenced, exam-panicked, automaton minds.

Outside the window, all my hard work was vanishing under a curtain of safe, empty white paint.

And, *and*, there was another bloody spider climbing over the edge of the desk, feeling for the surface with its thick black legs. I clenched my fists and then snatched up a piece of paper and took a swipe at it.

"Get *off*!" I hissed, not even caring if anyone noticed me sulking and talking to a bug.

Although I did care a bit, deep down, when nobody did.

"Oh my *Lord*, Mags," Ameera said, as we headed for Classics together after registration. "Last night was epic. I am so hungover!"

She didn't look all that hungover. She'd obviously had the time and energy to do her makeup that morning, and choose shoes that went with her handbag – blue and white, with a wedge heel – and do whatever it was she did to her hair that made it so glossy and bouncy.

She nudged me, amiably, in the ribs.

"You should come with! You know when you don't come drinking with us, the terrorists win. Why do you hate freedom, Mags?"

That got a snigger out of me, and she grinned in triumph.

"Yeah, see? You can't be good all the time."

I don't know why I never tried to explain to Jewel and Ameera that I wasn't spending my evenings studying, or reading *War and Peace*, or whatever else they thought "being good" meant. I don't think they would've thought less of me for creeping out at night and artistically vandalising stuff. I just never wanted to share that part of my life – except as *Thatch97*, on graffitilondon.com. I told myself I was quite happy living a bunch of totally separate lives.

"Oh, crap," Ameera stopped abruptly in the middle of the corridor and her shoulders sagged like a puppet with its strings cut. "Forgot my Ovid. It's in my locker." She rolled her eyes dramatically and turned on her heel to head back to our form room.

A cold twist of nerves hit me right in the gut, and I found myself saying "I'll come with you," before I really knew what I was doing. Ameera looked at me with a questioning twitch of her eyebrow, and I shrugged. "I left my notebook, might as well pick it up now. Plus, you're so hungover you might wander into the wrong room."

My excuse made her smile, and I followed in her wake as she made her way back against the stream of people heading to their first lessons.

It wasn't that I believed Ameera was going to go into my locker and find the stone. I knew, with every rational part of my mind, that she wouldn't.

It was just that I'd remembered that she *could*, and now I couldn't stop the vision from playing over and over in front of my eyes. All she'd have to do was jiggle the door just the right way. All the lockers in the school were the same, pathetically unsecure, possibly in a calculated attempt to stop us bringing in anything illicit. I'd learned that one the hard way, when Cath Forbes planted a porno mag in there the day before end of term inspection. Out of pure luck, I escaped a fate worse than detention by a margin of about thirty seconds. I took the moral high ground and didn't retaliate, which is Liar for "I couldn't think of a good enough revenge that was worth the inevitable escalation".

I'd never have left anything valuable in my locker if I'd thought about it for more than two seconds. I felt like an idiot for even considering leaving the stone there. My blood felt like it was running hot, super-heated by my relief as I reached into my locker and my hand closed over its cool, smooth surface.

For a second, while Ameera dug through enough Starbucks receipts to wallpaper my house looking for her Classics textbook, I ran my fingers over the smooth surface of the stone and felt its weight in my palm. It wasn't particularly heavy, and yet...

Perhaps I was imagining it, but the stone felt as if it was weighing me down, anchoring me to the ground, as if gravity wasn't what it used to be and if I put down the stone I would just float away on the breeze. It made my fingers twitch.

I pocketed it, swearing I'd find a better hiding place later.

Despite the detour, we made it to the Classics room before the teacher, and I got out my Ovid and started doodling over the back cover.

"Also, you need to get laid," Ameera said, glancing over my shoulder at the swirls and jagged lines.

I'd been hoping she'd forgotten about trying to get me to go out. I felt the heat rise in my cheeks, and hated myself for it. I made a sort of non-committal "Eehhh," sound.

Unsurprisingly, Ameera wasn't put off. "Falco's was crawling with hot guys last night. You'll have no problem hooking up with someone. Me and Jewel'll totally be your wingmen," she pressed.

"Where is Jewel, anyway?"

Ameera didn't seem to mind me changing the subject. "She was even more wasted than me," she shrugged. "She's probably lying down in a darkened room. I wish I was." She ran a hand dramatically over her face, although not so hard she smudged her eyeshadow, and groaned.

Jewel did turn up, eventually. She floated in halfway through double English, just as Mr Strummer was gearing up to launch into *Henry IV, Part 2*. Her sunglasses seemed fused to her face, two deep greenish pools beneath a sweep of choppy black fringe. She clutched a can of Red Bull in one hand and a piece of folded paper in the other.

Mr Strummer looked up from his preparations, smoothed back his floppy grey-brown hair and held his other hand out to receive the note. When he'd read it, he harrumphed, but didn't question her.

"All right, sit down," he said, "and take those shades off. You're indoors now."

Jewel sighed, deeply and loudly, and reached up to take off the sunglasses with all the urgency of a particularly unbothered sloth, shaking her hair forwards over her face.

She sat down beside Ameera, and Mr Strummer found his place in the text and drew in a deep breath.

"Ahemhem. *Open your Eares!*"

Which was our cue to do the exact opposite.

Ameera waited a prudent thirty seconds before turning to Jewel.

"You OK?"

"No. I'm *dying*." Jewel squinted across the desk at us. "I ought to be in bed – or preferably a coffin."

I turned my eye roll into a glance up to check on Mr Strummer. He was still droning on, his voice rising and falling unevenly over the poetry and fifteenth century puns. We think he's a failed actor – he'd always rather act our set texts out than have us work on understanding them for ourselves. If you were careful, you could talk right through his performance and never bring him back from his private Bard-world.

"How come you came in, if you're so sick?" Ameera asked.

Jewel shrugged. "Ugh. Mark bribed me with a family emergency note and a shopping trip if I'd get out of the flat so he could have the Duchess round for lunch."

"Is he *still* going out with her?" Ameera winced.

"Don't even." Jewel waved a hand weakly, as if gossiping about her brother's girlfriend was just too much for her delicate constitution. To be fair, she looked a lot sicker than Ameera. Her eyes were bleary under her fringe.

"I do not get it. She's such a munty, sourfaced bitch," Ameera said, loyally.

"Last week she bought a Chihuahua," Jewel stated, hanging her head and holding up her hands in defeat. "She called it *Mr Pooches*."

"Oh my God," Ameera gasped. "An *actual Chihuahua*. Has she got like, *no idea*?"

Handbag dogs are like, really 2000, you see. Everyone knows if you can't rustle up either a sugar glider or a giant Afghan hound, you just aren't trying.

I turned my gaze to the window and watched the branches of the birch tree outside shake as a flock of mangy pigeons dropped in from the grey sky. For a moment they sat there, about five of them all together, twitching their feathers and twisting their necks. Then they took off again, scattering in all directions. One lone pigeon was left squatting in the tree. It glared in at the window. It was almost looking right at me.

Could it be a person too? Could it stretch and flex its wings into elbows and fingers, until it was a naked stranger, sitting in a tree? I could visualise it more clearly than I would've liked.

But it didn't have a stone, so maybe not.

"Right, Mags?" Ameera said, bumping shoulders with me.

"Huh?"

"You're coming out with us on Saturday night." I opened my mouth to disagree, but she didn't stop for breath. "I'll come over to yours and make you over and then we'll go to Falco's for pre-drink drinks, and then on to that new place, with the ice, and finish off at Nobilis. And if you don't find a man in one of those places I'll, I'll..." she paused, and I seized the moment.

"No," I said. "Thank you, really, but no."

"Look," Jewel leaned over, and then sat back quickly as we realised Mr Strummer had fallen silent.

"So," he said, snapping the book closed, which was quite impressive really since it was only a flimsy paperback, "What do we think is Shakespeare's *dramatic purpose* in beginning the second part of Henry the Fourth's story like this? Hmm?"

I frowned at my copy, as if deep in thought, and waited for someone else to answer. Luckily, Alice Thurso accidentally caught his eye from the back row, and while he was engaged in trying to extract an answer she didn't have, Jewel scribbled a note and passed it to me.

If you don't have fun we'll never ask again, it said.

Ameera grabbed it back almost before I'd read to the end of the sentence and scrawled an addition underneath.

LOOKING HOT + YUMMY MEN – INHIBITIONS = A GOOD TIME OR YOUR MONEY BACK.

She drew a little heart, and then scribbled it out and drew a cock instead. I cringed.

Jewel seized the pencil, crossed out the cock and drew some boobs, and a question mark. I cringed even harder and shook my head.

Jewel underscored the words *we'll never ask again*, and passed the note back with a flourish of finality.

I looked out of the window again. I tried to give the idea fair consideration, but my mind kept going blank. For a moment I just sat there, staring. The pigeon was gone. There was yet another spider on the window ledge, hanging from an invisible thread and drifting slightly in the wind.

My stomach rumbled. The wardrobe had made me too late to grab my usual second breakfast from Mr Patak's on the way to school.

I picked up the pencil, pulled the paper in front of me and scrawled down *FINE*.

Fine. I didn't feel much like going out tagging right now anyway, and it'd be better than staying at home. Surely.

As we were going out for lunch, I made an excuse about leaving my bag behind and slipped out into the playground.

The memory of that night hit me like a falling meteorite. The bins, with the motion-sensor light. The picnic tables. The grass. The wall.

I stared at the patch of grass by the fence, where a group of Year Sevens were sitting cross-legged eating sandwiches. That was where he fell, where his blood seeped into the ground.

I turned and looked up at the back wall, a vision in negative of my artwork floating in front of my eyes. The men with paint-rollers had done a brilliant job. Nothing was left of all my hard work. Two year nine girls saw me staring at the wall, pulled *OMG, what a weirdo!* faces at me and giggled behind their hands.

The school had won this one, but I'd be back. One day I'd finish what I started.

A little huddle of Year Eights jumped out of their skins as I rounded the corner of the Kit Shed, and totally failed to hide their cigarettes behind their backs.

"Miss Wolfcliff's coming," I said, and they dropped the cigarettes and scattered like a flock of starlings.

I knelt down on the patch of earth by the shed, and dug out the triangular plastic protractor from the bottom of my bag. It served pretty well as a mini shovel – it'd certainly never been any use to me in lessons – and I used it to dig a hole about the length of my hand by the wall of the shed. I dropped the stone in and covered it over, arranging a clump of weeds to cover the dug earth. It wasn't all that deep, but it would do for now.

Thump thump thump thump thump whirr whirr screech clang thump.

A DJ in mirrored sunglasses was mangling a popular song on the raised turntables at one end of the bar, while at the other end I sat frozen on a violet leather sofa, nursing my cocktail and watching Ameera and Jewel flirting with a pair of C-list boyband singers twice their age.

I cursed myself for forgetting that there *was* something else I could have done on a Saturday night: I could have taken the stone home and tried to magic myself into a fox in front of my mother. That would've been more fun than this.

"Maggie?" A man flopped into the sofa beside me. I tried not to shy away. "Your friend said you were called Maggie," he yelled, over the *thump thump thump skree whinge thump*.

"It's Meg, actually."

"What?"

"Meg!"

"What?"

"Meg!"

"Sure," he nodded and smiled a blindingly white smile, as if he'd understood what I was saying, when we both knew he hadn't. "My name's John."

"*Meg*," I said, under my breath. I gave him a tight smile. He seemed to expect me to say something else. I didn't want to be rude – apart from the fact that he was obviously at least five years older than me, and he'd come up to a bunch of young girls in a bar for no reason except the obvious, and he was smiling at me like the Cheshire cat that got the cream, I had no reason to feel so wary of him.

I just suck at this, I thought, miserably. *I just don't care about you, John, or about this music, or about this stupid drink. I just want to think if a guy's chatting me up it's because he's interested in me as a person. Is that seriously too much to ask?*

I realised I'd gone silent and tried to think of something to say. "Nice shirt!" I managed eventually.

It was a polo shirt with a graffiti motif coiling up around one arm – a bit cheap-looking, which probably meant he'd paid way too much for it, but I liked it.

"Thanks. Nice top!" he grinned, staring at my boobs. I tried to sigh without encouraging him. It'd been a whole five minutes since I'd regretted letting Ameera talk me into the bright green lowcut Roberto Cavalli dress I had hidden in a drawer and hoped never to have to wear in public again. I almost didn't blame him for staring at my chest: it was very much the star of the show.

"How old are you?" I yelled.

"Twenty," he lied. "You're at college together, right?"

Yeah. Except you're thinking Oxbridge and I'm thinking sixth form. "Uh huh," I said, not wanting to ruin it for Jewel and Ameera. After all, they looked like they were having a good time. The boyband were buying them champagne cocktails with little fizzing stars at the bottom of the glass, and when one of them ran a hand over Ameera's bottom she wriggled and laughed.

I never wanted to be a prude. I didn't wake up one day and think, *From now on I shall be really uptight about boys and take myself way too seriously and not think any of this is fun.*

It's just... not fun.

John the Supposed Twenty Year-Old was saying something about boats. I nodded and smiled, my face forming a kind of frozen death-grin.

Oh God, please don't be telling me about your yacht. Oh my God, you're telling me about your yacht.

My parents had a yacht for a while. My friends' parents had yachts. Jewel had one of her very own, it was called *Tinkerbell*. I was not impressed by his yacht.

"Are you in college?" I asked, going along with his lie about his age – I don't even know why.

"No, I'm in politics," he shouted. "I'm one of their, y'know, Senior Policy Wonks."

At twenty years old. You really must think I'm stupid.

"I work with the Poverty Tsar," he declared, looking pleased with himself.

OK, that's it, thank you and goodnight, it hasn't been fun.

I stood up.

"I'm just going to… er…" I gestured vaguely in the direction of the bathroom.

"I'll hold your drink," said John the Yachting Poverty Wonk.

"No!" I clutched it protectively to my unfortunate cleavage. "I'm good! Back soon."

I had to brush the traces of cocaine off the toilet lid as I sat down so they didn't stain my dress, but at least it was quiet. The muted sounds of *thump thump snort thump* were practically restful by comparison with the bar.

There was some graffiti on the toilet stall door, mostly just scrawled writing, names and dates.

My purse was quite tiny, but it had room for the essentials – phone, mace, keys, Oyster card, and four fat marker pens. I untipped the black one and started to draw a fox on the back of the door.

It evolved, as these things usually do, unfolding in front of me as I drew. I'd say that the drawing started to come alive, except that metaphors like that are tricky once you've actually seen a fox turn into a person. The fox on the door didn't come alive – my strokes just got wilder and more confident, until he was sitting up on his haunches, his ears alert and his eyes a scribble of bright red among the black muzzle lines. He seemed to be watching me, maybe waiting for something.

I signed the drawing with *THATCH* scrawled in the top right hand corner, as usual.

Back in the bar, Ameera and Jewel had gone. I should've seen it coming, but I still felt a stab of icy panic when I couldn't see them anywhere. I walked around for a while, trying to look purposeful. *My friends are just on the other side of this barstool... I know exactly where I'm going, they're just over there... 'scuse me, I'm very busy and purposeful and my friends are waiting for me, just outside...*

They'd gone. I stood outside the bar and caught my breath, while the unlicensed minicabs crawled along the pavement and the bouncers refused entry to people with the wrong colour Gucci sandals on. The panic crumbled into a heavy layer of weary bitterness. It lined the bottom of my stomach like the sticky blue stuff in my cocktail that tasted like cough syrup.

I tapped out a text to them both.

Can't find you. Gone home. Have a good night ☺ M

I probably should've hailed a taxi, but the club was about a ten minute walk from a bus stop that would drop me right at the end of my road, and I'd rather keep the cash. If Mum thought it was a good idea to press drinking money into my hands, she didn't get a say whether I spent it on cocktails or spray paint.

I set off walking, my short heels clicking heavily on the pavement. I cringed slightly away from open bar doors, which spilled desperate smokers and thudding music out onto the pavement. A blinding flash lit the air, and I realised I'd been caught in the corner of a paparazzi photo of someone leaving a club. I couldn't clear the afterimage quick enough see who it was.

I was nearly at the bus stop when I stumbled to a halt with a *click-clack*, gazing into an alley between two glass-fronted bars. There was a piece of graffiti on the wall, large enough and close enough to the road that I could see it clearly in the pulsating blue-purple-yellow light that filtered out through the frosted glass.

A labyrinthine maze of hot pink arrows curled around each other, forming the shape of a giant brain. Bright blue-white sparks flashed between the arrow tails. Strange shapes seemed to flicker in and out of sight, like the way you can see faces in tree bark or creatures in the shadows. I could see animal shapes, and building shapes, and things that could've been hands reaching out – but I couldn't tell what was really there, and what I was putting there.

Right in the middle of the brain there was a four-pointed star in bright, sunshine-yellow.

It was an E3. I would've known his style anywhere, even if it hadn't been for his tag: two mirrored swirls of white in the centre of the star.

I looked around at the other people staggering down the street, wondering if any of them had seen it. Even though I was in the middle of bitterly stalking off home alone, part of me wanted to share this.

One of a group of women glanced down the alley as they passed me and saw the amazing painting, but she didn't pause, didn't even smile.

I whipped my phone out and strode into the alley to get a photo. I got up close and took one of E3's signature that filled the whole screen, then backed away to get the whole painting into the shot, my eyes on the floor so I didn't trip on the uneven paving. I backed up against the wall and raised my phone up almost to my eyes to get as wide a shot as I could.

Something knocked the phone from my hands, I felt a juddering pain in my shoulder and I fell down. I landed hard on my bare elbows, pain and pavement scratching across my arms, and looked up. Two men, their faces covered, their hands grasping for my purse. I felt it tugged from my hands, almost before I could blink. The mace was in there – worse than useless, now they had it. I tried to scream, but my chest felt constricted and no breath seemed to come. One of the men kicked out at me, I ducked away and his shoe missed my face by millimetres. I was on my feet now, backing down the alley, knowing that going deeper was stupid, that I was going further from the bright lights and the crowds that could help me, but the two men were blocking my way out.

My right ankle twisted and I staggered with a yelp. The heel of my shoe had slipped into a crack in the pavement. As I tried to regain my balance there was a plastic splintering noise and it broke off. I could feel my hands and arms and knees trembling, like an earthquake was passing through me. One of the muggers grabbed for me and I couldn't move quickly enough – as I tried to duck away his hand struck the side of my head, all the bones in my jaw ground together and flashing white dots swarmed in front of my eyes. I felt one of them grab my hair and push me back, further away from the road.

I tried to lash out, not much more than a desperate flail – but my arms twitched all over and wouldn't move right. A giant, body-shaking shudder ran all the way down my spine and I convulsed under the man's hands, so hard he actually let go. My legs wobbled and gave way and a juddering shock of impact ran through my whole body as my knees hit the ground. My face felt numb and tingling at once.

Was I having some kind of fit?

I can't feel my fingers.

One of the men made a choking noise and dropped my purse. I lunged for it with all my might, but I only managed to roll onto my front, my legs kicking out behind me. He leapt away, turned and ran, with his friend not far behind him.

My stomach churned and I tried to crawl forwards but my arms and legs just twitched and jumped. I felt something slide across my back and looked down to see the dress hanging off me – my cleavage, my arms, all of me, shrinking and changing and...

When the orange fur burst from my hands, I finally understood.

For about five seconds, panic turned my mind into a swirling pool of madness and I twisted, scratched and bit at anything I could still reach, my mouth full of Cavalli silk and my claws scraping along the pavement.

But then I breathed in, and I lay down on my side, keeping still except for the heaving of my ribs. The world rose up all around me, like time-lapse footage of mushrooms ballooning in the forest. I let out a yelp as my arms drew back into my body and my elbows clicked into their new positions. I could feel myself flattening against the concrete. My ears twitched involuntarily. I screwed my eyes tight shut and yowled, feeling my tailbone lengthening and pushing out of my back. I could feel the hairs on my tail, feel it swishing beneath the fabric of my dress.

I opened my new eyes onto a different world.

Chapter Four

I was a fox.

Everything smelled. And not just in a bad, back-alley way – although there was a patch of stink just to my left that set alarm bells ringing in my mind. *Human territory*, it said, *foul, keep away*.

But *everything* smelled – the pavement carried the scent of sand and metal and dirt and heat, a city-smell, underlying everything around me. I could faintly make out a tangy, fizzy airborne smell coming from the electric lights out on the street.

I bent to sniff my dress, intrigued. On top of the synthetic, *fabric-dye-smoke-alcohol* I could smell from the dress itself, my human scent was floating, unmistakeably animal. My instinct told me *female*, and comparing it with the foul patch to my left confirmed that as *male*, and *mature*, and something chemical – which, after a second's puzzled thought, I realised had to be *drunk*.

My muzzle stung, and I remembered the mugger's blow to the side of my head. My tongue flickered out, and on my chin I could feel hair matted with a trickle of blood. My jaw ached when I moved it.

I suppose that made sense – after all, the fox-man had obviously been hurt as a fox, and he'd died as a human.

I sat back on my haunches and looked around. I could see the edges of close things with a sort of razor-sharp clarity, although the colours were muted. It was the scents that guided me along the alley, toward the main road, and the scents and sounds that blinded me when I drew closer. Delicious food-smells, terrifying chemical car-smells, the sounds of feet pounding on the pavement and buses screaming past. I could hear the human chatter, and weirdly, I could still understand it – but there was much too much to make out any one thread. My ears flattened and I cringed back into the shadow of the alley, away from the racket.

Did you and her brother my boss in the bar I don't think hey loved it great time no by the police in the way doctor most exciting coffee Greek place...

I backed away. I couldn't go out there. My head was already spinning. I padded back down the alley to my dress, and sat for a second.

There was another sense, much more important than just sight. Not exactly a sixth sense – more like the same sense of perspective that I'd always had, but magnified a thousand times. I glanced up at a council dustbin, towering far above my head. My whiskers twitched, and my tail – my brush – swished against the ground.

I can make that jump.

I took a run up and sprang. I flew through the air, my front legs extending, as naturally as breathing. Except suddenly, as my claws clutched at the plastic lid, it was as though my body remembered it was supposed to be a girl, with short nails, and no fur, and ears that didn't move independently – and I couldn't make the jump, because that was absurd.

I missed hard, the edge of the lid smacking into my ribs. Pain and panic filled my head and I scrabbled with all four feet, my front claws leaving jagged grooves in the plastic, and my brush waving madly out behind me... and then I was up, on top of the bin, panting but safe. I'd made it.

I looked down at my dress, my shoes, my purse. They looked so small, like pieces of coloured paper that could blow away in a strong gust of wind. My whole life was down there – my friends, my mother, my house, my graffiti.

Can I change back?

What if I tried to change back, but found that I couldn't? What if I changed back, but then couldn't be a fox again? Wasn't it better to seize the moment? Whatever the next few hours might bring, right now, I was a fox, and I was *free*.

I looked up at the orange-black city sky. There was a fire escape I was pretty sure I could reach from here and climb all the way up to the roof of the building.

I glanced down again at the dress, and back up at the window ledge. My legs twitched with the desire to jump. Almost without my input, I felt myself crouching back on my haunches, ready to spring.

Could I ever change back?

In that moment, I didn't care. I leapt.

The night air was much cooler up on the roof. There was a stiff breeze that hadn't made it down between the buildings. It ruffled my fur and made the hair on my brush ripple like water. I sat and curled my brush around me to watch it, entranced by the way I could feel and not feel every strand moving at once.

The whole sensation was bigger than just the flow and pull of the fur. The wind brought scents from far away – tarry smog mixed with more of the gritty dirt and a hint of something juicy and delicious.

A restaurant? I sniffed. *Meat... salt, and fat.* Maybe it was a fast food restaurant. It smelt divine.

And underneath that, even more layers of smell drifted past and around me. I thought I could taste far-off rain.

Although I couldn't make out fine details, the view from the rooftop was just as incredible as the feeling of the wind in my fur. The twinkling lights in the distance, the tiny hurrying forms of clubbers down below... The whole human world felt so far away to me now.

I could do anything I wanted.

I could raid the bins outside that fast food place for some of those sweet, juicy, greasy bones. I could run and run through the streets and over the rooftops. I could see things humans never saw. I could run away forever and live my whole life as a fox. I could take a running leap off the top of this building and end my life in a splatter of red fur, blood and bone on the street below, and nobody would ever know what had happened to me.

I sat back on my haunches, my brush curled around my paws. I wasn't going to jump. I didn't *want* to jump.

I could just feel... something. The pull of the edge, the urge to leap out into the air and fly.

No – I had to enjoy this. I had no idea how long this would stay fun. What if I'd traded my new skin for the one thing that'd made any sense of my life so far? Could a fox handle a stencil and paint?

And then I knew where I wanted to go first. I turned on the spot, trying to find my bearings, and then set off, springing across the roof along the line of shops, heading west.

I reached Acton much quicker, and much less tired, than I'd expected. My paws were hardly even sore, even though I'd been running along the half-empty streets for at least half an hour.

I found E3's masterpiece, hidden from the road down a cut-through alley crowded with weeds and rubbish, and I sat back on my haunches and stared. My ears flattened against my head in disappointment and a sigh turned into a hiss as it escaped my jaws.

I'd seen photos of the *Arabian Dragons* on the forums. I knew that the painting was intricate and beautiful, two dragons entwined in a fight or a dance, in vivid red and green. And they were there alright – I could make out the faint shape of their outline against the brickwork over my head, the dim, fuzzy sweeps of colour taunting me with their shades of brown and more brown.

Foxes were colour-blind. I don't know how I'd not realised – I guess on the night-time streets everything was orange-tinted and dim. Their – our – sense of smell was like a second sight. It made up for the indistinct edges of things and for not being great at traffic lights. Even now I could scent dirt from the path, oil and smoke and sharpness rising from the nearby train tracks. I could smell the water in the drains, full of *foul* and *fresh* all at once. There was a sticky kind of plant smell coming from the weeds by the fence, and I could smell an animal scent too, something acrid but vividly alive and strangely mouth-watering. I wondered if it was a rat.

But none of it was any use to me now. I'd come all this way to see the *Dragons*, liberated by my new body – but to really see them, I needed my old eyes back.

Well, I thought. *I have to know, anyway. I had to try it sometime.*

It was strange to realise it, but clubbing and spiders and wardrobes aside, there were a lot of things about my human life I would miss.

Like red, and green.

I drew in a deep breath and shut my eyes, concentrating, trying to remember what it felt like to be human. My rib cage stretched out... and kept stretching. My claws scraped the dirt as my fingers spread and lengthened. I flexed my back muscles and they started to twist, my spine clicking weirdly as new vertebrae popped into existence.

It stopped being like stretching and became a feeling like air flowing into a void. I could feel cold, exposed skin on my arms and legs and stomach. I opened my eyes.

Just for a second – less than a second – there was a burst of light. It was too bright. The scents were too sharp. I could see everything, scent everything. I could do anything. It was too perfect, too much.

Then it was gone. I couldn't smell the water or the dirt. My mouth felt shallow and soft. I could still feel the bruise across my lips. It tasted of purple. My teeth clacked together and my knees shook as I stood up.

Two things hit me as I shook off the change.

First – my God, it was *so beautiful.* I had no idea. The dragons were both made of letters. Arabic lettering, words and sentences coiling around themselves, forming wings and claws. "Vivid" barely scratched the surface. The colours seemed to radiate heat and movement and life off the bare brick wall in front of me.

And then, second – oh God, I was *so naked.*

I gasped, swallowing a mouthful of cold, dulled scents. I threw my arms up awkwardly across my chest, as if my *chest* was my biggest problem, and twitched away from the road, pressing back against the wall. It was rough and freezing on my skin, but I didn't dare move away. Shoulder-to-shoulder with the red dragon, I shivered with every beat of my pounding heart.

Stupid. *Stupid.* What did I think would happen? I'd left my clothes in an alley.

A clatter sent shocks like electric sparks shooting up my spine, and I flinched back and changed again.

The first few times, every change felt different. Instead of panicked writhing or intense stretching, this time it was pure animal instinct, and it felt like taking a great leap backwards into my own body. There was a second's confused twisting and then I landed on the rough ground on all four paws, crouched and ready to run. And just in time, because a man rounded the corner and opened his fly, peeing a solid stream of *foul-male-drunk-urine* against the wall.

With a sigh – a huff of air through my muzzle that tickled the fur under my nose – I turned and slunk away.

I was just a few bus stops' distance from my house when I saw the patch of fog floating down the middle of the deserted street.

I'd just turned onto one of the little side streets off the main road, where antiques and jewellery shops huddled together like they were sharing a secret they didn't want the upstart fashion boutiques next door to hear. Dickensian carved signs cast elaborate shadows over steel shutters with high-vis security logos.

The fog was like a fixed, contained column of smoke, or a cloud that had come down to earth – or as though the legendary London fog of the 1800s had returned to one incredibly specific spot.

I was staring at it, wondering if something in the road was on fire, when it moved. I gasped, scenting something tangy and sparkling on the back of my tongue, and crouched back on my haunches. Tendrils of fog reached out, like a thousand tiny tentacles, and then the rest of the cloud followed, rolling along the street.

Another movement: a man in a leather jacket turned a corner and came walking down the street, right towards the fog. I watched him walk right up to it and not give it a single glance. As he passed it, the fog swirled its tendrils out around his head, but then drew back.

Hadn't the fox-man said...?

"Please. The fog..."

Was this something only fox-people could see? What *was* it? What was he trying to tell me about it?

I got to my paws and took a deep sniff of the air. That tangy scent again – something like electricity, but less physical somehow. It tasted of bright lights. It filled my jaws with imaginary fizzing. I couldn't feel it, I just *knew* it.

Magic? I wondered.

I took a step forward.

"Hey! Vixen!"

I skittered around, my claws clattering on the pavement. There was another fox standing behind me. He was a male, with a grey streak between his eyes and deep red socks on his paws. He smelled of *male* and *fox*... and something chemical I didn't recognise. There was something at his feet... a small black bag with something lumpy inside.

"Yes, you," he snarled. His black lips drew back, showing me his teeth. I felt my fur bristle and my throat tighten. "Get away from that thing," the fox barked.

I turned back. The fog was closer now. It reached out its tendrils and rolled forward, faster, right towards me. I took a couple of faltering steps away. The fog kept coming.

"What is it?" I asked.

"Don't ask bloody stupid questions, just run!"

I felt something snatch at my brush and yelped, tugging it away from the grasping tendril of fog. The other fox turned and bounded away in a flash of orange. I leapt after him. He turned into an alley like a fuzzy bullet and I skidded along in his wake. He was all line and muscle and grace as he jumped up onto the back of a car and a tall council bin and the low roof of a garden shed. I tried to follow, but I slipped on the car, leaving ragged scratches in the paintwork and sliding off again.

"Come on," he shouted down from the shed. I looked back. Fog-tentacles were coiling around the corner of the building, glowing bright and dirty orange in the street light. I took a shaky step back and jumped up onto the car, steadied myself and made the leap up onto the bin, and then to the thankfully rough and graspable roof of the shed.

As soon as I'd made it, the fox was off again. He jumped down into a scrubby garden and headed for a tiny hole under a fence.

"Wait," I called, jumping down after him. The impact was hard on my paws, but I recovered.

He hesitated for a moment, tossing his head. More of his composure seemed to return to him and he preened, looking down his nose at me. "Do you want to lose it or not, darling? Let me tell you, that thing'll do more than pull your pigtails if it catches us."

I followed him across two gardens, up a slippery climbing frame and over a row of garages. Finally he jumped up through a metal railing onto someone's private balcony and came to a halt. I clambered after him and sat, panting and staring.

He smirked at me. He still looked like a fox, but I

could read his smirk in the way his eyes narrowed and his ears twitched. I felt so clumsy next to him, and it wasn't just that I was new at this. Something told me this fox had more grace and poise than I'd ever have.

"What was that? Who are you?" I panted. "Are you like me?"

"If by 'like me' you mean 'a shifter', then yes," said the fox.

"Shifter." I rolled the word around my mouth. "Wait, how are we talking? Are we making sounds?"

"My word," said the fox, "you really are new to this, aren't you, love?"

"I have absolutely no idea what's happening to me," I admitted.

"*Well*," he said, sitting back on his haunches and curling his brush neatly around his paws, "it's certainly lucky for you I came along. Top tip: you don't want to get caught in the fog."

"Um. Thanks," I said. "Um. My name's Meg."

"James Farringdon," the fox said, getting to his paws and giving a deep bow. "It's been a pleasure, but I should really be going." He picked up the bag in his jaws again. It rattled.

"What, now?" I sprang to my paws. "Can't you... I mean... can't you tell me more about this? What's a shifter? Is it just like shapeshifting? How did this happen? Am I... am I safe?"

"Ish," said James through the mouthful of bag. He blinked at me and then put it down again. "Look, dear, I've been doing this for a while, and there's not much more to say. We're people who can change into foxes. What you choose to do with that is entirely up to you." He licked his muzzle thoughtfully with a thin pink tongue. "Although... which one died?"

"What?" I shook my head.

"You're new. So one of the others must have died."

"There are others?"

James rolled his eyes. Fox-face and everything, they actually rolled.

"Well, *yes*. Did you think it was just you and me?"

I sat back on my haunches and scratched my ear. After a couple of scratches, I realised I was doing it with my back leg.

"So, what? I got it from the dead guy? Like a disease or something?"

"That's how it works."

So, it wasn't the stone. I frowned. *But then the stone and the fog and the shifting – how are they connected?*

"Can you describe him?" James Farringdon asked, his claws flexing impatiently on the balcony. "Was he black?"

"Um... no, er, he was white. Short hair. Brownish."

"Ah. That would be the nurse chap. Too bad, he was a bit of all right. Now, please don't take this the wrong way, but I'm going to leave now and I don't mean for us to meet again."

If there was a right way to take that, I couldn't figure out what it was.

"Why not?" I whined.

He narrowed his eyes at me – I thought I could sense another little smirk. "I generally avoid the Skulk. I don't play well with others. Good morning." With that he took up his little bag, turned and leapt off the balcony, sprang from fence post to car roof and disappeared into the darkness.

I stared after him for a few minutes, my mind racing.

He hadn't mentioned the jewel. Could it be it had nothing at all to do with the shapeshifting? But then what was it? The man had been a nurse.

One of the Skulk.

Chapter Five

The next morning, Gail barged into my room to wake me up for breakfast at half past eight, even though it was a Sunday. The full strangeness of the night's adventure came screaming back as I sat up to glare blearily at her, and I got my legs tangled in my blanket and faceplanted onto the floor. Then when she'd finished tutting at my gracelessness and left I made it to my chest of drawers only to find there was a spider in my bra.

The day only got worse from then on.

There are a couple of problems that shapeshifting into a fox just doesn't solve. Lack of sleep is one. Replacing lost keys and Oyster cards and mobile phones, without having to explain how the "mugging" also left you naked, is another.

And then there's my mum.

"...ready by five," she said, at breakfast. I blinked. She gave me a look as though, hangover or not, I was getting on *simply* her *very last nerve*. I'd been wolfing my muesli and not listening to her. "Margaret, will you please come back to planet Earth for just two minutes?

The party starts at six, so I'd like you to be ready by five, understood?"

Oh God. What party? I crunched slowly on my mouthful of wholewheat grains to cover the fact I was racking my brains.

"I'll have Gail lay out your outfit," Mum went on. My heart sank.

"Mum, there's no need–"

"No excuses, I won't have you turning up in jeans like last time." Her lips pursed and her thin fingers tightened on her knife as she spread a violently thin layer of jam on her wholewheat muffin. I braced for a rant – how she didn't care if it was *fashionable* it had been so *embarrassing* and the people had been so *important* and how everyone was *shocked* and she was *humiliated* by my *constant rebellion* and...

Gail saved me, for once.

"Excuse me, Mrs Banks," she said, taking a respectful loitering half-step into the room. "I have the Chief Whip on the telephone."

Mum rolled her eyes, took a long and deliberate sip of her tea and then stood up.

When she was out of the room, I turned to my dad.

He was there too, depending on what you mean by "there".

My dad was like the Invisible Man, if all the Invisible Man wanted to do was read the paper and not pay corporation tax. Once in Year Nine he came to a Parents' Evening and met all my teachers, sitting and listening attentively as they went through my aggressively mediocre grades. I saw them shake his hand and make eye contact with him. And then I'd been summoned to the Year Head and told off for not bringing anyone.

He wasn't mean. He never shouted. He was just a vague pinkish presence at the dinner table and in the hall, like a walking man-sized copy of the *Financial Times*. I used to think he wanted a son, but actually I don't think he would've been much better with a boy. I don't think he cared for children at all. Maybe if I'd been a better daughter he would have cared more – but far more likely he would have been vague and useless at the back of piano recitals and school awards ceremonies.

"Dad," I said, "what's the party for?"

"It's a Party thing," Dad said. I heard the capital P – when you live with a Member of Parliament your ear becomes attuned to it. He didn't seem to care that I'd forgotten. "Something to do with the budget."

Good old Dad. It's nice to have a parent who doesn't freak out about every little thing I do.

I mean, it's hard to freak out about anything – or anyone – you never take the slightest bit of notice of. Still, hooray for my dad not being my mum.

I rubbed my eyes. So my presence was required at a Party party.

I should've let the fog get me.

I was asleep on my bed, curled up around a sketchbook, when Gail knocked on my door and walked in without waiting. I think she has delusions of being Jeeves. Except that if Jeeves' boss had said "don't do that, it's creepy, and while I'm at it can you stop going through my drawers looking for reasons to get me in trouble with my mother", Jeeves would've listened.

I lurched awake, gripping on tight to the biro I'd had in my hand when I'd dropped off. Gail waved a dry-cleaning hanger at me.

"I have your outfit for this evening."

"Wass time?" I mumbled, and glanced at the clock. 4.28. Damn. I dug my hands into my hair and sat up, closing the sketchbook on the page full of star-stones and swirly living fog. She laid the dress in its white plastic on the bed and told me to hurry up and get ready, then left.

I glared after her.

What if I turn into a fox, right in front of you, and jump out the window instead? What would you do?

I bet the Skulk doesn't have a dress code.

I sighed and unzipped the plastic dry-cleaning bag. Would it be the weird broad-shouldered navy blue one that reminded Mum of the Good Old Eighties? It seemed appropriate for the occasion.

It was new. It was pink. I wanted to cry.

I squeezed into it and tied the shiny pink ribbon at my back, staring in the mirror. It had a built-in corset – which was at least the second best thing after a dress that actually fit – and little pink and white ruffles over the shoulders.

I wondered if she'd had it made specially. Because what were the odds that a dress bought off the rack would make me look this much like an undercooked sausage?

I slathered my hair in anti-frizz and went downstairs just in time to hear Mum give a yell and something hit something else with a *smack*.

I edged into the drawing room with my back to the doorframe, ready to make a hasty exit. Mum was standing by the big gold-framed mirror over the fireplace. She turned, brandishing a rolled-up copy of the dinner menu. Her eyes lighted on me for a second and then slid away to the stairs.

"*Gail!*" she shrieked.

Gail hurtled down the stairs, faster than I thought it was possible to go without losing her professional poise.

"There's a spider in the fireplace. Get the trap and kill it."

"There was a spider in my room, this morning," I volunteered. "And at school on Friday. It might be the time of year."

Mum frowned at me, as if I was a lampshade that had come to life and tried to make a political point. I felt pretty much like one, considering the ruffles. "Yes, I suppose so," she said slowly. It was like conceding the point actually caused her pain.

Suddenly though, I wasn't sure I was right. I mean, it *could* have been the time of year. But... that made about six spiders in three days. That's not normal.

I didn't know about the one that Mum had seen, but the five that I'd seen had all looked the same. Not just has-eight-legs, is-a-dark-colour, basically-it's-a-spider the same. They were *exactly* the same colour, the same size.

I could easily be imagining it. Maybe I was just seeing weird stuff when there was none. It was probably the least crazy reaction I could have to having turned into a fox last night.

Surely it was more likely than the idea that I was being stalked by a spider.

Gail scuttled off to get the spider trap – a gleaming chrome thing that I had never seen actually catch anything except lint – and Mum brushed down her little black dress and turned to me.

"I'm glad you're here," she said. As if I had even the slightest choice in the matter. "I've invited two of the young people who've been campaigning to help us pass the amendments to the budget. I'd like you to look after them this evening."

Oh good. Young Conservatives.

I'm sure there are young Tories who are nice, thoughtful people who want to get into politics to make a positive difference to other people. There are, I'm vaguely aware, young Tories who are sweet, polite, non-white, even female.

Those are just not the ones my mum invites to parties.

She looked me up and down again, and smiled in her stretched-out, thin-lipped way. "Please... try to be a good hostess. If they empty their glasses and you can't see the staff, volunteer to get them a new one yourself. Try not to let them feel as if you're not paying them attention. They're our guests, and they're boys, so let them do most of the talking and try not to insult them."

Sometimes I wonder how my mother got to be a successful career politician and yet still had parts of her brain hardwired straight into the 1950s.

She was straightening the flowers on the mantelpiece now, still talking, but in a thoughtful way, almost to herself.

"They're both charming young men. I'm sure they'll like you. They're both at Cambridge, you should ask them about their colleges. I'm sure they'd be happy to show you around. Wouldn't that be nice?" She turned and looked at me again, and gave a miniscule nod of approval.

I suppressed a shiver. If my mother approved of me, something must be up.

The party was one of Mum's political schmoozing affairs. A gang of black-shirted waiters emerged from the kitchen, as neat and regimented as if Hilde had just unpacked them from a plastic box at the back of a cupboard. They passed out glasses of wine to the guests as they arrived, and circled the room with little gourmet nibbles on square black plates.

The guests were mostly politicians; friends and collaborators of Mum's. Ministers chortled over their glasses at lobbyists. A few of Dad's colleagues and clients turned up too, and stood in the corner of the room, chomping on little green pastries and talking about furniture and concrete cores and Qatari finance. They were mostly white men in suits, but eventually they were joined by a woman. I couldn't help staring a bit as she walked in. She was black, and wearing a peacock-coloured dress, her hair thickly braided and shimmering under a sprinkling of gold glitter. She was overdressed for the occasion, and I caught Mum giving her a doubtful side-eye, but somehow she carried it off with such panache that she made everyone else in the room look underdressed. I found it hard to believe my Dad knew anyone that interesting.

I lurked by the window, very slowly drinking the lemonade one of the waiters had pressed into my hand and staring at the pointy porcelain ornaments on the windowsill while I listened in to their conversation. It was disappointing: the woman joined right in with Dad's talk of steel, land deals and billion pound loans. I was willing to bet she was disgustingly rich, just from the way they all seemed to fall over themselves to agree with everything she said, but I couldn't make out what it was she actually did. I was focused on the polite chatter, trying to catch the woman's name, when I suddenly heard loud voices on the front step. I peered out of the window, trying to see who was there. I could make out two shadowy figures, but not much detail. They were braying with laughter, like posh donkeys. Mum disappeared to open the door and halloooed them down the hall and into the drawing room.

"Margaret," she cut across the room towards me with two boys in her wake. "I'd like you to meet Richard and Warren."

I tried to smooth down my dress and smile pleasantly, though my face suddenly felt like it was made of stiff plastic and I hated myself a bit for caring whether or not they thought I looked like a sausage.

Richard was the taller and better-looking of the two. I observed his square jaw and artfully curly blond hair with the dispassionate gaze of someone who knew that fancying him would make her mother happy and had *no intention whatsoever* of making her mother happy no matter how fit he was. He was wearing a tweed jacket, suspenders and glasses without lenses in them. Textbook hipster – such a classic look I had to wonder if he dressed like this all the time or if it was some kind of elaborate fancy dress. I decided to call him Hipster Dick, at least in the privacy of my own head.

I realised I was staring and turned my glance to Warren. In contrast to Hipster Dick, Warren was short and stocky. He was wearing jeans and a yellow Paul Smith shirt. I noticed Mum didn't seem to be *utterly humiliated* by the denim as long as it was on one of her guests.

"Call me Rich," said Hipster Dick, with a sweet half smile.

"Meg," I said, in a nice loud clear voice so Mum could hear me.

Warren replied by smiling at my boobs. I only hoped they were enough to keep him entertained for the rest of the evening, because God knew I had no idea what to say to him.

Mum was looking at me. I was supposed to be doing something. Oh, right.

"Can I, um, can I get you something to drink?" Mum rolled her eyes at me before she walked away. Obviously I was already a total disaster. I turned to wave over one of the waiters with a little tray. Warren and Hipster Dick both took glasses of red wine. So that was that part done.

The three of us hovered by the window sipping our drinks in silence, smiling awkwardly.

This was excruciating.

"So, er, Mum said you go to Cambridge?" I asked.

"We're in first year at Trinity," said Hipster Dick. "Are you applying?"

"Well, Mum wants me to."

"I'd be happy to introduce you to a couple of the right people," he said. "You should come up for a couple of days."

"That's what Mum said," I agreed, without much enthusiasm.

"You don't sound very sure."

"Oh, I mean, thank you, really, it's just..." *It's just that I don't want to go anywhere that'll take me just because my mother introduced me to all the important people.* It even sounded rude in my head, so I just trailed off.

Hipster Dick's pretty amber-brown eyes narrowed. "It sucks that who I introduce you to might be what gets you in."

I blinked at him. "Yeah, it really does."

I felt my face warming under his gaze. I guess I'd misjudged him. I guess not everyone Mum knows has to be completely morally bankrupt.

Warren made a deeply unattractive spitting sound in the back of his throat. "Ugh, Richard, don't be such a fag. Hey, you were at Conference this year, tell me Jenkins didn't do his usual two hours on NHS reforms."

I blinked at him. I instinctively tried to formulate a reply, despite the fact I'd rather die than attend a Party Conference.

But Hipster Dick laughed, and just like that, I realised my five seconds of being relevant to the conversation were over. Warren had very deliberately changed the subject. He kept smiling at my boobs as if they were making a contribution, but after the third time he'd made Hipster Dick laugh and I had no idea how, I drew my own conclusions.

"I was helping out at the EDYC last week, surgery was full of crackpots as per, then Glenn and Alex took Barrows and Robinson out to lunch to grease them up for the IDK and sprung prescription allowances on them over the milk-fed veal, they nearly crapped themselves but the GNE is solid," said Warren, without apparently stopping to breathe.

I tried to smile when it seemed appropriate and laugh whenever Hipster Dick did, but I could feel my eyes glazing over. I traced patterns in the condensation on the side of my glass until my fingers were dripping wet and I had to surreptitiously wipe them on a discarded napkin.

I'm not stupid. I'm politically engaged. It'd be hard not to be, when I live with the MP for Kensington and Chelsea. She named me after Margaret Thatcher, and I've been searching for a suitable revenge for that ever since. I can follow real politics. It's just the backroom insider talk that makes my brain try to crawl away and hide under the sofa.

"Glenn says we're going to screw them on copyright reform," Warren said. He followed up with a vivid description of just how hard and against their will they were going to get screwed that made me glare at him and grip onto my glass for fear I might accidentally chuck my lemonade in his face. Hipster Dick caught my eye and gave a tiny eyebrow-twitch.

An apology, for his friend's douchebaggery? He wasn't sorry enough to try and make Warren shut up, though.

Warren carried on speaking and I tried to tune him out again.

A dark scuttling shape moved across the windowsill and I bit back a yelp.

Another bloody spider.

I don't like spiders. Nobody likes spiders. It's the legs, they're just wrong. But I didn't want to run away or squish it this time. Maybe I was getting hardened to the creep-factor, or maybe I'd just lost all feeling in my brain after listening to Warren for – I glanced at the clock – oh God, almost half an hour.

Warren was saying something about someone called John getting lynched by a select committee, and Hipster Dick was smirking knowingly. I could hear the tone of Mum's voice rising and falling silkily on the other side of the room as she sucked up to Sir Douglas Ross, the Chief Whip. He was a thin, scary man who always wore a thin blood red tie – according to the Westminster legend he threatened to strangle people with it on a regular basis.

The spider climbed to the top of one of the pointy white ornaments, on the side that meant only I could see it, and sat there. Its two front legs rubbed together, but it didn't move.

Did that mean something? Was it looking at me? Did the spider *want* me to see it?

OK, now you're just being mental.

Still...

"Hey," I whispered, no louder than a breath, trying not to move my jaw. "If you can hear me..."

"Er, did you...?" Hipster Dick interrupted Warren in mid-crow. He stared at me. "Did you just say something?"

"I was just..." I stupidly let my eyes flicker to the spider. Hipster Dick and Warren both clocked the spider and then stared at me.

"Did you say something to that spider?" Rich's golden eyebrows drew down together. I didn't dare look at Warren – he was smirking, I knew it, and probably formulating a joke involving Prozac and Disability Living Allowance. But looking at Rich was almost worse. He looked... worried.

I've only known him half an hour and now he thinks I'm crazy, as well as a stupid girl, wearing a stupid horrible dress that doesn't fit and laughing along with Warren's awful jokes just because I don't know what else to do.

"It's, er, been hanging around here, you know, when you keep seeing a bug it's like, it's kind of like become a bit of a, like, a nemesis–"

Smack!

I jumped about a foot in the air and only narrowly avoided throwing my lemonade over Warren after all. Something had hit the window, right beside me. Heads turned all around the room and conversation died.

Warren, Rich and I stared out at the flapping shape on the outside windowsill.

"Just a pigeon," Warren said. "God, they're stupid." He rapped his knuckles on the window right in front of the pigeon's face. It cringed back, then tapped on the window with its beak as if it could bite his fingers right through the glass. Warren laughed.

"If I never see another pigeon it'll be too soon," said one of Dad's men in suits. "Window cleaning on the Shard is like painting the Forth Bridge. Only worse! I don't care how amazing the view is, I wouldn't live up there with only those mangy birds for company."

The woman in the peacock dress laughed. "Peter did offer me special anti-pigeon window protection, but I said no. I rather like them."

Usually, I quite liked pigeons too. But something about this one was giving me the creeps. It *was* particularly mangy. Most of its feathers were ruffled up, several were missing altogether. Plus, it had red eyes – they must've really been deep orange, but they looked red. It twisted its head weirdly up and down, as if it was searching the inside sill.

"Maybe it's after your nemesis," Warren said. Rich laughed, and I felt the blood rush to my cheeks. I looked down at my shoes. I smiled a cute, modest little apologetic smile. I hated myself.

Dinner was pretty awkward, but at least there was something I was supposed to be doing with my hands and my mouth so I couldn't say or do anything too ridiculously humiliating. I ate my noisettes of pan-glazed lamb in miniscule bites and took tiny sips of cranberry cordial.

It was nearly enough distraction, but Rich leaned over to me as the waiters were clearing the main course and lining up with their plates of artfully-arranged desserts.

"Hey, I'm sorry if I embarrassed you," he said.

"Er... when?" I tried to bluff.

"You know. With your arachnid nemesis." He smiled at me.

"It's funny, you don't look like you're mocking me," I said. "But how could you not be? I'd be mocking me if I were you."

"I'm not," Rich said.

There was a weird, semi-uncomfortable silence between the two of us. The rest of the guests chattered and laughed across the table. A waiter slipped a plate of pomegranate parfaits in front of me.

"I am sorry if you were embarrassed," Rich said. He lowered his voice. "Warren really is a massive wanker. I didn't mean to let him ramble. I really would like to take you round Trinity if you're still interested."

I was saved from having to say yes or no as Mum stood up and started to make a speech. I tuned it out, focusing instead on the reflection of light through my drink dancing in little circles on the tablecloth.

Finally she finished, we all ate up our desserts and people started filing back out into the drawing room. They were all laughing a bit louder, walking slightly less straight than before.

I stood up. Only another hour or two and then I could vanish upstairs and this whole horrible evening would be over.

There was a soft *rrrrrr* sound and a cool sensation on my right hip.

I looked down and saw a smooth blob of flesh about the width of my hand poking out through the ripped seam of my dress. It was right at Rich's eye level. His nose was practically touching it.

Oh. My. God.

Pinpricks of freezing sweat broke out all over my back and the room seemed to drift in and out of focus. I felt like I might faint. I took half a step backwards and nearly fell over my chair, bracing my feet on the floor and clutching at a passing waiter. There was a pinging feeling as another one of the stitches gave way.

Warren burst out laughing.

"Oof, had a few too many canapés, Maggie?" he said, incredibly loudly. Heads turned. People stared. Everything went blurry and tears stung in my eyes. I slapped my hand over the tear in my dress and made a dash for the door.

The cool air flowing off the tiles in the hall was a relief for a few seconds. I leaned against the table and nearly knocked over the vase of flowers. I grabbed for it and set it down, only slopping a little bit of cold, mucky water onto the varnished table-top.

Goosebumps started to pop up on my bare sausagey arms and the patch of exposed skin where I'd burst the seams of my dress, but my face and shoulders still felt like the blood underneath was slowly coming to the boil.

"Meg," said a soft voice.

"Oh God."

It was Richard, and I couldn't look at him. I shifted against the wall, so the table was between me and him, hiding the rip in my dress.

"Are you all right?"

"Ugh. Other than the fact that I look like an idiot, sure, I'm *fine*."

"Listen, seriously, don't worry about it." He was coming closer.

He was coming really, really close. He put his hands on my arms. They were hot and very slightly clammy against my goosebumps.

"It's OK. We can still make out. I like chubby girls."

For a second, the party seemed to go silent and all I heard was white noise in my head.

"I'm sorry... what?"

I couldn't have heard him right. *Make out?* Now, with me? Now?

"Come on, like you weren't thinking it too."

"I, I wasn't..."

Was I? I hadn't totally dismissed the possibility of seeing him again, some time when I wasn't squeezed into this dress, when I wasn't on my least-bad-behaviour on pain of wardrobing, when we could *talk*, like *normal people*.

"Well, you weren't listening to Warren. I know I wasn't. I was thinking about you."

I felt like I was floating somewhere just behind my head, watching all this, just not sure what the hell was going on. The words, themselves, were kind of flattering. So how come they felt so thoroughly *icky*?

My heart thundered in my chest, my mouth went dry. I licked my lips to try and fix it, to say something, and he just grinned at me. I tried to shrink back into myself, but he pressed his skinny pelvis up against mine.

"OK, no, Rich... I think..."

"Come on, let's go upstairs," he said, leaning in. His hands were moving. One of them slid down to my waist, tracing little circles on the dress, pulling the fabric with it.

Wait, was he–

The dress was creeping up my legs. I moved to pull it down and he laughed and held my hand in his, which is when I realised my hands were shaking.

It was the stupidest, most illogical thought I think I've ever had, but just for a second I told myself *I'd better not try to pull my hand away because I don't want to find out what he'd do next.*

"That's enough, this is... Hey, stop it." I didn't recognise my own voice. It was like a child's. I sounded pathetic! How could I not even find the words to tell him to sod off and stop groping me in my own hallway, not five metres from where my mother was standing drinking champagne cocktails with the Chief Whip?

There *was* something I could do. I felt my ears prickle and my spine begin to move...

I stopped it, forcing the change back. I couldn't do it. If I turned into a fox with him watching, with Mum and half the Cabinet in the next room, I'd probably be abducted by government scientists and live out my life in a cage or something.

Anyway, there was no way – no *effing* way – I was going to let Hipster Dick know my secret.

He raised a hand to cup my left breast and squeezed.

I reached out and grabbed the vase, shoved him away hard and chucked the stagnant flower water over his crotch.

He staggered back, righted himself and stood still for a moment, staring down at himself. The greenish-yellow water stained his light grey trousers as it trickled to the ground. There was a limp pink daffodil caught on one of his suspenders.

I brandished the vase like a club.

"Get out of my house."

"What the *hell*?"

"You heard me."

He swiped down his trousers with his hands, which did nothing to improve the look, tore the daffodil off and threw it to the floor like a kid chucking a toy out of its buggy.

"Well, you certainly don't have to worry about me getting you into Trinity. You stupid cow," he spat, turning and heading for the front door. "If you think your dumb, fat arse is getting *any* help from me–"

"Shut up," I snapped, still clutching the vase. "Shut up and get out."

He was on the front doorstep when he turned back.

"And tell your mother next time she wants to set you up she should warn the potential victim you're such a frigid bitch."

I slammed the door in his face.

Chapter Six

She set me up.

I put the vase back on the table with great care, because I was afraid if I didn't I'd hurl it against the wall.

She set me up with *that*.

I stepped lightly over the scattered flowers and crossed the hall to the cleaning cupboard. I unpacked one of the new rolls of paper towels from its neat row and spread the paper liberally over the floor.

She obviously didn't *know* that he'd – what he'd – what he'd try to – that he'd be…

I knelt and scrunched up soggy paper towels in both hands, squeezing them so hard the water leaked out again, which sort of defeated the point.

I couldn't even find the words for it in my own head, and I didn't want to anyway. I wanted to clear this up, change into some proper clothes and then hide in my room until either Mum sent Gail to drag me out again or I turned eighteen and could move out.

The nearest bin in the house was back past the drawing room and I didn't want to risk Mum or her guests spotting me. But there was a street bin on the pavement just in front of our door, despite Mum's increasingly frantic attempts to get the council to move it down the road.

I scraped up the paper towels and wet daffodils in my arms, managed to open the front door with my elbow, descended the front steps and dumped the rubbish into the bin.

When I turned back, there was a fox on the steps in front of the door, not more than a couple of feet from me. I froze, in case it startled, but it just sat still on its haunches and stared dead at me.

Normal foxes don't get that close. And they don't stare – they'll stop to make sure you're not a threat, but they've got things to do, bins to raid. They're busy. They don't sit and stare, certainly not for this long.

It looked smaller than the one I'd seen yesterday. It was definitely scruffier, its fur standing up on its back and a bit of mud caked around its paws.

"You're not James Farringdon," I said. The fox huffed air out of its nose. A snort? A laugh? "Are you from the Skulk?"

The fox nodded.

A sound slapped through the air and a gust of wind whipped my hair around my face. The fox gave a screech and reared up as a pigeon fell on it, claws first, beak pecking viciously. It was the one from earlier, its mangy wings leaving trails of dust and bits of feather in the air as they flapped madly to keep it hovering over the fox's head. The fox tried to snap at the pigeon and bat it away, its fangs shining yellow in the street light, but it had to keep turning away, squeezing its eyes shut to protect them from the pigeon's raking claws.

I seized the closest liftable object, a thin clay plant pot about the length and shape of a baseball bat, and swiped at the pigeon. It swooped out of the way, almost tumbling to the ground before shooting back up into the air. It flapped around my head, and I caught a glimpse of a sharp grey beak and mad red eyes, and then felt a needle-thin lance of pain just over my ear. I could taste blood. That was weird – had I bitten my tongue?

There was no pain, and no time to investigate. I lashed out with the plant pot again. This time there was a sick *clonk* and the pigeon slapped down on the steps. The fox pounced, snarling, but the pigeon half-rolled, half-flapped out of its reach and managed to take off. I jabbed at it with the spiky cactus fronds sticking out of the pot, and the pigeon flew off, dipping and reeling in the air until it disappeared over the roof of the house opposite.

I ran my tongue around my mouth but didn't find anything bleeding. Something trickled down behind my ear, though. I reached up and my fingers came away wet and red. The wound was small, when I found it – a single violent peck under the nest of my hair.

I looked down at the fox. It shook itself out, like a dog, and panted up at me.

"The Skulk," I said, because I couldn't think of anything else. The fox nodded again, jerked its head – a weirdly human movement – and looked away down the street.

I glanced back into the house. Amazingly, nobody had heard or seen the fight on the front step. The sounds of politicians chatting drunkenly wafted out to me, the sound of wine glasses clinking and my mother planning both her prime ministerial campaign and my wedding to Hipster Dick.

"Give me two seconds."

The fox nodded again.

I put down the plant pot, ducked inside and into the small toilet under the stairs. I peeled off the necklace, the shoes, the sausage dress and my underwear, bundled it all up and shoved it down behind the cistern. When I came back, if I could just get inside the house I'd be able to change back and nobody would be any the wiser. It'd be just like Superman or something.

It was a crap plan, but it was better than leaving my clothes in a mysterious pile in the street.

I changed curled up on the bathroom floor. There was the skin-prickle of fur bursting out all over me, the stretch and suck of everything inside me shrinking and rearranging... the weird too-bright moment of painful perfection where the sharp edges and scents of everything crowded in on me all at once...

In that moment, just for a moment, I scented something bizarre. It was like the fog, that smell-feeling of fizzing in my muzzle, but this was bigger – like a million sherbert lemons bursting in the back of my throat all at once.

Then the change had finished, and the strange scent had gone.

I twitched all over and got to my paws, half-blinded by the fluorescent pink stink of scented bleach with an overlay of something differently chemical that made me sneeze. Someone at the party had been doing lines of cocaine off the back of the toilet seat. My money was on Warren. As I trotted out of the door, I fervently hoped Mum would find out and chuck him out on his ear.

The fox was at the bottom of the steps now. She turned to look at me. "You coming or what?"

"Um, yes, I'm coming." I bounded down the steps, but before I could reach her she'd turned and raced down the street. I put on a burst of speed and drew level. She twitched her ears at me as we ran around the corner.

"You live here?"

"Yep. I'm Meg," I added, feeling we'd missed a step somewhere. "What's your name?"

The fox hesitated for a few seconds. She led me down an alley, around an obstacle course of recycling bins.

"Addie," she said.

"Nice to meet you."

She huffed again.

"What happened back there? Are pigeons always like that?"

"I dunno. I dunno if that was a pigeon."

"What? I mean, what was it then? Another shapeshifter?"

"No. Ain't no pigeon shifters. Didn't smell like a pigeon, though. It stank of, like... rotting meat. And blood."

I thought of the taste of blood in the air, after it'd hit me. A shiver rippled through my fur and my ears twitched back. Could I have been smelling blood on the pigeon – even in human form?

"Well, *that's* incredibly creepy," I said.

Addie didn't seem to want to talk about it. We ran for another five or ten minutes in silence. I tried to relax and let it all wash over me – the scents of the city, the night time air rushing coolly through my fur, the way I already felt steadier on my paws than last time. Pigeon-attack aside, I already felt more comfortable in this skin than I had in my human one for the last few hours. Addie's scent moved along beside me, almost like a warm creature independent of her fox shape. I could smell dirt and dust and concrete on her, and a musty dampness like mouldy fabric. There was a spicy food-scent too, a bit like the smell of a kebab shop.

I wondered what she'd smell on me.

"So where are we going?" I asked eventually, though as long as it was away from the house and the party – and the pigeon – it was fine by me.

"To the Skulk," Addie said.

"And, er... what *is* that?"

"*Us*, innit? Fox shifters. You'll see." She seemed like she was going to go silent again, but then she said, "We meet up Willesden Junction, on the siding, every week."

We stopped on a dark street lined with small shops and she stopped to scratch behind her ear. I got my first really good look at her, up close. There was a wide scar over her forehead and she had fleas; I could half-see and half-scent them moving around on her. She was noticeably smaller than me, when we sat side by side, and I could smell... something that wasn't so much a smell but a feeling of tension and energy moving through her.

She was young, I realised. Younger than me – but not a pup. Not actually a child. Maybe fourteen, in human years?

I realised I was staring at her, but I figured it was probably OK since she was staring at me, too. I hadn't thought to wonder what I looked like as a fox, before.

"That boy," she said suddenly. "With the wet trousers. He called you a frigid bitch. He feel you up, yeah?"

I sat back on my haunches, surprised. Was it that obvious?

"Yeah," I said.

Addie's tail lashed against the pavement. "You batter him?"

"No, I – I threw a vase of flowers at him."

She made a low growling sound in her throat and huffed more air through her muzzle. I was right, it was a laugh.

"You're OK," she said, and turned a wide, canine grin at me, then got to her feet and trotted off again. "Even if you are a princess."

'I'm not a princess," I said, trailing after her.

"What, living in one of them big houses? Whatever, Princess," said Addie.

"No really. I should know. My friend Jewel is a princess, a real one."

Addie's tongue lolled out of her jaws. "You are shitting me!"

"Nope. Her second cousin's the King of Bahrain."

"Oh my *days*. Does she know the Queen? Does she live in a palace?"

"They've met. Actually, she lives in an apartment building near Hyde Park, not that far from here." We'd turned a corner and suddenly come out onto a wide main road. I recognised the huge towering trees and boutique shops. Instead of darting across the road and back into the shadows, Addie turned left and we headed along the pavement.

"Don is going to flip his shit when he meets you," Addie said. "A real princess!"

"Who's Don?" I asked.

"Well, we haven't got a *leader*, cause we don't, but like... Don knows the rules."

"So how many of you... us, I mean..."

"Six. Same with the others."

This threw me. "Er, others?"

"Yeah, you know. Oh right, you don't. Other shifters."

"Spiders, by any chance?"

"Yeah, and rats, ravens and butterflies."

One of those things seemed kind of out of place to me. "Butterflies? Really?"

"The Rabble." Addie ran off the main road into a parking garage under a hotel. I followed her around and underneath the cars, through the labyrinth of metal and rubber. "You know like we're the Skulk? Butterfly shifters are the Rabble. Bunch of posers, think they're so superior just cause they've all got pretty wings. That's what Don says."

I was starting to look forward to meeting Don. He certainly seemed to know what was going on. Maybe he'd know about what happened to the other fox shifter – and what I ought to do with the blue stone that was still buried in my school playground.

My nose twitched as Addie led me through a cloud of petrol scent, out through the back of the parking garage and onto a thin walkway beside a main road. I thought we were heading north again, but I was starting to lose my bearings.

"Then there's the Horde – rats. We hate them," said Addie. "And they hate us. They live down the old Aldwych tube station. Fran caught one coming into our meeting place once; bit it so hard on the tail, half of it fell off."

Fran. I filed the name away and let Addie go on talking. She seemed to be enjoying the chance to impart her knowledge to someone.

"And the Cluster are the spiders. Take my word, don't trust the spiders. They're always *watching*."

"I think there's a spider following me," I blurted out. "I keep seeing it – it was at school, and then in my house..."

"Yeah, sounds like the Cluster." Addie shuddered, her fur rippling along her bony shoulders like bright orange water. "They're probably interested in you cause you're new. And cause you're young and pretty. Perverts."

I choked. "Really?"

"Don says," Addie shrugged.

"And the ravens?" I prompted.

"The Conspiracy," said Addie. "Only, you'll never see a raven shifter. Never come out of their tower, do they?"

"Wait!" I actually skidded to a halt on the side of the road. Cars roared past, stirring up tidal waves of *hot-dirt-metal-dust-mud-rubber* that washed over us. "The ravens in the tower? Not *the* Tower?"

"Of London," said Addie. "Innit."

"They're shapeshifters?"

"Six of them, yeah. The rest're just creepy old birds. Come on, it's a way yet and Don'll think I've lost you."

I managed to put one paw in front of the other again, as fast as I could go without tripping over something.

"There are always six?" I said. "How come?"

"I dunno. Not even Don knows. We just know shifting passes on when you die. That's how we knew... about Ben."

There was an awkward silence. I felt it was my responsibility to break it.

"Um. Did you know him well?"

"Fairly."

"I'm really sorry. That he died. Do–"

"Save it," Addie snapped, not looking at me. "Till we're with the others," she added.

We ran underneath a huge flyover, past a yard full of scrap metal that gleamed in the light from cars passing overhead, past a trailer park and a community sports centre. Addie bore left and we made our way alongside a train track in silence for a while, then climbed back up the bank to a small road crowded with grimy shops.

Addie stopped dead in front of me, sniffing the air.

"Fancy some dinner?" she asked. I sniffed. I could smell fried food. My mouth filled with drool and I instinctively opened my jaws to taste the air. It was delicious. My stomach rumbled. I guess it shouldn't have done, I had had dinner – but every fibre of my fox-being told me this was different, an opportunity not to be missed.

Addie led me into an alley beside a fried chicken shop. Its red and yellow and white lights shone out into the dark like the place was on fire. Addie and I shrank back into the alley between two shops as a pair of humans walked past, their legs rustling in baggy black tracksuit bottoms. One of them dumped a cardboard packet into a street bin.

An acrid, smoky smell followed them, but as it faded I could taste an amazing, juicy, meaty scent coming from the bin. There were chicken bones in that packet. I could practically see them, dripping and crunchy and gorgeous...

Addie darted forwards, reared up with her paws on the edge of the bin and thrust her muzzle deep inside. She drew back, her teeth clamped down on a bundle of bones, ran back into the alley and dumped them triumphantly in front of me.

My human brain did try to kick in, but I felt a rush of animal instinct and the next thing I knew I was digging in, crunching the bone and sucking out the marrow and chewing up the leftover peelings of skin and flesh.

It sounds rank, I realise that – but it just wasn't. Everything about me was fox, now. The smell from inside the bin, which I knew should've been foul, was actually like walking into a busy restaurant kitchen, or sniffing a bag of sweets. A mix of smells and flavours, not all yummy, and not all food, but all really *interesting*.

The chicken bone was one of the most delicious things I'd ever tasted. Not quite up there with Chef Duchamel's famous plate of international chocolate puddings, three of which I'd gleefully wolfed down under Mum's disapproving glare at my last birthday dinner. But pretty damn good.

I licked my lips, my large dark tongue flicking over sharp fangs and tickling on the fur at the edge of my mouth.

If my body-obsessive, food-fascist mother knew I was turning into an animal and eating out of a bin...

She'd probably strangle me with her bare hands.

But she doesn't know, and she never will. This is my life.

I crunched up the bone and sucked out the marrow, savouring every last greasy bin-scented bite.

Chapter Seven

We squeezed under a tall metal fence, around the back of Willesden Junction station, and I found myself at the top of a steep overgrown bank. It was covered in weeds, thistles and rubbish. For a second I couldn't see a way down. Then Addie led the way around a blackened tree-stump and I followed her through a tunnel in the weeds, between discarded beer cans and thorny branches that pulled on my fur when I got too close. A violent roar and a burst of hot air buffeted us as a train hurtled past.

The tunnel opened onto a scrubby clearing surrounded by dark trees and tall bushes. Three foxes – the rest of the Skulk – turned to stare as Addie and I emerged.

"I found her," said Addie. "This is Meg."

"Hello." I stopped on the edge of the clearing, suddenly shy.

Two of the other foxes were male, and one was female. One of the males was larger than the rest, his fur a vivid dark red flecked with white. He stalked towards me. Instinct flattened my ears against my head and I shrank back, pushing my front haunches down. Everything about him was dominant, intimidating. His scent was sort of spicy, and full of *male* and *power* and a sort of... *prime*. His eyes glinted yellow as he fixed them on me, and he was growling, almost too low and quiet to hear. I looked at Addie, but she had stepped back.

Over the large fox's shoulder, the other two watched. The other male was smaller, wiry, and almost all grey. The female looked sleek and poised, and had a white patch running down her muzzle.

"My name is Don Olaye," said the large fox. "This is the Skulk. You are the girl who took the shift from Ben Cohen."

"Um, yes."

He lowered his head till it was level with mine and his lips drew back.

"You will tell us what you saw," he snarled.

"Oi," the other male fox snapped. "There's no need for that."

Don didn't move his gaze from me. "One of the Skulk is dead, Randhir, don't you think we ought to question the only person who was there?"

"It could've been an accident. How did Fran get her shift? How did I? She's just a teenager!" The other male – Randhir – trotted up to us. He didn't quite get between Don and me, but he sat close enough that Don couldn't fail to acknowledge his presence. The larger fox's body language shifted and he drew himself up, looking imperiously down his nose at me.

"I'm Rand, love," said Randhir. "And that's Francesca. You've met Addie. And James."

Don's top lip peeled back and his ears pointed down and towards me, anger and disapproval coming off him in waves.

"Answer my question please," he interrupted. "What happened to Ben Cohen?"

"We want to welcome you here," Fran put in, padding up to stand on Don's right. "We just need to know what happened to our friend. Can you tell us about it?"

I glanced at Addie. I'd rather talk to her than either of these two – Don was still looming over me and Fran was talking like a nurse trying to coax a child to explain how the Lego block got up its nose. Rand sat back and scratched himself behind the ear with his hind paw.

"It was a couple of days ago – about three in the morning. I was at school."

"Why?" Don demanded.

"I... I was..." I hesitated. But then a mutinous streak flared up in me. What was the harm in telling the truth? What was he going to do to me? He wasn't my mother, or my head teacher. And I didn't want this part of my life to be built on lies, like everything else I did. "I was painting graffiti on the wall," I said. My heart raced. I'd never told anyone straight out like that before – other than on the internet, which hardly counted. Don growled, deep in his chest, but Fran nudged him and he quieted. I stole a look at Addie. Her head quirked to one side.

"What happened then?" she asked.

"I turned around and there was this fox, and it was hurt – and I wanted to see if I could help, except... then it turned into a man, right in front of me. He'd been hurt.

Stabbed, I think, in the chest. He died, and I ran away. He didn't tell me anything about this – I didn't know what was going on till the next night. I was out with some friends and I got mugged and turned into a fox by accident."

"Where'd you say your school was, love?" Rand asked.

"I didn't – I mean, it's in Kensington," I said.

"She's a princess," Addie put in helpfully.

"I am not–" I snapped, and then caught the look in Addie's eyes.

Oh, so you're trolling me. I stuck my tongue out at her. She gave me a panting grin, lay down on her stomach and licked her paws.

"Adeola," Don snapped. "Someone is dead. Please be serious."

"Oh, like you were such a fan of Ben in the first place," Rand muttered.

"He was one of us," Don said. "That's all there is to it."

"But what was he doing in a girl's school in Kensington?" Fran frowned.

I shook my head. "I asked if he... if he had anyone I should tell, you know, that he died. He just told me to..."

I stopped.

I don't know if it was Don's overbearing scowl, or Fran's wide, concerned eyes, but I decided to keep the sapphire to myself. Just a *little* longer. Nobody here apparently knew anything about it – nobody had said anything about any stone.

"He told me to watch out for the fog," I said.

"What did he mean by that?" Don mused.

"He must've been delirious. You said he was stabbed, I certainly don't think fog could have cut him," Fran said, slowly, as if explaining to a small child.

"No, I saw it. When I was with James the other night. It was like... fog that was *alive*. I felt it pull my tail!" They all gave me blank looks, so uniform they were almost comical. "Didn't James mention it?"

Don growled again. "James is a traitor, a liar, and a thief. And no, he didn't mention it."

"I... oh." I thought of the little rattling bag he'd been carrying when we ran from the fog. But that didn't change what I'd seen and felt...

"Well, *anyway*," Fran sighed, bowing her head slightly, "if you don't know anything more about what happened to Ben, I suppose there's nothing we can do. Perhaps he was simply mugged, or involved in some kind of fight."

I didn't think so. Unless he'd been the mugger, and got hurt while stealing the giant sapphire from someone else.

I hadn't thought of that before.

I wriggled uneasily.

"If we're finished, Don?" Fran asked. Don sat back on his haunches, drawn up tall, and nodded once. "Then let me welcome you to the Skulk, Meg," said Fran. She stepped forward and sniffed at my muzzle, touching her nose to mine. She smelled strongly of expensive soap, like my mum used. Rand ducked close, but didn't actually brush against me; he stank of petrol and cigarette smoke. Addie stepped up and nudged me in the shoulder with the top of her head, affectionately, but hard enough to make me wobble.

I caught my breath. If I'd been human, my face would've been turning bright red. Even considering that Don was still looking at me as though I'd done something deeply suspicious, this was probably the most welcomed I'd been anywhere since I left Brownies when I was ten. I had no idea if the feeling could be read on my fox face, but I found myself shuffling my paws and turning my face away from the others.

"Thank you," I murmured.

"You are one of us now," said Don. "And so you must live by our rules."

Rand's ears flew back and he growled. "Not this rubbish again."

Don's head snapped around and he bared his teeth at Rand. Rand looked small, skinny and scruffy next to Don, but he stood his ground.

"I've had enough of your tongue today, Randhir," Don snarled.

"And I've had enough of your rules," snapped Rand. He turned to me. "Don't you listen to him, Meg. He makes them up to suit himself. Nobody ever elected you leader of us, mate."

"The Skulk has been in my family for a hundred years."

"Oh yeah, I forgot, because you haven't mentioned it in ten minutes. Your father was a shifter before you, and his father before him, and his father walked fifty miles to school in the snow uphill each way and lived in a cardboard box," Rand sneered. "It don't make you better than us, kid."

"Randhir," said Fran, in a voice like grease on a squeaky door, "please, let's not argue about this." She glanced at me, and back at him. Her yellow eyes narrowed, the first time they'd been anything but wide and full of concern. I guessed she meant *not in front of the new girl*. "Don's rules are quite sensible."

"Don's rules are *bollocks*," Rand sniffed. "He makes them up to suit himself, but, God forbid any one of us amend them slightly..."

"Your wife's cooperation is not crucial to the survival of the Skulk. You should never have told her," Don barked.

"Now, Don, we've been over this. Rand said he was sorry," said Fran.

"I did not."

The three of them turned in on each other, snarling and bearing their teeth, leaving Addie and me on the outside. I backed off. They didn't notice.

"It's pretty crucial if you want me to keep coming to your precious meetings. She thought I was shagging around!"

"You should have thought of a better explanation."

"Why should I not tell my *wife* about something like this? What harm could it do?"

"Because the more people who know, the more complicated this becomes."

"Just because your sister couldn't cope," Rand snarled. "I don't blame her, either, from what I've heard..."

Don's hackles shot up and he bared his teeth at Rand. "You leave my sister out of this."

"Please, let's try to see each other's point of view," said Fran.

I turned to Addie. "Are – are they always like this?"

She looked at me with a hangdog expression, then jerked her head and slunk away to the other side of the clearing. I followed. The others didn't stop arguing, or seem to notice we'd moved away.

"Yeah. It's not Don's fault," she said. "It's not easy to lead a bunch of foxes that don't want to be led. I'd never leave the Skulk, but... some days I don't blame James for refusing to show."

I watched the three foxes – Don and Rand literally snapping at each other's throats now, and Fran wheedling at them like they were naughty children – and my heart sank like a stone. This was the Skulk. My amazing new world. It was a selfish thief, one young girl, and three bickering adults.

I caught my breath. My eyes were wet.

It was ridiculous. I guess I didn't realise how much I'd been hoping that I'd walk into this world and find... what? A whole new family? A ready-made group of friends to have wacky adventures with?

I felt so stupid.

"Aw, don't feel bad," Addie said. "It's not always like this. New people stir Don up. Fran was the last one in before you and he was just like this. He gets hacked off with everything cause he can't actually be God and stop people from dying, and then he takes it out on Rand because Rand doesn't know when to shut up. But he'll come around to you, long as you don't get in his face and disrespect him. Believe."

"I just... I was looking forward to finding out more about all this. I mean, why is this happening to us? Why can we do this? Why are there six of us, and not more or less?"

"Well, sorry, but even Don doesn't know that," Addie shrugged. "He says there's something important about meeting in this place, but I think he's just parroting what his dad told him."

"This place?" I looked around at the messy, overgrown clearing. It didn't look like anything special.

"Look," Addie said, scratching her side against a nearby tree, "Normally Don tries to run this like a church group or something, and we hang out and talk for a bit, but... I don't think this is going to be one of those times. You wanna slope off? We can tell them you've got to get home. I can walk you."

"Yeah, I think that'd be good," I said.

I stood back as Addie managed to slide in between the three foxes – still arguing fiercely – to let Don know we were going. He turned and looked at me and, for a second, I thought he seemed upset. Then his eyes went hard again, and he nodded.

"We'll see you next week," he said.

"Yes," I replied.

We walked back up the tunnel of weeds towards the road. I glanced back, but the Skulk was already lost in the tangle.

Chapter Eight

As we were walking under the huge flyover roundabout, between the trailer park and the sports centre, Addie stopped.

"Are you all right on your own from here?" she said. "It's just kind of out of my way to go any further. My den's really nearby."

Her den? I wondered if it was human slang, like crib, or if I'd come to call my house that when I'd been a shifter for a while.

"Oh – yes, I think so," I said.

"Just go on down the main road and then you're on Holland Park Avenue. Turn off at the Hilton, you can't miss it. Or spend the night there," she added, cheekily, "I bet five stars is like home, right, Princess?"

I laughed and snapped my teeth playfully beside her ear. I pulled back at once, afraid I'd overstepped – it'd been pure instinct. But maybe she'd be offended, or scared?

Addie panted, happily. "See you next week," she said, and trotted away without looking back.

The journey down the main road was scarier without Addie there, knowing exactly where it was safe to walk. Cars roared past dragging hot waves of stinking air along behind them, dulling my senses. I half-felt my way along the hard shoulder, pressing myself to the metal barrier just in case.

I wasn't unhappy, though. The Skulk may have been a bit of a disappointment, but – not to jump way ahead of myself, or anything, not to be overconfident, not to assume anything – I thought I'd made a friend.

The warm glow followed me down to the Holland Park Roundabout, up behind the Hilton, and along Holland Park Road. I decided to take the shortcut home – what was the harm, while I was still a fox? – and headed off the road between two embassies.

My pace slowed as I got closer and closer to home, and I was dawdling down a Kensington back-street, lined with little boutiques, jewellers and shoe shops, when something scuttled across my path.

The spider.

It stopped right in front of me. It was the same one. I tried not to shiver. With my fox eyes I could see it was very dark brown, its legs spindly and covered in miniscule hairs, its abdomen striped with tiny lines of a lighter brown colour. Tiny brown fangs poked out from the front of its face and eight shiny black eyes circled its head. It crouched low to the ground, its eight knees high in the air over its body. I couldn't get much of a smell from it – there was something totally alien about its scent that made me think of *fast*, and *very still*. I guessed that just meant I'd never smelled *spider* before.

"Hey, Skulk girl," it said. It was male – it wasn't the sound of its voice that told me, more a feeling, resonating somewhere near the back of my skull. My ears twitched.

"You've been following me," I growled at the spider.

The spider's fangs chipped together, exasperation in its voice. "I needed to talk to you. I was waiting for you to change, but I couldn't go outside when the pigeon was there and then you ran off with the other girl from the Skulk before I could get to you." The spider's back legs scraped the ground anxiously. "My name is Angel. I need to talk to you about the stone, the one you left in your locker."

I blinked. "My stone? But what's it got to do with…?" I trailed off.

Something was moving behind him. Something flowed out from under the door of the closest jewellers shop, stretching its grey tendrils across the road towards us.

"The fog…" I muttered.

"*What*? Where?" The spider leapt in the air and turned in a split second. "*Dios!* Run!"

I backed off, still staring at the fog. I felt that strange fizzing again and shook my head to clear it.

"What *is* it?"

Angel paused, his four closest eyes looking back at me – and that was when the fog struck out, one coiling tentacle twisting around Angel's back leg. He screamed. The fog sucked him in, like he was caught in an undertow. His scream cut off as the fog swallowed him.

I should have run, right then, but I didn't understand. I didn't know what I was about to see.

The fog formed a column in the middle of the silent street, with Angel hanging weightless in the centre of it, twitching, his eight legs clawing at the air. For a second, through a red haze of panic, I thought he might be drowning and I half-crouched to spring in after him.

Then his front and back legs splayed out, and the middle ones drew in. His body ballooned, the thorax swelling into a head and the abdomen squaring out into a torso. Hands and feet and fingers and toes burst out of the ends of his legs like flowers blooming.

I saw him change, silhouetted against the orange street light, in the grip of the fog. I barely had time to register his human form – he was young, brown-skinned, his hair a dark shadow across his skull – and then he writhed, flailed, clutched at his head.

And it burst.

A violent splash of red hung in the fog. It was like a galaxy: shards of bone, strings of skin and muscle, spiralling around a slowly-expanding cloud made of a million droplets of blood.

My back legs fell out from under me and I sprawled on the pavement. I coughed, and then slammed my jaws together: no time for vomiting.

The fog pulsated, contracted, and then relaxed. His body dropped to the ground. Blood fell like rain.

I scrambled up and ran, blindly, stumbling over my paws. My vision closed in and the buildings seemed to curl up and around me, a tunnel of brick and concrete with a roof of leaves. The shadows of trees clawed the ground as it passed underneath me. My paws thudded a drumbeat on the hard road. My bones jangled together.

I didn't know if the fog was following me, if it was falling behind or right on my tail. I couldn't look back.

A burst of light, a banshee screech and a blur of movement right in front of me. Pure instinct threw me to one side, my left flank coming down hard on the pavement, as the metal monster swerved and hurtled past.

Just a car. I got up, looked around. The street was full of shifting shadows and patches of light. The windows of the tall houses glowered down at me like a hundred cold, dead eyes. But I couldn't see the fog. I paused, panting, turning round and round on the spot and peering into every gap and shadow and turning for any sight of a searching tendril. There was none.

The time for vomiting finally arrived and I threw up, messily, and for what felt like a long time.

It took me a long time to get home, even though I was just around the corner. I could hardly move an inch without stopping, trembling, to look all around me. At one point a gust of wind stirred the hairs at the end of my brush and I fell down, paralysed, convinced the fog had found me, the end had come, my head was about to be shattered like an egg. I retched and threw up again, a trickle of hot bile stinging the back of my throat, and couldn't move for five minutes.

When I made it to my house, there was no way in on the ground floor. I had to go around to the back gate, climb up the fire escape to my window and turn back into a human, naked and shivering, to lift the frame.

After I'd climbed inside I caught my reflection in the mirror. I had a fine spray of Angel's blood spattered across my shoulders.

I suppose I should've showered. I couldn't. This wasn't like last time. I could *feel* what I would do if I could bring myself to do anything at all. I walked to the door of the bathroom and just looked inside, I don't know how long for.

I felt like a shell of frozen stone, with a hot core of molten fear boiling deep inside. I pulled on the first clothes that came to hand and sat down on my bed.

My hair stirred in the breeze from the open window, and I gave a little squeak of a yell and almost fell off the bed, clutching at my head. It was just the wind. I turned and clumsily slammed the window down.

There were running footsteps on the stairs. My door burst open and my mother stood there. She had the bunched-up sausage dress clenched in one hand, like a hawk with a limp corpse in its talons. Her face was scarlet, which made the tiny face-lift scars around her ears stand out white and proud, and her blue-green eye shadow look ghoulish and wrong.

She hurled the dress at me. The material fluttered through the air and fell limply at my feet, but one of the earrings flew out of the folds and struck true, stinging the side of my neck. I flinched.

"Where have you been? How did you get..." her eyes flashed to the window. She sucked in a lungful of air through her teeth. "You ungrateful sack of... of..." she stalked across the room to the window and threw it open. I didn't move, didn't even follow her with my eyes. "This used to squeak! Why doesn't..." She grabbed my shoulders, her fingernails digging in hard, and twisted me around. "Answer me, did you put oil on this? Have you been sneaking out? How long has this been going on?"

I didn't answer. I didn't meet her eyes. She drew her hand back and slapped me, hard.

"*How dare you* run out like that? I was *humiliated.* Where did you go, eh? You haven't been drinking." She sniffed. "You smell disgusting. What did you do?"

I didn't answer, and she slapped me again, and then again, harder. I felt her ring catch on my cheek and a dull ache settled there, like an insect burrowing in. I felt tears running boiling hot down my face. Mum was saying more things, but I didn't hear her anymore. I felt her coil her fingers in my hair and shake me, felt the pinprick-sharp pain on my scalp, but I tuned out her words. What could she possibly be saying to me that was worth my while listening to? I focused on a shiny button on her dress, through the watery haze in front of my eyes, letting the way it glinted fill my world.

She calmed, eventually. She always does. After all, if she were to beat me black and blue, there would be questions asked. She can't have people thinking she's not a good mother.

After she drew away, her hands shaking, I looked up at her. I could just about make out that there were tears on her face, too.

A hot ribbon of rage curled itself around my spine. She always does this. She always makes me think I'm the one that's done something wrong, that if she's mad it's because I've driven her there. I'm glad the window was shut, because if it had been open I might have pushed her out. I would've happily gone to prison. It wouldn't have affected my plans, and I didn't need people to love me. I didn't have an election to win.

"How dare you?" she moaned again, backing away. "You are grounded for *life*. I'm going to have that window boarded up. I'm going to... I can't look at you." She staggered out of the room and slammed the door.

Let her. Let her ground me for life. Let her lock me in the wardrobe until I was thirty. Let her pull my hair until it all fell out. I didn't care.

I never wanted to go outside ever again. Outside, there was fog that could make my head burst open and leave my decapitated naked body spraying blood across the road. There were mad pigeons that smelled of death, and shapeshifters who would bicker over how to run their club while the world rotted all around them. It wasn't an adventure any more. It wasn't freedom. It was just death.

I curled up on my bed and shut my eyes and swore, on everything I had ever held dear, on my life and on art and chips and freedom, that I would never shift again.

Chapter Nine

I didn't sleep. I lay on my bed in my clothes, staring into the darkness until exhaustion crept up and slipped underneath my skin like a sheet of ice, but I couldn't shut my eyes. They were raw and stinging – every so often a wave of tears swelled up and burst through, and I'd let out a strangled sob or two, and then swallow the tears again.

Every time I tried to go to sleep there was a swish, a thud or a tiny click, and my stomach twisted itself up, pushing my thundering heart into my throat. I clamped my eyes shut and tried not to think about heart failure. I was waiting for the fog to catch up to me, just waiting for the worst – but meanwhile, the routine noises of the night were going to kill me.

There was a rushing sound outside the window. I gritted my teeth and threw my arm over my face. I wasn't going to look. It was the wind in the tree, out in the courtyard. I knew that. I didn't need to check.

I was sweating, the wetness prickling in my hair and at the base of my spine. When I shut my eyes, all I could see was Angel's blood and bone hanging in the air. I could still taste the vomit, the corrupted taste of horror and chicken fat lingering at the back of my throat. I hadn't brushed my teeth. I hadn't even washed his blood off my shoulders.

Something outside rattled and scraped.

I wasn't going to look. I wasn't. There was a line, and this was me drawing it – I might be shivering and sweating and planning to run and hide, I might be throwing away the best thing I'd ever had, but I wasn't going to sit and stare all night, waiting for my death to roll up to the window.

Taptap. Taptaptap.

I sat up like a puppet pulled on strings. Panic blinded me for a second and I grabbed the first thing that came to hand – my pillow – and held it in front of me.

My room shifted into focus, full of the dim orange light from the streetlamps outside.

Taptaptap.

There *was* something out there. I bit back a scream and crawled backwards up the bed. There was a patch of twitchy blackness perched outside, almost pressed right up against the glass. I could feel it watching me. It tapped on the window again.

It wasn't the fog. It was a bird – enormous, as big as a buzzard, with sleek black feathers that gleamed with a weird blue-orange iridescence.

A raven.

It tapped again, with a thick black beak longer than my fingers. I clutched the pillow to my chest, uselessly, and wiped at my eyes.

You'll never see a raven, Addie had said. *They never come out of their Tower*. And yet, here one was. It tapped once more and turned a glimmering yellow eye against the window, staring in at me.

I went over, my knees quivering underneath me, and opened the window a tiny crack.

A flood of questions rose in my head.

Who are you? What do you want? Are you from the Conspiracy? Do you live in the Tower of London? How does that even work, do you fly around the White Tower all day being stared at by tourists? Why are you here now?

No. I ran a hand into my hair. I didn't want to know. I didn't want anything except to be left alone.

"Go away," I said. "Shoo. I'm not interested."

It opened its beak and gave a long, deep croak. Then it tilted its head. "Skuuuuuulk," it said. "Maaaaagraaaat."

I stumbled back, hugging the pillow, horror rising in my throat.

But then I remembered Year Nine English. Mr Howard had insisted that ravens could mimic speech like parrots, so it was entirely possible that the one in the Edgar Allen Poe poem had been taught to say spooky things to wind up the narrator, possibly by an angry neighbour.

At the time we all thought he was crazy. Right now, I could've hugged him.

"What, 'nevermore' wasn't creepy enough?" I snapped. "I'm serious. I don't want to talk to you. Sod off!"

Quoth the raven: "Naooo."

I shut the window and threw myself down on the bed with my head under my pillow. But it was no good. The raven started tapping again, a long tattoo of annoying chipping noises. I couldn't leave it doing that. What if Mum heard? What if it broke the window?

"Oh God," I sighed. "I don't want this. I don't want anything to do with any of this."

The talking raven outside my window glared in at me with its piercing yellow eyes, and I glared back with my watery red ones.

Then I got up again and opened the window.

The raven hopped in and fluttered over to perch on the top of my computer, its massive wings sending scraps of homework fluttering across the floor.

"I'll..." I coughed, cleared my sore throat. "I'll change so we can talk properly. Wait there. And don't look!" I slipped into the bathroom, pulled off my clothes and twisted myself into fox-form. It was almost easy now. I hesitated in the bathroom for a second and pawed at the carpet, my flanks heaving. It felt so natural. My ears twitched and I raised my head to taste the air.

My room smelled mostly of me – my own body scent with a hefty chemical overlay of cleaning products, pencil shavings, a little make-up and sticky, sweet hairspray – but the raven's scent was in there too. He smelled of old, wet stone and wood.

And you're still so new, said a mutinous voice in the back of my mind. *Imagine how much better at this you could be in time. Imagine the worlds that would be open to you if you weren't such a coward.*

But I am, the rest of me retorted. *I'm a chicken and a yellowbelly, and this is the last time I'm changing for anybody.*

I padded back into my room and stared up at the raven perched on my computer screen.

"What do you want?" I asked. "I can't talk long. If my mother hears something..."

I hesitated, bleakly entertained by the notion of Mum finding a fox and a raven conversing in her daughter's empty bedroom in the middle of the night.

The raven tipped forward, his yellow eyes glinting in the streetlight. "My name is Yeoman Warder Blackwell." I blinked at him, surprised – his voice was softer than I'd expected. There was none of the harsh raven's caw in it. He shuffled his talons on the edge of the computer screen and dipped his head again in a sort of salute. "I need to know what happened to you tonight."

I needled the carpet uneasily.

"Margaret, I know it doesn't seem like this right now, but I promise if you can talk it through you will feel better."

"Meg," I corrected him automatically.

"Meg, I'm sorry," he repeated.

"How do you even know anything happened? Were you following me?" I whined.

I don't care, I reminded myself. But I knew it wasn't true.

A boy died. He *died*, and I still had his blood on my fur. Another shifter's corpse, right in front of me, and I had no idea who they were or why they'd died. Again.

"I was following the spider," he said. He took off, fluttered over to the window and hopped out. "Shall we continue this outside?" he said, twisting his head at an inhuman angle to look up at the roof.

The cold breeze coming through the window stirred my fur and my ears twitched. I realised how stuffy and stifling my room had become. It couldn't hurt to just step out and feel the air on my face. We were high up, so I'd probably see the fog coming.

Of course, I wouldn't have much chance to escape, unless I sprouted wings like Blackwell's and flew away.

I shook myself, twisting head to tail like a dog coming out of the sea.

"All right, fine," I said. "Let's go."

I always wanted the roof of my house to be a secret, romantic getaway spot where I could sit and look out over London and sketch and not think about my mother. The reality was a bit different. The fire-escape that ran past my window ended in steps so steep they were almost a ladder, and it hadn't been a pleasant climb, especially when my vision was blurred with furious tears. It'd been freezing cold, uncomfortable and not the least bit romantic.

It was actually slightly easier as a fox – the steps were almost on a reasonable scale, and my brush helped me keep my balance. Blackwell circled above while I was making the climb, a black hole of a shape against the grey-orange sky.

It was darker up on the roof, and I kept my muzzle low to my paws as I padded carefully up the sloping tiles to the flat section that ran the length of the house. I smelled traffic and the deep green scent of leaves in the trees that lined our road, pigeon shit and the faint scent of something salty and sizzling. Was one of our neighbours cooking at this time of night?

When I got to the flat part of the roof and looked up I could just make out the yellowy urban starscape of lights that never went out in the skyscrapers beyond Hyde Park. The wind chill made my eyes water, but even as I huddled in the lee of a chimney stack I felt a little better for having the open sky over my head.

Blackwell circled once more around the roof and then landed in front of me and folded his wings close to his body, hunching a little to shelter himself from the wind. He blinked, and I realised he had a thin set of sideways eyelids, like a lizard. "Awrite. Meg. If you're ready, I need to ask you: when did you first see the spider?"

"No, I want some answers first," I said, taking a deep breath of cool air as if it was a stiff shot. "I want to know who you are and why you care about what happened to Angel."

Blackwell let out a soft *cawwww*. "Was that his name?" He shifted his wings, flapped once and settled again. "I've been following him for a few days. I thought he knew something that could help me."

"Help you do what?" I asked.

Blackwell hesitated. He was still and silent for nearly a full minute, so long that I started to swish my brush around my paws nervously, wondering if he'd heard me. "Help me do what?" he said eventually. "That's actually a good question, one I don't have a very good answer to yet." He sighed. "Stopping the fog and saving the world. That's what I wanted Angel to help me with."

"Oh, really." I gave him my best, most withering foxy glare.

"Well, close enough." He flapped his wings and took off, fluttering up to perch on the chimney stack. He looked all around him, over the glimmering lights of London, and fixed his gaze in the direction of the City. "Have you wondered yet what this is all about? *Why* you have the power to turn into a fox? Where that power comes from?"

"Well, I… I Googled it," I said weakly.

Blackwell chuckled. "Ach. And how did that go for you?"

"I gave up pretty quickly," I admitted. In my defence, I'd barely had time to breathe since last night, let alone ponder the mysteries of the universe. Still, I felt a bit foolish for never thinking to ask Addie or Don. "Does it… does it have to come from somewhere?"

"Shall I tell you the story as it was told to me when I was initiated?"

Initiated? I thought of Don's little speech about the rules. Was that all the initiation I was going to get? I felt a little jealous of Blackwell. It sounded like the Conspiracy did things properly.

"I was told that long ago – *long* ago, before the Romans, before there was anything here but scattered villages and the river – a magical weapon was forged."

"OK, *wait*." I couldn't let him just go on like this. "Magic? You're talking about a magic spell. Like, *wizards* and stuff?"

Blackwell gave a low croak. "You're a fox, talking to a raven about killer fog. What, exactly, makes *wizards* so hard to believe?" He hopped from one foot to the other.

"They roamed the countryside, fighting constantly, tearing great wounds in the earth and building their towers taller and taller. The taller the towers, the more powerful and more competitive they became."

I followed his beady black gaze over to the skyscrapers in the City, and my ears twitched back involuntarily.

"All-out magical war raged for years," he went on, "Until one man decided to put an end to it. He created a weapon that brought together five points of power… five elements of the universe, if you like."

"If I like," I muttered. This was all sounding a bit *Lord of the Rings* to me, but he had a point: how could I know what was a fairytale and what was real, anymore?

"I know," he said, presumably reading my expression. "It gets a wee bit worse before it gets better – will you bear with me?"

"I haven't got a lot of choice at this point," I pointed out, settling down with my brush curled around me and my head on my paws.

"Aye, in for a penny," Blackwell acknowledged, giving a short nod. "Well, this wizard and his weapon were quite prepared to wipe out every living thing in a hundred miles. But the wizard wasn't alone; he had an apprentice. And she had a change of heart. She took control of the weapon and turned it on the wizard. She threw down the towers and sent their warring masters away; then she tore the weapon apart. Her own power wasn't enough to destroy it, so she hid the pieces. She set the five weards, one to guard each of the elements and keep them separate."

I'd decided not to interrupt again, but I couldn't let this one go. "Weirds?"

"We-ards, with an A – from 'ward'. That's us. She took five animals and borrowed their shapes, lending the weards the ability to change and blend in with both humans and animals. And the wizard's assistant set herself as the first leodweard – the ward of the land. She was a metashifter. She could change into any one of the five shapes she'd picked, to help and advise the weards and make sure the stones were safe. Once the weards had hidden their stone, she was the only one who could see or move it."

A shiver ran down my back, from my ears to my tail.

He could talk all night about weirds and wizards and towers… the magic word was *stone*, and he'd just said it.

Little details flashed into my mind like fireworks going off. When I first saw the fog it was near the jewellery shops, with James, who'd had a bag that rattled suspiciously. There were jewellery shops on the street where I'd met Angel. The fog had actually come out of one, before it killed him.

"What were the five elements? I thought there were only four – earth, water, wind, fire," I said, examining the fur on my paws closely. If I could have crossed my fingers at this point, I would've been crossing them that the Skulk didn't have something rubbish and made up like "heart".

"Those aren't the elements we're dealing with. The way the Conspiracy tell it, we guard the element of Mind in the wizard's own tower – rebuilt a hundred times over the centuries, but essentially in the same place. The Skulk guarded the Hands. The Rabble had the Sight, the Cluster had the Shadow, and the Horde had the Spirit."

"How come nobody mentioned any of this to me? I was with the Skulk this evening and nobody ever said we had any kind of sacred duty."

Blackwell shook his head. "I wish I knew. If what the Conspiracy has told me is right, we should be helping each other remember and keep our elements safe, and instead…" He made a disappointed clicking sound with his beak. "As far as I can tell, ours is the only one that's locked away, safe in the White Tower. They've been lost and forgotten, and now I believe there's someone using at least one of them. Exactly what for, I don't know yet."

He flapped back down to stand in front of me, his feathers puffing out around his chest.

"The fog you saw kill that poor shifter is a creation, a spell, most likely made with the power of at least one of the stones."

All my fur stood on end and I clawed at the rough surface of the roof, tears springing to my eyes as I remembered the fleshy thud of Angel's body hitting the street in front of me. "But – but someone *made* the fog? On purpose? It *ate his head.*"

"Not exactly. It consumed his mind, swallowed all his thoughts and memories. It – and its master – now knows everything he knew."

A shuddering chill ran down my back. My tail swished to and fro almost of its own accord – I felt like there was a buzzing insect I needed to brush away.

Angel was on my locker when I put the sapphire away. If the fog was looking for it…

I swallowed hard. "I first saw Angel at my school," I said.

Blackwell's head twitched to the side. "When was this?"

"On Friday. And then I saw him here, I think, earlier this evening. But I wasn't changed so he couldn't talk to me. And then when I was coming back from the Skulk I was walking down the road and he ran into my path. He stopped me. I was…" I felt a twist of guilt and turned my head so I wasn't looking at Blackwell. "I was angry with him. I mean, he was stalking me, I thought. But he said he'd been waiting. He wanted to talk to me about something that I'd found."

I risked a look at Blackwell. His head twitched again as he realised I'd trailed to a halt.

"Go on. It's all right," he said.

"I found a giant gemstone," I said, and Blackwell nearly fell over. He righted himself with a massive flap of his wings and gaped at me.

"You've *got* one of the elements?"

"Well, I – well, yes. Apparently. The Skulk shifter had it on him when he died." Blackwell looked like he was going to speak, but then shut his beak with an audible click. He gestured with one wing for me to go on. "Angel told me he knew I had the stone and I'd left it in my locker. And then I saw the fog, and… and he was sucked in."

Blackwell tipped his head back and shut his eyes for a moment. "So it knows," he said weakly. "We may already be too late. Another one lost."

"Not necessarily," I said. Blackwell gave me a piercing glance.

"What do you mean?"

"I put the stone in my locker on Friday, morning, but I moved it later that day. I put it–"

"*Waaaark!*" Blackwell flailed with both wings, buffeting me with cold air. "Don't tell me! We're all in enough trouble if I get caught in the fog as it is." He started to pace, his head bobbing as he took each step back and forth across the roof. "If you put it somewhere else but Angel thought it was still in your locker, there's hope that whoever's controlling the fog won't have found it yet."

"What do I do with it?" I asked. "If I get it tomorrow and bring it to you, can you–" "No, don't bring it to the Tower," Blackwell said sharply. "It's best if you take it straight back to the Skulk."

"But you said the Tower was safe." I got to my paws and stretched. "I don't think the Skulk even know about all this; how are they supposed to protect it if the fog comes after them?"

Blackwell said "Ach," again and shook his head. "Awrite. You go to where you left the stone tomorrow and see if it's still there. Then come and find me at the Tower and we can talk about it. And I'll… I'll do my best to help you. *Don't* bring the stone. If the fog's master hasn't found it yet then it'll be safer where it is."

My eyes narrowed as I watched his feathers rustling in the stiff breeze. Was it my imagination, or did he seem even more twitchy than before?

What aren't you telling me?

I didn't ask – after all, he wouldn't have told me. But a prickling feeling of unease settled in at the back of my neck.

"Are we agreed?" Blackwell asked.

I nodded. "All right. I'll meet you at the Tower tomorrow, after school."

"I'll be looking out for you." He leapt into the air, his wings stretching out to their full span, and flapped away. I stared after him until he was just a dim shadow against the orange-black sky, then lay down and rested my head on my paws.

This was crazy. It was something beyond horrifying – it was *absurd*. Magic spells, wizards, towers and magic jewels?

I growled at my own stupidity, the sound resonating low in my chest. This wasn't absurd at all. Angel was dead. Whatever had killed him, I had to take it seriously. I owed him that much.

I climbed back down from the roof and in through my bedroom window, then shifted back to human form and took a shower, watching as the last of Angel swirled away down the drain. Afterwards I gazed at my reflection in the mirror for a second.

I was still weak from exhaustion and shock, but my strength was starting to return, slinking back like a loyal dog that'd been shut out in the rain.

Blackwell was right – crazy as our talk had been, I felt better for it. I wasn't sure if I could trust him or believe his fairytale, but it was better than nothing. I wouldn't just wait here to be eaten by weather. If there was a mind behind the fog, it could be stopped. Maybe it could be reasoned with, or thrown in jail, or *something*. At the very least if I kept the Skulk stone safe, perhaps I could stop it getting worse. Maybe I could even find a way to do what the metashifter hadn't been able to – destroy it, for good.

I had absolutely no idea. But I knew I had to try.

Chapter Ten

I vaguely heard the click of the key turning in the lock, and then Gail's bony fingers gripped my shoulder and shook me awake. I surfaced scowling.

"What?"

"Get up," Gail said. "You've got ten minutes."

"What?"

"Don't give me 'what'. It's Monday. You're going to school."

I groaned and tried to burrow back under the covers, clutching at my head. I didn't remember going to sleep.

"Your mother says she doesn't care how hungover you are. She's calling the builders to fix your window today and she doesn't want you underfoot."

"I'm not hungover," I grumbled, before the second half of what she'd said hit home. I sat up, my mouth sagging into a shocked semicircle. "She's really going through with that?"

"Up," Gail snapped, and walked out.

I sat up, burying my hands deep in my hair. I'd rather not go anywhere within ten miles of school. In the piercing light of the morning, the whole encounter with Blackwell felt like a weird dream, whereas Angel's death felt more real than my own skin.

I could still see the blood hanging in the air, still feel vomit and panic in the back of my throat. I could feel Hipster Dick's hands on me, and the instinctive cringe in my spine at Don's growl, and a hot stinging patch on the right side of my face where Mum slapped me.

Everything was so wrong.

I hadn't really agreed to go and check on the stone with the fog still out there, had I? What the hell had I said I'd do that for?

Normally I'd stay home sick on a day like this. I'd spend it curled up in a duvet watching DVDs on my computer and sketching the awful away. I have a whole sketchbook buried at the bottom of my trunk, full of artistic interpretations of whatever was bugging me. Every other page is a portrait of my mother, each less flattering than the last.

Something told me "I feel sick" wasn't going to cut any ice today.

I couldn't have just *one day* to hide under the covers and feel sorry for myself?

No, of course not.

When I stomped down the front steps, I was planning to bunk off and go straight to the Tower and tell Blackwell I wasn't going anywhere near the stone by myself. But by the time I'd got to the end of the road I'd changed my mind. The fog or its master might have tracked down my hiding place somehow. I needed to know *what* I was going to tell Blackwell, and if it was going to be "I had the Skulk stone but now it's gone" it was better to be prepared.

Besides, I thought, *maybe the wizard will have come in the night and razed my school to the ground. That would be worth seeing.*

The tall white brick building was still standing. I walked up to the front door more slowly than I ever had in my life, even back in Year Nine when Shauna Harris was going through her I-dare-you-to-expel-me phase and my school life was so hellish I was "sick" on average three days a week.

Ameera appeared at my elbow and bounced us both through the door and up the stairs.

"*Meg*, oh my God, are you OK? I'm so sorry if me and Jewel left you on your own on Saturday night. It's just Nick and Deshawn said we had to come and see their studio, and we did a couple of rounds of shots and frankly it's all a bit of a blur but we had the *best time* – did you get home OK?"

"Yeah, I was fine," I said. *Actually, I had one of the best nights of my life*, I thought. *Seems so long ago now...*

Our form room didn't look like it'd been ransacked. I went over to the window and peered out. There was no sign that anyone had been digging up the grass. I slumped against the frame and let out a long breath as Jewel jumped up to give Ameera a good-morning-hug.

I looked over at the lockers. A ghost of shock and revulsion ran through me as I remembered the spider, climbing down over the top of them just as I was putting the stone away.

He wasn't just a spider, he was a real person, and he died because he was there that day.

At lunchtime I slipped behind the Kit Shed again and scrabbled in the dirt, my heart beating a frantic rhythm against my ribs, until my fingers brushed something cool and smooth.

"Oh my God," I breathed. "Thank God. Hi," I whispered to the stone, stupidly but happily, as I pulled it from its hole and wiped the dirt from its surface with my thumb. The sunlight glinted clearly on the star in its depths.

I felt that strange lightness again, just for a second.

The Hands, I thought, turning it over and over. *What does that even mean?*

Just one of the many things Blackwell hadn't gone into last night.

I reburied the stone, deeper than before, and rearranged the weeds so that they covered the newly-turned earth. I was suddenly very glad I'd come to school. Just for once, I was a step ahead. The wizard hadn't found the stone. I could do this. I could keep it safe. Whatever Angel's killer was after, I could keep it from them.

It had never felt so good not to be helpless. I found myself actually looking forward to telling Blackwell all about it. I even smiled all the way through Double Politics. It was so unusual that Ameera kept asking me what was going on, in a more and more insistent voice, until finally Miss Freiboden snapped and gave her detention on the spot.

••••

I set off for the Tower right after school, only pausing to wave goodbye to Ameera, who was staring out of the detention room on the third floor with a comically forlorn look on her face. I hopped on a bus headed towards High Street Kensington tube, clinging to the yellow rail and squeezing from side to side to let gangs of schoolkids and mothers with buggies get past me, going over and over what I'd say when I got there.

It hadn't occurred to me earlier, but I realised that I didn't know quite how I was going to find Blackwell once I got to the Tower. What if none of the warders had heard of Blackwell, or they knew him but they didn't think he'd want to see me? What could I say to convince them it was important without blithering about magic stones and just crossing my fingers that I'd found one of the Conspiracy? I could pay to get in to the Tower and go straight to the ravens – and then what? Stand there asking them if they were secretly people? Maybe I should change into a fox, but if I was spotted by the human warders they wouldn't want me anywhere near their birds...

My mobile bleeped in my pocket. I jumped. I didn't get many texts, and the ones I did get were usually from Ameera – but they always confiscated phones at the start of detention. So who was texting me? I guessed it was going to be spam from the hairdresser's again, but when I looked, the little blue box said:

Dad

Come home ASAP sweetheart.

My heart juddered in my chest.

Sweetheart?

Dad never called me sweetheart. Hell, Dad never texted me at all.

What was wrong? Had something happened? My mind hopped madly from theory to theory. Had Mum finally had a total breakdown? Was I in trouble? Were they splitting up? Were we skipping the country? Was Granddad dead?

The bus pulled up outside the tube with a hiss and I stepped out. I looked at the tube, and then back at my phone.

Then I kicked myself, and crossed the road to the bus stop going back the other way. I was probably a bad daughter, but I wasn't *that* bad. The stone was safe for now. Blackwell could wait.

The back gate was open, and a sleek silver Jaguar was parked haphazardly inside, blocking in Mum and Dad's huge black beetle-cars. I hadn't even thought, until just then, how weird it was for them to be home at this time of day.

Dad usually stayed late at work, overseeing his firm's latest construction project or helping to sell off the leftover office space – either that or he'd have to take the Qatari finance minister out to dinner or meet Rupert Murdoch in a strip club or whatever else CEOs did.

I sometimes wondered if he was having an affair. I hoped he was. Having Mum as my mother was bad enough, I couldn't imagine being *married* to her.

Mum should be at work, too. She would usually rock up in time for dinner, take an hour from terrorising backbenchers to terrorise Hilde and Gail, scream at me for something so minor it made my blood boil, scream at me again for getting angry at her, and then shut herself in her study and go back to running the country.

All in all, this was looking bad for someone.

My hands started to shake as I fished my keys out of my pocket and held them up to the front door. I paused, clutching on to the handful of cool, pointy metal, focusing myself into the feeling in my hand until I calmed down a bit. Then I forced myself to slide my key into the lock carefully, turn it slowly, step deliberately into the hall.

I breathed in, and my hand flew to my face as just for a second as I smelled something tangy and strange on the back of my throat, like fizzy sweets. It felt like I needed to sneeze. But the feeling vanished in a blink.

There were voices coming from the drawing room, but they sounded... happy. I could hear Mum, Dad and another female voice I didn't recognise. Dad chuckled. Mum said, "Of *course*."

I followed the voices and hesitated in the doorway.

I expected a stone-faced policeman handing out sympathetic cups of tea; maybe some lady in a suit bearing tidings of our impending bankruptcy; maybe just my mother with a face like death, breathing fire.

The third person in the room was the black lady who'd worn the peacock dress to Mum's party. They were all sitting on the white Queen Anne sofa, sipping cups of tea. It looked like perfectly ordinary tea between friends – although they were drinking it from the best china, the genuine antique china from China. Mum looked up at me, and smiled.

She smiled. Her cheeks actually wrinkled. I nearly dropped my keys.

"Er. Hi," I said.

"Ah, hello, Margaret," said Dad, also smiling. "This is Victoria Martin, do you remember? She bought the penthouse in the Shard."

"Hello."

Victoria Martin smiled at me too, over the rim of her teacup.

I stood there for a few seconds, my hand in my pocket clutching at my phone. I raised my eyebrows at my Dad, and he raised his right back.

"Do you want to join us, Margaret?" Dad asked. "We're just having a nice chat."

A nice chat, with the woman who owns one of the most expensive flats in the world. I guessed it had to be Party contributions. Whatever Victoria was selling, Mum's government would be right behind it, in exchange for a couple of million a year. No wonder she'd broken out the antique teacups.

...But why text me? Why invite me to join them?

"I got your text," I prompted. "I was going to pop out, but I came straight home."

"Ah. Yes, I wanted to see you, didn't I? Come in, have a cup of tea. There's sugar," he added, taking the lid off the Chinese china sugar pot. I rolled my eyes. *Right, I'm allowed to have sugar. And the flying pigs, when are they getting here?*

But Mum didn't shut him down, didn't make any snide comments or even glare at me to make sure I knew I was expected to politely decline. She was still smiling, as if she had not a care in the world. Victoria had to be offering her money beyond her wildest dreams. Campaign money? Was this Prime Minister money?

And she wanted me to join her new contributor for tea?

It occurred to me, with a nasty jolt, that this had to be some sort of scheme. Perhaps I was going to be sent abroad or pensioned off into a job at Victoria's company, whatever it was. Perhaps this was her backup plan after failing to get Hipster Dick to seduce me into buggering off to Cambridge.

I didn't entirely want to know what it was, but if it was something bad enough that I was going to have to run away from home I decided I'd rather just know now. I dumped my bag in the doorway, walked into the room and planted myself in a chair opposite the sofa.

"Hi," I said to Victoria, with a tight grin.

"I have a couple of questions, actually," said Victoria.

"Um. Oh?" I was a bit thrown off my sulk. What kind of questions would she have for me? She took a sip of tea and a bite of biscuit, clearly not in any hurry to explain.

I looked her over while she swallowed. She was looking a lot less glamorous than she had at the party, but she still carried the tell-tale signs of someone with more money at their disposal than they could possibly ever use. Her loose cream shawl was probably Spanish cashmere, draped neatly over a silky rust-coloured A-line dress – I would've guessed retooled vintage. She was wearing her hair pressed down flat at the front with a wide black band so it fanned out behind her ears. Her shoes were polished black Leboutins.

"You go to Kensington School for Girls, don't you?"

"Yep," I said, taking a biscuit, catching Mum's eyes – still blankly calm – and taking three more.

"Wasn't that where they found that man?"

"Yeah, last Thursday. He'd been stabbed. Or something." I imagined just carrying on, nibbling on my biscuits between statements of fact. *I was there. His name was Ben. He was a shapeshifter. It turns out he gave me more than one thing that night... Now I've got to get to a raven in the Tower of London to save the world. Or something.*

"Terrible shame," said Dad. "Gang violence, I expect."

"In Kensington," I deadpanned. Dad nodded and smiled at me again as if I hadn't just cheeked him. Victoria's eyebrow quirked up and she gave me a little smile.

"I was just wondering, you see," Victoria said. She took another sip of her tea and set it down on the saucer with a little *chink*. "I was just wondering where you put the sapphire, Margaret."

My hand spasmed and the biscuits crumbled between my fingers, crumbs dropping all down my trouser leg and scattering on the carpet. I half-braced myself for Mum to shout at me about the mess – and she didn't.

"What?" I breathed.

Victoria smiled at me again. "The stone, with the star in it. The one that was in your locker. It isn't there now. I want to know where you've put it, Margaret."

I stared at her, and then I looked at Mum and Dad, waiting for their reactions to this. But their faces had both gone blank. They both seemed like they'd drifted off into a pleasant daydream.

"Mum? Dad?" I reached across the coffee table and shook my Dad's knee. He didn't react. "What did you do to them?"

"They're not here right now."

I looked at the pleasant half-smile on Mum's face and wondered if they'd been here at all since I'd got here.

"I know you have it, Margaret," Victoria said, her voice still calm and reasonable.

"It's *Meg*." I closed my teeth over the words. Victoria raised her eyebrows at me.

"I'm sorry. Meg. You know how I know, don't you?"

"You killed Angel. You're the –" I stopped. I wasn't going to say "wizard" out loud to this person, sitting on my sofa, drinking my tea. I just refused. "You're in control of the fog?"

"I know it's not at the school." She turned and looked out of the front window, and I twitched back as I followed her gaze. There was a pigeon outside, its red eye pressed up to the window. "My fog has just been there, it found nothing."

A thrill curled in my stomach, something like victory – and nothing like it. I'd outwitted her so far, but it wasn't much comfort. I looked up, certain I'd find the grey tendrils of the fog hovering over my shoulder, just waiting to drag me in. The air was clear.

"Now, you will tell me where the stone is," Victoria said. "Or I'm afraid I'll have to hurt your parents."

I glanced at Mum and Dad's blank faces again. "Hurt them?" No. She'd been to my house, she'd done business with Dad – probably with both of them. She'd voluntarily attended one of my mother's parties, for God's sake. "You can't be serious. They're your friends!"

"They're scum," said Victoria.

The words *They're not* crowded up to my lips, like screaming passengers trying to escape a sinking ship. But I wouldn't let them out. I looked Victoria in the eyes. I saw what she was doing. She wanted me to leap to their defence, to think of everything I loved about them, so I'd get all sentimental and hand over the location of the stone.

Well, joke's on her, I wasn't going to do it. She could explode my head if she wanted. She wasn't going to hurt her friends, and I wasn't going to defend them.

I forced out a shrug. "You won't hurt them," I repeated. "I'm not telling you anything."

Chik.

I looked up. The pigeon outside the window was tapping on the glass with its sharp, curved beak.

Chik. Chik.

Was that supposed to put me off? I turned my gaze back to Victoria, fixing her with what I hoped was a steady, resolved glare.

"Is it in the house?" she asked me. "I could tear the place apart, but I'd much rather not."

I shook my head. "I'm not telling you."

Chikchik. Chikchik.

My eyes were drawn back to the window. Another even grottier-looking pigeon, tapping on the glass, its rhythm not quite syncing with the first one. As I watched a third flapped down, trailing dust and blackened feathers, and joined in with the others. *Chik chikchik chikchik chik chik.*

"Is that... what are they doing, like Chinese water torture or something? Am I supposed to be scared?"

"No, dear," said Victoria. "They're not for you."

Chikchik chikchiktap.

Tap.

Mum's long, thin middle finger pulled back and then swooped down, every tiny movement seeming huge and terrifying, and tapped a slow rhythm on the side of her china teacup.

I felt as if the breath had been stolen from my chest.

"Mum?"

Her face was blank but her finger kept tapping.

Taptap.

"Dad. Stop it."

His finger came down on the coffee table. His face was as blank as Mum's.

The chorus of chipping from the window was growing louder. I tore myself away from my parents' blank eyes and glanced up. There were more pigeons – five, six, eight of them. And Mum and Dad were staring ahead, their eyes empty and their fingers dancing on the table.

Chikchiktap chiktap chikchiktapchikchiktap

A crack snaked across the window.

"Stop it," I hissed at Victoria.

"It's too late," she said, and leaned back in her seat.

The glass shattered around the pigeons and they flocked into the room, a flapping and fluttering crowd of dirty pecking clumps of feather. I shrieked and ducked my head, threw my arms up to shield my face.

A crackling sensation shot through my sinuses and there was that taste again, stronger this time, like fizzy sweets dipped in battery acid.

Air buffeted my shoulders and pulled at my hair, and I tensed for the feeling of claws raking my skin and beaks stabbing into my neck. But they didn't attack me. I peered through my fingers, my eyes watering, and saw them settling on Mum and Dad's shoulders, flapping all around them, totally obscuring both of them from view.

I lunged out of my chair and made a grab for the iron tools beside the fireplace, seized a heavy black iron shovel and whirled around to swipe at the pigeons.

My weapon sliced through the air, and the fluttering mass of birds scattered to the far corners of the room, taking up positions on the sideboard, the back of the sofa, the mantelpiece.

Mum and Dad were gone.

Chapter Eleven

My hand went limp and the shovel crashed to the floor, leaving a black wound on the carpet and a resonant *thunnng* ringing in the air.

"I did tell you." I turned to see Victoria standing up, brushing a mottled grey feather off her cream shawl. "I'm not messing around, Meg, I want that stone."

"But they're–"

"My friends? I wouldn't go that far. I did get on with your father," said Victoria. "They've both been very useful to me over the last year or so. That's the only reason I didn't kill them."

"But they..." I spun around, searching for any sign she hadn't disintegrated Mum and Dad, but I saw nothing but pigeons.

One of them flapped down onto the arm of the sofa.

I looked into its red eyes and saw twitchy rage staring back at me. It was... familiar, but twisted, filtered through a mad, feral animal.

I mouthed the word "Mum", but no sound came. I cast around the room for Dad, but I couldn't pick him out of the crowd. Any one of the pigeons could have been him. I felt dizzy and clutched my hands in the empty air, feeling like I was trying to hold on to my sanity by my fingernails.

How many other people's dads were staring at me now with their weird orange pigeon eyes?

Victoria reached out a finger and touched Mum – the pigeon – on the back of the head. She – it – opened her beak and let out a long *cooooo*. "Now, be a sensible child and tell me where you've hidden my stone, or I shall have your mother peck you to death."

"Waterloo Bridge," I said.

Victoria's eyebrows shot up. "Oh, good girl! I really thought I might have to murder you." She scooped up a brown handbag and hooked it over her shoulder. "Let's go," she said.

"Wait," I croaked. I swallowed hard. "If I help you find it, will you turn them back?"

"Of course," Victoria said. "I've no need to hurt you if I've got the stone, right?"

I didn't believe a word of it.

"OK," I lied right back. "Then let's get this over with."

The back seat of Victoria's silver Jaguar smelled of new leather and made a low squeaking sound as I scooted along to try to keep my distance from the two evil pigeons that used to be my parents.

I don't know what was wrong with me, but I hadn't really freaked out until the car started to pull out of the drive.

Then I looked down and saw that my hands were shaking. A throbbing pain stabbed into my ribs. I felt like I'd just run the full length of Oxford Street. I couldn't look at the – at my – at *them*. I twisted away and huddled up to the window to watch my house vanish as we cruised away down the road.

It was all gone, just like that.

My mum. My dad. My house. My room, with my laptop and my paints and my horrible bathroom carpet. The party fridge. The wardrobe. Dad's study. Mum's Cabinet memos, all her secrets and plans.

My life as I knew it had just come to an abrupt, feathery end.

And Hilde and Gail… where were they right now? Had Victoria got rid of them already? If they were dead, how long would it be until someone called the police? Until the police came round to my school asking who'd seen me last? How long until the papers got hold of the story? Where would I be, when the happy family picture hit the front pages? Who was going to explain to my Granddad that his whole family was missing?

I felt too frozen with panic to really cry, but two big, splashy teardrops fell on the cream leather seat back, and I balled my hands in my sleeves to soak them up.

It took a few tries, but eventually I forced myself to turn and face my parents.

Mum looked madder than Dad. She was mostly grey, and she looked sleek – but not like a well-looked-after pet. More like she'd been caught in a clear oil slick. She was emaciated. I could see her ribs through the thin down on her breast. She dug her talons into the seat, the claws tearing through the leather just like they'd tear through skin.

Dad was bigger, darker-grey and brown, and messy. The down stuck out between the feathers of his wings. He pecked around in the foot well of the seat. He didn't seem at all interested in me. I guessed if Mum decided to peck out my eyes he'd be right there with her, tearing at me with that heavy grey-yellow beak.

Story of my life.

Victoria had said we should bring them along so she could turn them back when she found the stone. I stared at their sharp beaks and claws, and I knew that as soon as she found out I'd lied to her she would have them tear me to shreds.

I forced myself to turn away, my eyes stinging with tears again as I stared at the City of London passing beyond the Jaguar's tinted windows.

It's my fault. Just for once, it really is all my fault. I'm so sorry.

Mum made a little bubbling sound in her throat and her body twitched. I could've let myself believe it was a response – one I couldn't translate, to a statement I hadn't even made out loud – but a thin, trembling line of rationality prevailed. She was a pigeon now. She was just being a pigeon.

I leaned forward, my head almost pressing against the back of the driver's seat, and tangled my hair in my hands.

We were drawing closer to Waterloo Bridge. So much had happened since I'd read the location of E3's latest graffiti on graffitilondon.com. It felt like a hundred years had passed. But the information had lodged in my mind and then risen to the surface, like a drowned corpse in a river floating up in the spring.

The corpse of an old life. Even if I survived the next hour, what was my life going to be like now, without a home, or a family? What the hell was I going to do now?

I had to get out of here. Abandon Mum and Dad, for now, and run for my life. I tried the handle on the car door as we pulled up to a red traffic light, hoping to just tumble out onto the road… but no luck. The child locks were on and I was trapped.

I'd have a better chance of getting away if I were a fox, but when could I change? Even when Victoria unlocked the car to get out, she'd be watching me. Plus, I'd be slowed down by my clothes. It was a shockingly practical thought. The trousers might be OK by the time my legs had shrunk to fox-size, but I'd almost certainly tangle myself in my school shirt and my bra, and by the time I wriggled free I'd be pigeon-food.

Victoria stopped the car and I raised my head to glance outside.

We'd pulled up right underneath the bridge, where it crossed over the top of the Victoria Embankment, parked half on top of the pavement. I was pretty sure you couldn't park here, but an hour ago I was pretty sure people couldn't be turned into pigeons.

On the other side of the bridge, the setting sun was glinting off the Thames and casting bright patches of light and shadow across the road, between the huge trees and the spiky forms of tour boat moorings. Under the bridge the shadows were dark, but the light reflected from the water danced prettily on the bricks. A young couple with matching Mohawk haircuts – except one was pink, the other blue – strolled along the river, hand in hand. I think one of them was singing. I watched them with tears in my eyes.

Victoria swivelled in the driver's seat to look over her shoulder at me.

"Where?" she asked.

"Um... I hid it..." I swallowed back the tears and stared out of the window, desperately trying not to look like I was making up the details on the spot. I pointed. "See there, where there's building work?" There was a tall plywood fence up around part of the wall, plastered with the logo of the coffee shop that was going to be there when the building was done. "I got through the fence and hid it, in a hole under some bricks."

"A hole," said Victoria. She stared at me for a second.

That's it, I thought, bracing myself and casting another terrified glance at Mum and Dad. *She's on to me. I'm going to die.*

"Stay here," she said, and got out of the car. I grasped for the door handle, but her hand shot into her purse before I could turn it and there was a *kathunk* from all four car doors. The lights on the dashboard went out. I tried the passenger door, then leaned over the driver's seat, tugging on the door handle. No good. I stabbed at the buttons on the dashboard, looking for an on button or a door release, but it stayed resolutely dark.

I was locked in.

My skin prickled and froze as she walked towards the fence without looking back at me. She wasn't going to let me out of the car at all. She wasn't going to let me out. I couldn't get out.

I couldn't breathe. My chest was hitching like a trapped animal, I could see it, I could hear the air passing through my throat, but I felt like I was drowning. A black haze swirled at the corner of my vision, and I tried to turn, thinking it was the fog again. A wave of dizziness carried me up and beached me with my head against the cold glass of the window.

I couldn't get out. She was going to find there was no stone and give the signal and I'd be pecked to death by my own parents, right here, pressed into the new leather seats. I'd die bleeding into Victoria's foot-wells, shreds of my skin scattered across the darkened windows. She wasn't going to let me out.

I yanked at the buttons on my shirt and tore it off. The pigeons flapped and cooed, but a terrified moment of staring out of the window told me Victoria couldn't hear them. She was inspecting a hole in the fence. I managed to undo my bra on the second try and then leaned into the front seat, running my hands over everything in search of something hard that I could pick up. I fumbled into the glove compartment and my heart pounded in my chest – there was an ice scraper with a hard, pointy end.

I grasped it and pulled back to the passenger window. I took a split second to brace myself, gather my strength.

The instant I hit the window Victoria would know. I'd have no more than a handful of seconds to make a hole big enough and change.

I felt a pinching, stabbing pain on my elbow and yelped as looked back. Mum had pecked me, hard, and drawn blood. I gripped the ice scraper like a dagger, and stabbed. The window cracked, but stayed in place. A moan escaped my throat and I stabbed again, and again, until finally the window shattered into a hundred chunky pieces of glass. They sagged out but hung on to the window frame, held together by the tinted layer of plastic.

"Hey!" Victoria's shout rang out, muffled, outside the car. "Stop her!"

Another shove with the ice scraper sent the whole shattered pane of glass toppling out onto the floor and I twisted into fox shape just as the pigeons' claws came down, raking across my back. I felt deep wells of pain open up in my flesh, jolting energy through me as my perspective shifted. The colours faded, and the scent of blood and foulness overwhelmed me.

My back legs scrabbled for a grip on the shiny leather even as they were still forming, and I pushed up and out, tumbling half-changed through the window. My tail burst from my back and my hands shrunk into paws, just as I came down hard on the shattered glass on the road. I stumbled, one of the shards slicing through my right front paw pad, but I heard Victoria shriek with rage and the flapping of two pairs of wings, and I didn't stop to look back.

I sprint-hobbled down Victoria Embankment, half-blinded by pain, in and out of the slanting shadows. There had to be a way off the road, somewhere I could hide, somewhere I would be safe...

I ducked under a bench, almost on pure instinct, and a second later, a fluttering thump hit the slatted wood over my head. There was a hoarse croak and a shower of foul-scented dust, and I looked up to see a snapping grey beak and one mad red eye.

Mum.

I opened my jaws and hissed, and she snapped at me again. I could feel blood trickling though my fur. This wasn't safe. I couldn't stop.

But Mum...

"Please," I whined. "Mum, don't you know me? Can't you..."

I stopped myself. There was no point. She wasn't really Mum right now. I'd find a way to put this right, I *had* to, but right now she would kill me if I let her.

I took a second to lap at the wound on my paw, and then braced myself to spring out of my hiding place.

I shot out from under the bench and ran straight into a warm, feathery mass – the heavier, mouldier pigeon that was now my Dad. He pecked at my flank and I swiped, my claws springing out by instinct. I felt one of them catch, and Dad fell back with a burst of feathers. My paw ripped away, a few drops of fresh blood trailing through the air after it.

Oh God. Dad!

A fresh wave of horror hit me.

Dad, I'm so sorry. Please be all right. You shouldn't be here. This is all my fault. I'm sorry...

Pigeon-Dad twisted back, black beak open wide. I got a split-second's glimpse of a freakishly pink tongue lashing like a worm on a hook, before he went for my eyes. I twitched away just in time and took off running again.

My heart felt broken, like it was hanging loose and useless in my chest. Like I'd died, and I just hadn't stopped moving yet.

There! Finally, I saw hope open up in front of me. A hole, a blessed, heaven-sent hole, right at the base of one of the buildings. It looked like it was supposed to have a metal grille across it, but it was open and dark. It smelled of dust and things that snuffled and scurried as I threw myself inside. It was just wide enough to take me, and so dark I might have been about to knock myself out on a dead end and I wouldn't know it, except that I could feel air rushing through my fur, stirring the sensitive hairs around my muzzle.

The pigeons were right on my tail, but the tunnel wasn't wide enough for them to flap their wings, so they were reduced to a bobbing hop, and I gained ground quickly. The tunnel grew cold and damp, and the scent of rats grew stronger, and I pressed on until suddenly I could see an orange glow. Literally, a light at the end of the tunnel. I put on a burst of speed and stumbled out into a vast space. I'd come out in the curved side wall of a tunnel with dim electric lights strung on the walls and metal rails along the ground that stank of electricity and grease and a black, sticky kind of dust.

This was a tube tunnel. Some deep-down part of my brain that apparently didn't have enough to worry about supplied: *probably the District and Circle lines*. I turned right and scampered up the tracks as fast as my aching muscles would take me.

Chapter Twelve

It was dark when I finally climbed out of Tower Hill tube station. I slipped between the feet of puzzled commuters and under the Oyster card barriers before the staff could react, and huddled in the bushes outside the station for a few minutes, catching my breath and hoping that nobody had called the RSPCA. The last thing I needed right now would be to be snatched up and imprisoned in some wildlife centre with a bunch of actual foxes.

I made my way to the Tower in short sprints, darting my way from shadow to shadow across the road and down the slope towards the gate and the drawbridge. A few straggling groups of tourists were still hanging around outside the entrance to the Tower, but the gate itself was shut. I hopped over the low wall around the moat and trotted down the blessedly soft, damp, grassy slope. I could circle the tower and get in through the holes in the portcullis across Traitor's Gate. It was a bit of a tight squeeze and I hissed in pain as the metal of the gate scraped over the wounds on my back, but then I was in.

It was obvious why Blackwell had smelled the way he did. Every corner of this place gave off the scent of old stone, old, wet wood and new varnish. If history itself had a smell, this place reeked of it.

I climbed the steep steps and slipped through the wooden gate that kept tourists from going down to the moat level. The stone was smooth and cool under my sore paws, dented by time and millions of visiting shoes. I was limping, one paw pad still stinging from the shattered glass, but even that felt better on the stone.

The raven cages were in the centre, near the base of the White Tower. I padded up to them with a growing sense of dread. I could see a group of dark shapes inside, pecking at their feed.

This didn't feel right. Why would a shifter live like that? But I couldn't see any Warders around, and I couldn't dismiss the idea that one of them might be able to help me.

Feeling self-conscious, I crossed the courtyard and slipped under the metal chain onto the patch of grass, passed an enormous black iron cannon and drew near the cages.

"Um, excuse me," I said.

The ravens ignored me.

"Excuse me? I need to talk to someone – I need to talk to Blackwell, is he here?" I took another step forward and one of the ravens flapped over to the front of the cage. It tipped its head and opened its beak, but all that came out was a long, loud caw.

Suddenly, as if at its signal, the cages came alive with flapping, cawing and croaking. I stumbled away, my heart racing, my fur prickling all along my back. I heard a door slam behind me and I tried to spin around, but put too much weight on my wounded paw and fell onto my side, blinded by pain for a moment.

When my vision cleared I saw a tall human shape hurrying towards me, thick woollen overcoat unbuttoned and flapping in the wind. The ravens quieted to an anxious background flap as the man hopped the metal chain and skidded to a halt a few feet away.

It was a Yeoman Warder. Deep blue coat that looked black in the darkness, dim brown trimming I knew was really red, flat cap in the same colours.

"Meg?" said the man. He leaned down and the shadows under his hat shifted so I could see his face.

It was the strangest feeling, like meeting a close relative of someone you know well – there was a shock of recognition along with the certain knowledge that I'd never seen this face before.

He had a thin face and pale, wrinkled skin, with a short ginger beard and small, light grey eyes.

"Margaret Banks? It's Arthur Blackwell," he said. He had a soft voice and a Scottish accent.

I twitched as the door behind him banged open again. But Blackwell twitched too, threw a glance over his shoulder, then turned back to me with urgency in his eyes.

"Please, hide," he hissed. "Get under the cannon and don't come out till I say. Please, it's very important."

I hesitated a split second. Then I did what I was told.

I wormed my way under the huge iron cannon with my belly flat to the grass. The underside of the gun was deep in shadow, and it smelled of paint and a far-off, possibly imaginary echo of blood and gunpowder. All I could see was Blackwell's boots, polished and gleaming in the damp grass. They turned and shuffled to attention, and a few minutes later another pair of boots – identical, but slightly larger – stepped into view.

"What's the alarm, Blackwell?" said a man's deep voice. I smelled cigarettes and expensive brandy, and wet wool and leather from both their uniforms.

"False alarm, sir," said Blackwell. "A cat. Just a stray. It spooked when the ravens sounded the alarm and ran off."

"They're a little sensitive this week," said the other voice.

"Yes, sir. Perhaps it's the weather."

Even from here, I could tell the other man was sceptical. He shifted his weight and made a "hrm" noise in his throat. "Old wives' tale. You should be careful what you believe, Blackwell – you sound like you've been talking to the Rabble."

So this was the leader of the Conspiracy. Why did Blackwell need me to hide from him? I wished I could've seen his face.

"Is there anything else?" said the man.

"No, sir. All's well, sir."

I frowned. All was not within a hundred miles of well.

"All right," he said. "Carry on, Blackwell."

Blackwell's boots slid together and his knees locked. I was pretty sure he'd saluted.

"Yes, sir."

I waited, breathing in the cool fumes from the cannon, until Blackwell's stance relaxed.

"Come on out, Meg," he said. I slunk out of my hiding place and looked up at him. He took off his hat and wiped his sleeve across his forehead. "We need to talk."

The inside of the Yeoman Warders' accommodation – part exclusive apartments, part barracks – smelled of varnished wood, tradition, leather and polished swords. Its scent was overwhelmingly male, though I was pretty sure there were a few female Warders nowadays. It was so thoroughly steeped in routine I could almost have traced the criss-crossing paths of the different Warders through the air.

Blackwell sneaked me inside at his heels and let me into his apartment, disappeared for a few nerve-shredding minutes and came back with a pile of clothes in his arms. He put them down in the bathroom – a neat, gleaming place with lots of wood panels, gold taps and polished mirrors – and said we could talk properly when I'd changed.

The change hurt.

I crouched in the gap between Blackwell's bath and his toilet, pressing my head into the wall and groaning. My legs splayed out on the cold tiles. I flung a still-fuzzy arm over the cool white bath and clung on while the change flowed through me.

The wounds on my back and my paw were changing with me, stretching out along with my skin. Each one stung like – well, like a rough hand stretching an open wound. Tears sprang to my eyes and I twisted my unhurt hand in my hair as it cascaded out of my head and settled on my shoulders.

When it was over, I struggled to my feet and turned, wrapping my arms around myself, to look at the damage in the bathroom mirror. Three small cuts on my back – much, much smaller than they felt from the inside – a scrape on my elbow and one puncture wound on my hip. There was a thin layer of caked-on gore around each one. The one on my left shoulder-blade was oozing fresh, red blood when I moved.

My parents did this.

I scraped my hair back from my face, as if I could brush the thought away.

No. Victoria did this.

The cut on my hand was longer, but not deep. I ran it under the cold tap and bit back my moans until the flesh went numb.

I picked through the pile of clothes Blackwell had brought me. There was a pair of pants and a bra that were slightly too small, but not so much they were painful – except where the bra strap ran over the open wound. I wondered where he'd got them, as I adjusted the straps to be as loose as possible. Maybe they were his girlfriend's. Giving me his girlfriend's underwear was kind of creepy. Then again, I was bleeding on another woman's bra. That was pretty creepy too.

The other clothes fit pretty well. I slipped into the pair of black trousers – cotton-nylon blend, with no pockets, a white T-shirt screenprinted with a picture of the crown jewels, and a large hooded jumper with the Historic Royal Palaces logo stitched on the breast.

I glanced at myself in the mirror before I went out. I was bleeding, my parents were pigeons, I was wearing another woman's pants, and the rest of my clothing had clearly been stolen from the Tower of London souvenir shop. But I was alive. And I was going to get help.

I opened the door and stepped out into Blackwell's apartment. Even though I'd spent a few minutes in there as a fox, I'd not really taken it in – it had just been a blur of scents and textures under my paws.

The corridor was painted in plain cream, with a couple of pictures hanging on the walls – a painting of a heather-covered mountainside, a framed photograph of him with the Queen and another of a group of young men with Seventies moustaches and regulation hair. They were gathered around a regimental banner with thistles on it. One of them had to be Blackwell, but I couldn't spot him in the sea of gingers. The sitting room beyond was oak-panelled and warm, with a large brown leather sofa taking up most of the floor-space. There were bookshelves on most of the walls. One of them was full of medals and certificates. I was crossing the room to get a better look when Blackwell emerged from another door, carrying two mugs.

He'd made tea. I could have hugged him. Instead I sat on his sofa, sipping at the sweet, hot caffeine while I told him everything that'd happened since he'd flown away last night.

He listened and nodded, and when I'd finished he put his mug down on the coffee table beside the sofa, and said "I'm very sorry."

"Thanks," I said.

"But..." he sighed and ran his hand over his eyes. "I'm not sure how much I can help you."

I stared at him for several seconds.

"But you've got to," I said. "I've got nowhere else to go," I added, trying to keep my voice level. "We have to help my parents. We have to stop her getting the stone, don't we? I thought that was what we were *for*."

"I'm sorry," said Blackwell. He scratched his ginger beard and shook his head. "You have no idea – you don't know what I might have done, bringing you here."

"What have you done?"

Blackwell stood up and walked away from me. He stood in front of the bookcase with all the medals in it, then gazed out through the thick, warped glass in the small window.

"I'm giving you the stone," I pressed. "If the Skulk can't keep it safe then you take it, keep it in the Tower. I'm telling you, it's at my school, in the back garden."

He raised his hands to stop me, too late, and groaned. "I wish you hadn't told me that."

"You just have to dig it up," I went on. "All I'm asking you to do is tell me how I can fix this so Victoria will turn my parents back and leave me alone."

"Oh, Meg, I wish it was as simple as that."

"*Simple*." I put my mug down hard on the coffee table. The loud noise made Blackwell glance out of the window again. "How is any of this *simple*?"

"The Skulk stone is Skulk business," Blackwell said, as if every word was being twisted out of him like a cork out of a wine bottle. "The Conspiracy cannot officially get involved in Skulk business. That's what Chief Warder Phillips says. He believes the other weards have forgotten their purpose and let their stones get lost, but he says we can't get involved, not even to help the others keep their stones safe. None of the Conspiracy knows that I've been investigating this sorcerer – this Victoria. I'd be punished for letting you bring us into this."

"*You* brought *me* into this," I snapped. "You're the one who turned up at my house in the middle of the night first, remember?" I twisted the edge of the Palace hoodie between my fingers.

"I know," Blackwell sighed.

"Also, I don't think it's particularly fair to compare a scrubby bit of land near Willesden Junction to the *Tower of Fricking London* when it comes to keeping things safe!"

"It's not just the Tower. There's something the weard can do to keep their stone safe from outsiders."

"Well, what is it?"

"I don't know," said Blackwell, and I rolled my eyes dramatically at him. "I'm sorry, the Conspiracy stone's never been out of the Tower, so the protection hasn't been broken. I haven't even been up to the vault since I came here."

"It doesn't make any sense." I shook my head, boggling at his strange leaps of logic. "If we've all forgotten our purpose, your duty has to be to help us remember it. What about the apprentice from your story? I can't remember the word..."

"The leodweard," Blackwell said.

"The metashift. Didn't that pass down like the shift? Isn't there still one of those out there? If the Conspiracy won't come down out of their tower and help the rest of us, isn't it the metashifter's job?"

"You're right," he said, "It should be. I heard whispers... gossip that there was a shifter out there with the power to be any one of the weards. I heard they'd been seen with the Cluster. But I was never able to find them, and if the knowledge of the elements has been forgotten, they wouldn't know there was anything they were supposed to do."

I threw my hands in the air and slumped back into the sofa, wincing as my clothes rubbed across the scrapes on my back. "Well then, you have the knowledge, you have to do it, don't you?"

Blackwell didn't answer for a second. He looked at the medals and certificates again. I peered at them over his shoulder. There was a red military cap in there, propped up at a rakish angle against the back of the bookcase.

"You're right," he said, very softly. "I have to share what I know." He turned away from the bookcase and sat back down in the chair opposite me, leaning forward. I sat up involuntarily and bent my head towards him. "I used to be military police," he said, meeting my eyes, speaking deliberately. "I know corruption when I see it." He shook his head. "I never expected to find it here."

Corruption? "How can a group of shifters be corrupt?"

"Power corrupts, doesn't it? We're sitting on one fifth of what may have been the greatest weapon the world has ever seen. And the elements are powerful enough by themselves – this Victoria has conjured killer fog and transformed your parents. And others, by the sound of it. We don't know which stones she's got, but we know it's no more than three out of the five."

He paused to let this sink in, and I shuddered. "But, are you saying the Conspiracy are *letting* her get the other stones? Why?"

"I'm not sure," he admitted. "I don't know what's in it for them. Maybe she's paid them off or she has some leverage with Phillips. Maybe it's not even that simple."

I took a long breath, putting it all together in my mind. "So, if they find out that you know there's something going on..."

"Or if they find out I've been disobeying my direct orders by trying to track down the other weards' stones," Blackwell continued. "I don't know what they'll do. Removing me from my position won't be enough. The only way to take away someone's shift is to kill them. I don't know yet exactly what I'm dealing with."

"God. Maybe I shouldn't have come here," I said. A cold lump of sadness settled in the bottom of my stomach. "I just – I had nowhere else to go." I looked down at my nails. They were torn. And one of them had dried blood underneath it. "My parents," I said. My voice had gone weak, almost mousy. I sort of hated it. "I don't even like them and now they're... gone." I dragged my hand across my eyes, roughly, as if I could deny the tears welling up if I wiped them away with flair.

"No, I told you that you should come. Perhaps I should have trusted you with this yesterday. Either way, you see why I cannae get the Conspiracy involved with this, not yet."

"So what am I supposed to do now?" I demanded.

"Maybe if you go and get the stone?"

I shook my head. "Oh no, no, no, I'm not going back there by myself. I just can't."

"Can't another member of the Skulk go with you?" Blackwell asked.

"I've only ever met them once – how can I ask them to come and maybe get killed with me? Plus I don't know where any of them live."

Blackwell went quiet, thoughtful, for a few seconds.

"I do," he said.

Chapter Thirteen

I stepped off the bus underneath the Westway flyover, the small change from the tenner Blackwell had given me to get here jingling in the front pocket of my hoodie.

"Go to the traveller site," he'd said, "And you should be able to sniff her out."

I knew where that site was. Right underneath the Westway roundabout, next to the stables and the sports centre, there was a big scrap metal yard and the only genuine trailer park I'd ever seen outside American television.

I pulled the hood up over my hair and hurried down the street. The quickest way to get there would be to change into a fox and slip through behind the houses, through the apocalyptic wasteland of concrete and gravel right underneath the flyover. I followed the advice Blackwell had given me and skulked around the backs of the houses, as close to their backyards as I could get without actually breaking and entering, looking for somewhere I could take off my clothes and leave them stashed somewhere safe. I finally found a dim corner where I could be alone, with a wheelie bin to hide the clothes under. I disrobed as quickly as I could, the chill night air and the fact that I was committing indecent exposure under the Westway roundabout competing to see which could make me shiver hardest.

As a fox I took a second to sniff around the base of the bin for scraps, hoping there'd be a bone or some stale bread, maybe even a mouldy potato. But there was nothing. My stomach rumbled.

I'd sometimes stared out of the car window as we shot across the flyover and wondered what kind of people lived in the trailers down below. Did traveller families live there permanently, or was it just a passing stop on the way to some better, greener place? Once or twice I'd seen children playing, chasing a ball or taking it in turns to ride a beaten-up bicycle round and round the gravel yard between the trailers. But apart from that there were gaps in my imagination where real life people ought to have been.

I hadn't given it all that much thought. Just written it off as something I didn't know, and would never need to.

But now I knew.

Addie lived there.

Blackwell was right: I crossed the threshold, under the metal arch, and I could immediately pick out her scent among the smells of traffic pollution, fast food and diesel oil. It was because she was younger, I guessed, as I sniffed around the edges of the trailers, trying to figure out which one belonged to her family. I could pick up the scents of *shifter* and *growing* and *female*, all tied up with fleas and something musty and sort of like wet paper.

I tried not to think about my house – comfortable, warm, furnished in the finest mix of modern and antique, and only a little bit like a prison. I tried not to pity Addie. After all, my house had been warm and safe right up to the point Victoria walked in. Now I might never be able to go back.

I followed the scent around another trailer. It seemed to lead around to the back – maybe they had a back door? The gap between the trailer and the wall of the park was tight, though, and only got tighter as I padded down it.

Addie's scent suddenly grew so overwhelming I had to look around to check she hadn't appeared out of thin air. There was a line here. I could almost *see* it – a line of marked ground. This place was hers. Her territory.

I stepped around the corner, and found myself in a little den. Cardboard boxes and a plastic sheet formed the roof. There were blankets on the floor. And Addie was curled up on top of them, her head on her paws, asleep.

She didn't even live *in* the trailers. She lived *under* them. Pity kicked in and I edged towards her, trying to make a sound loud enough to wake her, but not loud enough to startle her.

"Addie? It's Meg. Addie?" I was close enough to touch her. I nudged the blanket a little with my nose.

One of her paws lashed out and her mouth opened in a violent hiss. I sprang away, panting, my heart hammering. She staggered to her feet, blinking hard, her eyes still full of sleep.

"Get out! Get out! I'll rip out your throat!" Her jaws snapped viciously in the air just where my head would've been if I hadn't jerked out of the way, then she dropped back into a defensive crouch, her back to the wall of cardboard and her teeth and claws bared.

"Addie, I'm sorry, it's me, Meg, I – I'm sorry!"

Addie sniffed the air and the slits of her eyes prised fully open.

"Meg? What the hell?" She sat back on her haunches, her flanks heaving. "What are you doing here?" She sniffed the air again, looking around jumpily. "Are you alone?"

"Yes, it's just me, I... I just came to..." I came to ask her to help me, but her eyes were glazed and panicky and I couldn't just spring my troubles on her like this. "It's OK. It's just me."

Addie panted a little more, and then seemed to relax. Her ears tipped back, sadly. "How did you find me?"

"Um. Blackwell, from the Tower – from the Conspiracy – he told me you were here."

"You spoke to a raven? And he knew where I was?" Addie's stance turned defensive again. "How did *he* know?"

"He's been keeping tabs on a few of us," I said. "He showed up at my window last night." *God, was it only last night?* "It's a bit complicated..."

Addie licked her paw and washed behind her ear. "I wish you hadn't come here." She didn't sound angry any more. She sounded miserable.

"I'm sorry. I didn't realise. Addie, are you... homeless?"

"What about it?" Addie snapped, and I cringed back, feeling blunt and stupid.

"N-nothing, I just..." I started backing away. Maybe this wasn't a good idea. Maybe I'd be able to find someone else to help me. Hell, maybe I'd brave the school again by myself.

Addie shook her head and sat back. "Hey, look, Princess... I didn't mean to. Y'know. Did I get you?"

"Nah. I'm fine."

"Good. You look hungry."

"Uh – yeah, actually."

"What happened, did the Ritz shut for the day?"

"I... actually..." I swallowed. "Something happened to my parents. I can't go home. Maybe ever."

Addie's eyes widened. She turned and rooted around behind a flap of cardboard and pulled out a small box. It had several half-chewed chicken bones in it. "Here," she said, pushing it towards me.

"Oh, Addie." I couldn't help giving another glance around at the cardboard walls and roof, the crumpled blanket. On a second look I was pretty sure it had been a jumper once. There was a cheery kitten half-chewed away on one corner. "Are you sure?"

She rolled her eyes at me. "Don't gimme that. I do fine. Take one."

I reached in and grabbed one of the lovely chewy, greasy bones, tugged it out and lay with it between my paws, gnawing gratefully.

"D'you run away?" she asked, when my chomping started to slow down. "Was it like – they hurt you?"

"That's sort of complicated," I said. I took a deep breath, swirling the scents of chicken and Addie and diesel and grime around my taste buds for a second, and then launched into my story. She listened attentively, punctuating every couple of sentences with a burst of passionate swearing. It was oddly therapeutic.

"Now there's nothing I can do except get the stone and hope we can keep it safe, but I'm too scared to go back there by myself. You can say no," I added quickly.

"Bollocks to that," said Addie. "I'm with you." I sprang forwards, fox instinct kicking in, and head-butted her affectionately in the side of the neck. She flinched, but then rubbed the side of her muzzle against mine. "You're all right, Princess," she said.

We hugged for a few seconds longer and then she pulled away, sniffing.

"We'd better get going. If this bitch knows you lied to her maybe she'll search the school again, right? If we go now we might still get there first."

I really, really hoped so.

I wanted to go back for my clothes, but Addie convinced me not to. She was right – we'd be quicker as foxes, it'd be easier to slip into the school, plus we'd be able to talk. Really, it was the last thing that convinced me. I had so many questions buzzing around my head I could barely make out which ones were the least rude.

"So, you live as a fox," I said, as we pounded along the pavement. "Like, all the time?"

"Yep," said Addie.

She leapt up onto a low wall and disappeared into a row of bushes, in one swift fluid movement, and I followed her lead. Leaves whipped past us, but we were hidden from the road.

"Can I ask...?"

"What, *why* do I live as a fox?" Addie snorted. "C'mon Princess, think about it. I'm fourteen and homeless." She gave a dramatic pause, letting this sink in. By the time she carried on, I knew pretty much what she was going to say, and I already felt a bit sick. "If it's not the druggies it's the preachers or the pimps or the creepy guys in cars who want you to blow them cause you're not in fishnets or anything, you're walking around looking like a little lost kid, and they like that. And if you get into a shelter for the night, there'd be guys outside giving out free drugs in the mornings when they kicked you out for the day, to get you hooked, so they could control you and get you on the game. The *instant* I had another option I took it and I didn't look back. I'm not homeless now, I'm *wild*. Being a shifter is the best thing that ever happened to me."

"How did you get it, then?"

"An old homeless guy, innit. Froze to death right in front of me one night. Couldn't have been less than eighty, and crazy with it. I dunno if he even knew he was a shifter. Don says he never came down the Skulk. Poor old guy should've been in a hospital. Sodding crime."

I concentrated on my paws for a while, letting all that sink in. I had a hundred more questions – how did she get to be homeless in the first place? Where were her family? How could this *happen*? But I knew, deep down, those were all stupid questions. More to the point...

"Did you know about the stone? About us being weards and having this sacred duty?"

Addie hesitated. "Never seen the stone myself, but I heard of it. Don knew. He'd hidden it in our meeting place, not told anyone. He went batshit when it disappeared."

"So Ben took it?"

"Well," Addie said, and then stopped to look around before leading the way back down onto the pavement and across the road. "Which way?"

I pointed with my nose and we headed off the main road, towards the leafy square where, until today, I'd gone to school. Something told me I wasn't going to go tomorrow. Somehow I thought my A-Levels were no longer my top priority in life.

Not that they had been before, either.

A whole roll-call of things I wasn't going to have to worry about now marched through my head. A-levels. Waxing. University. A burst of something like triumph hit me, although it was a really sick, hollow triumph.

"Thing is, Don says James took it," Addie said. "Cause he's a thief. I mean really, that's what he does, like for a job, he thieves."

"I suppose that makes sense," I said. "I think he might've just stolen something when I met him."

"So... I dunno, maybe Ben found him and they had a fight and Ben took it back off him," Addie said.

"But – does that mean *James* killed Ben? And not Victoria?" I shook my head. "That's weird."

"I think it's bollocks," said Addie. "Don knows a lot of stuff, but–"

"But what?"

"Well, James wouldn't stab anyone for a start. Believe. He's just not like that."

"And...? You said for a start."

Addie shook her head. "Don's a bigot. He hates James cause he's camp and gay and he's not ashamed of it. Don thinks that makes him untrustworthy. You try arguing with him, if you've got a spare lifetime. Aren't we nearly there?" Addie squinted up at the road signs.

Actually, we were. I led her along one side of the square and soon we were looking up at Kensington School for Girls. Some of the lights were on, and a window was open on the ground floor. I guessed some of the teachers were still there, or maybe the caretakers. With a bit of luck, we'd never have to disturb them.

But maybe something already had. There was something else overlaying the scent of glue, bleach and flaking paint from the doors and iron railings.

I could smell blood.

Chapter Fourteen

Addie shivered at my side as we padded softly across the garden. It felt surreal to be back here, seeing it all with brand new eyes for the second time in twenty-four hours. I sniffed the damp grass and caught a whiff of old blood like rust among the scents of nature. I glanced up and blinked as the piercing light over the bins came on, throwing everything into stark light and shadow. Was this how Ben had seen it all, that night?

The smell of fresh blood seemed to follow in my footsteps, like a dog, whining for me to pay it attention. But I couldn't see anything out here. Maybe that was just the scent that the fog left behind when it searched the place. Perhaps it had killed recently. I pushed the thoughts away. We didn't need to be here long. We could get the stone and get out.

"It's just down here," I whispered, leading her around the woody, varnished scent of the Kit Shed. Ash flew up into my nose as I sniffed around for my own scent, looking for the right place to dig. Addie stood guard, her ears pricked for the slightest sound. I could hear nothing but my own breathing and the scrape of my claws in the earth.

I started to think I'd got it wrong and I was digging in the wrong place, but then my claws hit something smooth and solid. I dug around it. It seemed bigger to me now – which would make sense, because it was about half the size of my head, except that the star seemed to shine brighter, too, a point of pure white in the slightly dulled world around me.

I plunged my muzzle into the earth and clamped my jaws around the stone. My mouth and nose filled with the scents of dirt and roots and something cool, like the tang of electricity but much gentler, coming off the stone...

"Meg!" Addie snapped. I pulled my head out of the ground, stone held in my jaws, and looked up. Something had settled in the tree above us. No, two – three somethings. Three flappy, grey somethings.

"Pigeons," I gasped.

"Run!" Addie yelled, and took off at a sprint towards the side-alley and the gate. I followed at her heels, the stone jarring against my teeth. I could hear the chaotic flapping of wings at my back and I put on a burst of speed, careening around the corner, right into the fog.

I tripped over my own tail in my hurry to stop and sprawled on the ground. The stone dropped from my mouth. The grey, shimmering cloud curled and pulsated in the air in front of us as it flowed through the bars of the iron gate. Addie skittered away from it as if her spine were attached to an invisible string, her paws dancing on the ground.

"Addie!" I screamed. I scrambled to my feet and backed off. "Back, this way!"

"But–" Addie looked over my head and I snatched up the stone and ducked out of the way just as a pair of bird claws raked the gravelly ground where I'd been lying. I took a hard swipe at the pigeon. It was fat and grey with a vivid blue-green streak across its neck. Neither of my parents. Someone else's? Right now, I couldn't afford to care. I lashed out again and caught my claws on the side of its head. Blood burst from just behind its eye and it flapped off, hissing.

The fog was after Addie. It flowed towards her and she leapt away from it, all the fur sticking up on her back. The fog moved slowly, as if it had all the time in the world, but something told me it would never stop.

The pigeons were faster. Another one swept down just as I was turning to see if there was a way around the fog so we could slip out onto the street. I heard flapping and when I looked up all I could see were grey feathers... and then a flash of orange fur crossed my vision, like a grubby shooting star. Addie caught the pigeon in mid-air. I saw her fangs dig hard into its neck, and as she landed she gave the pigeon a violent shake. The pigeon's eyes went dim and it thudded to the ground when she let go of it. Dead.

Someone's dad? I thought. *I'm sorry. That's not enough, but it's going to have to do.*

Addie nipped at my throat.

"Come on!"

The fog was rolling around towards us. It was about to corner us against the wall. I head-butted Addie gratefully and we ran back into the garden.

"There's a window open," Addie yelled. I looked up. Thank God, she was right.

"There was one open at the front as well; we can get through." I took a running leap up onto the windowsill and tumbled headfirst through the gap, into the school hallway.

My paws splashed down into a lake of blood. I skidded, landed on my belly and rolled over and over in it.

Addie let out a guttural howl as she came down beside me with a splash.

The scent of blood filled every pore; every halting breath I took just pulled in blood and more blood. It was blinding. I could feel Addie scrambling beside me and hear her panicked gasping. Her fur pressed, stickily, to mine.

We could see all the way to the front door, from here, down the long main corridor. All we had to do was run down it.

But through the haze of blood I could make out shapes, scattered along the hall. Bodies. One of them lay right beside us under the window, hands outstretched. A shirt, a simple gold necklace, and serious grey tights. A teacher. Her head was missing. Her blood had flooded out over the floor and splashed up onto the walls.

A dark halo gathered at the corners of my sight.

No. I won't black out. If I do, I won't come up again.

I forced myself to look up. The fog was at the window, its tendrils creeping through. And through it I could make out more swooping shapes against the dark sky.

"We," I said, "have to keep moving. Addie. *Addie.*"

She was shaking harder than I've ever seen a living thing shake. I put my head down and prodded her forwards. She scrabbled for a foothold and turned to me. Her eyes were black and her jaw hung limp.

"We've got to get out. That way is out. *Go.*" I leapt forward, my feet slipping in the teacher's blood, and shouldered her towards the front door.

Time seemed to stand still as we made our way through the river of blood. Limbs like islands forced us to slip and slide around them. Gory handprints littered the walls like messy children's finger paintings. I couldn't look back, couldn't do anything but reach deep inside and take myself by the throat and force myself to push on. I had no idea how close the fog was, or if there were vicious beaks and claws crowding through the window. I could have had all the sulphur-stinking demons of hell on my tail and I wouldn't have known it.

"I know it's not at the school. My fog has been there." Victoria's voice floated through me. Then my own thoughts: *Maybe the blood scent is what the fog left behind. Perhaps it killed recently.*

I held on so tight to the stone in my jaws I could feel my teeth squeaking against its smooth surface.

Even though I tried not to look at the bodies, a few details seemed to bypass my brain and eyes, stabbing me straight in the heart.

There were students here. One of them was younger than the rest, her white socks scarlet with blood, her regulation-length skirt splayed. I climbed over a denim-clad man's leg. The caretaker was here too.

In front of me Addie tripped and let out a wail. I walked into her brush, which was fluffed up like a bloody feather duster. She lifted her paw. There was a little clot of red-grey matter clinging to it.

We were almost at the front door, so close now to the open window, to the street. I could hardly imagine it any more. Barely a minute in this place, and I could no longer conceive a world not made of red.

We passed the foot of the stairs. Blood had cascaded down them and now lay thickly on every step. The dripping scarlet river drew my eyes, even as I became aware of wings beating in the corridor behind us. At the source of the red tide, a crumpled figure sprawled. White shoes with blue straps, and a white wedge heel. Dark-skinned ankles in black tights. A blue and white handbag dangled from limp fingers.

I stopped. Stared.

It was Ameera.

She'd been in detention. Making that face like she just wanted to *die*. I'd waved goodbye. And now... this ruined, faceless object on the stairs, spilling down.

She didn't know anything. None of them knew anything. None of them should have died.

Victoria's face swam in front of my eyes.

She would pay.

"Meg!" Addie wailed.

Pain exploded in my shoulder and I toppled sideways, a pigeon's claws digging deep into my fur. Addie took a slippery run up and leapt, trailing drops of Ameera's blood through the air. She and the pigeon fell together, splashing and sticking. I got up and looked back down the corridor – Addie about to bite down hard on the pigeon's grey head, the fog swirling through the back window, and the pigeon itself... it was thin, angular. Though it was spattered with blood and flapping madly I could make out the sleekness of its feathers.

"Addie, no!" I screamed. It was enough to make Addie hesitate and I dropped the stone from my jaws to snatch at her tail. "Don't hurt it! That's my mother."

The pigeon looked at me, its mad red eyes like mirrors reflecting the blood, and I gasped. Did she know my voice? Did she know it was me?

She took off in a great flapping of wings and dived for the stone.

"No! Mum, no!" I threw my body in front of her and her claws raked down across my back. "Addie," I gasped, "The stone, get it out of here!"

Addie snatched up the stone in her jaws. She gave a whimper and shuddered, but took off for the open window. I threw Mum off my back and swiped, catching her on the wing. She landed in the blood, opened her beak and gave a vicious hiss.

"I'm trying," I screamed. "I'm trying not to hurt you! After everything–"

I stopped. I didn't have time for this. The fog was rolling through the red mire towards me.

I turned and leapt for the window after Addie.

The cool, clear air burned the back of my throat as I pushed up and out onto the front steps of the school. A razor-sharp rainbow of scents burst across my muzzle, cars and trees and people and electricity.

Addie was waiting for me on the pavement, dripping and trembling, her eyes wide and her teeth audibly chattering against the surface of the stone.

"Go," I breathed. "Go go go."

We washed off the blood in the Princess Diana Memorial Fountain.

I'd led us towards Hyde Park, hoping that we'd lose the pigeons as we crossed through the crowded streets of Notting Hill and negotiated the traffic circling the park. I don't quite know when we did lose them. But when we leapt through the iron bars of the fence and huddled together under the bushes that lined the park, there was no flapping or cooing, and no tentacles of fog crept through the leaves.

I tried to lie down gently, but my legs went from under me and I sprawled on my side, my chest heaving.

I'd known Hyde Park like the back of my hand since I was about six years-old and I used to spend Sundays trying to lose Gail among the hydrangeas. It was the best spot to loiter on a sunny afternoon when I was pretending to be staying late at school. Sometimes I'd come alone with a sketchpad, sometimes with Ameera and Jewel and we'd sit on our coats by the Serpentine, surreptitiously drinking rum straight from a bottle and feeding Waitrose bagels to the ducks.

Ameera was gone. There was no point trying to tie the bright, bubbly party girl I'd known to the mess the fog had left behind. She was gone forever. The sheer weight of it seemed to fill the world, pressing me down into the earth. She'd never pester me to be more fun again. She'd never pass another exam while hungover. She'd never have another hangover. She'd never be at any more of Jewel's recitals, or make fun of the Duchess, or coordinate her handbag with her shoes.

In the morning, there would be screaming, and sirens. The school would close. Maybe for good. There would be reporters, press conferences, calls for witnesses. There might be public hysteria. There would be funerals.

I wondered whether Jewel would ever get over it.

I wanted to lie in the earth with them and never get up, but then I looked over at Addie and dragged myself to my feet. If we were going to lie down and die, we might as well have given ourselves up to the fog. I'd dragged us both through that horror; I might as well drag us a little further.

I led her to the Diana Fountain, by the banks of the Serpentine. The thin, cool stream of the fountain shimmered over a constantly changing pattern of wet stone and brick in a looping ribbon, sparkling in the moonlight and the shifting headlight beams of the cars crawling along Exhibition Road. I guess it was supposed to be a metaphor for the Princess' life, but all I was thinking about right then was which part would make the best fox bath.

The blood on our paws had long since stopped leaving prints behind on the pavement, and now it was sticky, flaking and clumping in my fur.

Addie and I waded into one of the deepest fast-flowing corners and she dropped the stone into an eddy with a little whimper. Her whole body shook.

I looked at the stone, its deep blue covered with a film of blood.

It had fallen in the lake of blood.

And I'd made Addie carry it all the way here in her mouth.

"I'm so sorry," I murmured.

Addie just whined and lay down in the gently trickling water.

I put my head down and rolled over. The water was cool on my fur. It clung to me in sparkling droplets and I writhed and splashed, trying to coat myself, to wash away the feeling that my skin and fur were being tugged together in sticky brown handfuls. Thin streams of blood peeled off me and shimmered away with the flow of the fountain.

Addie lapped up the clean water, running it over her muzzle, then turned and rubbed her head against the shining bricks.

My paws were going numb from the cool water, but slowly parts of me started to feel clean again. My heart ached for soap.

Addie and I didn't speak.

When I thought I'd done all I could do, I stepped out of the fountain and trotted a little way across the grass to shake myself off, keeping Addie and the stone in the corner of my eye.

Blood welled up under my paws, flowing thickly between the blades of grass, and I jumped back, a scream forming behind my teeth...

It was so real. But a split second later, there was nothing there. Just grass and dark earth. I swallowed the scream and shook myself again, as if I could shake off the memory. There was nothing here but the long lawns, the dark skeletons of trees and the whisper of the water as it washed away the worst of the horror from Addie's back and cleaned the stone.

I trotted back to the side of the fountain and gazed down at the stone. The blood had mostly gone now, but it still looked almost black in the dim, shimmering light. The star glinted like a diamond at the bottom of a deep well.

Addie got to her paws. She took a few faltering steps downstream to stand beside the stone.

She seemed weak, and looked half-drowned. I wanted so badly to gather her to me and wrap her up in a warm towel. I fought off the urge to tell her everything was going to be all right. I couldn't find the words for the lie.

She dripped shakily into the water for a few seconds, regarding the stone in silence.

Then she raised her head.

"That ain't ours, you know."

"Excuse me?"

"That's not our stone. Don said our stone was a ruby." She grabbed the stone out of the water and plonked it down on the edge of the fountain. It shimmered, deep and mystical and very definitely blue.

"But..." I opened my mouth, closed it again, and waited for my brain to stop spinning. "But if this is... So where – and who–?"

"What the hell was Ben doing with someone else's stone?" Addie said, cutting through my waffle.

"Whose *is* it?" I croaked. "And where's ours?"

"I don't even care to be honest." Addie hopped out of the fountain and shook herself, splattering the grass and me with cold droplets. "I've had enough of this shit."

I nodded. "I'm so sorry," I said. "I shouldn't have brought you into this. You don't have to – you shouldn't have to see any of this, I mean, you're..." the words *just a kid* wisely revolted on my lips before I could say them.

Addie's ears pricked up and her eyes narrowed.

"Meg. I dunno what you're talking about, but I'm talking about getting off our arses and going and messing that bitch's shit *up*."

I blinked at her.

"I'm serious, she is one sick, nasty piece of rat crap and I say we go round her place right now and make sure she never, ever does *that* ever again."

I had to take a second. I sat back on my haunches and rubbed my paw over my muzzle.

I felt shamed, more than anything. I'd underestimated Addie, but also... I had no idea how we could get to Victoria. None. I wanted to make all this right, but I hadn't a clue where to begin. Addie's pure, disgusted drive made me feel sluggish and dithery.

"The Conspiracy won't help us," I muttered.

Addie hissed through her teeth. "Bunch of old white men in a tower whose most important job is giving guided tours to the Queen's bling. They wouldn't help us even if they weren't crooked."

"I thought I could take it back to the Skulk and we could hide it somewhere, but if it's not even ours... We can't go and face off with Victoria until we've found somewhere safe for this," I said, pawing warily at the sapphire. "This is what Victoria wants," I added, when Addie shifted impatiently. "I'm not taking it anywhere *near* the Shard."

"Hey, d'you think she's already got ours?" Addie asked. "I mean, it's been missing for weeks and she's got to want to collect them all. For that ultimate weapon thing, right?"

"All the more reason to keep this out of her hands," I said. "Hopefully if we can find out which group of shifters it belongs to, they'd be able to keep it safe."

"Hopefully," said Addie dryly. "Look, I think I know a place where it'll be safe for a bit. But I don't know if it's the *best* plan ever."

"Oh yeah?"

"Yeah, well. It depends. On how you feel about taking the big giant sapphire you've just literally waded through blood to get back, and handing it to a jewel thief."

Chapter Fifteen

I crouched in the shadows between a crumbling brick wall and a rusty Mini with no tyres or engine, with the stone between my paws, watching the end of the alley for any sign of James Farringdon.

A railway bridge loomed over us, with four large archways underneath that had been converted into storage spaces. Every so often a train would hurtle across the top, clattering out towards the East coast or back into the City. The noise was like a moving, living creature sweeping past, shaking me to my aching bones and leaving a cloud of sparks and dust in its wake.

The stale scent of old petrol, metal and rotting wood filled this place, but it was a comforting, familiar kind of decay. I wasn't exactly Banksy, but I'd spent my share of time hanging out in London's industrial nooks and crannies, and this was a perfect example.

The arches showed little sign of criminal activity, or any activity at all. They looked pretty much like any other railway arches, like there would be nothing inside but old car parts and dust.

I spotted the first sign myself, scanning the place on a totally different instinct from the one that made me sniff out the ground and turn around three times before settling down to wait. Even with the fox's dim eyesight, I could make out the black gleam of glass hidden in the corners of the archways. I instantly marked this place off on my mental map: *Looks like a great location, quiet and deserted, four great matching canvases, but too much CCTV. Not worth the risk.*

Addie had to point out the other clue that this place might not be what it seemed. I'd actually seen it, and not realised what it meant besides the fact that all four of the arches would make great blank slates for paintings.

I couldn't see a door in any one of them.

I said I would've assumed there was one somewhere else, and Addie smirked and told me that was exactly the point.

A long time passed as I lay in the little gap, with Addie's warm body breathing next to mine. I wondered what time it was, and how long it'd been since I last slept. Even the roar of the trains started to sound oddly soothing, the longer we stayed there. The stone was smooth and cool when I laid my head on it.

There was a pigeon right in front of me. It didn't attack. It just stared at me with one red eye. I could see myself, in human form, reflected in its mad depths. Then the black space began to fill up with red, and the red spilled over, and blood began to pour from the eye of the pigeon and flood out over me. It was up to my waist. It was up to my neck. It lapped at my lips and poured down my throat, choking me. It tasted of old petrol.

Addie nudged me awake.

"He's here," she said, getting up and arching her back stiffly. "Let me do the talking, OK, Princess?"

I shrugged, picked up the stone and followed her, bleary-eyed, hanging back as she stepped boldly out into the pool of yellow street-light.

James Farringdon was slinking down the alley in fox form, the little black bag between his teeth.

His whole body flinched when he spotted us and he crouched back as if to run.

"Jimmy, it's me," Addie said.

James paused. His body language shifted, his shoulders slinking forwards a little into a stance that could flow easily into running or leaping at us, fangs bared. He growled.

"Adeola, if you've brought that bigoted cur down here..."

"No, I wouldn't! Look, it's just Meg. You remember Meg?"

I stepped forwards. James' head tipped to one side.

"The new girl," he said. His eyes flickered to the jewel in my mouth.

"She's with me," said Addie.

"And you're both with the Skulk," James said. "So why should I believe she won't betray me to Olaye the first chance she gets?"

"Because we need your help," Addie said. "Also because I say so, you paranoid twat," she added.

James gave us a toothy, canine grin. His stance finally relaxed and he trotted up to us, the bag swinging from his jaws, as if he'd never thought we were anything but his best friends.

"Darling," he said, brushing his muzzle against Addie's, and then – to my surprise – against mine. I gripped the stone a little tighter in my jaws but he seemed to be pretending he hadn't noticed it.

"Can we talk about this inside?" Addie asked.

James gave me a long look, then bowed deeply to us. "Anything for my favourite girl. If you'd like to show our guest the way in..."

Addie walked up to the closest arch, right up to the plywood wall that had been put up to seal the arch shut. I still couldn't see anything that looked like a door until Addie suddenly pounced forwards and head-butted one of the corners. It flipped up, leaving a hole just about big enough for a fox to squeeze through. She paused on the other side, so I could just see her legs through the hole, and jumped up. A light came on behind her.

"Come on!" she said. Despite everything, there was a thrill in her voice, like a kid who's discovered something *awesome* and can't wait to share it.

I put my head down and stepped through into James' den.

It was all I could do not to allow my jaws to drop open and let the sapphire tumble out.

This place was an Aladdin's cave. A dragon's lair. It was *full of diamonds*.

A bright fluorescent strip light hung in the centre of the room. In any other place, the light it cast would be harsh and unforgiving. It would make furniture seem institutional and turn skin pasty and dull. But in here, the plain, unfussy quality of light was perfect. No romantically flickering candles could have done justice to this number of diamonds. It was like standing in the Milky Way, with thousands of coloured sparks glinting and glittering around me every time I moved, even just to breathe.

There were cabinets full of tiaras, shelves and hooks dripping with necklaces, low tables scattered with rings and bracelets. Rubies and sapphires and emeralds and garnets and every shade and shape of diamond you could imagine.

The furniture must've been brought in some other way, but every shiny piece of stolen property was small enough that it could be slipped into James' little black bag and carried safely through the fox-door.

Addie trotted through the scintillating forest of jewels and flopped down on a silky couch draped with velvet. I hopped up beside her and dropped the sapphire, putting my paws on it protectively, and staring around. If anything, the view from this angle was even better.

"You stole *all* of this?"

"What a question to ask a gentleman," James smirked. He was in one of the corners, doing something with what looked like a box of miscellaneous, unsorted loot. He slipped the black bag off over his head and put it down carefully on top of a glinting pile of rubies. "Of course I did."

He came over to the couch, jumped up and sat back on his haunches, his brush swishing happily around his paws.

I tried to come up with an appropriate expression of stunned appreciation.

"*Dude*," I breathed.

"Why, thank you," said James.

"Do you sell *anything*?" I asked.

"Well, you tell me, what's the point of having it all if I can't look at it? I sell the ugly pieces, to keep me in the style to which I've become accustomed. Other than that, I just like to come here and polish them. You can't blame me, right?"

"Nope."

"So," James said. "I can't help but notice you've brought me an enormous sapphire."

I clenched my claws around it, protectively. "It's not really mine. Exactly."

"Oh yeah? Who'd you bounce it from?"

"I don't know."

"Sounds like there's a story there."

"I don't want to tell him," Addie said, turning her head sharply to me. I blinked.

"Really?"

"It takes knowledge, right? So the less he knows..."

"Oh, right. Yeah, she's right." I thought James already knew enough for Victoria to have every reason to send her fog after him, if she ever knew that he knew. But Addie was looking at me with huge, puppy-dog eyes and throwing worried glances at James. I supposed it couldn't hurt to play our cards close to our chests, for the moment.

"If we tell you, you could die," Addie said to James. "I'm not kidding, people have died."

"Fine," said James, tossing his head impatiently. "So what do you want from me?"

"Just to keep it safe," said Addie. "This is like the safest place in the *world*, right?"

James shook his head. "I don't know about that, love. Maybe the safest place in Bow, but that's not saying much."

"It'll have to do," I said. "We can't keep carrying it around. Someone's looking for it. Someone really dangerous."

"Uh-huh." James washed behind his ear, over-casually. "And I can't help also noticing that it's pretty much the same as the stone Olaye carelessly misplaced. I hear that was a ruby, though."

"Did you take the ruby from the Skulk?" I asked.

"Ooh, blunt. No." James licked his muzzle. "I prefer at least a *bit* of a challenge. I knew it was there, I mean Don was keeping it under a *rock*, for God's sake."

"We want it back. It's important."

"Important, eh? What's so important?"

"I said, didn't I?" Addie growled. "If we tell you, she could come and... it'd be really bad, OK?"

"All right," James murmured. "All right, babe. I won't ask."

"You're sure you didn't take the Skulk stone?" I pressed.

"Can't help you there," said James, with a flick of his head.

"But you'll hide this for us, right?" Addie said. "You remember when you said if I ever needed anything, anything *at all*, I should ask you?"

"I pretty much meant cash, sweetie, but sure. I'll hold onto it. I'll put it away in a drawer and I won't let anyone take it but you. How's that?"

My gaze wandered over James' cave and then lighted on Addie. He'd promised her cash, any time she wanted... and she was living under a trailer in the Westway Traveller Park, and she'd never taken him up on it?

I didn't get it. Pride could only take you so far, surely? But then, one thing I'd noticed about rich people: they could have dignity by the bucketload, but they were often not big on pride.

Addie squeezed past me and snuggled up to James, rubbing her muzzle against his. "You're the tits, Jimmy."

"I know," said James, with another doggy grin, licking the top of Addie's head affectionately.

He showed us out, but before we could walk off he called to me.

"Hey, Meg. Can I have a word?"

"Don't talk shit about me," Addie warned.

"*Never*," James swore, so deadpan that it could only have been sarcasm. Addie stuck out her tongue and trotted away to wait at the end of the alley

"Look," James said, "Addie's telling the truth about people dying, right?"

"Dying, getting turned into evil pigeons," I said, a little hysterically. "Yeah."

James hesitated for a second. "Well, if you ever want to clue me in on exactly what's going on and why these things are so important, I'm here."

"We'll be back," I promised. "It's Skulk business. And

I think that makes it your business, whether you want it to be or not."

I thought he'd deny it, but he just nodded.

"Actually, there's something else you can help me with," I said. "Do you know where the other shifters meet? The Cluster and the Horde and the butterfly one?"

"The Rabble? Kew Gardens, I think. In one of the big greenhouses. Last I heard the Cluster were meeting in a derelict pub in Hammersmith, the Saracen. And the Horde meet up in the abandoned tube station in Aldwych, but – you don't want to go visiting."

"Why not?"

"They're not friendly. At all. Trust me on this. And look, this might come under the heading of 'talking shit', but take care of Adeola."

"I'll try," I promised.

"So, what do you think that sorceress bitch's deal is?" Addie asked. We'd followed the train tracks down to Limehouse, and now we were looking out over the river at the dark knife-edge of the Shard, slicing through the London skyline.

"I… I don't know," I said. I scratched hard behind my ear with my back paw. "I guess she wants this weapon that Blackwell told me about. The one that got split up into the five stones."

"Yeah, but why?" Addie's nose twitched and she glared down at the reflections of the lights glittering in the river. "Is she a terrorist or what? I mean, what kind of person lives all the way up there and still wants *more* power?"

The taller the towers, the more powerful they became, Blackwell had said.

And even though I knew that, I couldn't help thinking the Shard was kind of beautiful.

My Dad helped build that, I thought, with a strange burst of pride. *If I ever see him again I'm going to tell him how pretty it is.*

"My mum, for one," I said. Addie gave me a sharp look. "One of her campaign managers once told me that wanting to be Prime Minister is perfectly sane, but nobody actually gets there without going some flavour of bonkers. It's like... a slippery slope of bad choices. You make allowances and concessions and deals. You go on *Newsnight* and kiss babies and pretend to be tough on immigration, or whatever it is everyone wants that week."

"How bad do your choices have to be to end up with you killing people for a bunch of magic rocks?" Addie asked.

"Pretty bad," I conceded.

"Well, whatever it is, we're going to stop it, right? How are we going to get up there?"

"I don't think we can, not yet."

"What?" Addie snarled. "She's got your mum and dad. I thought we were going to go and sort her out?"

"I know," I said. "I want revenge, believe me, but we have to be smart about it. I've got a plan."

"So what's the plan, Princess Smartarse?"

I was pretty sure it was a rubbish plan. But it was the only one I had.

"We need help," I went on. "I need to know more about what's going on. I'm going to see the other shifters. Blackwell said we had this duty, to look after the stones, and we've all forgotten how to keep them safe, and that's why Victoria could do all this. So maybe someone in one of the groups remembers and they'll help us put it right. Or maybe I can find this metashifter person and they'll be able to help, somehow. I've got to find out."

"Meg," said Addie, shaking her head. "You've got to be kidding me. Your plan is asking random strangers for help? You want to ask the *Horde*? We're going to get massacred, I hope you know that."

"Actually, just me. You know the rest of the Skulk, right, you know where you can find them?" Addie nodded, slowly. "I want you to go and get them to meet us. I guess... tomorrow night, midnight. Can you do that?"

"Well, yeah. But, listen, they may technically be our crew, but I'm warning you, they won't want to climb a massive tower and attack an evil witch just cause you say so."

"If she's got our stone, it's all of our business. It has to be. Don will help persuade the others, won't he? I mean, he wants to get it back, right?"

"I s'pose," said Addie.

"Your confidence is overwhelming," I muttered.

"I wish." Addie stood up and brushed against me. "And you're going to go in the Horde nest all by yourself, yeah?"

"How can they be scarier than what we've seen tonight?"

Addie shook her head. "You're *nuts*, Princess."

"Yeah. I know. But you know what, I think I like being nuts." I gazed out across the rooftops at the Limehouse basin glinting between tall apartment buildings. "I feel OK right now. You know how long it's been since I felt OK?"

Addie tilted her head at me and her ears flattened to the sides of her head. I blushed – not that she could see it through the fur, but I felt the heat down the back of my spine.

"It may be stupid deathwish nuts, but that's way better than gibbering wreck nuts, right?"

Addie made a *pssht* sound between her teeth. "Right. When I left home I didn't give a toss what happened to me next. I'd got out. I felt invincible. *It wore off.*"

"My mum used to lock me in a wardrobe whenever she thought I'd done something wrong," I said. "Which was a lot of the time." My voice sounded kind of distant and dreamy – I sounded pretty crazy, even to me. "I should've gone mad years ago, it's pretty liberating actually."

Addie stared at me. "A wardrobe, huh?"

"Yeah."

"I didn't think rich people who were going to be Prime Minister did that kind of thing."

"I think that's what she was counting on. She... she wanted me to be perfect, that's what's so stupid about it. She wanted me thin and vain and clever, just like her." I shook myself. "I should hate all this, the shift and the magic. It's taken my parents. It took Ameera. We weren't… I mean, we weren't soulmates or anything, but she… she was my best friend…"

"Oh," said Addie softly. "Was she in the school?"

I nodded, unable to speak.

After a second, I felt a warm weight on my back. Addie'd laid her head on my shoulder.

I felt her throat vibrate against me as she spoke. "Don't hate the shift. Hate Victoria."

"That's just it. I love the shift. Love it. And I know I should be afraid, but I'm just glad to have a problem that makes sense. Mum despises me and everything I am for no reason at all, that's… that's hard. Evil sorceress wants magic stones, killed my friend, I've got to stop her: simple. Got it."

Addie pulled away. Her ears twitched and she scratched behind them with one of her back paws. "People are bastards. My dad hit me a lot. There was a lot of Bible stuff. Pray the gay away, y'know, only with more shouting." I flinched, and then felt horrible about it. "God. I'm sorry."

"Ugh. Don't be. Screw it. It was horrible and I'm a fox now. I've got my own place, I've got Jimmy. Worst I have to deal with now is Don. I know he's a bigot, but he's not a deep down awful person, he's just a bit of a dick. I'm just saying…" she shook herself. "I'm saying, parents are people and people are bastards."

"That is surprisingly insightful."

There was an awkward silence. Then she licked my shoulder roughly. "Well, you're not a bastard and neither am I, so we're probably doing OK."

I head-butted her affectionately in the neck. "Yeah, we're OK. We'd better get going, if I'm going to sort this mess out before Christmas. I'll see you tomorrow, right?"

"Tomorrow, midnight, in the Skulk meeting place. I'll get everyone. Take care of yourself, Bugnuts," she said, and turned and ran off towards the river.

Chapter Sixteen

The Saracen squatted on Hammersmith Road with a pawn shop on one side and a porn shop on the other. For a pub it was a thin, cramped-looking building. It had once had glossy black fake-Tudor beams painted on it, but the paint was flaking away. All the windows were shut up, sealed over with those grey metal shutters the council put up to stop people actually using derelict buildings for illicit activities like *living*. Peeling posters dotted the walls and there was a strong stench of urine and musty sweat around the doorway. I couldn't pick up any of the skittery spider-scent I'd smelled on Angel through the general funk.

I hugged the edge of the pavement to the end of the street and slipped down the alley behind the shops. Gravelly dirt crunched under my paws as I made my way past the back doors of the shops, under vans, between towering rubbish bins and in and out of a maze of old bits of fencing. A door creaked open as I passed, throwing a warm spike of yellow light across my face. I froze as a shape moved into the light. It was a human, carrying a large bag that rustled... and then the scent hit me, the most delicious salty, fatty, bready smell, with a far distant echo of slippery, glass-eyed things.

Fish and chips. My stomach rumbled. I was about to sneak up to the bin, to see if I could break into that bag when the man had dumped it, but then a barking shout broke me out of my trance. The man snatched up a stick and ran at me, slashing it through the air in my direction.

"Garn! Get out! Vermin!" he yelled. I cringed away, and he stopped coming after me. He put the bag into a plastic wheeley bin and slammed the lid down. I turned tail and ran on along the alley, before he came at me with that stick, and tried to ignore the awakened rumblings in my belly.

It suddenly occurred to me as I slipped in and out of the shadows that I didn't know if I'd be able to figure out which of the buildings was the Saracen from the back. The dim brickwork all looked the same and more than one of the buildings had its windows covered over. If it had been a working pub, I probably could've picked it out a mile away – but now that I was looking for traces of alcohol, I started finding it in every bin I passed, splashed up against fences and even pooled underneath an old car. The warm tang of it was everywhere. I passed a homeless man, huddled in about four different coats, cuddling a bottle as if it were a child. When he saw me he muttered something in what I thought might be Spanish, but didn't move to chase me away.

In the end, it was easy to spot the back door to the Saracen.

I just followed the smell of death.

There were metal shutters on the ground floor windows, but not on the door. I peered up at one of the top windows and could just make out that one of the shutters had been pulled away, just a little. That room was where the scent was coming from – a foul tang that was almost sweet, that made my skin creep up and down my spine. It wasn't the recent, crimson scent of blood, not like at the school. This was something different. A long exhale. Decay.

I head-butted the door and it shifted a little, enough for me to squeeze through.

Inside, the darkness settled over me like a warm, mouldy blanket. I sniffed my way forwards, dust clouding up around my paws, scented with years of stale beer, mice... and something fresher, more human.

A cramped, carpeted stairwell led up to my right, and I hesitated for a second, wondering if I really needed to know. I could draw my own conclusions. The Cluster had been here, and now there was nothing but death.

I drew in a deep breath of cool, stale air, and began to slowly climb the twisting stairs.

Something scuttled away from me in the darkness. I froze, sensing the movement of many-legged things.

"Hello?" I tried to bark, though it came out as more of a whine. "I'm – I'm from the Skulk. I'm here to see the Cluster. Is anyone there?"

Silence, except for the faintest sense of vibrating air. I sniffed, and there was a definite scent mixed in among the dust and decay – it wasn't quite like Angel's, but it was definitely insectlike.

I cringed back, imagining a thousand spiders rubbing their legs together, rushing towards me in a tide of skittering, biting *things*... but nothing happened.

The black walls loomed over me and I caught my claws on the worn, patchy fabric as I moved forward, following the death-scent to the top of the stairs. It was coming from a gap underneath a door, like invisible wisps of smoke.

There was a little more light here. A spattering of dim yellow spotlights hit the carpet at the other end of the landing, where a shuttered window would have looked out onto the street.

There were spiders. Lots of them, hanging in great drooping webs from the ceiling, scuttling along the edge of the carpet. One huge one, its body the size of my paw, picked its way slowly up the wall beside me, putting one thick, hairy leg unhurriedly in front of the others. It was so close I could see its shiny black eyes, like globes full of nothing but void on the top of its head.

I froze again, but the spiders didn't seem to care that I was trespassing in their house. This wasn't the Cluster. They were all just normal spiders, getting on with their spidery business while I caught my breath.

I followed the path of a tiny black spot, almost so quick and small I couldn't even make out its legs moving, up the side of the stairs and over something that gleamed and caught my eye. I peered up, sniffing. It was a metal chair, attached to a thin rail that ran down the stairs. I could still taste a faint tang of old electricity, like a ghost haunting the place where it was plugged into the wall.

This place was never going to pass an accessibility inspection. I wondered who'd felt the need to put in a stairlift.

I padded carefully across the patchy carpet, my hackles rising with every step, and put my head down against the old wooden door. I could feel my fur bristling all over my body, from my brush to my nose. I flattened my ears against my head and gave the door a firm shove. It shivered open and the scent reached out and curled around me like a pair of loving, decaying arms.

I could barely make out the naked human shapes of the three bodies on the floor of the room. The forest of spiderwebs was so thick it was like peering through cloud. Cloud with a thousand black specs hanging suspended in it, as if they were floating in the air.

I didn't need to go inside. I didn't need to do more than glance into the room, and then I turned tail and bolted, whining, scrabbling my way back down the stairs, my ears pinned to the back of my head. The dark walls banged around me, twisting, like I was running through a hall of mirrors, and I longed for the wide outdoors, for scents other than death and decay, and sounds other than the buzzing of flies.

There were three bodies. That is... I'd seen three torsos. I assumed there were six arms, six legs. But I hadn't stayed to find them all.

The three people in that room had been dead a while, and the circle of life was in full, disgusting flow: maggots had turned into flies, had fed the spiders, had laid their eggs right next to the next generation of maggots. I couldn't even see them – it had just been a clear scent of something *tiny* and *blind* and *hungry*, a sense of wriggling at the ends of the Cluster's torn, scattered limbs.

I sprang out of the back door of the Saracen and sucked in breath after breath of cool, grubby air. The dim light in the alley seemed like bright daylight after the claustrophobic darkness inside, and I turned my muzzle to the open sky, letting the faint breeze shift the fur on my neck.

Then something moved, a little crawling something in the fur on my back, and my whole body twitched. I jumped and rolled until I saw the spider drop off and shoot under a pile of bricks, and then pranced a couple of steps sideways, my whole body revolting against the idea of touching anything, ever again. I stumbled against the rough wood of one of the broken-down fences and sprang away again.

I let out a long whine.

It was too late for the Cluster. At least for four of the six. These three, and Angel... What had happened to the other two? And what about their replacements? When they'd died, others must have been chosen, people who happened to be close by. But by now they could be anybody, anywhere. Did they even have any idea what they were, what they'd been sucked into?

For a second I wondered what could've torn the Cluster's arms and legs from their bodies. But then it hit me, and I shut my eyes, trying and failing not to visualise the pigeons swooping in unannounced, catching the

Cluster in their spider form, pecking and tearing, and then the bloody blossoming of flesh as they transformed at the point of death...

Is this it? I wondered, my breath hitching in my chest as I walked away. *Is this all I'm going to find, more pointless death? Has she already destroyed the Horde, and the Rabble too?*

I stumbled to a halt.

Has she already destroyed the Skulk?

What if she's already found out where they live? What if she's sending the fog there right now?

What if I've sent Addie to her death?

I turned on the spot, my paws dancing in an agitated circle, and then forced myself down onto my haunches and scratched at the back of my ear until my skin stopped trying to crawl in all directions.

I had to be practical about this. It wasn't as if I had a choice, unless you counted lying down right here and waiting for Victoria to find and kill me as a choice, and somehow, despite everything, that was becoming less and less attractive. I didn't know where Addie had gone. But I did know where the Horde and the Rabble were supposed to meet. If any of them were still alive, then maybe they could help me, and if they were all dead... at least I'd know.

I set off for Aldwych Tube Station under a spreading cloud, my paws feeling heavier with almost every step. Maybe the Horde would be OK. Maybe they'd have their stone and it would be safe and everything would be fine.

But the odds seemed to shrink the closer I came.

Aldwych is an abandoned station just around the corner from Somerset House, near to the Victoria Embankment and Temple tube – and yet, it didn't occur to me until I was standing right underneath Waterloo Bridge, that I was going to pass the very place I'd escaped Victoria that afternoon.

Had it only been that afternoon?

I imagined for a split second, as I passed under the shadow of the bridge, that she would still be there, waiting, somehow knowing I would come back to this spot. I thought she might lunge out of the shadows towards me, the pigeons that were my parents flapping at her Leboutin heels.

I stopped on the far side and looked up. The side of the bridge was fuzzy to my fox eyes, but I could make out the scent of aerosol paints and the faint, shining swish and curl of the graffiti high overhead. E3's latest, the Icarus figure falling through the clouds.

I ought to keep moving. I certainly shouldn't linger here, where I'd only escaped death by the skin of my teeth a couple of hours ago, looking at the pretty pictures.

Except there had to be room in my life for this, because I was probably going to die soon. The knowledge felt innate, like if you cut me open you'd find it written through my bones like a stick of Brighton rock, but it came with a steely certainty that if there wasn't time for this, there was no point trying to find the Horde or the Rabble, and I should throw myself into the Thames right now and have done with it.

I crossed the road and looked out over the river for a few minutes, as if by staring at the deep black waters I could wash my memory clean, like a palate-cleanser. I could make myself ready for whatever flavour of horror was waiting for me up the hill at the disused Tube station. The cold flowed off the water and I sucked in a few hard breaths.

I was getting tired. I wasn't sure what time it was, but it had to be after 2am, and I'd spent most of the night running. My paw pads glowed with exhaustion. I really wanted to stop, to lie down here and let the gentle lapping of the Thames and the roar of traffic sing me to sleep.

I walked on towards Aldwych.

The station had been closed for decades, but it still had the iconic Tube entrance with its huge oxblood-red bricks, and the words STRAND STATION in black and white letters under the arched window.

I'd actually been inside once, two or three years ago. Transport for London rent it out to people who want to film in a tube station. They were making that film with Carey Mulligan, and Dad's company was putting up part of the finance, so we went along on a family outing to watch the pivotal scene where she thinks about throwing herself in front of a train. By the end of the day Dad had made so many inane suggestions to the film crew, and Mum had made so many jibes about how many of Carey Mulligan I weighed, that I wished it was a working station so I could leap onto the tracks myself.

As I passed the side entrance on Surrey Street, heading for the main entrance on the Strand, I stopped dead and took a deep sniff.

I'd suddenly caught a strong, fresh smell of rat, as if out of nowhere. But then it had gone again. I snuffled all around the station, trying to figure out where it was coming from. High above my head I could make out more big black letters: ENTRANCE written over a metal concertina gate, and EXIT over two brown wooden doors with a modern lock. But the rat scent wasn't near either of them. I retraced my steps, and there it was again, as I passed the front door of the next-door building.

Apart from the station, Surrey Street was lined with thin, tall Georgian town houses. Each one had an area – a deep ditch in front of the house that let light into the basement and allowed servants to take deliveries straight into the kitchen, so the lower class never had to come to the front door. Mum has a similar arrangement with the back gate and the Ocado man. Or... she had.

I shook off the vision of groceries piling up at the back door over the next few days, of milk going sour in the fridge, and Mum's answerphone filling up with anxious calls from members of government. I tried to concentrate on what was in front of my nose.

The rat scent was coming from the bottom of the steps. It was strong and fresh, full of scrabbling and nibbling creatures – and oddly, a blast of strong, fruity perfume.

My heart lifted. Perhaps the Horde were all right. Perhaps they'd have answers for me, perhaps even somewhere safe for me to rest.

"Hello?" I called down. There was no answer from the darkness, so I started to gingerly climb down the incredibly steep iron stairs. There was barely room for me to stand on each step. Tall windows loomed up over me, with white-painted bars bolted to them. At the foot of the steps there was a tiny corridor, strewn with leaves and bits of old newspaper. It was barely wide enough for a person to stand in, but at the far end there was a little hollow arch, and at the base of the arch...

A rat hole and a pile of clothes.

I leapt at the clothes, almost burying my head in them. Jeans, a white shirt that carried a clinical, hospital kind of smell. A bra, knickers, socks rolled up carefully inside bright blue crocs. She'd been here recently, and... yes, there was a fresh, female rat smell leading into the hole.

One of the Horde was here. Right now.

I pushed my head inside the hole, careless in my excitement, and got a face full of pure blackness. My heart hammered and I tried not to think about what would happen if I got stuck. I had to try. I started to crawl inside. My shoulder-blades hit the top of the tunnel every time I reached out with my front paws, and my belly scraped along the floor. I was all the way inside, stretched out to my full length, my head in utter darkness, when I pushed forward a little and a tiny, bright point of light appeared to my left. The tunnel curved gently around and down, and thank goodness, it started to open up.

When I pushed myself out, blinking in the bright electric light, I found myself in a dusty broom cupboard, stacked with teetering piles of paint-stained buckets and old mops.

The lights were all on. Was that normal? This place was supposed to be deserted.

I heard something skitter, like claws on tile, and I froze and then spun around, my own claws clattering.

"Hello? Hello! I'm from the Skulk, I just want to talk," I said. There was no reply, and no more sound.

Had I imagined it? Maybe it was mice, or just some ordinary London rat. It wasn't as if the Underground didn't have its fair share.

I stood, frozen, for a few more minutes. But there was nothing.

I stepped out of the open cupboard door, into a deserted corridor just like any other one in the Tube. Except it was completely empty.

You almost never get an entire corridor to yourself, in the London Underground, and even if you do, you can sense the working station all around you. There are sounds of other people's feet coming up in front of you or behind, of trains clattering through the tunnels or escalators humming. You get warm breezes off the tracks, smells of yesterday's chips, and the far-off echo of buskers strumming guitars. In the Underground, even if you're by yourself, you're never quite alone.

Here, the curved corridor was silent, apart from the sound of my paws padding along the concrete floor, following the rat trail to the top of the spiral staircase. I could smell only rats and dust and the flow of electricity through the thick black cables that ran along the ceiling.

I couldn't see how far down the staircase it went – it curved around a thick, tiled column so I couldn't even see around the next corner. But I remembered it being a long climb down, and feeling much longer on the way back up to the surface.

I hesitated there for a little while, listening for any hint of movement. But the scent went this way, and I couldn't do anything but follow it, to the end.

I lost count after about seventy-five steps and stopped for a moment, pressing my back to the cool tiles, waiting for the tremble in my limbs to subside. The staircase was utterly silent except for the loud rasp of my own breath. I felt the urge to stifle it, so as not to disturb the dusty nothingness. Grime and brick dust crept into my nose and I let out a sneeze that echoed for what seemed like eternity.

I counted another eighty-two steps, hugging the outside of the curve and trying not to think about anything but counting and not tripping over my own feet or the little pieces of debris that littered the stairs, before a flat patch of concrete finally came up to meet me. I'd hit the bottom, at last. I sank down onto it and lay there, panting, for a few seconds.

The corridors down here were brightly lit, too. Coloured signs and Thirties advertising were pasted to the walls, presumably props from the last time the station had been made up for filming. The walls curved up over my head, almost perfectly round.

The silence was even more oppressive when my breathing had calmed. The loneliness of it, the knowledge that I was so far down under the earth with nobody to see or hear me made me shudder.

Even the rat scent seemed to be fading out in all directions. The corridor led off at least four different ways, and there were two barred alcoves in front of me in total shadow, looking like prison cells for the darkness.

Something skittered.

I twisted around, looking for the source of the sound, but there was nothing there.

Then, again – a scuttling, claws-on-concrete kind of sound. It seemed to circle all around me, like a ghost, right behind me and gone as soon as I turned around, building to a rattling crescendo. I whipped about, faster and faster, twisting my head up and down, and still I couldn't smell or see the source.

And then, suddenly, there were rats all around me.

Chapter Seventeen

I stumbled, dizzy, bracing my paws on the concrete, and just about managed to focus on the sharp teeth of the one in front of me as they snapped at my nose. I jerked away. The rat reared up, its pink tail whipping out behind it, and raked its claws down over my muzzle. It was a stinging pain, like a bad paper cut, and it made my eyes water.

"Invader!" the rat snarled. "Trespasser! Tell us what the Skulk sent you for, and we might let you live."

"The Skulk didn't... I mean – I'm from the Skulk, but..." I tried to turn my head, to count how many rats there were around me. The one who'd spoken, a big grey female with a glossy coat, was flanked by a black-furred male and a smaller female. This was the one I'd followed down from the surface. I could still scent the faintest hint of medical soap on her. I was pretty sure there were three more behind me. The entire Horde.

"Answer her," the male chittered.

"I came to... I..."

I didn't know where to begin. It hadn't occurred to me to work out what to say, if I actually *met* the Horde.

"It's about the stones," I blurted, before the lead rat could give me another swipe with her sharp little claws.

She narrowed her eyes to gleaming black slits, and the female beside her bared her teeth.

"How dare you?" the leader growled. Her whole body seemed to vibrate. "Filthy Skulk, breaking into our territory to accuse us of being thieves."

"I – no, I wasn't." I tried to look around at the other three, but the male leapt, snapping his teeth close to my left eye.

"Face front when Amanda is speaking to you."

"I wasn't accusing you of stealing our stone!" I barked. "I just want to know if you've got yours."

"Well if you were planning on stealing it, you're out of luck, honey," said one of the rats behind me, another female.

"No," I whined. "Listen, there's a sorceress, and she's killing people for their stones, and I have a blue stone that I found – it's hidden, safe for now, and I want to know whose it is so I can give it back, that's why I came here."

"She's lying," said the black male beside Amanda. "Just like the Skulk to make up some farfetched nonsense about a sorceress to get us to let our guard down."

"Get out," said Amanda, rubbing her front paws over her whiskers. "And don't come back here."

My heart sank. "You can't throw me out," I said. "Not without giving me a chance to explain!"

"Orion," Amanda snapped, and pain blistered across my tail. I yelled and tore my tail away from the teeth of the rat she'd called Orion, and lashed out, without thinking. My claws weren't drawn, but I caught him hard on the side of the head and he tumbled through the air and skidded up against the wall of the tunnel. He was on his feet again in seconds, but it was too late. I felt claws digging into my back as one of the rats jumped and clung on.

"Leave Orion alone! You'll pay for that, Skulk vermin," she growled. It was the little female. Her teeth clamped down on the scruff of my neck and I bucked and twisted, trying to shake her off.

"I don't want to hurt anyone," I growled. In hindsight, probably a mistake. The rats piled on, biting and scratching. They were pulling their punches, trying to teach me a lesson rather than kill me – if they'd gone for my eyes and throat, I realised, I would be a goner. As it was I could barely move and my skin was stinging all over, bleeding from thousands of tiny punctures.

"Let me go," I finally shrieked, "I'll go, just let me go!"

"Back," Amanda's voice commanded. The weight lifted and I staggered over to the foot of the spiral steps. I turned back to see all six rats advancing on me, their little razor-sharp teeth bared and snapping at me. "Get out, and tell the Skulk if we see you here again we'll bite to kill," she growled.

"You don't know what you're doing," I whined.

The rats lunged, their jaws snapping. I turned and hurtled up the stairs as fast as my tired legs could carry me.

I had no idea how close I was to the surface when my legs gave out and I lay, gasping, my head drooping onto my paws.

At least they weren't all dead. It was better than finding them dead. And the stone couldn't be theirs, could it? I racked my brain for any rat that'd pricked up its ears or seemed interested when I'd mentioned that it was a sapphire. None of them had.

So this was good. I'd learned something. And perhaps the Skulk and the Horde could reconcile, in time.

I just had to keep telling myself that.

A scuttling noise sent me leaping to my paws, swaying madly in a rising cloud of brick dust, and a second later a wriggling rat's nose appeared around the corner of the central column.

"Oi, Skulk girl," said the rat. I shied away, crouching to run – or to spring and sink my teeth into its mangy little neck.

That's hardly going to help Horde-Skulk relations, is it?

Save it for Victoria.

"I'm going!" I growled at the rat. "Give me a minute, for God's sake."

"Shh, do you want them to hear you?" the rat hissed, clambering up over the step and into view, fixing me with a glittering black stare. It was large and brown, and male. It was the other one that'd been behind me, with Orion and the female that called me honey.

This one hadn't spoken.

"I just want to give you a message," he said.

"From Amanda?"

"In a way." He sniffed at the air, glancing up and down the stairs, and then took a couple of steps closer. "The Horde and the Skulk have been at war for decades and it's ridiculous. You don't know what the Skulk did. *I* don't even know, nor does Amanda or Ryan."

"So this is like... you offering a truce?"

"If you like," said the rat. "I'm offering you information. You want it, or not?"

I nodded.

"The blue stone's not ours, ours is black. That's all I can tell you about that."

"Fine," I rasped, glad of the confirmation, though I felt far from fine.

"You been to the Cluster and the Rabble yet?"

"I've been to the Cluster. Four of them are dead – for days, at least. And I have no idea where the new ones are, or if they even know."

The rat hesitated, blinking his black eyes at me. He washed his ears. "That's... unfortunate."

I just looked at him blearily. *Unfortunate. Right. My whole life is unfortunate right now.*

"But I can tell you where to find the Rabble."

"I already know," I muttered. "They meet in Kew Gardens, right?"

"Well yeah, but you don't wanna go up the Gardens at this time of night. You won't find anything. You want to go round their leader's house. She'll talk to you."

I felt a yawn crawling up my throat and tried to strangle it. "What time is it, anyway?"

"Nearly four," said the rat.

"And the Rabble leader will let a strange fox into her house at 4am?"

"I think so. She's a bit like that." There was a scrabbling sound. I tensed, and the rat sat up on its haunches like a meerkat and peered down the stairs. "They're coming up. I said I had to get off home. Let's not be here, eh? You want Susanne Dirden, 42 Pacific Road, Acton. Got it? Repeat it to me."

"Susanne Dirden, 42 Pacific Road, Acton. 42 Pacific Road."

"Right," said the rat, and vanished up the stairs like a mangy, furry rocket. I gathered my strength – though it felt like it was about enough to fill a small teacup – and scrambled after him.

This time, the feeling of twisted déjà-vu kicked in when I was still a long way from my destination. Here I was, passing through Acton in fox form, at 4am, again. It was like the world was mocking me by sending me back here. How long had it been since that first night, when the night had opened up in front of me, promising freedom, a wide open world where I'd never have to answer to anyone? It couldn't have been long, but when I tried to think back, I realised I couldn't even think what day it was today.

Last time I was here, the night had been full of excitement and adventure, and I'd been full of nervous energy, looking forward to seeing E3's masterpiece. I hadn't been cold. Now, that deep bone-chill was catching up to me, curling around my joints, pulling my muscles tight so I couldn't even bring myself to move quickly to work up some heat.

I trudged past *Batman with Rainbow*, hardly looking at it, and didn't even think about trying to go back to the *Arabian Dragons*. I just had to get this done. If I survived tonight, I'd find some clothes and I'd find the time and I would go back to the dragons. I would.

Pacific Road was a very ordinary street lined with terraced houses with cramped, hedged front gardens. I could smell ordinary cats and dogs, leaving their domesticated scent in a complex chessboard of overlapping territories, and a couple of other, sharper scents, mostly around the bins. Other foxes. Real foxes. I hoped I didn't meet any tonight. I wasn't up to defending my territory. I was starting to think about curling up at the bottom of a random garden and sleeping till morning. But something bitter and steely was creeping into my spine, overcoming even the exhaustion and the trauma.

I had to keep going. If this was going to go horrifically wrong – if Susanne Dirden was going to have been violently murdered, or not want to listen to me – there was no point trying to put off finding out. I just wanted to *know*.

Number 42 had a blue front door and the front garden was full of overgrown bushes. I sniffed carefully around the door, bracing for the increasingly familiar taste of death and blood and doom, but all I got were the scents of mud on the welcome mat, old paint on the door, and a hint of spicy food from within.

I wondered how I ought to announce my presence. Other than with a full symphonic choir singing *Dies Irae* and a round of cannon fire, obviously. It would be polite to ring the doorbell. But that would mean turning human and naked in the middle of suburban Acton.

I might be full of insane bravado, but I still wasn't up to getting naked in the street.

I settled for barking, as loud as I could, and scratching at the bricks beside the door, raking my claws over the uneven surface.

After only a minute or two, light burst overhead. That was quick. Perhaps she was already awake. The window flew open and a head and shoulders appeared, frizzy hair forming a brown halo around a face in shadow.

So far, so human. But I couldn't see her expression from down here.

The figure didn't speak. I looked up at her and held her gaze, trying to convey that she was the one I wanted purely by acting unnatural and unfoxlike. Was it working? I couldn't tell. And the staring into the light was starting to give me a headache, although it occurred to me that I was long, long overdue for one. I yapped, scratching again at the ground by the door, trying to look as intelligent as I could – although I wasn't sure I could manage to look intelligent right now even if I had my human face on.

For a few seconds, the figure didn't move. Then it pulled back and the window thudded shut.

I waited. Should I bark again? Did she think I'd gone?

No... I heard the soft thumps of feet on carpet. She was coming down. I braced myself to run – in or out, I hadn't decided yet.

I heard the metallic clicking of locks being pulled back, and then the door opened. Fingers of warmth crept out onto the chilly street and I looked up at Susanne Dirden: a pair of black ankles in fuzzy blue slippers, worn grey pyjama trousers with stars on them, a brown dressing gown. Her face was still shadowed against the light in the hallway.

"Hey," said Susanne. "Are you from the Skulk?"

I nodded, so hard it made me dizzy.

"What could possibly bring you here in the middle of the night?" She frowned down at me. "Are – are you all right? You look hurt."

Did I? I hung my head, feeling the sting of the rats' claws across my muzzle and my back. I didn't realise it showed...

"But why would you come to... I'm sorry, I'm just a little... Come in, please." She stood aside and I half-trotted, half-fell over the threshold.

I got a muzzle full of the spicy food smells, and reeled, drooling. The scents were warm and inviting, lived-in. I could taste ginger and cardamom and a bunch of scents I couldn't even identify. My stomach rumbled and I let out a small whine.

"Are you hungry?" said Susanne shutting the door behind me, and putting on the chain. I twitched as it jangled into place.

"Come into the sitting room and let me get you some clothes, and then we'll sort you out."

My skin crawled. She hadn't said it with a malicious cackle, but the words *we'll sort you out* made me shiver. Who was that "we"? How would they "sort me out"? The door was shut and locked. *If I'm screwed, I'm heartily screwed.* I glanced about, looking for other ways out of the building. At the end of the hall there was a door into a dark place with a linoleum floor. The kitchen? Maybe there'd be a back way out through there.

Susanne waved me through a door into a carpeted room that was almost completely taken up by two squashy-looking sofas, a wide wooden coffee table and an enormous plant that was basically a small indoor palm tree. Its fronds brushed the ceiling and trailed over the back of one of the sofas.

"Wait just a sec," Susanne said, and vanished. I heard her softly thumping back up the stairs.

I shook myself, and shifted from paw to paw. With an odd, dispassionate coolness, I registered that my legs were starting to shake and my fur was creeping up and down my spine on a near-constant loop. I didn't know how much longer I'd be able to stand. If I was going to get "sorted out" it'd better be now. I didn't know how much longer I'd be able to keep running.

Susanne came back with a pile of neatly-folded clothes in her arms.

"I'm afraid they're my son's," she said. "I hope they fit. I'll take them into the bathroom and you can change in private. Then we can talk, OK?"

I nodded.

She led me to a door under the stairs, turned on the light and placed the clothes on the floor next to a toilet, a tiny sink and a fluffy white bathroom mat. I walked in, and Susanne closed the door.

So far, no attacks. No blood, no shouting. I felt like I was walking a razor-sharp wire over a pit of alligators that were on fire, but I was still alive. And that had to be enough for right now.

I stretched out my neck and my limbs, and tried to push into the change.

It wouldn't come.

Panic shredded my very last nerve and I dropped to my belly on the soft mat, burying my head under my paws, every muscle in my aching body shaking. I wept, my shoulders heaving, curling my fingers over my ears, tears springing to my eyes. My spine curved up, my elbows pressed out. Sharp points of pain stung my face and neck and back, like bad paper cuts. Hair fell over my face and I shivered as my toes pressed out and touched the cool tiled floor.

Oh. I sniffed and sat up, blinking through the film of tears at my hands, my human hands. I reached out and grabbed a fistful of loo roll and dabbed at my eyes and blew my nose. *Oh, thank God.*

I had to get up in stages, curling my shaking legs under me, pulling myself up to perch on the cold wooden loo seat, then gripping the edge of the sink and leaning hard on it as I pushed myself to my feet. I looked at myself in the mirror and blinked at the alien girl who looked back at me.

Christ, I looked a *state*. I gaped at my reflection for a bit, wondering when I'd got so many shallow cuts across my face, when my eyes had got so bloodshot and darkly shadowed. And my hair – it was never non-tangled unless I'd spent an hour blitzing it with anti-frizz conditioner, and that was pretty much fine with me, but right now it was elevating tangled to an entirely new level. There ought to be awards for this level of commitment to tangling.

I scooped up the clothes, praying Susanne's son wasn't a skinny ten year-old. But they looked OK, and I suppose she wouldn't have given them to me if she'd thought they wouldn't be a good approximation for an average person.

If I thought pulling on some woman's knickers and bra didn't feel right at the Tower, climbing into this boy's Batman boxers felt one hundred per cent more wrong, even though they fit pretty well. His tracksuit bottoms and faded Foo Fighters T-shirt were soft and comfortably baggy.

I ran the taps and splashed warm water on my face. The little cuts stung as my fingers ran over them, and turned pink around the edges. I tried to pull my hair out of my face and make myself look, if not presentable, then at least not completely mental.

It was pretty much a lost cause.

Then I turned, curling my toes in the soft bathroom rug, and opened the bathroom door.

The hall was empty.

I glanced into the kitchen – the light was on now, and I could see a cramped row of counters, piled with pots and pans and spices and recipe books, and a wooden dining table that would've seated about six. But Susanne wasn't there. I guessed she was waiting in the sitting room, and stepped slowly towards the door.

There were pictures hanging on the walls all along the hall. They mostly seemed to be posters, modern art – and a large, lovingly framed photograph of the *Arabian Dragons*.

My heart felt like it swelled about four sizes, and I went into the sitting room with a smile on my face.

Which froze and died when I saw Susanne standing in front of the coffee table with a hard look in her eyes and a shovel clutched in her hands.

Chapter Eighteen

"What," I breathed. I backed away, my hands shaking violently as I raised them between me and Susanne. I braced myself to go fox again, except maybe I should run for the kitchen and smash a window and *then* go fox, or perhaps I could get to the front door, except the lock and the chain would slow me down.

But Susanne was staring at me, at my face and then at my hands.

And she was lowering the shovel.

"You're just a kid," she muttered. "What do you want?"

"Help," I moaned. "I swear, I just, I need help!" Tears hitched my chest and I dragged my hands across my eyes. "The... one of the Horde said I could come. Someone's after me. She took my parents. Please," I hiccupped, "just say you're not with Victoria, please."

"Oh, my *dear.*" Susanne dropped the shovel onto the sofa. "I'm so sorry. You have to understand – you turn up here in the middle of the night and of course I had to let you in but you could have been a robber, or *anything*. You understand, right?"

I nodded, but I'd started crying and there was no stopping it – the tears seemed to have been lying in wait for me, and now they were pushing and shoving down my cheeks. My lips twisted and my shoulders hunched. I couldn't see a thing – Susanne could've brained me with her shovel and I wouldn't even have seen it coming. But instead of a cold *thunk* and then nothingness, I saw a dark blur moving towards me and felt strong, soft arms around my shoulders.

I melted into the hug and wept all over Susanne's dressing gown.

Her voice took on a faint Jamaican lilt as she rubbed my back in firm but gentle circles and made comforting noises of the "oh, shh, there" variety. I wondered, distantly, if she'd mind just how sticky and soggy her dressing gown was getting.

After a little while she steered me gently towards the sofa and I sank into it, next to the shovel. I've sat on antique Chesterfields and £800 duck-down pillows, but right then, collapsing on Susanne's saggy sofa, with the soft brown leather cracking a little underneath me, was like being cradled in the arms of giant, saggy, cinnamon-smelling angels.

Susanne disappeared for a couple of seconds and then set a glass of water down on the coffee table and handed me a roll of kitchen towel. I blotted at my nose and eyes, and tried to pull myself together enough to take a drink of water.

"You must be exhausted," said Susanne.

"Uh huh," I nodded.

"Is this something we can fix tonight?" she asked. I thought about it. Yet another wave of tears lapped at me. I tried to fight them back, looking up at her through eyelashes that were still wet and clumpy.

"No," I managed to squeak.

"Then I think you should get some sleep," Susanne said. "I'll make you up a bed here and we'll talk about in the morning. How about that?"

I tried to express just how much I liked that plan, but only came out with a strangled "Aaahh." I coughed, took a little sip of water, and tried again. "That would be amazing."

"You just wait there, I'll grab some sheets and pillows."

She left, quietly taking the shovel with her. I took another sip of water, put it down on the coffee table and then let myself sink sideways, into the soft embrace of the sofa.

Dear? Oh, dear. Here you go.

Warmth, and the clean smell of someone else's laundry. My head lifted, and then lowered onto the coolest, softest cloud in the sky.

Slosh-clonk. Zzzzip. Rustle.

I turned over, rubbing my eyes with a balled fist. It wasn't time to get up yet. Five more minutes. The bed smelled oddly of cinnamon, but that was OK. The room was still dark. A line of moonlight sliced across the room from the open window. It wasn't open before.

Mum would be angry if I didn't shut the window.

She'd be so angry if I couldn't stop the bleeding.

But I didn't know how. I buried my head in my pillow. The blood was everywhere. It poured in through my bedroom, down the stairs, all over the kitchen. I huddled in to myself and tried to be a mouse. If I stayed quiet, it wouldn't find me here. It was safe here in the dark. The wardrobe was uncomfortable, but it was safe: nothing else would happen while I was here in the dark.

I felt a breeze and stirred again. A small shape fluttered through the window, coming down the shaft of moonlight into the room. It hovered over me and then set down briefly with the lightest of touches on my hand. I twitched and it flew away.

I woke up to the sound of tea happening in another room: a kettle boiled, and there was the distinctive *tingting scrape ting* of a spoon swirling around a mug.

The room was full of warm light and the detritus of everyday living. The coffee table was crowded with books, mugs, pieces of paper, remote controls, a large biscuit tin with scenes of children skating on a frozen pond. A glass-framed poster over the mantelpiece glinted in the sunlight, drawing my eye with its striking red-and-black collage of a full moon and the words *Take Back the Night, Philadelphia, October 1975*. It was printed on crumpled A4 paper with a tear on one corner, but framed with as much care as Mum's original Rembrandt sketches. Not that Mum would ever do anything as careless as hang the Rembrandts on the wall where just anyone could enjoy them.

Even if she wasn't currently a pigeon.

I sat up and rubbed my eyes.

A tall boy walked into the room, carrying a mug. Our eyes met and I gave him a nervous, hi-there-complete-stranger, sorry-I-collapsed-on-your-sofa kind of smile.

"You're up," he said. "Susanne said I should bring you some tea." He set the mug full of steaming tea down on the coffee table in front of me. If my eyes had actually sparkled, or filled up with little red hearts, I would barely have been surprised.

"I didn't know if you wanted sugar, so there's some in the pot," he said, gesturing to a little brown ceramic pot with *Coffee* written on the side of it.

"Oh, my God," I muttered, sitting up straighter and folding down the duvet. "Thank you." I spooned about five sugars into my tea, stirred and took a sip. That first mouthful of sugary caffeine and tannins was beautiful. I felt my brain kick into gear and let out a long sigh.

The boy went out of the room and came back with a mug of his own, and another one that must be for Susanne.

It was clearly his clothes I was wearing. He was in jeans and a baggy pre-distressed Rainbow Dash T-shirt. I guessed he was about my age, maybe a couple of years older or younger, I couldn't quite tell. He had a dusting of stubble on his cheeks, short black hair in loose curls, brown skin, South Asian features. There was a single wide earring in his left ear.

"So," he said, perching on the arm of the other sofa, "you're a fox? I mean you're from the Skulk?"

I nodded. "I'm Meg."

"Mo. Mohammed, but call me Mo," said the boy. He held out his hand and I shook it, awkwardly.

"So, er. You know about the Skulk and... stuff?"

"Oh, yeah, Susanne didn't tell you? I'm a shifter too. With the Rabble, like Susanne."

"Oh." I tried not to look confused. A mother and son who were both shifters? It wasn't way out of the realms of possibility or anything, but it threw me a little.

Plus there was the fact that they really didn't look anything like each other. But maybe Mo had got all his looks from his dad...

I caught Mo's eye, and we both looked away again. I suppose I couldn't begrudge him a good stare. I was the one who'd turned up on his sofa in the middle of the night covered in scratches. I looked up, a half-smile readied on my lips, but he was looking away.

"Ah, you're awake," said Susanne, appearing at the doorway in the same dressing gown she'd had on last night. "Would you like some breakfast – I'm sorry, I don't think I caught your name."

"Oh, Meg. Meg Banks. Um, if you're sure..."

"I'll put on some toast," said Susanne. "Jam, Marmite, or butter?"

"Jam, please," I said.

Susanne vanished again and I sipped my tea, concentrating hard on the sugary taste as it flowed over my tongue and the feel of the smooth handle between my fingers. I had to reassure myself I was awake. I'd never been in a situation so surreally *ordinary*. From the jam toast right down to the awkward pauses.

I tried to run my fingers through my hair and spent a pleasingly busy few minutes getting out the very worst of the tangles and not trying to think of something to say. It occurred to me that if I'd been sitting here last week looking like this in front of a boy like Mo, covered in wounds and bruises, with bird's nest hair and probably smelling pretty weird into the bargain, I would've been burning up with embarrassment. It wasn't as if I was exactly happy about it now. I just didn't have the space in my head for it.

"So..." Mo began, and faltered. "We should wait for Susanne, like, before you tell us what's going on with you," he said.

"Yeah, I think so," I nodded into my tea.

"So..."

There was the clatter of toast popping out of a toaster and a rattle of cutlery.

"So, are you at school?" he asked.

I swallowed another gulp of tea. He probably had no idea how complicated that question was. "I'm in lower sixth. Year Twelve," I said. It wasn't quite the real answer, but it was as close as I wanted to get. "You?"

"Thirteen," he said. "What're you taking?"

"History, Classics and English," I said, without much enthusiasm. "Boring, but... I kind of miss the boring right now."

"I'm doing Art and Design Tech."

"Oh?" If I'd been in fox form my ears would've literally pricked up. I sat up a little straighter and met his eyes. "You want to go into design?"

"Fine art," said Mo, with a sheepish smile. "I'm applying

for the Central St Martin's foundation course," he said, but he didn't look particularly enthusiastic. He shrugged as I raised my eyebrows at him. "Even if I get in, I'm going to have a billion pounds of debt and I'll end up working in McDonalds either way."

"Don't say that," Susanne shouted from the kitchen. "Nandos, at least. You've got to aim high."

Mo rolled his eyes, and I giggled. It felt surreal. When was the last time I giggled? Before all this? No, longer. I hadn't giggled since I was about ten.

"I love art," I said. "I wish I could've taken it, but my mum wasn't a fan."

Mo smiled, looked away, and then looked back and regarded me with a slight frown.

"What?" I asked.

Mo scratched the back of his neck. "Well, this is going to sound kind of weird, but do you mind if I sketch you?"

There's leftfield, and then there's "can I sketch you?" I blinked, while my brain went over its response options:

Yes.

No.

Me?

Why?

Like one of your French girls? Oh, my God, Meg don't you dare say that. This is as awkward as it needs to be already without weird Titanic *jokes.*

"You want to draw *me*?"

"If you don't mind. I need to practise my faces, for my portfolio, you know. And you've... got a face. And kind of amazing hair."

"You want to practise drawing cuts and tangles?"

Mo hesitated, but then his face split into a sheepish grin. "Well, yeah. What's the point of drawing faces if they're never, you know, lived-in."

Some distant part of my brain suggested I ought to feel insulted, but I didn't. I mean, I'd seen my face last night and I could objectively state that "lived-in" didn't really cover it.

"Sure. Why not?"

"Now?"

"Er... I suppose," I said.

Mo dived for the coffee table and produced a thick ring-bound sketchbook and a 2B pencil. He leafed through the book to an empty page.

Susanne walked into the room and grabbed her mug of tea. She gave Mo's sketchbook an affectionate side-eye. "Always working," she said, her voice overflowing with fondness. "But I'm not sure this is completely appropriate, Mo. Poor Meg's only had about four hours' kip."

"No, it's all right," I said. "I get it. Actually I draw things too."

"All right," said Susanne, heading back to the kitchen. "But tell him to sod off if you get tired of it, won't you?"

"Yeah, I promise."

"What kind of thing do you draw?" Mo asked, his pencil moving across the paper at lightning speed.

"Well, I'm not going to art college or anything, I just..."

I hesitated. And then I remembered the *Arabian Dragons* photo on the wall, and I also remembered that I was probably going to die soon. Cuddled up on Susanne's sofa, with the warm sunlight and the tea and Mo looking at me over his sketchbook, it seemed inevitable and impossible all at once. Either way I should live in the moment.

"Actually, I do a bit of graffiti. Here and there."

Mo's gaze shot up and his eyes met mine. His fingers were sketching, but his eyes didn't leave my face for a few seconds. He looked down before he spoke again. "Oh, really? D'you live round here? Would I have seen any of your stuff?"

"Well, I live in Kensington." *Lived.* "But I've been trying to spread things out. So, I dunno, maybe." Ah, OK, here came the blushing – it was a little late to the party but it seemed determined to make up for lost time. I hoped Mo wasn't trying to sketch my skin tone because it was probably shifting and changing like a blotchy lava lamp. "I – I go by Thatch."

Mo sat up straight, a broad grin spreading over his face. "I have seen your stuff! I've seen it on graffitilondon. You're good. I loved the Thorn Queen one, that was *scary*."

"Oh, my God," I laughed. "Erm, thank you! It, yeah, it was..." *A fairly accurate depiction of my mother.* "Supposed to be pretty freaky. But I'm not E3 or anything."

Mo dropped his pencil. He bent down to pick it up, grinning sheepishly. "Oh, you know E3? That's nice. That's, um... me."

I felt like a computer overloading. Too much information. Does not compute. *What do I do with this insane mess that is my life? How can I even begin to fit this in with everything else that's happening to me? It doesn't fit. It's the wrong shape. It's too brilliant.*

I can't even tell you what I did in that moment. All I can tell you for certain is that the next coherent thought I had was:

I'm wearing E3's boxer shorts.

I'm wearing them on my arse.

Oh, my God.

"I love your work," I whispered, because if I didn't keep my voice down I thought I might scream it out at the top of my lungs. "So much. I love it... *a lot.*"

"Wow, thank you!" Mo said, and his cheeks darkened, and he went on sketching my face.

Because that's what was happening to me, right then. My absolute art hero was sketching my grubby, beaten-up face. I froze, trying so hard not to pull a stupid expression I was probably pulling the *mother* of all stupid expressions.

Susanne came back in and handed me a plate with two slices of toast with jam. I gave her a weak smile. "So you're an artist too, Meg?"

"Oh, *no*, I mean not like Mo," I protested.

"Pretty much exactly like me, I thought," Mo said, frowning down at his sketch. "She's a graffiti artist, too."

I glanced warily at Susanne. "You... know about..." I stopped myself. Of course she did. The *Arabian Dragons* was hanging on the wall in her hallway! I'd seen it, the night before, and not known what I was really looking at.

"As long as he doesn't get in trouble, and he's making the community a nicer place to live, not a worse one, I don't have a problem," said Susanne.

Apparently, there was still a little part of my mind that hadn't yet been blown, because it was now.

She didn't just know. She was *proud*.

"Now, Meg," said Susanne. "I think it's time you told us what happened to you, if you're ready. You said you needed my help."

I sighed and shifted my legs under me on the sofa. I suppose the illusion of comfort couldn't last forever. I couldn't stay here on Susanne's couch, exchanging art tips with E3 and drinking her tea for the rest of my life.

Victoria would find me. And then they would both die.

I steeled myself, cradled my toast in my lap, and began to tell my story in the most concise, logical form I could manage.

"So, I need to know – the Rabble stone. Is it safe? Or is it the one Victoria already has – or the blue one I left with my friend?"

Susanne glanced at Mo, and sighed. "Our stone is yellow. But I don't know where it is. One of the Rabble took it, a couple of months ago."

Mo looked pained and started to flip through his sketchbook. "Helen," he said. "Helen Crossman. She sold it for crack." He held up the page. It was dotted with sketches – facial studies, movement studies. The woman was gaunt and her face was dirty, but there was life in the way she pulled on her jacket or the way she ran her fingers through her dark hair.

"We don't know exactly what she did with it," Susanne corrected him. "But she was an addict, that much is certainly true. She'd been clean a whole month – then suddenly Helen disappeared, and so did the stone. We haven't seen it since."

I sighed. I suppose I didn't expect anything else.

"So..." I ticked off on my fingers. "The Skulk stone is red, the Rabble stone is yellow, the Horde stone is black. I don't know about the Conspiracy stone, but that's locked up in the White Tower. It has to be the Cluster stone I've got. But that leaves me... exactly nowhere. The Cluster are dead, and I don't have the faintest clue how to find their replacements." I pressed my knuckles into the corners of my eyes. "And I don't suppose either of you know where I can find the metashifter? Blackwell called the first one the leodweard. Someone who can be any one of our shapes."

"No, I'm sorry," said Susanne. "I met one once. He enjoyed being a butterfly the most, I think; he spent some time with the Rabble back in the day. But that was decades ago."

So there was still a metashifter, in theory. I sighed. That was good news, I supposed... but it didn't seem like it was going to be worth my while to chase after them.

"Thank you," I said. "For the bed. And the tea. I should probably get going."

"Going?" Susanne shook her head. "No, I don't think so. This Victoria," she said, her lips twisting with distaste. "We need to call a meeting. The others need to hear about this." She stood up and reached for the landline phone on the coffee table.

"Are you sure?" I blurted. "I don't want anyone else to get hurt, maybe it'd be better if–"

"Will not knowing protect them, if this woman comes looking for our stone?"

I flushed and looked away.

"It's all right," Susanne said. "But we need to talk it through. I think we might be able to help you." She left the room, dialling.

"I'm really sorry about your parents," said Mo. "I hope you can get them back. My, uh, my parents died. In a car accident. When I was eleven."

"Oh, God, I'm sorry."

Mo waved a hand, swatting away my sympathy. "I'm fine, I've got Susanne, I just... I know. Kind of. How much it sucks."

"Right," I whispered.

"D'you wanna see?" he said holding out his sketchpad. My heart thumped, and for a moment I considered saying no.

I always had this feeling, right before clicking or scrolling to see E3's latest work – I don't know where it came from, this almost crippling sense of anticipation, of fear that the streak would be broken and he'd finally produce something that wasn't good, that I didn't love. And now there was a whole other level of investment in it: what if the drawing was good, but I just looked completely awful?

I was sure a couple of minutes ago I'd been feeling totally Zen about how I looked. Where had my Zen gone?

I took the sketchpad and dropped it into my lap to hide my trembling hands.

"Wow."

It was pretty amazing. There were three of me, from different angles – one without much expression, one staring morosely down at my hands, one with a broad smile I didn't remember actually giving. He hadn't exactly skimped on the details – the tangles were particularly well-drawn and the bruise on my neck looked livid and painful – but somehow, I didn't come out of it too badly. Actually, I looked sort of OK. I felt my cheeks burning.

"It's great," I managed to say. I would've gone on, but something caught my eye on the bottom of the page. He'd signed it, with his usual tag, and it was...

I tried not to let my jaw drop. How had I never seen it before? It wasn't "E3". It was two equal curly shapes face to face – a pair of butterfly wings.

Chapter Nineteen

Susanne insisted on buying me some proper clothes before we met the rest of the Rabble. I couldn't argue with her logic – I couldn't really go walking through Kew Gardens in Mo's old clothes. I thrust my hands in the pockets of my new hoodie as Susanne and Mo led the way down the neat raked gravel path towards the giant Palm House.

"I keep stashes of clothes all over London," said Mo as we strolled past a line of statues of heraldic animals – a dragon, a dog, a sort of demon goat thing. "It's a pain in the arse to organise but it's not like I can carry anything in butterfly form. It's worth it."

"I should do that," I agreed. "I haven't had time to think any of this through, it all..." I waved my hands in the air in the universal symbol for *went absolutely batshit.*

Mo dug his hands into the pockets of his jeans and kicked some gravel. "Well, maybe when things are a bit, y'know, calmer, I can show you some of my good hiding spots."

"That'd be amazing," I grinned. I couldn't see that far into the future, right now – I could hardly see past my next breath – but it was kind of nice to know that the potential was out there, somewhere. Comforting.

"Here we are," said Susanne. I looked around, wondering where we were going to change, and caught the eye of two men who were sitting on one of the benches along the path, staring at us as we approached.

Wait...

The Rabble met in human form? It'd been strange enough to me that they'd meet in daylight, somewhere so public. I suppose the Skulk had never outright *told* me they never met as people, I'd just assumed it wasn't done.

We drew level with the two men and they stood up.

"This her?" said one of them, a white guy with hair so thoroughly gelled-up he looked a bit like he was wearing a hedgehog on his head. He folded his arms in his Super Dry blazer and gave me an unconvinced kind of look.

"Meg, this is Aaron, and this is Marcus," Susanne said, indicating the white guy and then the other man, who was black and about seven feet tall and wearing a T-shirt with an Eighties wrestler on it. He had veins like steel rope running all the way up his arms. He shook my hand as Susanne introduced me. "This is Meg. She came to me for help – the Skulk are in some trouble. It sounds like it could be serious."

"Shall we?" said Marcus, and turned to lead us off the path and up into the enormous greenhouse.

The heat and dampness hit me as soon as I stepped inside. I could almost feel my hair frizzing up around me, like one of those cartoons where fright literally curls people's hair. The forest of palm trees seemed to stretch away from me, endlessly green and dripping with moisture. Brown strings of fern fronds wrapped around the massive trunks and the odd bright flash of red and yellow peeked out between huge rubbery leaves. It smelled of green and of earth, even to my dulled human sense of smell. I almost wished I could go fox right now, just to breathe it in for a second. Another thing to put on my if-I-survive to-do list.

As we were pushing past the palm fronds my curiosity got the better of me and I leaned close to Mo. "Hey, er, looks like there's four of you – and Helen makes five – isn't there another one coming?"

"Peter's eighty-nine years old. He's not well enough to come out to meetings. We visit him in the home sometimes. Susanne keeps him up to date."

"Oh."

Susanne led us up an ornate white-painted spiral staircase to the balcony that ran around the top of the building, and we gathered on eye-level with the giant pinkish seeds on one of the tall, deep-green palms.

"So, Meg – what's going on?" asked Aaron, folding his arms across his chest.

I swallowed and glanced out of the windows, over the lake and the gardens and the wide gravel paths cutting through the trees.

"It's about the stones," I began. Every time I'd told my story, it sort of amazed me that people believed it. Maybe I had a very honest face. I suppose right now the scratches and bruises were doing that job for me.

Something had obviously gone very bad for me. Why not killer pigeons and fog that liquidises your brain?

"Victoria wants the stones, and if she hasn't got yours already, I'm certain she'll come for it soon," I said, after I'd given them the quickest version I could manage. "I think we need to work together to stop her. I have what must be the Cluster stone, but the Cluster are all dead. I just don't know what we can do. If there's nothing else, I'll be going up to the Shard myself."

Marcus and Susanne shook their heads and Mo muttered, "You can't."

"I have to – I can't do nothing, and I really don't have any other options, unless you can help me."

"We may be able to," said Susanne. She turned to the others. "I'd like to ask permission from the Rabble to share everything we know about the stones with the Skulk. Any objections?"

Mo and Marcus both shook their heads at once. Aaron shuffled his feet and tapped his fingers on the white railing.

"I dunno. I suppose there's no harm in it, it's not like we even have our stone anymore."

Susanne nodded. "All right. Here's what I know – boys, please leap in if there's anything you know that I don't mention. I know that our stone is yellow, and that it governs over the element of sight."

"So Blackwell was right about that," I said. "But what does it actually mean?"

"It meant that anyone who possessed the stone could use it to alter other people's perception," Susanne said.

"You could make things appear, or disappear. I think in theory you could use it to make yourself invisible, though I don't know anyone who ever tried it."

"Wow," I said. "So, if Victoria's got it, maybe she's using it to hide the fog from ordinary people?"

"She could be," said Susanne.

"So, did you use your stone, when you still had it?" I asked, fascinated with the idea of altering the way people saw things. You could take visual art to a whole new level...

"What would we use it for?" Marcus shrugged.

"I... well..." Mo reached up to fiddle with a palm leaf that was dangling over the balcony railing. "I thought about it."

"Mo," Susanne gasped. "You didn't."

"I never actually did it," Mo held up his hands. "I just thought about it. Come on, it would've been amazing. Imagine using it to make paintings move or set up sculptures that weren't really there..." he turned to me. "Back me up, Thatch, you have to see where I'm coming from."

I grinned. "Yeah, I have to say, that sounds awesome. I mean, of course, you couldn't actually *do* it. Cause we have to keep them safe."

"See? Meg's an artist. She gets it." Mo held out his hand and I met it in a fist bump, trying to keep my cool and not let the dangerous levels of fangirl glee that were building up inside me spill out all over this very sensible conversation.

Marcus shook his head. "I know it seems tempting, but just think what the wrong person could do with the power to change how you saw the world."

"Deception and trickery," said Aaron. "You'd be walking off cliffs thinking there was a bridge there."

"Or believing you were talking to your best friend – or your boyfriend – when it was really some stranger," Marcus added.

I shuddered. "OK. So, not at all awesome."

"And it's out there right now, who knows where, being used for who knows what." Aaron folded his arms. "And all because Helen couldn't be bothered to stay on the Methadone."

Susanne gave him a sad look. "Please, Aaron. Blame the disease, remember?"

Aaron shrugged. "I don't know, Su. Why didn't she come to us for help this time? I think she just wanted an excuse not to have to try anymore."

"No. I give her more credit than that," Marcus rumbled, lowering his voice about two octaves. "She must have been desperate to think this was her only choice."

I shuffled my feet, feeling for the first time that I'd really intruded on something not meant for me – this was Rabble business. I'd never even met Helen, it didn't feel right for me to stand and listen in while her surrogate family talked through her issues like this.

"Where did you keep your stone, when you had it?" I asked, hoping it didn't seem too much like an obvious change of subject.

"Here," said Mo.

"Where?" I frowned.

Mo crossed the walkway to my side and leaned over the railing, pointing down at the beds of dripping ferns. "In the dirt, down there."

"But..." I stared down at the winding paths around the beds below. Two old ladies hobbled slowly along one, while a group of school kids in matching maroon jumpers were being herded down another. "But this is a public place!" I looked up at Mo. "They must have hundreds of thousands of visitors every year, weren't you afraid someone would find it?"

"It was protected," said Susanne. "Marcus, Peter and I are the only ones who saw it done who're still in the Rabble."

"This was back in the... what, the late Nineties?" Marcus said.

"Yes, it must be." Susanne sighed. "We all gathered here in the middle of the night, in butterfly form. Peter brought the stone. He gathered us all around it – we all had to be touching the stone."

"As soon as I touched it," Marcus said, "I felt something happen. It was like the surface of the stone became soft and I could reach inside and grab one of the points of the star."

But the points aren't really things you could grab, they're cracks in the gem...

I stopped myself from saying it. We obviously weren't in the realm of physical logic any more.

"Peter and Lena talked us through it," said Susanne. "They said we should just hold on and let the power of the stone flow through us, and we did, and the next thing I knew, I was opening my eyes and the stone looked different. Opaque."

"Lena stayed with us, remember?" Marcus added. "To show us that it'd worked. We stayed in butterfly form until the Palm House opened the next day, and watched the gardeners and tourists pass the stone by without even looking at it."

I tried to ignore a pang of jealousy. The Rabble seemed so… *functional.* Though I suppose that was before one of them vanished and took their stone with her.

"So, do you think the Skulk could do the same thing, but it'd have a different effect?" I wondered aloud. "Blackwell told me it was 'the hands' – does that mean it's about touch? Like, you can physically change things?" I thought of Mum and Dad, and felt my heart sink. Victoria already had the Skulk stone, I was sure of it.

"I bet it'd be pretty similar, anyway. As long as you have every member of the group on board," said Aaron. "The problem is that you can't protect it against each other."

Because shifters are people, and people are bastards, I thought. My heart thudded, hit with a one-two punch of fondness and worry. *Please be all right, Addie…*

"That sounds about right," I said, thinking back to Blackwell's lack of knowledge. If none of the Conspiracy had moved their stone for decades, there'd be no need for him to know their ritual.

So I was going to have to make Don and James work together, trust each other enough not to break the spell.

But probably only *after* I'd scaled the tallest building in Europe and stolen the Skulk stone back from an evil sorceress, so that was a relief.

"Can we only protect our stone?" I wondered aloud. "If we've got the Cluster stone but I don't know how to find the Cluster, is there anything we can do to keep it safe?"

The Rabble all gave me apologetic looks. They had no more idea than I did.

"Well, it's got to be worth a try," said Susanne, "Can you get the Skulk together?"

"I've called a meeting for tonight. Whether they'll all turn up... we'll have to see." I glanced out through the massive steamed-up windows, out over the perfectly organised lawns and flowerbeds, and wondered what Addie was doing right now. Had she found them all? Had she found them all alive?

I shook myself. I had to act as if she had.

"All right. We could all join you," said Susanne. "As a gesture of goodwill. Then we can talk you through it."

"Good idea," said Marcus.

Aaron shook his head. "I don't trust the Skulk. No offence to you, kid. I just don't see this doing much good. And if they don't even *have* their stone... I'm not going into any witch's tower for the Skulk's sake, I'm sorry."

"But you'll come with us tonight," Susanne said. She smiled at Aaron and Marcus, and her voice was like steel wrapped in sponge cake. "All you boys will, won't you? For the Rabble?"

Mo said, "Of course," and Marcus shrugged and nodded. Aaron rolled his eyes. "For the Rabble," he replied. Mo caught my eye behind Susanne's back and smiled.

It'd started to drizzle while we were inside the Palm House, and the shock of the chill as we stepped outside made me shudder. I pulled my hood up and balled my hands in my sleeves.

"What are you going to do now?" Mo asked. "Before we meet up with the Skulk?"

I hadn't really thought that far. I was struck with a sudden, intense longing to go home – to run up to my room and kick off my shoes, put on some of my own clothes, log onto graffitilondon and boast that I'd met E3 and I knew what his signature meant.

The knowledge that this was impossible, at least for a little while, ached dully in my chest.

But if I couldn't go home, what was I going to do until midnight?

"I should try to reach Blackwell, tell him what I've found out. Maybe he'll have figured out something more about what's going on with the Conspiracy."

"We'll go with you," said Susanne.

"Oh, you don't have to," I said, automatically, and instantly regretted it. The very last thing I wanted right then was to go running off to the Tower of London on my own. Not least because the Shard was right across the river, so close you could probably swim it if you didn't mind catching a few horrible diseases and a touch of hypothermia.

Luckily, Susanne took my polite refusal for what it was and clicked her tongue at me. "Don't be silly, of course we'll come." She turned to Aaron and Marcus. "We'll meet you later – where, Meg?"

"Willesden Junction," I said, trying to ignore the tiny stab of guilt. This wasn't a betrayal – bringing the Rabble there could only help the Skulk. I was pretty sure of that.

Even in the middle of a drizzly autumn day, Tower Hill was busy with tourists. We came out of the station into a sea of backpacks and bumbags and hastily-purchased Tower of London-branded umbrellas.

The Shard loomed up just to our right, across the river; grey and monstrously big from such a close viewpoint. The top few floors were lost in the clouds. I wondered if Victoria was up there, staring down at us through the shifting grey mist.

"There's some good graffiti round here," said Mo suddenly, breaking the silence that'd fallen between the three of us as we crossed the road towards the Tower.

"Oh yeah, I saw a photo," I said, happy to turn part of my brain away from Victoria for a second. "Didn't that team from South Africa come over and leave one of their goblins behind Fenchurch Street?"

"Yeah, last year. I wonder if it's still there."

As one, we stopped and turned back to look up the hill towards the train station.

And then, pretty much as one, realised what we were doing.

Mo gave a jerky, bashful shrug. "Maybe we can go and look for it later. Some other time."

"Yeah. Not so much at this minute." I sighed as we turned back towards the Tower. "Although you have no idea how much I'd rather run off and look for goblins right now."

There were two Warders out by the main entrance, dressed in their identical dark blue coats with red trim spelling out ER across their chests. Their wide-brimmed hats kept the soft rain off their faces. One was old and bearded, and one was slightly younger and wore glasses. Neither of them was Blackwell.

I squared my shoulders and walked up to the ticket barrier.

"Excuse me," I said, leaning across and giving the closest Warder, the one with the glasses, a polite smile. "Can you help me? I'm looking for Arthur Blackwell. He's a Yeoman Warder here."

"Blackwell?" The bearded Warder came over. "Can I ask why?"

"He's a friend of my dad's," I lied cheerfully. "They were stationed together in Scotland for a bit. I was just passing, I wondered if I could say hello, give him Dad's love, you know."

"I'm afraid Yeoman Warder Blackwell is on leave today," said the Warder, with a beardy smile.

"Oh, that's a shame. Um – would you mind letting him know I was here?"

"Of course. What's your name, dear?"

"My name's Meg..."

I hesitated – probably not for more than a second, but in that second I thought:

If I give them my real name, they could look me up and find out my dad's never been anywhere near the army.

If they look me up, they might find out my family is missing.

They might find out about the school.

I don't even know how it's being reported yet.

They might not look me up, they might be totally trustworthy and just pass my name on to Blackwell and that'll be it.

But if one of the dodgy ravens guesses Blackwell's been talking to another shifter…

"Meg Grantham," I added, giving the Warder a bright smile. "My dad's name is Ned Grantham."

"Lovely," said the Warder. "I'll be sure to tell him all about it."

"Thanks," I said, and turned away.

Mo and Susanne were standing a little way back, and I gave them a shrug as I walked up to them.

"Apparently he's not here."

"Do you want to go fox and sneak in?" Mo asked. "I could come with you."

I smiled at him, but then cast a wary glance back at the Tower. "I think let's leave it for now. I'll try again once we've met up with the others."

"All right. Let's go home," said Susanne. "If there's nothing else we can do until we've met the Skulk, then you should try to get a couple more hours' sleep."

The very mention of sleep sent a huge yawn crawling up my throat. I tried to stifle it.

"Actually, there's something else I need to do. I want to see the news about my school. I want to see..."

What did I want to see? Photos of the outside of my school, police tape, shocked interviews with parents and students, statements from the police?

"I don't know, I just want to see it."

"OK," Susanne said, but she seemed doubtful.

"I'll be all right," I said. "I'm not going to see pictures of it and faint or anything." *They're not going to show pictures of what I saw last night on the news.*

"Let's not do it here," said Mo. He was looking up at the Shard. I followed his eyes and saw that the clouds were parting, as if the building was a sharp edge slicing through grey candyfloss. I nodded hard.

We headed back underground and I resisted the urge to snatch Mo's phone out of his hand and try to get onto the Tube Wi-Fi. Nothing would have changed by the time we got to Acton. I folded my hands in my lap and tried to be Zen.

I think Mo could tell I wasn't feeling very Zen. He'd pulled his phone and he was Googling Kensington School for Girls by the time we were halfway up the escalator. I was pathetically grateful. We stood outside the station, waiting for the page to load while Susanne went into the newsagent's over the road to see what was in the printed papers.

It wasn't raining any more. The sun was starting to filter weakly through the clouds. I put down my hood and scooped out my hair, scraping it into a ponytail, twisting it, trying not to look over Mo's shoulder, tangling my fingers in it, curling it over my shoulder, pulling it straight and letting it bounce back, wondering how the hell the internet was taking so long to load.

I gave in and stepped closer to him so I could look at the screen of his phone. He was scrolling through search results, scanning them with a frown creasing his brow.

KSG Sixth Form entry

Kensington fee paying schools

Jobs at Kensington secondary schools

KSG netball team storms London Championships

Kensington School for Girls Ofsted 2013

Royal Borough of Kensington and Chelsea private schools

There was nothing about any attack. Nothing from the BBC, nothing from the police... nothing at all.

"I don't understand," I muttered. "Someone *must* have found them by now. It's the internet, this is news – people died, they were... It was..." I thrust my shaking hands into my pockets and tried not to think about red handprints on the walls. I could still feel my fur sticking and clumping together. I couldn't fall apart now; I had to get a grip. "How can there be nothing?"

I looked up and saw Susanne coming across the road, holding a stack of papers and looking concerned.

"Is there anything?" I asked. "Any mention at all?"

"Not that I could find," she said. She handed the papers to Mo. "Let's go home, we can look again."

"No. It's not going to be there." I tangled my fingers in my hair. "Google me. Or – no, do my mum. If one of us is missed, it's going to be her. Sarah Elizabeth Banks."

Mo typed, his thumbs moving swiftly across the screen, and then hit go. I shuffled my feet while the results came up. "Sarah Elizabeth Banks, MP Kensington and Chelsea..." he raised his eyebrows at me. "Your mum's the Secretary of State for Business and Enterprise?"

"Does it say anything about her being missing?" I pressed.

"I can't see anything."

I let out a long breath.

"Come on," said Susanne quietly. "We can talk this through at home. Come on." She put a gentle arm around my shoulder and I let her steer me away down the street.

I sank back into the cracked brown leather sofa with another steaming mug of tea at one elbow and Susanne's creaky old laptop balanced on top of the pile of newspapers in front of me. I'd scanned them from cover to cover and found nothing, not a single word about my school or my parents. But I still refused to believe that nobody on the entire internet had noticed anything strange about a school suddenly closing. I Googled every combination of words I could think of, I scoured Facebook and Twitter, but everything seemed normal.

"Why so quiet?" I muttered. "Why is it so quiet?"

Mo shifted beside me, still scouring the internet on his phone. "Look at this."

I leaned over. "The school website? That doesn't say anything, I looked already."

"No, but that's just it. It doesn't say *anything*. If the school was closed for the day, wouldn't it say so?"

"Doesn't it?"

He shook his head.

My shoulders slumped and I stared at him. "But it has to be closed. The hall is full of... it has to be."

Mo met my eyes. "It looks like someone's kept this out of the papers, right?" I nodded weakly. "Well, if it's Victoria doing this, she can do magic. Maybe she's got the Rabble stone and she can change how people see things, or the Skulk stone and she can... I don't know, change the debris into something harmless. We don't know all the kinds of magic she can do. Wouldn't it be simpler for her to make it look like nothing happened, rather than letting people find out about it and then keeping them quiet?"

"I hate how right you are about that," I muttered. "Can I borrow your phone?"

He handed it over. I clutched one of Susanne's sofa cushions hard in one hand as I dialled the school secretary's number with the other.

"Hello, Kensington School for Girls?"

"Are...?" my voice came out strained and squeaky. I swallowed, coughed and tried again. "Hi, sorry. Is the school open today?"

"Of course," said the secretary. "It's a normal school day."

"Can I...?" my hand crept up to my mouth. I racked my brain for a way to ask if anyone was missing today that she would answer to a stranger on the phone. *Did you by any chance come in to work this morning and find a bunch of bodies in the hallway?*

"Hello?" the secretary called. "Are you all right? If you're a student calling in sick you really should have had your parents call this morning."

Inspiration struck. It was horrible.

"Actually, I'm looking for Jewel Al-Naham. I have an urgent message from her brother Mark. It's... about his house keys."

I forced myself to shut up before I could accidentally invent a whole, rambling, suspicious backstory.

"I'll take your number and have her call you at lunchtime."

"Actually, it's a bit more urgent than that – it'll only take a second but I really need to talk to her now."

"All right," the secretary sighed. "I'll fetch her. Let me put you on hold."

The line went dead for a second and then a blast of tinny Mozart made me hold the phone away from my ear.

"I don't know what I'm doing," I muttered, cradling the phone in front of me. "This is – I should just hang up."

"Jewel's a friend of yours?" Mo asked.

I nodded.

"Will you regret it if you don't talk to her?"

I tipped my head forward, letting my hair dangle down and shield me from his earnest, surprisingly insightful face. Then I nodded again.

We sat in silence, with the phone blasting twiddly klavichord runs at us, until it cut off and a very faint voice said, "Hello?"

I slapped the phone back to my ear.

"Jewel?"

"Meg, is that you? They said Mark needed me."

"No, it's me. I just, um…" I dried up. My free hand tapped out a nervy rhythm on my knee.

"Meg, are you all right? Have you got the bug too?" Jewel sighed. "Ameera's off today as well, and Miss Walter. I swear if you two breathed this thing all over me and I have to spend the weekend all red and puffy and vomiting…" She clicked her tongue. "D'you want me to bring over the English homework? I'd take the out, if I were you, it's only going to be about the Henrys again. Worst. Kings. Ever."

I opened my mouth, and no sound came out.

It was like listening to someone speaking another language, one you used to know, from a country where you used to live a long time ago.

"Meg?" Jewel called. "Have you died?"

I sucked in a breath and blinked until the tears clinging onto my eyelashes trailed off and ran down my face.

"No. I'm here."

"Want me to bring round the homework?"

"No! Nah. You're right, I'd rather not know. Don't come round, I'll only infect you," I croaked. "Have you… heard from Ameera?"

"Nope. I expect she's conked out in front of Jeremy Kyle or something."

"Yeah." I forced a tearful grin, for whose benefit I wasn't sure.

I felt something warm and soft on my free hand and looked down. Mo had taken my hand in both of his. And I was glad of it – I felt earthed, like I was a ball of messed up lightning that'd been crackling wildly around the room. I glanced at him, but he was looking away, staring at the newspapers on the coffee table.

"You should probably get some Kyle time in too," said Jewel, her normal snarky drawl turning a bit gentler. "You seem pretty out of it."

"Ugh. Yeah. I – I should go."

"OK."

"Jewel..." I sucked in a deep breath and steadied myself. "Listen... if Ameera and Miss Walter have both got this I bet it's all over the school. If I were you I'd bunk off sick right now and go and stay with your dad for a bit."

"Dad's in Dubai," Jewel said sceptically.

"I know – but what better excuse, right? Can't come to school, you'll get sick, and you don't want to stay home and get under Mark's feet."

"Ha!" Jewel chuckled. "You are an evil genius. How long did it take you to cook that one up? You amazing nerd. I'll totally email you from the plane."

"Gotta go," I said. "*Bargain Hunt*'s on."

"Love it. See you later."

She hung up. I dropped the phone into my lap.

"She's really going to get away with that? Just leaving the country for a week because there's a bug going round?" Mo said.

"Yeah. Jewel's just like that. Ameera is too, they can get away with... with anything..."

I tried to hold it in, to pull myself together. Then I pulled my hand away from Mo's and bawled into my sleeves.

Susanne came back a few minutes later and found me snivelling into one of her cushions with Mo looking on helplessly, and convinced me to get some sleep. I didn't need much convincing. She made up her own bed for me. I lay and stared at the ceiling for about ten seconds, imagining Jewel getting on a plane and flying a long, long way away from here, before I slid into the best sleep I'd had in days.

Chapter Twenty

Willesden Junction at midnight was chilly and damp. Marcus and Aaron were both there waiting for us by the time we arrived, and I led them around the corner to the place where Addie had showed me the hole in the fence. I stared down the hill towards where I knew the Skulk clearing had to be, but I couldn't see anything except the dark-on-dark shadows of scrubby plants.

One by one, the Rabble disappeared into a thicket of weeds and bushes, rustled about for a moment, and came out as butterflies.

Aaron went first: he fluttered past my head and landed, batting his intricately blotchy brown wings gently, on the fence. Marcus came out as a huge, swallow-tailed butterfly with vivid blue and white and black patterns and long fur all over his body. Then it was Mo's turn. He fluttered out and settled in Susanne's hair, waving his antennae at me, his big black bug eyes seeming kind of friendly, despite the inherent strangeness of looking into the eyes of an insect. His wings were bright yellow with black spots.

I went next, folding my clothes as neatly as I could beside the three other piles, shivering on the cold dirt for a second, and then curling into the change. I tasted a slight tang of blood as my skin rippled and shifted, but my fur was so much warmer than bare skin, my nose much more useful than my eyes in the dim light by the fence.

Mo landed on the bottom of the fence, at about eye-height to me. He smelled a little of Susanne's cooking – I probably did, too. She'd cooked us up a feast of chicken and spiced sweet potatoes and insisted we ate the lot before we went running around all night doing God knew what. But Mo's scent also had a startlingly familiar chemical tang that I recognised as the smell of aerosol paint, with an undertone of something more natural – green, growing things and cool shady places.

His legs were thin as a hair and the light fluff on his body caught the glow from the streetlamps and lit up like a halo.

"Hi," he said.

"Hi," I replied.

"Shall we?" said Marcus. I wouldn't have thought butterflies would be all that expressive, but I could read the sardonic edge in the way his wings dipped. I led the way through the fence and down the slope, the Rabble flitting around my head.

The clearing was empty.

I raked my claws in the dirt and whined softly.

"Do you think they'll come?" asked Mo.

I didn't answer. It wasn't the stubbornness of the Skulk I was worried about right then.

I trotted back and forth across the clearing, sniffing for any sign of Addie or the others, but the only scent was old and faint – it must have lingered from the last time we met.

Maybe I was wrong to send Addie off on her own. Maybe her bravado had made me overestimate her. She was only a kid. But, no, that wasn't fair – the fog didn't give a damn how old you were, and Susanne and Don probably thought I was just a kid.

But if Victoria had got to the Skulk first, if she was lying in wait for Addie, if she'd found James…

If she's found James she has the Cluster stone already and all this is for nothing.

Suddenly, I scented something, coming closer… petrol, expensive perfume, soap. The Skulk was here. I raised my head, desperate to catch a sight or smell of Addie.

"Meg!" someone barked. I spun around just in time to see her bounding across the clearing before she hit me like a grinning cannonball, licking my ear. I rolled to my feet and head-butted her hard in the chest.

"You're alive! Thank God," I whined. "I thought I might've – she might have got to them already, and you'd..."

"What, me? Never." Addie nipped playfully at my shoulders. I flinched as her teeth brushed one of the rat-wounds. Addie drew back. "You OK? What happened? Why'd you bring the Rabble?"

"Yes," said Don, stalking out of the bushes with Randhir and Francesca at his heels. "What are they doing here?" He bore down on me, and I shook my head and met his eyes. He was actually a little bigger than

I remembered. "How dare you bring another pack of shifters here without my permission?"

"They're here to help," I said, deciding to bypass the issue of whether he was in fact the boss of me.

"And you're sure we need their help?" Fran asked.

"If you don't want us here, we'll go," said Aaron, one antenna twitching irritably.

"All I'm saying is we should try not to get hysterical about this," said Fran.

Addie pawed the ground. "Fran doesn't believe me," she snarled. "Tell her, Meg. Tell her about the school, and the blood."

"It's true. Something's happened to cover it up, but we both saw it... someone's willing to kill us all to get hold of the stone I found."

"*You've* got the Skulk stone?" Don barked.

"No, I think I've got the Cluster stone," I said, calmly. "That is..." I looked around, my heart sinking, as I realised for the first time that James wasn't with them. I looked at Addie, and she swished her brush.

"He said he was coming," she whispered.

"Well, I left the Cluster stone somewhere safe," *I hope,* "and I went to look for them – and found them. They were dead. Have been for a while."

"Well, that's unfortunate, but I still fail to see what their failure could possibly have to do with us," Don growled.

"How can you be so shortsighted?" Mo snapped.

Rand snarled agreement. "That's cold, even for you."

"Randhir didn't mean that," said Fran.

"Is your leader always this stupid?" Aaron said to me in an irritating fake-whisper, not even really bothering to lower his voice.

Don raked his claws through the dirt. "How *dare* you come here and–"

"She's got my parents!" I howled. "She's used our stone to turn them into monsters, doesn't anyone care? I don't even know how many people have died, but I know there will be more if we don't try to *do* something. The stone we've got is the Cluster's, we have to find a way to keep it safe until we can get ours back."

There was a second's pause, and my fur prickled as they all turned to stare at me.

Last time I was here, Don and Rand were bickering about their sisters. Things are a bit different now.

"Don," I said, crouching back submissively, "You have the longest history with the Skulk – you said your father and grandfather were shifters, right?"

"That's right," said Don, sitting up straight.

"So you must have some knowledge of the stones," I prompted. "We have the Cluster stone. Does that mean we can hide it, like we could with our own one?"

"I don't think that's the question we should be asking," said Don.

Something about the way he said it made me almost want to laugh. I felt like I could see right inside his head. *What you mean is, you don't know and you don't want to admit it.*

"We have the Cluster stone," Don mused. He squared his shoulders and bared his teeth. "And if they're too weak to hold on to it, isn't that our gain? The way I see it, these stones have power." He paced up and down the clearing, looming over the Rabble for a second then turning to stare down the rest of the Skulk. "We can use that power, just like this sorceress. Why shouldn't we?"

"We don't even know what the Cluster stone does," I said. "What would we use it *for*?"

"Well, how about fighting this woman and getting our stone back?" Randhir said. "I hate to admit it, but he's not wrong. Maybe we shouldn't hide this thing away if it can help us."

"He's got a point," said Aaron.

"But would it be worth the risk?" Susanne asked. "It sounds to me as if the only way to beat Victoria for good is to make sure she can't get any more of the stones. You may well say you can use them against her, but isn't it better not to bring them anywhere near her?"

"Susanne and Marcus were both there when they last hid the Rabble stone," I said quickly. "That's why I brought the Rabble here. They know how to do it, they can show us and we can try to put the Cluster stone out of Victoria's reach."

"All you need is your stone and all six shifters," Susanne said.

"But we don't have either," said Fran, her voice dripping with reasonableness. I sighed, raking my claws along the earth in front of me. Even more than Don, I was starting to dread her weighing in.

Don planted his paws firmly on the ground. "And we're not likely to, with that thieving scum on the loose."

"Well, if you don't *want* your precious stone..."

There was a scrabbling of claws on earth as we all turned to look at James. He padded down the tunnel through the bushes, his little cloth bag hung around his neck, drooping with the weight of something inside.

He sniffed and his ears pricked up with amusement. "Guess who's come to save the day?"

"Thief!" Don barked. "Traitor! Get out of here before I rip your throat out."

"Oh hush," James purred, strolling past Don – at a safe distance, out of pounce range – and heading for me. "I'm a thief but I'm no traitor. I've brought your sapphire back. And I can tell you where the Skulk stone is, too."

"What?"

"I saw it in a jewellery shop I was robbing a couple of weeks ago. Recognised it at once, of course, and I was going to steal it back and post it through Mr Olaye's door, with my deepest and most sarcastic compliments. Unfortunately, I was interrupted."

"The fog?" I asked.

James nodded. "It crept in while I was working on the safe – scared the living daylights out of me when I turned around and saw this misty tentacle monster crawling in through the windows. It was between me and the stone and I wasn't about to argue. I got the hell out of there. Some other shifter must have sold it to the shop in the first place. I have my theories," he added, "but I wouldn't want to *wrongly accuse* anybody."

I pounced on James, knocking him to the floor, pinning him under my paws. I licked and nipped at his throat, not sure whether I loved him or wanted to give him the hardest bloody slap.

"Why didn't you *tell* me when I turned up with the sapphire?" I yipped. "You knew there was something important going on!"

"Oof. Princess – let me..." I laid off a little and he rolled to his paws. "It wasn't as if I had the thing to give you. I'd been accused of stealing it, darling," he said, and cast a sharp look over my shoulder at Don, who was still bristling. "I saw it, but I didn't take it – who'd believe that?"

"You – you..." I was trying to come up with a suitably affectionate insult when my gaze fell on Don, who was quivering with rage, his fur rippling like he was standing in the middle of an earthquake.

"I *don't* believe it," he growled. He bared his teeth, wolf-like and furious. He stalked forwards. His muscles bunched and I crouched to spring, to put myself between him and James – but then a fluttering burst of colour slammed into the air in front of him.

The Rabble flew around his head, forcing him back.

"Just stop it," Susanne said. "I don't know what your issue with this young man is, and right now I don't care. You can accept our help and try to do what's right for the Cluster and make their stone safe like any true shifter would, or we can go – but I won't stay here and watch you tear each other apart, like *animals*."

Don glowered at her. I stepped forward to accept their help and screw him for just assuming he had the authority after everything Addie and I had been through...

"Perhaps we should see if it works," said Fran, gently. "If it does, wonderful. Meg's sorceress won't be able to touch it."

She is not my sorceress, I thought. *She's not a figment of my imagination!*

"And if not, we'll decide how best to use it for the good of the Skulk, while Meg keeps looking for its rightful owners," Fran finished.

"That sounds reasonable," said Randhir. "I'm up for trying it if you are, Don."

Don shook his head. "You trust these people? They're *butterflies*. What are they good for except spouting pretty platitudes? I'm sure you're all very nice people, but…"

Marcus threw his wings up behind him with a snap. The fur on his body puffed up like an angry cat's.

"I'm not staying here to be insulted," he said. "Not by someone so cowardly he doesn't think he can take a bunch of butterflies."

Don snapped his teeth. "I could take any one of you."

"In human form?" said Marcus.

Ooh, Don. I tried to stifle my urge to smile. *I dunno what you look like as a human but unless you're secretly the Rock you might be in trouble…*

"Marcus, don't do this, you remember what happened last time," said Susanne, fluttering with theatrical concern. "It's humiliating for a man to be naked and concussed in front of his friends."

My gaze flickered over to Mo and even though he was a butterfly, with no obvious eyes to glint or mouth to grin, I had to look away because I was pretty sure he was enjoying this even more than I was.

"Typical Rabble," Don muttered. "Your brains can't handle more than one thing at a time, can they? I never said I wanted to fight you. I just want some assurances before we try this scheme."

I could have done a little dance right there, but I managed to control myself.

"How do I know you're not playing some trick on us – you'll convince us it's worked and then come back and take it when we've gone?"

"You'll be able to tell," said Mo. "I swear on my mum's life. Our stone went all shiny and translucent – maybe the Cluster stone will do something else, but if the Skulk do it together then none of the Rabble should be able to take it."

"Then let's try it," said Don. "But if I find it's disappeared again, *someone* will pay." He bared his teeth at Mo and then at James. James shrugged it off with a smooth movement of his shoulders.

"Everyone, gather round," said Susanne, and took off so she was fluttering above our heads.

As Fran, Randhir, Addie and Don gathered around the Cluster stone, I bent my head down so my muzzle was brushing the earth beside Marcus.

"Thanks," I whispered.

Marcus gave a heavy sigh. "I know the type. Thinks he's a big man."

I nodded a little and joined the group.

It was sort of odd, seeing the whole Skulk gathered together, circling the gleaming stone. Even if it wasn't ours – six shifters and a stone together felt... satisfying, like clicking a tricky jigsaw piece into its rightful place.

Except there was something missing. I could feel something tugging on me. It was like the feeling when you realise you don't know exactly where you've put your keys, when your mind spins out of control imagining pickpockets and locksmiths and long, cold waits on the doorstep.

Maybe this wouldn't work. The jigsaw piece was the wrong one, after all.

We still had to try, though.

I gazed around at them, wondering if they were having the same feeling, taking in Addie's small frame next to Don's big, dark-furred body, next to Rand's shifty grey-tinged paws digging into the earth, next to Fran's sleek stillness, next to the way James seemed to hang back, twitchy of getting too close despite his camp bravado. And then me – I still hadn't really examined myself as a fox, but if it was anything like my human appearance it'd be long-furred, well-fed, and covered in bruises.

"Now, each touch one leg – well, paw I suppose – one paw to the stone," said Susanne.

There almost wasn't room. Don and James' fur brushed mine.

"Shut your eyes and concentrate on the feeling of the stone."

We did. It was smooth and cool, and a tiny bit grainy under my earth-splattered paw. Susanne's voice was deep and calm.

"Try to clear your minds, just feel the air on your fur and the stone under your paws... imagine you're reaching deep into it. Feel the gem part around your hand... you reach out and grasp part of the star... feel it tingling under your fingers..."

I could feel it. It *was* working. I could feel my fingers tingling, even though I didn't even *have* fingers right then.

"Feel yourself holding the star in your hand. You can feel the power… the element of shadow. The star glows brighter. Bring it up, out through the surface of the gem. It flows out and envelops the stone like a net of blinding light, and digs deep into the earth. It keeps your stone safe, and shades it from the eyes of anyone but you."

I could see it in my mind's eye – the light flowing from the centre of the stone, glimmering across its surface and then piercing the ground like razor-sharp pins made of light and magic.

There was a silence.

"Erm..." said Mo.

"Keep your eyes closed," said Susanne, her voice rather less deep and mellow. "Bring it to the surface... keep hold of the light, bring it up..."

"What's going on?" said Addie. "I can't feel anything."

"Isn't it working?" Fran asked.

"What?" said Don. "Let me see."

There was a clamour.

"Don't open your eyes!"

"Did you open them? Don?"

"Can I open my eyes now?"

I looked. Fran was looking already, and one by one the other three did too. The stone was still there. It wasn't transparent or translucent. I reached out and nudged it with one paw.

Mo flapped over and landed on the stone. He could see it, all right. He hopped down on the ground and with a groan of effort he put his front legs on the side of the stone and pushed. It moved just a little bit.

"I can move it. It didn't work," he said.

Susanne started to say "We can try a–"

"I told you, these people don't know what they're talking about!" Don took his paw off the stone and jumped in the air, his teeth snapping dangerously close to Susanne's wing.

"Hey, get off her," Mo yelled, taking off and flying around Don's ears. It can't have done much more than tickle, but it clearly annoyed Don, who cringed back, pawing at his own face.

"Stop it, all of you! This isn't your stone, there was always a chance it wouldn't work," said Susanne.

"No, I think you wanted to trick us. You wanted us to do it wrong so you could come back and take it," Don growled.

"Don't be absurd!" she cried. "Why would I? Mo, come away from there this instant."

Mo darted out of Don's reach and hung over my left shoulder, flapping agitatedly. "He could've killed you," he complained.

Susanne landed on a thorn bush a little distance away. "I promise you, sir, I gave you the instructions I knew. It's always worked for the Rabble. I'm sure the only reason it didn't work for you is because you are not the Cluster."

"Come on, Susanne, let's go, if these ingrates don't want our help," Aaron complained.

"I don't know why we trusted them," Fran muttered to Don. "They can't even take care of their *own* stone."

"That's not fair," I said. "Their stone was taken by one of their own. It's not their fault she was a junkie."

"Wait..." Fran turned to me. "Are you saying one of *us* made this not work?"

I opened my mouth to say "no", but then I hesitated. "I did feel something," I said. "Didn't the rest of you? I thought it was working, but–"

Don cut me off with a furious bark.

"James!"

"Don't look at me. I brought it here, didn't I? If I wanted it I would've kept it."

"Why should I trust you, you admit you're a–"

"Oh, *a what*, Olaye? Don't pretend we don't both know why you *really* can't stand me."

"Now, come on, let's not get into this," said Fran. "Surely we can agree to disagree. I mean we're all entitled to our beliefs."

James' fur bristled and he hissed at them both. I cringed so hard I felt the fur on the back of my neck curl, wishing Fran would just *shut up*. I gazed at her for a second, so sleek and poised and supposedly friendly – and yet every time she spoke she seemed to make everything worse.

"Oi, guys. *Guys*." It was Rand. He was staring at the sky. I followed his gaze.

A black speck was circling, shadowed against the grey-orange clouds overhead. Now there were two of them, now three, four, five... a whole *flock* of flapping, circling pigeons.

They dived.

Chapter Twenty-One

Addie shrieked and flinched away as a pair of talons sliced through the air where she'd been standing. The clearing was engulfed in a storm of beating wings and stirred-up dust. Grey and brown and green streaked through the air, red and yellow eyes gleaming in the moonlight like horrid perversions of gemstones. They fell on us, pecking and tearing.

"Hide," I yelped. The Rabble scattered. One of the pigeons was chasing Marcus, following his evasive twists and turns, and then suddenly he folded his wings and dropped to the ground. He rolled over and his whole body burst out of itself. His wings folded tight against his back and vanished, and his body smoothed and grew massive. He staggered to his feet, towering over all of us, as his antennae shrivelled back into his head. The pigeon flapped away, no match for a six-foot-plus human with muscles on his muscles. Marcus showed no sign of his nakedness bothering him in the slightest – he grabbed a fallen branch and swung it like a broadsword.

One of the pigeons tried to dive for the stone. I heard Addie give a furious hiss and saw it pulled down out of the air. "Protect the stone!" I growled. My heart hammered as I saw that Addie was the only one standing over it, but then Don thundered across the clearing, shrugging off the attacks of the pigeons, and stood protectively against her, his teeth bared.

"Meg!" James yelled. I looked around for him and then he collided with me, pushing me out of the way as a pigeon – a slick-feathered, thin, grey thing – went for my head. It shot past us with a sound like tearing paper.

"James, get the bag," I hissed. "Get the Cluster stone out of here. Take it and run!"

James nodded and sprang for the black bag. The pigeon was coming back. She was diving for me. I felt the tears well up, unhelpful, unwanted, and useless.

"Mum," I whined, even as I jumped into the air and batted her down with sheathed claws. She hit the ground with a thump and staggered dizzily for a second, but she was back up and flying after only a couple of seconds, wheeling away across the clearing.

"Mo?" Susanne yelled. She and Aaron were hiding deep inside a thorn bush – two pigeons were flapping and pecking at them but they couldn't get past the twisted prison of twigs and sharp thorns. Susanne's voice rose from their hiding place, high and panicked: "Where's Mo?"

I felt like someone had grabbed my heart and squeezed until it burst.

"Mo!" I screamed.

"Help!"

A burst of yellow shot across my vision and I spun around, following in dismay as a huge grey-black pigeon hurtled after Mo, right on his wing-tips, its beak open, ready to snap down on him.

"Over here," I yelled. Mo flipped over and shot back towards me. The black pigeon took the corner clumsily and came hurtling after him, screeching. I waited till I could smell the scent of foul decay on it, till I could see its tiny red worm tongue curling in its mouth. Then I leapt, claws out, and knocked it to the ground.

Its throat was right under my jaws, its head twisting back and forth... it would be so easy to rip it open. Even a simple, hard shake would break its neck. My lips drew back into a growl, my long canine teeth bared.

I twisted my head to catch the bright yellow spot that was Mo vanish into a thick thorn bush, and then reared back and let the pigeon go. It hobbled away, in pain, and tried to take off.

"Oh, for – let go, you–" I glanced around. James was gripping the black bag in his teeth, but a heavy, messy-feathered, brown-chested pigeon had landed right on top of it. *Dad*. James tried to pull the bag out from under him, but Dad went for James' eyes with his sharp, wide beak. James let go of the bag to avoid being blinded and Dad took off, the bag dangling from his talons.

I twisted to look at Addie and Don, and sucked in a deep breath. They still had the Cluster stone. Addie was standing over it.

Aaron shot out of the bushes like a tiny brown bullet and circled Dad's head. Dad flapped back and forth, a confusion of snapping beak and feathers.

"It's just the bag, let it go!" I yelled.

I was too late. Aaron yelled, a hoarse and throaty cry of agony, and I felt my jaws go slack with horror, as my Dad's beak pierced his wings and one of his legs. The pigeon's eyes flashed as it deftly flicked Aaron up and into its beak. Aaron sucked in a gasp, and choked. The beak closed. Aaron went limp.

The body blossomed, ballooning out of Dad's beak and thumping to the floor. I danced out of the way as Aaron's wings crumpled and his body swelled, limp and broken, his back twisted horribly out of place, one leg barely hanging on at the knee by a few strings of muscle and cartilage.

"No, oh my God, Aaron..." Susanne wailed. I looked up just in time to see the pigeon that had once been my own father flapping away from the man he'd just killed, vanishing into the shadowy treetops.

My blood thundered in my ears. I gazed down at Aaron's body. His skin gleamed almost blue and blood gushed blackly from his leg. Marcus ran over to him and then hesitated, sinking to his knees, not too close to the body. His eyes were wide and liquid with horror. His shoulders slumped.

Something hard and furry smacked into me and I fell to the ground. The scent of damp blankets and old bones told me it was Addie, before I could turn my head. "Meg! Are you deaf or what? I said get down!" Her jaws clamped gently but firmly around the scruff of my neck and pulled me down again, as another pigeon swept over, its wings scoring the air.

"Help!" Fran screamed. "Oh dear – help!"

Fran was all by herself and standing over the stone – the Cluster stone, which I'd been given to keep safe, which I'd walked through a river of blood to get back. I scrambled to my feet, pushing Addie aside. Fran was on her own, snapping and swiping at two viciously clawing pigeons. Why weren't Don and James with her? They were being mobbed, standing back to back and fighting off four more. The pigeons had separated Fran from the others. "Help them," I yelped to Addie, and she shot off trailing dirt and fury, barrelling into the crowd of pigeons like a bowling ball.

I ran towards Fran. I had to reach her, I had to – but determination gave me tunnel-vision and I didn't see the pigeon swooping down on me until it was too late. I felt it smack into me, claws first, sending me rolling. I looked up, dizzy and sickened, into Mum's crazy red pin-pricks of eyes. Her claws came down on my face and she clung on. I tried to bite her but she bucked out of my reach. I rolled and twisted and shook my head but Mum wouldn't let go.

I could feel the freezing porcelain digging into my ribs as she held my head down, her sharp fingernails raking through my hair and across my scalp. Hot, thin vomit and stinging tears mingled in the bowl in front of me.

I howled and threw my head down, smacking Mum's back hard into the ground. Her claws loosened and I tore my face away, grabbed her in my jaws and threw her as far as I could. Her wings snapped open and she soared off into the dark sky.

"Come back here," I screamed. "I'll kill you, get back here, you heartless bitch!"

My voice rang around my ears in the cold, silent air. I gasped, looking around at the others. They were gathered around Fran. She was on the ground, licking at a gash on her leg. They were all staring at me.

"They – they took it," I whispered. "Didn't they?"

None of them answered, but they didn't need to.

"Sorry," said Addie.

I shook my head. "It isn't your fault." *It's my fault. I let her distract me.*

"Aaron," said Susanne, somewhere behind me. I couldn't look. I couldn't look at any of them. I turned and limped across the clearing, pain I'd hardly had time to register flaring in my front legs, and sank down with my head on my paws.

Susanne, Mo and Marcus alighted on the ground beside their dead friend.

My dad killed him.

Marcus was in butterfly form again now. Don and Addie were attending to Fran, helping her stand. I looked around for James. He had paused on the edge of the path. He was leaving. I caught his eye and couldn't bring myself to nod to him. But I think he knew I didn't blame him. He turned tail and vanished in a blur of orange fur.

"Go," said Susanne. Marcus leapt into the air and flitted away towards the street. I followed him with my eyes until he vanished.

"Meg." I looked up. Mo was there, his wings trembling.

"Where'd Marcus go?" I asked. My voice sounded low and hoarse.

"To find the new shifter," said Mo, in a flat, dull tone. "We have to find whoever was closest when Aaron died. Marcus'll follow them until he knows where they live. We'll make contact, tell them what's happened to them."

"That's very efficient," I said.

"It's... what you do," said Mo.

I glanced over at the Skulk, just in time to catch Don snapping at Rand and Fran pushing Addie away, insisting she didn't need help. For a second, I deeply wished I could've joined any group other than them. Then I remembered the Cluster.

"What about the body?" I asked.

"Susanne's going to get changed and call the police. She'll report that she saw a body and leave them to it."

"Right."

"This isn't your fault," Mo said. I thought about denying I'd ever thought it was. Mo hopped a bit closer and put one tiny leg on my paw. I barely felt it, just a slight movement of the fur.

His antennae brushed my whiskers and I fought back a shudder. But it wasn't an unpleasant shudder. Just a feeling of being so *close* to him I could almost feel his tiny body quivering with every breath.

"What are you going to do now?" he asked.

I swallowed. "I don't know."

Mo's eyes glittered. "I'm going to stay and help," he said.

"What? I don't think you should do that – look at what happened to Aaron..."

"Marcus and Susanne would do the same, if they could. They've got to deal with this. I'm going to stay with you. Anyway, I want to and you can't stop me."

A smile tugged at my face and I bowed my head, accepting his offer, even if I didn't need to. Then I got to my feet, reluctantly untangling my whiskers from his antennae, and turned to the rest of the Skulk.

They looked up as I walked over, Mo fluttering at my shoulder.

"I hope you all believe me now," I said quietly. Even Don had the graciousness to look a little bit ashamed of himself. "Victoria's got our stone, and now she's got the Cluster's. She might have the Rabble's and the Horde's too." I sat back on my haunches and looked at them. They watched me right back. A creeping unease chilled my spine. They were waiting for me to continue. Three grown adults and Addie, and they all wanted *me* to do something about it. As if I had any idea what we could do. Where was Fran's constant butting-in right now? Where had Don's leaderly initiative gone?

Well. All right. Fine.

"The only stone I'm sure about is the Conspiracy stone. Blackwell is sure it's safe in the Tower, and that's why the ravens aren't interested in helping the rest of us. He thought they might be corrupt, like they might have some vested interest in letting Victoria get away with all this. I think it's time we confront them about it. I'll go back to the Tower and talk to

Blackwell about everything that's happened. Maybe he can help us."

"I might be able to help," said Fran. I blinked at her.

"Really?"

"I know a Warder in the Tower. One of the Conspiracy."

"What?" I bristled. "You could've mentioned that."

"I didn't know it was relevant. I'm sorry, dear. But I think he's trustworthy, and I'm sure he'll listen to me. I should go and see what he says before we rush in to attack them without any proof that they even know any of this is happening. Don, can the others come back to your house to wait for me?"

"All right," said Don. He sniffed at Mo. "I suppose you can join us, if you're determined to stay with Meg."

"I should go with Fran, shouldn't I?" I said. "I mean, if I can convince Blackwell and you can convince..."

I paused, leaving a gap for Fran to drop the name of her Warder friend. She missed the cue.

"I don't think that's a good idea," she said. "Just as you said, the Conspiracy may need to be very carefully approached. I think it'll work better if I can bring your friend Blackwell in when the others already trust me."

My claws dug into the earth and I made a vague "ehn" of protest. I didn't want to let her go off on her own. But I couldn't think of a good enough reason to go with her, so she steamrolled right over my indecision.

"Don't worry, I'll tell them everything Addie told us. I certainly believe her now," she said, with a benevolent little smile down at Addie. "That's decided then. I'll get going right away and meet you all at

Don's house as soon as I've got some kind of answer from the ravens."

She trotted off, without waiting for anyone to reply.

I sighed, as her brush vanished into the undergrowth. Maybe her attempts at conflict resolution would actually play out this time and the Conspiracy would decide to help us after all and everything would be fine.

Hmm.

"If the Conspiracy are against us," I muttered, "We may need to fight Victoria ourselves. I've had a pretty firm sod-off from the Horde already."

"Then let's hope they will," said Randhir darkly. "Cause you won't change the rats' minds, and there's bugger all we can do against them pigeons for very long."

I couldn't quite bring myself to glare at him. I was sure there was something we could do. I was just out of ideas.

"I think Meg and I should change back," said Mo. "Since we've got clothes up top. Why don't you give us the address and we'll meet you there. We'll only slow you down otherwise."

"Fine." Don's fur ruffled and he drew himself up to his full height. "But if you give away my address to the other shifters, if I so much as see a Cabbage White in my back garden..."

I could just see James' face if he'd been there right then. *Oh, you'll what?* I thought.

"Scout's honour," said Mo. "I won't tell a soul."

"109 Hendon Road," said Don. "Near Finchley."

"I know it," Mo said. "We'll see you there."

I trotted over to Addie. Her shoulder was bleeding. Not badly, but enough to form a messy clot of fur and blood that could catch on the twigs of the bushes. I licked it a couple of times.

"Be safe, OK?" I murmured.

"Pssht," she said, without much feeling. "I'm only going round Don's. You worry way too much, Princess."

"Too much?"

"Well... whatever. I'll be fine. Don't take too long, though."

There was no sign of Susanne when we reached the top of the slope, but I could hear sirens in the distance. Don, Addie and Rand slipped away into the night and I went behind the bush. Marcus and Aaron's clothes were still there and I shivered.

The change was stiff, but nowhere near as terrifyingly difficult as it had been in Susanne's house. I cringed and yelped as my shoulder-muscles crunched into place and hissed at the feeling of the new cuts on my face – from Mum's talons – stretching into their places on my human face. The air was cold now and I tugged my clothes on as quickly as I could.

I slipped my shoes on and stepped out of the bush. "Your turn," I said, walking over to the fence, where Mo was perched with his yellow and black spots lit up under the street lamp.

He fluttered off to the bush and I stood there, gazing down at the dark clearing below. I couldn't see Aaron's body. And I couldn't hear the sirens, any more. Had I been hearing them from far away, or had they simply been heading somewhere else?

I hoped Aaron was OK. Which was nuts. He was dead. But I still, somehow, hoped that he wouldn't mind that we'd all left him there alone. "They'll be here soon," I whispered. "I'm... I'm sorry."

There was a rustling from the bush, and I glanced over. I didn't mean to. I was distracted. And I didn't see anything before I quickly looked away again. Nothing much, anyway. Just a strong, brown back, the muscles and shoulder-blades shifting as he bent down to pick up his shirt. Nothing interesting.

Mo came out of the bush at a hop, one of his shoes still undone.

"So, er," he said. "Listen."

I tried to put myself in a listening position, and ended up folding my hands in my hoodie, and then unfolding them again, and then trying to lean on the fence which was too loose and sagged worryingly underneath me, and trying to stand up straight again without losing too much dignity, and I almost missed the next thing he said.

"Can I have a word, I mean, alone?" He ran his hands through his tight black curls and looked at me with a sort of intense, worried stare. I tried to swallow. "That's part of why I suggested we change. I didn't really want to say this with the others here."

"OK," I croaked. Not very attractive. I sounded like a frog.

"It's just... it's about Fran."

"Fran?" I stared at him stupidly, while my brain performed a clumsy three-point-turn. "What about Fran?"

"How much do you trust her?"

I frowned. "She irritates me. But *trust*? I don't have any reason not to, I guess."

"Why does she irritate you?"

"It's probably irrational," I hedged. "It's just that she encourages Don, and eggs him on, and then he argues with Rand... and she's patronising to Addie. It's just like every time she speaks, she's *trying* to make things better and stop them arguing and she just makes everyone more angry."

"Yeah, like when James was trying to challenge Don about hating him for being gay. She just seemed to say, like, exactly the wrong thing for both of them."

"Exactly." I shrugged, feeling my face going a little red. "It's probably really unfair. I've only met her twice. But it's almost like..." I trailed off. What could I put at the end of that sentence that didn't sound insanely paranoid?

"See, there was this thing that happened when the pigeons were attacking. I don't think anyone else actually saw them take the stone. You were all fighting them off and Marcus and Susanne were so focused on Aaron..."

"What? What did you see?"

"I wouldn't swear it meant anything, except, it just looked like Fran kind of held out her leg to the pigeon to scratch at. It didn't look like a bad wound, but she fell down, and that was when they took the stone."

My blood crawled in my veins like it'd turned into a hundred miniscule insects.

"You think she *let them* have the stone?"

"I dunno," Mo shrugged, unhappily. "But I know she made the Skulk stay split up and she wouldn't let you go with her to the Tower. I know that it's possible you could have hidden the Cluster stone but someone kept the ritual from working."

I hissed through my teeth, and turned and kicked the fence. It rattled and bounced back at me. "We've got to follow her. Maybe we're wrong and she'll be there with her Warder friend and everything will be fine."

Mo put a hand on my shoulder. "Yeah, maybe."

He didn't believe it. Neither did I.

Chapter Twenty-Two

We hired a minicab from the station to take us to the Tower. This was no time for faffing about on night buses. I instinctively reached for my pocket even though I hadn't had any money on me for days, but Mo dug around and came up with just enough cash to get us across London. He winced as he handed it over. It was only £40, but it was all he had.

He smiled and muttered to me, "Never bring a bank card if you're going to shift in case you have to leave your clothes, but carry a bit of cash if you can."

I nodded, wishing I could think of a way to tell Mo I'd pay him back a thousand times over, if my life ever stabilised enough for me to actually be able to get at my bank account.

The driver made vaguely insinuating comments about late nights and "your place or mine" all the way to the Tower. Mo said "nah mate, just friends", and then nothing else. I stared out of the window at the bright lights of shops flashing by, hoping we'd find that Blackwell was wrong about the Conspiracy, and wondering if Mo could hear my heart hammering.

The cab left us by Tower Hill tube station, looking down towards the Tower itself. I shivered a little and huddled deeper into my hoodie. Last time I was here it'd been a grey, drizzly afternoon. This time I took a second to gaze at the floodlights around the White Tower and the moat, the way the pinpricks of light over on the south bank were reflected, gleaming and dancing in the river. The Shard was lit up like a beacon in the darkness.

Was the Cluster stone up there right now? What would she do with it when she had it?

"Do you think we beat Fran here?" Mo asked.

I shrugged. "Let's go and look."

We strolled down the slope and crossed the almost-empty road, and then walked around the chest-high wall that encircled the grassy moat.

Even in the middle of the night, there were a couple of people about. A few cars whooshed by and we passed a young couple strolling arm in arm, chatting in some East-European language with a map in their hands and huge smiles on their faces. I thought it must be nice to be so happy to be lost. It must be nice to get lost with someone you loved.

"Wait," Mo put a hand on my shoulder, drawing me back into the shadow of a tree. "Can you see that? There's someone coming out of the gate."

I looked. We'd just come around the corner and I could see the main gate of the Tower, and the figure of a woman walking out across the bridge. She was white and an adult, though she could've been anywhere between twenty and fifty, from here I couldn't quite tell.

She was wearing a knee-length pencil skirt and a tailored blue woollen coat. Her hair caught the street light and glowed a glossy, probably synthetic chestnut brown.

"That's Fran," I said. "I'm sure it is."

"Where's her friend?" Mo muttered.

Fran paused on this side of the drawbridge and looked at her watch. Then something black shot across the corner of my vision and I grabbed Mo's arm and pointed. It was a raven. It circled over Fran's head for a second, and then landed on the barrier right by her elbow.

She spoke to it, bending her head so her hair swung between them like a soft, glossy curtain.

"How come he hasn't changed?" I whispered. "He can hear what she's saying, but he won't be able to answer."

The raven didn't hang around for a long one-sided conversation, either – it took off again as soon as Fran stopped talking and soared up and over the moat, over the wall, into the Tower.

Fran immediately turned and walked away, her shoes clicking on the paving stones as she crossed towards the deserted ticket booths on the other side of the wide cobbled space. She slipped into the shadows and vanished.

"Was that it?" Mo wondered. "What did she tell it?"

"She's not heading back to the Tube." I strained my eyes towards the ticket booths – they were housed in a low, thin concrete building with parts that were open to the outside. "D'you think we should follow her?"

"I don't – wait, look." Mo pointed. I turned back to see a Warder leaving the Tower by the main gate, hurrying along with his coat pulled up high around his face. "Did he change?"

I shrugged. It seemed likely, and yet it had barely been a few seconds. Could he have changed and dressed so quickly? I bet a Yeoman Warder's uniform wasn't simple to get on, either.

Mo looked down at me, his eyes soft in the darkness and a little worried frown creasing his forehead. "Maybe she was telling the truth. You think we made a mistake?"

I looked again, and then shook my head. "There's something wrong," I said. "That's not her mysterious Conspiracy contact. That's *mine*. That's Blackwell!"

His ginger beard gleamed gold in the street lights and he huddled deeper into his coat as he hurried over to the ticket booths, where Fran had gone. I frowned. Did he know her after all? Why would she say there was some other Warder she knew?

"Put your hood up," Mo said. I pulled the hood over my head and tucked my hair away inside, and then he put his arm through mine and before I knew it we were strolling, arm in arm, across the cobbles. We slipped into the same covered space, but a couple of booths up from the one we'd seen Fran go into.

"Meg?" I heard Blackwell's voice, and frowned. Why did he think I was here? Had we been seen?

I met Mo's eyes and he shook his head – *don't go to him. Wait.* I nodded my agreement.

"Meg? What's happening?" Blackwell called. "Are you here? Phillips said you were out here asking for me. I hope it's worth letting him know you're–" he broke off.

I stuck my head around the corner as Fran stepped out in front of Blackwell and stood close to him in the little space behind the ticket booths.

Blackwell blinked at her. "Who are – aren't you Francesca, from the Skulk? Is Meg all right?"

Fran didn't answer. Then there was a sudden movement and Blackwell let out a gurgling gasp. He staggered against Fran. Her hand pulled away, wet with blood. A blade flashed, twice more, deep into Blackwell's belly. I tensed and breathed in, but I was too late to spring or cry out. Mo's hands were on my shoulder, gripping on tight. His breath stirred my hair, shallow and shocked.

Fran stepped back from Blackwell and let him drop to his knees. Blood dripped from her hand like glittering jewels and splashed on the pavement.

"You will give it to me," she said, in a normal speaking volume.

I frowned. There was something off about the way she'd said it – not, "*give* it to me", but "give it to *me*".

Blackwell shuddered. She reached over and knocked the Warder's cap from his head.

"I'm ready," said Fran. She knelt down. She peeled off her coat and cast it aside, and she raised the knife again and...

I twitched, nausea rising in my throat. She was cutting herself, somewhere around her stomach, around the same place she'd stabbed Blackwell. She let the pain out in a long hiss between her teeth.

"Come on," she said. "Just stop fighting. Don't make me cut your throat, too. Come to me."

I leaned forward a little, my whole body shaking. Fran seemed to be waiting for something. Blackwell stared over her shoulder, towards us, his eyes heavy-lidded. Something changed. His eyes widened and he refocused on Fran.

"Why?" he muttered, his throat rattling with fluid. "Why now? You have Phillips, you have the Tower. And you already... have... the shift..."

"I'm destined for bigger, better things."

"You think... oh, you think this will make you a metashifter?" He coughed and doubled up, clutching at the blood welling out of his stomach. "You have no idea. The leodweard is... nature, part of the design. You can't *make* one."

"Nobody as powerful as Victoria has ever tried it," Fran smirked. "And she's only using a fraction of the power we'll have when we've gathered all the stones."

Blackwell shook his head.

"Come... closer..." he dragged in a breath, blood bubbling at the corner of his mouth. Fran hesitated, and then leaned a little closer. "There's... no such thing as *enough power*. They will write that... on your tombstone."

"Oh, hurry up and die," said Fran, her voice suddenly much less smooth, reaching for the knife again. She raised it to Blackwell's throat and sliced across, hard and violent. A little spurt of blood splattered against the wall and then the flood cascaded down and soaked his uniform.

"Now, give it to me." Fran sat back, her shoulders rising and falling as she took a series of deep breaths. My hands crawled to my mouth and I chewed on my index finger. What if Blackwell was wrong, and the metashifter *was* made? Was she going to turn into a raven? Could she already be a spider, or a rat?

Blackwell's corpse fell sideways. I stifled a moan in my sleeve.

"OK." She rolled her shoulders and clicked her neck from side to side. She leaned forwards, the growing pool of Blackwell's blood lapping at her knees. "OK, let's go, *raven.*"

She hunched over. I held my breath, until my throat stung with the tension, straining my eyes in the dim light to make out the first sign of the change. Her arms might shrink back and burst out in feathers, or her hair could slick back and turn iridescent-black. Perhaps her nose and mouth were growing long and sharp and hard. Maybe her eyes were turning into tiny onyx gems in the side of her face.

But none of those things seemed to happen.

"*Raven!*" Fran growled, through gritted teeth.

Nothing happened.

Fran's shoulders sagged and she threw the knife to the floor. It clattered and skidded in the pool of blood. "Fuck," said Fran.

"Is someone back there?" A man's voice. Fran looked up, her chestnut hair bouncing around her face, and then shrank into herself. She was just a thrashing pile of fabric for a few seconds, then she burst out of her shirt in fox form. For a terrifying second she looked like she was considering running right past us. I reached blindly behind me and found Mo's hand clutching for mine. But then Fran turned again and vanished into the shadows on the other side of the ticket booths.

"Oh my God." The man's voice sounded again. A deeper shadow fell across Blackwell's body, and then a circle of light so bright I blinked and looked away. It made him seem like an impressionist version of a corpse – patches of deeply lined white skin, a golden halo of hair, a splash of red-black at his throat. "999, request immediate assistance. I'm opposite the Tower – there's been a murder. Oh yeah, he's dead all right. Multiple stab wounds." The man leaned down. I caught a glimpse of dark skin and short black beard against a neat black uniform. Not a Warder – an ordinary security guard.

A thrill of anger shivered through me. *Where were you ten minutes ago?*

Then I softened. *Where were you, Meg? You were right here. Could you have stopped it?*

I didn't know.

Mo tugged at my elbow. I looked back at him. He looked like he might be about to be sick, but he made a little gesture – he pointed towards the security guard, and then flapped his hands at his sides.

My eyes widened. He was right – if the shift passed to the nearest human, if it wouldn't go to Fran or me or Mo, then that security guard had just inherited Blackwell's shift. He was the new raven in the Conspiracy.

I ached to give him something, a clue about what was going to happen to him, to tell him that it was going to be OK – but that he should run, far from the Conspiracy, and not let them find him.

But Mo whispered to me, so close I could feel his lips moving. "We have to get back to the others."

I nodded and climbed to my feet, as silently as I could, trying to ignore the fact that my stomach had turned into a writhing mass of hot snakes at the touch of his lips on my ear.

I'd always wanted to know what it was like to actually fancy someone. But if I ever ran into Cupid I'd strangle him with his own bow string for choosing to give me a practical demonstration at a time like this.

109 Hendon Road was a large semi-detached house on a main road near Finchley. The lights were on, like a beacon drawing us along the street. It looked warm in there, inviting. I visualised a sofa as welcoming as Susanne's, maybe a cup of tea, and then... the bad news. I shivered. The night chill was starting to get to me and I wished I'd thought to buy a coat as well as a hoodie. But I wasn't nervous. I suppose because I knew exactly what I was going to say. "Fran is working with Victoria, I saw her kill a man." There was really nothing else to say.

I rang the bell and after a few minutes, Don opened the door.

I was as certain that this was him as I had been that the woman at the Tower was Fran. Where she was sleek, he was solidly built. His skin was a dark reddish brown in the soft light of his hallway and he was standing tall and tense in his doorway, like a warder in his own little suburban tower.

But he was younger than I expected. I'd seen him as a middle-aged bloke, a patriarch in his home life like he was trying to be with the Skulk. I'd thought he must be some kind of successful businessman and family man, used to getting his own way.

He was about twenty-one, maybe twenty-five at a stretch. He was dressed like an older man – a shirt, shiny shoes, like he was auditioning for *The Apprentice*. Who arrived home at 1am with a pack of foxes in tow, and immediately put on a shirt? I remembered his posturing, his hostility, and I *got it*. And at the same time, the little store of respect and tolerance I'd been carrying for him was melting away. He didn't have the excuse of being a middle-aged man, set in his ways, used to control. He was just a bit of a dick.

Also, he was scowling at me.

"*You*," he said. "What have you done?"

I blinked. "What?"

"Are you some kind of spy?" he hissed. "How did you do this?"

"Don, what the hell? I've got something I have to tell you, can we–?"

"Damn right you have," Don growled. "Why did you tell us he was dead?"

"Who?" I racked my brain. Aaron? Blackwell? Angel?

"Me," said a voice from the hall behind Don. A white man, in his thirties, quite short, with brown curls and glasses. I had never seen him before in my life.

"I have no idea who this is! Come on, Don, let me in, we have some really important–"

"This is Ben Cohen."

My train of thought ran smack into a brick wall and I reeled. Don was staring at me, expectant and angry.

"No, he's not." My voice sounded far off and small.

"Excuse me," Ben said, "I think I know my own name."

"But that's not him," I babbled. "That's not the man who was a fox. It's not him." I blinked at the man he'd called Ben. I couldn't doubt myself – the sight of the man who'd given me the shift had been burned into my memory like a brand on my soul. He didn't look like Ben. But he'd been a fox, so he *had* to be one of the Skulk. Didn't he?

"There cannot be seven in the Skulk. It's impossible. There are only six. Me, Randhir, Francesca, James, Adeola, and Ben." Don counted off, each name like a nail being driven into a coffin. "So where did *you* come from?" Don snarled.

Six in the Skulk. Seven fox shifters.

"It's one of us." Don and Ben gave me identical blank stares. "The metashifter. The person who can be any one of the weards. It's got to be one of us!"

"What are you talking about?" Ben muttered.

"When the wizard's apprentice split up the weapon and made the different shifters she gave herself the power to become any one of them," I said, impatiently, and with a hint of *duh*. Then I paused. "That's what Blackwell told me. He told me it was called the leodweard and there should still be one. Seven shifters in six places, that means one of us isn't really in the Skulk."

"We know who's not really in the Skulk," growled Don.

"No. It's not me, it's one of you, it's got to be. Maybe Randhir, or – or Ben, or you."

But Don wasn't listening.

"No, all this trouble started when you arrived, didn't it? *You're* the one who stopped the ritual from working."

"What? How do you figure that?" I couldn't keep up with this – I just wanted to address the last thing he'd said but he carried on talking, getting more and more worked up, his face getting redder and more puffed-up. "It all makes sense now. You summoned the pigeons. All that rubbish about your parents, you made it all up and convinced poor Addie to go along with your lies–"

"What? No, it's not Meg who's the traitor, it's Fran," Mo snapped.

Don gave him a look so contemptuous it was almost pity. "You must think I'm a total moron. *Fran*? Fran's been part of the Skulk for *years*. She's been nothing but loyal."

"That's exactly what she wants you to think," I said, more than half to myself. As soon as the words had tumbled over my tongue I knew there wasn't a chance in hell Don would ever believe me. "She murdered Blackwell, we were *just there*. She wanted to absorb his powers and become the metashifter but it didn't work – if course it wouldn't, the metashifter is *here*."

My head was spinning. I raised my hands to run them through my hair, as if the solution to all this weirdness was in there somewhere.

Mo stepped up close behind me. "She said she was with Victoria. We heard her. She said it!"

Don shook his head. "Why would she say that if there was nobody but a corpse there?"

I rolled my eyes. "He wasn't dead yet, he..." I stopped. *He asked her. He must have seen me. He asked her so she'd tell us. Thank you, Blackwell.*

"You're just picking on her for your scapegoat because she's not here to defend herself. Just like Ben. How long did you think you could get away with pretending to take his place before he came back?" Don reached for the door and started to shut it. "Get out, whatever you are. The Skulk doesn't need you."

"Wait," I shoved my foot in the door just as Don tried to slam it, and let out a yelp of pain. "It's not me, it's got to be one of the others. You've got to make them tell you who they are. They're supposed to be the one in charge of fixing all of this."

"I won't spread any more of your nonsense," Don snarled.

"I'm not leaving. I want to talk to Addie, where is she?"

"She's sleeping," Don hissed, "And you're crazy if you think I'm going to let you disturb her. Get out." He gave a great heave and I had to move my foot to avoid being crushed as he slammed the door in our faces.

"You'd better watch out!" I yelled, hammering on the door with both fists. "You can't trust Fran. Addie, please, don't let them trust her!"

"Oi!"

I looked up. Don's neighbours' windows were open. A man was leaning out, shirtless, his hair sticking up at all angles.

"Keep it down. It's gone midnight!"

"Sorry," said Mo, taking my arm. "Wrong house." He pulled me away.

"She killed someone, don't trust her!" I yelled, one more time, before Mo steered me off down the street, one arm around my shoulders. I shook him off and stumbled to a halt, burying my face in my hands. "I don't believe – I can't believe they won't even listen."

"Well, I'm listening," he said. "We'll work this out."

I nodded, miserably. "Maybe." I took a long deep breath and let it out slowly.

"You know what, vandalising my school seemed like such a good idea at the time," I said. "I sort of wish I'd just stayed at home."

Mo laughed. It was a brief, throaty sort of chuckle.

I stared into the middle distance, my shoulders hunched. "I've got to get into the Shard and get those stones back. I'm not going to get anything from the Skulk, or the metashifter. Blackwell's dead. The Cluster stone is gone." My voice was low and cold. "I've got to just *do* it. I don't know why I thought I could get this bunch of idiots to help me. I have nothing now I didn't have two days ago. Actually I have *less*."

Mo didn't even hesitate. "You have me."

My heart melted so fast I could practically feel it dribbling out of my chest cavity and pooling in my shoes.

I looked up at him. "You shouldn't come. It's dangerous, I'll probably die. I don't want you to die. I mean, think about the loss to the art world. You're E3. I can't–"

"Bollocks to that. All great artists die tragically young, right?" He smiled. "We can go together. Come on, let's get warm and come up with a plan."

He turned and strode off down the road, without waiting for me, and sure enough I ran to keep up.

Maybe, just maybe, we could keep each other afloat in this churning sea of total insanity and death. In any case, we could keep each other warm until we drowned.

Chapter Twenty-Three

The Finchley Road all-night McDonalds was warm and welcoming, once Mo had found enough loose change in his pockets to buy a small cup of coffee. The manager didn't seem to mind that we made it last nearly five hours. I guessed she was pleased to have someone in who wasn't falling-down pissed or liable to try and strangle the staff.

Mo called Susanne.

"This is all screwed up now, Mum," he said softly. "One of the Skulk has betrayed them, it was the one called Fran." I heard the tinny echo of a raised, angry voice. "She's killed Meg's Conspiracy friend. We're fine! We're in a McDonalds. Yeah, is he... oh? Oh, good. OK." He moved the phone a little away from his mouth and looked up at me. "Marcus thinks he's found the new shifter. He's not sure yet though. Him and Mum are going to stake them out." He put the phone back. "Yeah, it's fine – we can wait here till the first Tube. I think so. I think... we've got to go up there, Mum. There's nothing else we can do, the Skulk are being useless. And Meg's pretty sure one of them is the metashifter and just hasn't told us. Yeah, I know. Yeah, we'll be OK. Honestly." He glanced at me and I wondered if that was as much for my benefit as Susanne's. "I know." He turned his face to the window. I watched the reflection of his eyes squeeze shut and then open and look out, deep and serious. A small, private smile crossed his lips. I looked away, feeling like I was intruding. "I know. They would. Anyway, I'll call you as soon as we get home, if you're not there." He swallowed. "Love you too."

He put the phone down on the plastic table and pushed it around with one finger for a while, the slight squeak only making the awkward silence more awkward.

I don't remember the last time I told my parents I loved them.

I don't know if I do love them.

You're supposed to love your parents, aren't you? Almost no matter what they do to you. It's supposed to be built in, like breathing. You only get a pass if you're a psychopath or they've abused you, or both. My parents could've been a lot, *lot* worse. So I was meant to feel *something* right?

Susanne wasn't even Mo's mother – not his biological mother, not the woman who was supposed to have the natural imperative to love him and teach him to be good and prepare him for whatever the world could throw at him – and he probably had a better relationship with her than I'd ever had with any adult, ever.

I dropped my head into my hands and stared at the speckled pattern in the plastic. Was that by design, or was it just corrosion from decades of bleach and salt and grease?

In my mind's eye, Dad's beak snapped down on Aaron's defenceless, furry body.

Dad was never violent. He wasn't like Mum. He didn't have a furious bone in his body. In comparison, he was the sane one. But he was useless at everything but making money: whatever skills he had in the office did not transfer to parenting. I think he saw me as Mum's problem, like a dog he hadn't really wanted. Nice to have around the place in a very vague sort of way, but not something he ever had to *deal* with – that was what staff were for.

Was there anything left of that man, now? The *worst* thing was obviously the fact that he'd been turned into an evil pigeon who had tried to kill me, but the second worst thing was not knowing if he could ever come back. Not knowing if I could fix it.

The truth coiled in my stomach, like a venomous snake.

I wished they were dead. I wished they'd just died. I'd have cried, and then I would have been free.

Some normal way, like a car accident? Like Mo's parents? Just what kind of an awful person thought like that? Hot tears of shame coated my eyes and I squeezed them shut.

I had hope that they might come back, that they might one day be able to make amends. That was more than Mo would ever have again. I didn't want it, but that was just tough. I had to make the most of it.

"Can I help?" Mo said softly.

I took a deep breath and spread my hands on the table, steadying myself on its inarguably real, sticky, pockmarked surface.

"I'm OK. Just thinking about Mum and Dad."

There was an awkward silence. Then Mo stretched hugely, his long gangly arms seeming to reach halfway to the ceiling. "All right. Tell me again. Tell me everything."

I talked him through it, focusing on that first night – but nothing I said seemed to strike him as out of the ordinary, once you'd discounted the murder and shapeshifting. I dragged a fine tooth comb through my memories, but there was nothing to suggest I wasn't a Skulk shifter.

"You're sure?" Mo frowned. "You've never changed into anything else?"

"Never," I said. "I went fox that first night completely on instinct."

"So who do you think it is?" Mo asked.

"Well, not Fran." I held out six fingers and folded one down at once. "We know she's only got the fox shape, because she tried to take Blackwell's. And," I realised, my heart lifting a bit, "she must not know the metashifter was in the Skulk all along, because it would be much simpler to just kill that one person than try to collect the set."

"What about Don?" Mo asked. "Didn't you say that shifting runs in his family?"

"Yeah... his father and grandfather were in the Skulk. But I don't think it's him. If he could change into a butterfly he would've been up at Kew telling you all what to do as well as us. It'd give him a legit excuse to be lord of all he surveyed. He couldn't keep something like this a secret."

"So who's left?"

"Addie, Randhir, James, and… Ben." I blinked as I said his name and the wrong face automatically sprang to mind. "The real Ben." I took the tiniest sip of coffee known to man, barely wetting my lips. It tasted of burnt plastic. "It could be him. I don't know anything about him. It could be Rand – but he didn't say anything about it. And if he could be in any weard he wouldn't pick the Skulk, because it means he has to hang out with Don."

"James?"

"Maybe." I thought of his glittering dragon's cave. "Do ravens like things that are shiny?"

"I think that's magpies."

I thought it might be ravens as well, but I shrugged. "He could be. But then wouldn't he fly away from the scene of the crime, rather than wearing a bag round his neck?"

"So what about Addie, then?"

"I want to say no."

"But you can't?"

"I…" I tapped my fingers on the table. "I think she'd have the most reason to lie about it. She has everything to lose. I wouldn't begrudge her not telling me, not for a second."

"So we think it could be Ben or Addie?"

"I think so." I leaned forward and let my head rest on the table, gently pushing the coffee out of the way with both hands as I slid down. "I don't know. I don't know what to do now." I took a deep breath and lifted my head. "My dad partly built the Shard, did I tell you that?" I said. Mo shook his head. "His company was involved in the inside architecture. The apartments are all custom-built. He knew Victoria, as a client, before I ever became a shifter. I've actually been up there. They had a party for all the architects on the top floor, right before they opened the View." If I'd only known then that there was a homicidal sorceress living right below me...

"Dad's plans might help us get in, maybe even show us where to look for the stones, and I can get them off his laptop, but that means we need to go back to my house, and I'm..." my throat closed over the word "scared" but I swallowed and plunged on. "I'm not sure that's a great idea."

Mo reached over the plastic table and put his hands on mine where they cupped the dribble of cold coffee in its paper cup.

"Well, I'm a little unsure about going up thousands of feet in the air to battle a sorceress," he said. "So how about I look after you in your house, and you look after me in the Shard?"

"It's a deal," I said.

Dawn eventually broke over the high street, and we staggered out, bleary-eyed, into the awful daylight.

••••

It was only 7am and still dark when we got back to Susanne's house – and both of us breathed a sigh of relief when we saw that the lights were on. Whether that meant they'd found the new Rabble shifter, or lost them, I didn't really care right then. As long as they were OK.

Mo slipped his keys in the door.

"Hello?" said a voice I didn't recognise.

As we opened the door into the hall, a woman stepped out of the living room. She was short and slight, with close-cropped black hair. She was wringing her hands, twisting a ring with a tiny diamond on it round and round her finger.

"Are you – who are you?" he asked. "Where's my mum?"

"She's not here," the woman said. "I had to break in. I'm so sorry, I'd never normally do this, nothing's actually broken, I promise."

"Who *are* you?" I repeated. She was wearing jeans and a white shirt, but I smelled something oddly familiar, even as a human – the smell of hospitals. Her shoes were bright blue crocs.

"My name's Roxie Shinawatra," the woman said. "I'm from the Horde." The shoes and the smell all clicked into place.

"It's true," I told Mo, "She was there when I went to find them. She did this to me," I said, pointing to the scratches across my face, which would've been much more dramatic if they'd been a bit bigger.

"You're the Skulk girl?" Roxie cringed. "Listen, the Skulk's never been good news for the Horde, and then you come – well, *skulking* into our meeting place in the middle of the night. What were we supposed to think?"

"Well, perhaps you could've heard me out before jumping on me," I snapped. "I was trying to tell you that you were all in danger."

Roxie's face crumpled. "And we should have listened to you."

"Let's go inside," said Mo, gesturing to the sitting room. "You can tell us what happened."

Roxie nodded miserably. As she turned away to go back into the sitting room I saw that she had a big plaster on the back of her neck.

Roxie settled on the sofa and Mo vanished for a minute and came back with a big jug of water and three glasses, only two of which had *Simpsons* characters etched on them. Roxie picked the Lisa Simpson glass and poured herself a drink.

"We were betrayed," she said, as if she were dragging the words up from somewhere deep inside her. "One of us turned. Ryan. I can't… I still can't believe it."

"What happened?" said Mo gently.

"He came to the meeting late. His fur was ruffled and he had a scratch on his ear. He told us the stone was in danger, and we had to move it. He said the Skulk was behind it all – that you'd just been the first, and the others were coming, and we had to get out..." She took a long swig of water and went back to twisting the ring round and round on her finger. "He was very convincing. I mean, he was one of our own, we – it never occurred to us not to believe him."

Mo and I exchanged significant glances. For all that I wished I could put this down to the Horde's insular, untrusting ways, it hadn't occurred to the Skulk to mistrust Fran, either.

What if she has spies in every weard? I wondered. *What if Helen was no drug addict after all?*

Roxie went on. "We took the stone, broke the shield and carried it with us–"

"Wait, so, you do have your stone?" I said, eagerly, and then felt awful. *They had their stone.*

"We were moving it, and then there was this... this *fog*."

My hands flew to my mouth.

"It came from nowhere," Roxie said. "We knew something was wrong, we were deep underground and it just surrounded us, like a solid wall. Orion tried to barge through it, and it sort of picked them up, and... and spat them back out."

I blinked. "He, um..." It suddenly occurred to me that Roxie hadn't said "he" – or "she". But that wasn't the mystery I was worried about right now. "They – Orion didn't die?"

"The Horde stone was right there," Mo pointed out. "Victoria wouldn't have needed to read any of their minds."

"It sucked us all in," Roxie said. "All except Ryan. He sat there, with the stone between his paws, and he cleaned his whiskers. While we all yelled for him to help us. He didn't look scared. He didn't even say anything. That was when I knew he'd betrayed us. The fog started to move. It dragged us away down the tunnel. Amanda and Olly both tried to change but they couldn't, it was like the fog was keeping them as rats."

"How did you get away?" I asked.

"Luck. Pure luck." Roxie raised a hand to her mouth, which twisted as if she might cry, but she sniffed it back and went on. "The fog was rolling along the tunnel, with all five of us writhing around inside it. I managed to catch an exposed wire on the side of the tunnel with my tail and tug myself around to grab it with my paws. The fog went on without me, I just fell out of it. I sneaked back, managed to creep up on Ryan. We fought. He bit me on the neck but I turned human and grabbed the stone, and legged it down the tunnel as fast as I could."

I realised I was holding my breath.

"I got away," she said, and I let the breath out.

"Do you have the stone?" Mo asked.

"I've hidden it. I didn't want to bring it anywhere there were going to be other shifters."

"Good," I said, slumping back in my chair. "That's two she definitely hasn't got."

"Who is this *she*?" Roxie said, her shoulders sagging. "What is going on?"

I glanced at Mo, and took a big gulp of water before launching into the situation as I saw it.

"So this woman has your stone," Roxie said afterwards, "She's got at least one other, maybe two, and Ryan and Francesca. And now she's kidnapped the Horde, everyone but me."

"Meg," Mo said. He looked up at me with an expression like a kicked puppy. "We left the Skulk. They were all together – apart from James – and they didn't believe that Fran was a traitor. If she's taking people now..."

I sprang to my feet, my hands tangling in my hair. "We've got to get back there. *God damn Don*, I told him not to believe her…"

Addie. Oh my God. Please be safe. Please don't be taken.

"Hang on, hang on," Mo said, scrabbling between the biscuit tin and the remote controls on the coffee table for a pad of paper and a pen. "I'm leaving a note for Mum." He hesitated, and then wrote: *We came home, we've gone again. Horde are in trouble, Skulk may be too. We're going to*

He hesitated for a long few seconds, and I knew what he was thinking. What were we going to do?

If Victoria had them all captive, there was only really one thing we could do.

see if they're OK. Mo wrote at last. *I'll call you when I can.*

Chapter Twenty-Four

They were all gone.

I banged on Don's front door and yelled for Addie, with Mo and Roxie both hanging back on the street, until his neighbour came out in a fluffy dressing gown and yelled at me again.

"Listen," he said, leaning over the front garden fence and clutching the dressing gown over his hairy chest. "I don't know what kind of drama you people have got going on – shouting and screaming at all hours – but I'm going to make a complaint if you don't shut it."

"Did you see where they went?" I asked him.

"Oh yeah. Could hardly miss it. Half past six in the morning, *yet more* yelling and carrying on, and then they all got into this big van and drove off."

"They – they got in a van?"

"Half of them were barely dressed," sniffed the neighbour. "I swear, that little girl looked practically feral with her hair and no shoes. What's going on, anyway?" he asked, about four hours too late. "The Olayes have always been good neighbours. Quiet. And then you lot show up."

I just turned away from him.

"Addie," I said, feeling hot tears prickling at the corners of my eyes. "Addie *lives* as a fox. She wouldn't have turned, not for anything."

"You think she was forced somehow?"

"I... I don't know." I folded my arms, trying to pin my shaking hands against my sides.

"Sorry, sir, it's a family issue," said Roxie, stepping forward.

"Do you think I should've called the police?" said the neighbour, all the fight gone out of him.

"No, no, we'll handle it." She put a clinically caring arm around my shoulders and steered me away. "Come along, dear, you need a rest, don't you?"

I did, actually. But I wasn't going to get one.

As soon as we heard the neighbour going back inside, she dropped my arm.

"I'm not abandoning my Horde," she said.

"Nor me my Skulk," I agreed.

"Why did she take them?" Mo wondered, shaking his head. "I don't get it, if she's got the Skulk stone already, how come she needs the shifters?"

I tried to imagine what horrible thing she was planning to do. "I'm not sure I even want to know," I said. "All I know is it's not going to be anything good."

"How do we do it?" Roxie asked. "Break in, get them back?"

"Break into the Shard," muttered Mo. He glanced at me.

"It's time, isn't it?" I groaned. "OK. All right. We need my dad's plans – he helped build Victoria's penthouse,"

I explained to Roxie, whose eyebrows shot up, and I didn't blame her. "And we need to find James, if he's still... around." I hated myself for even thinking it, but we couldn't make any assumptions. I took a deep, steadying breath. "My house probably isn't very safe. Roxie, can you meet us at London Bridge?"

Mo pulled out his phone and checked the time. "It's nine now. Call it midday, by the ticket queue inside the Shard."

"Mo, do you want to go with Roxie?" I said. "It's my house, after all. I'm sure I'll be fine."

"Haha, nice try," he said, seeing through my pathetic attempts to let him off the hook. "You're not getting rid of me that easily."

Mo started to look around warily as we approached my house, as if he'd been willing to follow me anywhere, but hadn't quite expected that to include leafy Kensington. He stared at me as I let myself in by tapping the code into the back gate and then turned off the alarm system.

"We should climb the fire escape, go in through my bedroom," I said. "It's not alarmed, so even if Mum did get around to gluing it shut, we can smash our way in."

Mo looked up at the tall, pristine whiteness of the house, and stifled a horrified look. "Why would your mum glue your window shut?"

"Oh, she found out I'd been sneaking out."

"So she *glued it shut*?"

"Remember the Thorn Queen?" I said, starting to climb the fire escape.

"Ye-es?" Mo didn't sound like he really wanted to know where this was going.

"That was a portrait of my mother."

Mo didn't reply.

"She was a human being and she deserved better than being made into a monster," I said. "But she was a pretty terrible mother."

The window wasn't glued shut. I guess she never got round to it. I tugged it open and climbed through.

The smells of home hit me as soon as I'd put my head into the room. Even as a human, it was almost overwhelming. It smelled of status quo and of safety, if not actual happiness. But it wasn't safe, not any more. I pushed through it as though through a cloud of smoke. I was here for Dad's files, that was all. Then, as I reached the door, I hesitated.

"Wait." I turned back, threw open my wardrobe doors and dug down into the trunk, throwing aside ballet programmes and secret sketchbooks, tugging out the backpack. I pulled out the plastic bag, and stared at the clothes inside. They were still crunchy with the mysterious shifter's blood. If I had a forensic lab at my disposal maybe I could figure out who he was with his DNA. As it was, I put the bag aside.

It was the backpack I was after. I emptied the paints out onto my bed and stuffed in a spare T-shirt, jeans, my secret emergency cash, and – shielding the drawer from Mo with my back – a couple of pairs of knickers and a bra.

Then I took the black and the white paints and stuffed them down inside the backpack too. Maybe they were good luck charms. Maybe I just wanted something to remind me I had a life, beyond Mum and Dad and school, beyond Victoria, beyond Don and Addie and the Skulk. I had something I'd chosen for myself.

Then I led Mo out of the room and down the long climb to the ground floor.

There was a foul smell on the landing outside my parents' room. The lilies on the table by the window were going mouldy. I wondered again what'd happened to Gail and Hilde, whether they'd been removed by Victoria, or by the police when they discovered we'd vanished into thin, feathery air. Had the police even come? Or had Victoria cleaned that up in advance too, faked a sick note for Mum and Dad like she'd done for me? Mo was trying not to stare at the massive rooms and the artificial cleanliness of it, the kind you only get with an honest-to-God housekeeper. I could tell by the way every time I glanced at him he suddenly looked at his shoes. I thought about telling him it was OK to look, that there really wasn't much to look at – the mirrors glinted and the little pointy ornaments gleamed, and the stern faces of old portraits glowered down at us, and nothing was out of place or wonky and everything matched. I bit down the simmering resentment. There should be bigger things on my mind than my mother's taste in home decor. I should be holding my breath for any sign of creeping fog, eyes and ears peeled for beating wings. But the air was clear and silent, except for our breathing.

Dad's study was on the first floor, looking out over the garden. I peered down the last flight of stairs to the empty front hall, before trying the door. It was locked.

I smiled to myself.

"Stand back."

I backed up to the other side of the corridor, twisted and brought up one hefty boot and smashed my foot into the door panel. It splintered, and fell out altogether on the second kick.

"You enjoyed that," Mo said. I didn't try to deny it. I reached inside and fished the spare key off the table by the door, and let us in to the study. It was neat and tidy, unsurprisingly, and furnished in a mixture of old and modern. Polished steel sat uneasily next to wood panelling and battered leather. I went straight for the top drawer of the big oak desk and rummaged while Mo stood guard, looking out of the window and then the door.

"Got it." I pulled my dad's iPad out of its protective sleeve and swiped my way in. Dad's four-digit password was written on a post-it note on the back of the sleeve, which was pretty typical. His company's app loaded in a couple of seconds, and I found the folder labelled "Martin, V, penthouse, floors 64-65". "Everything we need ought to be on here. Come and have a look." I put the tablet down on the table and Mo sat on the other side of it. We leaned over to both get a good look, and our foreheads brushed for a second. His skin was warm. I tried to remember what I was doing. "This is the plan for her first floor. See how everything's labelled?" I double-tapped and the image zoomed in. I moved it around, showing him her bedroom suites, library, sitting room, the cavernous dining room. “The lift’s just off-centre, here – here’s where the lift up to the viewing platform goes, though it doesn’t stop on these floors.”

“It’s enormous,” said Mo. “She could be keeping ten people in any one of these rooms. What’s on the second floor?”

I zoomed out and flicked to the next page. “Not much, actually. Just her master bedroom, and a great big mezzanine room.” They were joined by a thin corridor labelled “gallery”. “It says the room is “reception”, but it’s huge for a sitting room. Maybe it’s for entertaining, like... a ballroom?” That didn’t exactly ring true. But it did seem as though Victoria was living on the 64th floor, and using the 65th for something else. I looked through the rest of the documents in her folder. There were a lot of budget spreadsheets and email correspondence. My heart leapt as I opened up *MartinVsecurity.doc,* but then it sank again. “He’s got the details of her alarm system here but I don’t understand a word of it. Good thing we know an expert.”

I shut my eyes for a second, praying our expert was all right, and not locked up in one of these rooms with the others.

I stood up and turned to shove the iPad into my bag, and my gaze flicked to the window.

There was nothing outside. It was as if someone had drawn a grey curtain down over the outside of the window. For a few seconds I just stood there stupidly, and then I swore and grabbed Mo’s arm.

"It's the fog."

"*Bollocks,*" Mo breathed.

We watched it swirl up against the glass for a few seconds. I thought I could see the currents within it, tiny particles of – of whatever the fog was actually made from. I was pretty sure it wasn't water.

"Get downstairs," I whispered, half-dragging Mo towards the door. I had to fight to tear my eyes away from the window. Then a burst of blue sky appeared in one corner, and my heart hammered in my chest. The fog was on the move. We had to go.

We slammed out of the study and rattled down the stairs, and I tore open the door. Grey mist filled my vision and I tried to leap back, but my feet got underneath me and I fell, my elbows banging down hard on the tiled floor. I tried to lash out with one foot and slam the door on the fog, but it bounced back from the doorframe as if it'd hit a pocket of compressed air.

"Meg!" Mo had his hands under my arms and dragged me to my feet. The fog rolled in, faster than I'd ever seen. It poured after us as we staggered down the corridor, towards the kitchen, swirling and roiling more violently. A smoky tendril shot out like the tongue of a lizard and caught a curl of my hair. I screamed and clutched at it. My scalp stung like hell as I tugged, but I managed to snatch it back and Mo pulled me through the kitchen door and slammed it behind us.

"That won't hold it," I gasped. Fog was already filtering under the door. "And it's worse than it was."

"*What?*"

"It's faster, stronger. She's got the Skulk stone; it's making the fog more solid." I grabbed Mo's hand and ran to the back door as the floor filled up with mist.

"We can't run forever," Mo muttered, as he turned to throw back the bolts and reached for the key hanging by the door. It leapt out of his fingers and clattered on the floor.

"I dunno, running forever sounds good to me." I seized the closest objects from the kitchen counter and started to chuck them into the approaching mist, while he scrambled for the key. Knives clanged and stuck in the floor and then twisted like they were made of plastic; salt and pepper grinders exploded and sprayed their contents into the fog where they were caught up, spiralling through the currents like streams of asteroids through space.

Mo jammed the key into the back door. The fog was almost on us. I swiped my backpack at it, just trying to buy us a few precious seconds more. The fog parted to avoid it and the backpack went *clank-clonk* as it hit the floor and the spray-cans rattled.

Wait.

I tore the backpack open, reached in, tugged out one of the cans, rattled, aimed and fired. The black cloud of atomised paint exploded out of the can, hit the roiling carpet of fog, and spread out at once, filling the entire cloud. It stained the translucent grey mist a deep and glistening blue-black.

The fog stopped moving towards us. It twitched. It pulsated and contracted, drew itself up into a writhing column and twisted around itself like a sponge wringing out. Flashes of light sparked from inside it like distant lightning.

"What the...?" Mo gasped. I backed up against him, pressing my back to his chest, and he put his arms around my shoulders.

The fog jerked again, and then once more, and the paint boiled inside it, and then the whole cloud burst, like a bubble, and was gone. Black paint rained down on the kitchen floor, and there was silence.

"You killed it," Mo whispered.

I blinked, barely wanting to acknowledge it in case he was wrong, scanning the spattered paint for any sign that it might twitch back into life. But there was none.

"Meg," Mo cried, and threw his arms around me and gave me a big, breath-stealing hug. "You killed it!" He spun me around and lifted me off the floor. Joy seared through me and I squealed and waved my feet in the air and laughed as I hugged him back.

He eventually put me down, and I staggered back, grinning stupidly.

I hadn't really wanted to let go of him. But that was a thought I could give some time to later – if there was a later.

My boots were spattered with drops of black paint. I glanced back at the kitchen, and another laugh bubbled through me. "Bloody hell," I sniggered. It looked like a gothic Jackson Pollock, only messier. The words "my mother's going to kill me" rose in the back of my throat and I fought them back, turning away. Maybe she was. But it wasn't going to be over the state of the kitchen.

"Come on," I said, turning the key in the back door and holstering the paint can in the front pocket of my hoodie. "We've got to get to Bow."

Chapter Twenty-Five

James was alive, and he was well up for breaking into the Shard.

We'd stashed our clothes under one of the broken-down cars outside his lockup and I'd nosed my way in through the fox door with the iPad in my mouth. I'd almost had my face clawed off.

"Oh, it's you. Well, I'm glad you're alive," he said coolly, as soon as I'd yelped my surrender. He sat back and let me and Mo clamber into his cave of wonders. "Are the others all right? Where's Addie?"

"We think Victoria's taken them," I said. "Fran's betrayed us. She's got most of the Horde, too."

James' silky veneer cracked right down the middle. "You said you'd look after her!" he barked. "I'm going to kill that woman. If she hurts Addie I'm going to feed her her own skull."

"We're going to get her back," I said. "We'll get them all back – but we've got to get into the Shard." I explained about my dad, and James' ears pricked up when I mentioned the plans.

"Is there a .vtf file?" he asked. "Have you got the lift layout in there?"

"I – I dunno." I opened the iPad and put in the code with my nose.

James scanned through the plans, and then double-tapped with one paw, zooming in on a side-on elevation of the lifts and staircases around Victoria's apartment.

"See here? This lift is public, it takes people up to the View, which is two floors up from Victoria's Penthouse. So all we have to do is go all the way up and then come down the fire exit stairs and break in through the fire escape on the right level."

"How do we do that?" Mo said.

James sat back and scratched behind one ear with his back paw. We waited. James didn't say anything. He scanned through the plans some more, and then blew out a snuff of air through his nose.

"What?" I asked. "What's wrong?"

James lowered his head. "I'm going to have to go in human."

"Well – yeah," Mo said. "Even if you could do the doors as a fox you'd have to be human to come up with us in the lift, right?"

I shuffled my paws. "You don't like being human?" I guessed. "Like Addie?" My ears went back and I hunched down. "But we really, really need you."

James gave me a sharp look, one foxy eyebrow twitching. "No, I'm with you. I'm just… I'll meet you in a second."

Mo and I had changed and were waiting outside the lock-up when there was a long, interrupted creak of hinges that hadn't opened in a while, and part of the wall opened.

The man who came out of the lock-up looked pretty much like Wayne Rooney's less attractive cousin. He was shorter than I was, maybe twenty-five, wearing jeans and a knockoff Adidas hoodie. He walked over to us, his shoulders hunched, his hands plunged into his pockets, with the iPad tucked under one arm.

He came up to me and Mo, and his lips twitched into a smirk. It was the first thing about him that seemed at all familiar. "I know, darlings, believe me." His voice made me blink. He had the vocabulary of Oscar Wilde and the accent of the Artful Dodger. "Sometimes I think I was swapped at birth. I was meant to be a fairy and instead I turned out a goblin."

"Hey," I managed. I wanted to tell him to stop it, not to talk about himself like that. But I tripped over the fact that actually he sort of *did* look like a goblin. "I didn't say anything," I pointed out.

"Yes, love, you did. Just not out loud. I'll have to ask you to keep it a bit quiet. I've got a persona to keep up. Can't have the other jewel thieves knowing the great James Farringdon is actually Ma Docherty's youngest from down Tower Hamlets. That'd never do."

Nobody who'd looked up at the London skyline in the last couple of years should be able to forget that the Shard is mostly made of concrete. For months its blocky central tower had loomed over the city, like a giant chimney stack with cranes and trucks buzzing around it night and day. But as soon as the glass had gone on and been polished up to a diamond shine, it was hard to remember the clumsy construction phase. Now it was all razor-sharp glass planes, edges not quite meeting in a cluster of points that caught and scattered the sunlight.

I glanced up at the giant LED board on the side of one of the neighbouring buildings as we came out of London Bridge station. It said it was Wednesday, 13.24. I couldn't remember the last time I'd known what day it was. Right now Jewel and Ameera would be sitting together in the square, eating chips and comparing notes on the weekend, or Facebooking in companionable silence.

Except...

My stomach turned over and I felt sick with guilt that for even a split second I could have forgotten. They wouldn't be there. Ameera was gone, and I hoped Jewel was on the far side of the world by now.

What had Victoria done with the bodies? What had she told Ameera's family?

There would still be *Aspects of International Relations* today, and *Eastern Europe in the 19th Century*. The other students would be pushing and shoving on the stairs, Facebooking, bullying, laughing.

And all the friends and families of those people Victoria had murdered would never know how their loved ones died or who was responsible.

But I knew.

My fingers tightened around the can of paint in my pocket, cool and solid and powerful.

The sparkling glass-walled public entrance to the Shard was full of people. Roxie met us in the lobby, waving four tickets.

"I bought enough for all of us," she said. "In case you found him." I grinned at her gratefully and James gave her a little half-wave, half-salute.

"Listen," I whispered to the three of them, as we walked over to the queue for the lift. "I don't want to even see Victoria if we can help it. I want to get the shifters out and take back the stones. I want to be the one with the power if I have to face her."

James nodded. "Sensible," he said. "And if we do run into Mistress Crazypants?"

We probably die, I thought.

Mo stuck his hands in his pockets. "Then we do what we can," he said.

I nodded. *That's good enough. It has to be.*

There were plenty of people swarming around the lifts to the office floors and the hotel reception, but the queue for the lift to the View was empty. My spirits rose as we filed along the rope line, and then sank back into my boots when I spotted the security guard at the little table right in front of the lift.

He waved for me to open my bag. I dragged my lips into a smile, though I could practically feel my heart thudding against my teeth.

The paint can isn't an offensive weapon, unless you're a patch of evil fog – or unless you're my mother and it offends you right in your sensibilities. But I bet it would be enough to get me banned from the ultra-pristine View.

I could feel a sheen of sweat prickling over the back of my neck as I pulled open the bag and the guard glanced inside.

The iPad was nestled on top of my clothes, between the cups of my spare bra. It wasn't even a pretty bra, it was a tatty old comfortable thing with a stain on one of the straps. The guard drew back with a nod, not meeting my eyes. I zipped the bag up quickly and let the blush flood my face, savouring the delicious embarrassment, because it was better than letting him see how relieved I was.

The lift arrived and the three of us stepped in, but before the doors could close we were joined by a boy, about twelve with red hair and freckles. I thought of Blackwell, and clenched my fists.

The boy's mother and father slipped in after him. The woman was holding the man's waist and looking deep into his eyes. The little boy was holding his mum's handbag and looking grumpy. As the lift shot up into space I caught sight of James in the mirrored surface of the opposite wall. For just a second he looked down at the boy and a slight smile crossed his face. Then he met my eyes and looked away, impassively.

I didn't know what he had to smile about. I would've thought the fewer people up there with us, the better.

The doors swished open and the couple almost ran out through the dim corridor and into the sunshine. They dragged the boy straight to the edge of the room.

"Oh, Stuart," the woman gasped. "Look!"

She wasn't wrong. I heard Mo's breathing shorten as we walked over to the floor-to-ceiling panes of glass that were all that stood between us and the clouds. It's almost impossible not to feel something at the sight of London spread out in front of you from such a ridiculous height. It wasn't a stunningly clear day, and the view came and went, patches of sudden visibility in the misty air drawing the eye to a stretch of river or a church tower or a grimy industrial estate.

"You OK?" I asked Mo.

"I'm not scared of heights," he said. "But this is – this is something else." He turned to me, and there was a slightly crazed smile lighting up his sleep-deprived face. "And you?"

"*I'm* not scared of heights," I echoed, gazing out over the grey ribbon of the Thames. Then my focus shifted and I caught my reflection in the glass.

What am I afraid of? Being crushed to death because I didn't see the fog coming? Being pecked to death by the creatures that used to be my parents? Finding out there's no way to save them? Finding out that the Horde and the Skulk are already dead? Letting this woman destroy my world without ever finding out why? Failing to live up to the responsibility that nobody ever actually gave me? Leading two of my new favourite people to their deaths because for some reason they keep listening to me?

I listed them off, fear upon absurd fear, waiting for the sense of release that always came when I faced up to the absolute worst that could happen.

What's she going to do, hit me? Yell? Shake me until I throw up? Strangle me and hide the body and tell the press I moved to Switzerland?

It wasn't something I'd consciously named before, but the release of tension always came. It was something like a swift breath that would leave my body and take my fear with it; and something like a self-fulfilling prophecy, because performing a deadpan, snarky commentary on life requires you to pretend to be calm, and then somehow you are calm.

I waited for the calm to settle on me.

It didn't.

Am I afraid of all those things?

Yes.

A million times yes.

I'd come a long way. But all that meant was that it was a very long way down.

Suddenly I couldn't move. My fingers locked on the metal railing and I couldn't uncurl them. Panic flowed up my arms into my shoulders and circled my head like a swarm of bees. My legs buckled. Red mist moved across my vision, like the cloud bank outside, shifting dizzily. London twisted beneath me.

I don't want to die. I don't want to be here. I want to go home and crawl into the wardrobe and eat nothing but salad for the rest of my life. I cannot be here. I'm not ready. We're going to die.

My fingers slipped from the rail, my palms trailing sweat, and I fell down.

"Meg," Mo's voice sounded blurred and far away.

"Are you all right, miss?"

A man in a neat black uniform with a high-vis laminated badge leaned over me, concern written across his face.

Oh God. It's Security. And I'm making a scene. A thousand volts of panic coursed through me and I sat up like Frankenstein's monster on the slab. "I'm fine!"

I wasn't fine, but now I was a whole different kind of not fine. Everything seemed razor-sharp and far too bright – the woman's red coat as she turned to look at me, Roxie's blue crocs, the guard's badge, Mo's wide and staring eyes.

"Now, just sit still," the security guard said. "Take a deep breath."

I tried, staring across the floor. Behind everyone else, the little boy's ginger hair burned on the back of my retinas, and the tight roll of banknotes James was passing him throbbed pinkly.

"She'll be fine," the guard was saying to Mo. "We get a lot of fainters up here. It's all just too much for some people. Let's just sit quietly and face ourselves away from the view, shall we?"

Mo put his arms around me and turned me so my back was against the railing. Coincidentally, that meant I had a wonderful view over the security guard's shoulder as the little boy ran across the room. He was clutching his mum's red umbrella, his fiery hair still leaving smoky streaks across my vision. He smashed the umbrella into the fire alarm and there was a sound so loud I was afraid the whole building might shatter into pieces.

The guard swore and told Mo to help me up, leapt to his feet, ran to the fire exit and threw it open. Then he spotted the boy, the broken glass, and the umbrella, and his face went a violent shade of purple. He seized the boy by the arm and dragged him over to his parents, shouting something about a maximum five thousand pound fine.

I felt Mo and James take an arm each and lift me onto my feet. "It's now or never," James whispered in my ear. We made a run for the fire escape and Roxie pulled the door quietly shut behind us.

"Down," he hissed. "Four floors, hurry before the guard thinks to look for us."

I wrapped my hand in the sleeve of my hoodie so I could cling on to the banisters for dear life without my sticky palms slowing me down, and started down the stairs.

Mo paused. "Meg, are you OK? If you need to stop..."

I shook my head. "Have to keep going. Adrenaline is good. Won't fall down again." *I hope.*

We clattered down four flights of stairs, the fire alarm still ringing in our ears. I half-slid down with my hand clamped around the banister. Roxie held back behind me and Mo went on ahead, taking the stairs two at a time with each stride of his long legs. James leapt down whole flights with the grace of a fox and the daredevil confidence of someone who's lived their whole life in a tower block.

We stumbled to a halt by the door to the 64th floor. The door bore a warning sign that read "PRIVATE PROPERTY, KEEP OUT, DOOR ALARMED AT ALL TIMES". James just smiled and dug in his pockets, pulling out a series of little bundles wrapped in dark grey silk. I leaned back on the wall, letting my brain catch up with my feet, while he unwrapped a couple of long silver things with wibbly-shaped ends and started sticking them in around the doorframe.

The fire alarm turned off. My breathing suddenly sounded deafening and I tried to calm myself. I could feel the same deep well of terror that I'd felt upstairs, just waiting to open up and swallow me. But maybe if I kept moving and I didn't look down, physics would forget me. The Roadrunner theory of survival in ridiculous circumstances.

"How did you get the little boy to set off the alarm?" Mo asked James.

"Never leave the house without a hundred pounds in used bank notes sewn into the lining of your coat," said James. "It's amazing what holding a ton in their hands will do to people."

"Thanks, I'll try and remember that in future," said Roxie, rolling her eyes. I flushed. I'd been thinking the same thing, but without the sarcasm.

James reached into another pocket and pulled out a little black box with a single LED on top. "Should take care of the alarm," he said. Mo and I nodded as if we understood how it could possibly do any such thing, and then caught each other's eyes, smiled, and looked away.

"How long's that going to take?" Roxie asked.

"Two minutes, four if you keep talking to me," James said, then held out his hand. "iPad." I fished it out of the bag and handed it over, and he started scrolling through the security files, so fast I could barely believe he was actually reading them, but he did seem to be doing things to the lock as he read, and eventually he pushed it away, readjusted his knees on the ground, twisted his longest, wibbliest silver stick in the lock, and there was a small but satisfying *click*. "We're in," he said quietly, retrieving his silvery metal things, tucking them away in their silk wrappings and pulling the door open. I grinned and squeezed his shoulder.

The fire escape opened onto a short corridor, panelled with light wood and polished steel. There was a lift door right across from us, a pattern of silver flower silhouettes etched into its surface and only one button – down.

And there were voices, lots of voices, coming from somewhere inside. It was too much of a clamour to make out individual people, but it had to be the Skulk and the Horde. They were here, and some of them at least were still alive enough to complain about it.

With my heart in my throat, I leaned in, holding my hand out to keep the others on the stairs, peered around to my left and right. To the left, the corridor opened out into a light, airy space where I could see low white leather sofas and a white rug. The sitting room. To the right, the corridor turned a corner.

The voices were coming from down there.

I oriented myself by my mental picture of Dad's plan – if the sitting room was to my left, and the Skulk and the Horde were forwards and right, they must be in the dining room. *Funny place to keep them*, I thought, until I remembered that the dining room was easily the biggest room on this floor.

I stood still as a statue and listened hard for a few minutes, but I couldn't pick out Victoria or Fran's voices among the general racket.

If there is a God, any god, looking down on me right now, let those bitches not be home.

I turned back to the others. "I think they're in the dining room. There'll probably be extra security on it," I whispered to James. He patted his pockets and gave me a thumbs up. I handed the can of white spray paint to Mo and he nodded and shook it up, muffled in his sleeve.

The light outside was diffuse and cloudy, but still bright enough for shafts of it to cross the corridor where doors to the outside ring of rooms had been left open. We reached the turning and I peered down it, blinking in surprise.

There was no door – the corridor ended a metre or two away, opening up onto the enormous dining room. And gathered there, in the middle of the room where the dining table ought to be, were five, ten… eleven people. I couldn't see any cell, or chains, or anything that was obviously restraining them, but they were all huddled together, standing or sitting on the wooden floor in an area about the size of a minibus. Half of them were partly naked or dressed in clothes that didn't really fit them. Don was shirtless and hunched, but still wearing his trousers and shiny middle-aged-businessman shoes. I scanned the crowd. Yes, there was a white man in a shirt that looked like Don's, but the buttons were stretched around his stomach.

They'd been forced to change, to be human. Some of them had been naked. They had to share their clothes.

I blinked back tears, selfishly glad I hadn't been there to see that. I looked for Addie, but couldn't see her.

I took a step down the corridor towards them, and then froze as I looked up and saw that the room had a balcony at one end, like a medieval minstrels' gallery but made out of the same pale, modern wood and silver and glass as the rest of the penthouse. That must be the passage between the huge reception room and Victoria's bedroom. Anyone on the second floor could walk into the gallery and look right down into the dining room.

"Roxie!" someone gasped, and the hubbub inside the dining room fell quiet. One of the people I didn't recognise was looking right at us: a white woman with blonde hair who was naked but tightly wrapped in a long woollen coat. She'd spotted Roxie and thrown her hands up to her mouth. The shifters were all turning to stare at us, all of them with wide hopeful eyes and our names on their lips.

In the hush, I heard other voices echoing down from upstairs. Victoria and Fran, and a male voice that must've been Ryan.

I listened, holding my breath. I couldn't quite make out words, but they seemed animated. Perhaps they were celebrating. Or perhaps Fran was trying to explain what had happened – or didn't happen – with Blackwell, and Ryan was explaining how Roxie had got away with the Horde stone. I took a second to send up a short prayer that Victoria would be really, really angry with them.

Then they, too, stopped talking. I heard heels clicking on wood and backed up into the shadow of the corridor. Roxie, Mo and James huddled back too. We drew closer together and I snaked my fingers into Mo's.

"Awfully quiet down there all of a sudden," called Fran's voice.

Roxie made frantic wheeling motions with her hands. A few of the shifters turned to their neighbours and tried to pick up their conversations where they left off, but it was stilted and false, like a crowd scene in a film where you can tell everyone's just saying "rhubarb" to each other.

One of the men glanced over and met my eyes. He was a wiry, greying Indian man who'd stripped down to his boxers and Doc Martins. He had a big tattoo of a fox on his upper arm.

Randhir...?

He turned to Don. "*Don't* tell me what to do!" he snapped, and he pulled one arm back and punched him right on the chin. Don went flying, sprawling into the arms of the woman behind him. Inspired, the rest of the shifters burst into chatter, taking sides, trying to calm things, restraining Don from retaliation.

Oh yeah. That's definitely Randhir.

Chapter Twenty-Six

"Randhir, you thug!" Don complained, holding his jaw. "You didn't have to hit me!"

"You shut up," Rand snapped. "It was your blind trust in Francesca that got us here!"

I closed my eyes and focused every part of myself on listening for the sound of footsteps upstairs. Sure enough, Fran's shoes could be distantly heard tapping away from us. I shuddered as I opened my eyes. That was too close.

And what were we going to do now?

James snuck up to the edge of the dining room, stepping silently and hugging the wall, and looked up at the gallery. He turned back to us and gave a thumbs up, and all four of us ran across the room to the group of shifters.

"Roxie," said the blonde woman again. I realised her voice had an American twang. "Thank God, thank God!" She held up her hands and leaned forwards on the thin air, like a mime pretending to be in an invisible box.

I held out a hand and gingerly tapped at the solid barrier in front of me. There really *was* an invisible box.

That explained why they hadn't spread out around the room...

"Are you all OK?" I asked. There was a general shrugging, a few nods and a couple of emphatic headshakes. "Where's Addie?" I couldn't see her – she must be behind the Horde shifters.

Roxie made her winding motion again. "Keep talking!" she hissed.

"Just keep away from yelling out things like 'thank God' and 'rescue' and we might be OK," muttered James.

The white man who was wearing Don's shirt gave Roxie a little salute and started talking to his neighbour, a black woman wearing a grey T-shirt and a brown cardigan wound around her waist like a skirt. He gathered the American lady into their conversation too.

"I don't know what to do," he said. "If it was a normal locked room, maybe there'd be something we could use..."

"I'm Amanda," said the black woman quietly, while the man went on, saying something about locked room mysteries and spy thrillers. "This is Olly and Cameron. On behalf of the Horde, on behalf of everyone here, I'm so sorry we didn't believe you."

I nodded. "I get it. Just hold on."

I crept around the side of the group with Mo behind me, keeping one hand on the solid surface so I could feel where the corners were and not walk headfirst into it.

"Are you from the Skulk?" said a plump man sitting near Amanda, with a skinny girl in a jumper and shorts leaning against his shoulder. She looked about my age. Her legs were curled under her awkwardly.

"Yes, but..." I did a quick count-off in my head. "You're not Rabble. Who are you?"

"Cluster," said the man. "Chandran, and this is Katie."

"Hi," said the girl. She waved an arm. Her wrist was limp at the end of it. "I've got cerebral palsy," she added, her speech a bit slurred. "I like to tell people early, it saves time. Don't worry, Chandran can carry me if we have to run. Bitch upstairs took my crutches."

Mo blew out an angry breath through his teeth.

I frowned. "Weren't you at the Saracen with the others?"

Chandran shuddered. "We were there. We managed to hide from the pigeons and we've been hiding ever since. Apparently not well enough."

"You the one that found our stone?" Katie asked.

I nodded. "I'm so sorry I couldn't keep it safe. We tried, but Fran was working against us."

Chandran shrugged. "You wouldn't have been able to do it anyway, it doesn't work like that. I'm actually relieved to find out someone knows where it is, after a year of just not knowing," he said, stroking his stubble with a rueful smile. "Even if it's in the hands of a maniac."

"You're looking for the girl, Addie," said Katie. "She's over there." She nodded towards the other side of the group.

"Thank you," I murmured. Addie must be behind Randhir and Don. They were standing over Ben, who was huddled in on himself, shirtless and trembling. Randhir caught my eye, looked me up and down and mouthed "Meg?" I nodded. He gave me a thumbs up and went back to berating Don for getting them all into this. I felt a little sorry for him, even though Rand was only doing it to keep up the noise… and he was right.

"Oh no, *Peter*," breathed Mo. He crouched to an old white man who was leaning on the invisible barrier. "Are you all right? It's Mo, from the Rabble!"

The old man looked up and smacked his wrinkled lips together. "Ah, Mohammed," he croaked. "What's going on?"

I saw Mo gather himself, his fists briefly clenching before he put a steadying hand on the barrier.

"The stones are in danger," he said. "The woman who brought you here is collecting them."

Peter tried to sit up straighter. His frail wrists looked like they might snap under his weight. "Mohammed, that can't happen…"

"I know. We're here, we're going to help you. Just hang on."

James sidled up to us, throwing wary glances up at the gallery. "Guys, I can keep an eye out for anyone up there, but someone ought to be back in that corridor keeping watch."

"Go," said Peter, looking at Mo. "I'll be all right. Don't let them catch you too."

"All right." Mo glanced at me, held up the paint can with a small smile, and then hurried back into the passageway.

I edged further around the box. "Addie!" I whispered. "It's Meg, where are you?"

"P-princess?"

Someone shifted aside, and I saw her. She was more fully dressed than most of the others, in a jumper and a skirt. But she was still curled up tight, her hands balled into fists. Her skin was dirty and spotted with old scars and bruises. She looked tiny compared to the others, more like twelve than fourteen.

I ran around the side of the box and knelt at her side. "Oh my God, Addie. Are you all right?"

"Is this her?" said a voice. I looked up and saw another person kneeling beside Addie. They had long, glossy brown hair that draped over their chest and they were wearing a big green shirt wrapped around their waist. The whole effect was quite mermaid-y.

"Meg, this is Orion, he's–" Addie broke off, rolled her eyes. "Argh! Sorry, *they*, I'll get it, I swear," she said weakly.

"Honestly, if 'he's' easier on you right now, you go ahead," said Orion. They gave me a sideways smile and tucked their hair back behind their ear.

"No way, no, screw that, I'm going to get it right, and so's Meg, aren't you, Princess?" Addie said, giving me a significant look. Her voice was croaky – I supposed she hadn't used her human vocal chords in a while – and her eyes were still darting about, full of wary anger. But she did seem to be getting it together.

"Why can't you go fox?"

"It was Fran, just like you said," Rand said quietly, looking down over Don's shoulder. "She came over to Don's house and the stupid bloody idiot let her in." I expected a sharp comeback from Don, but he stayed silent.

"It was like the shift just... turned off," Addie said miserably. "I hate being human. So what're we doing, Meg? How are we going to get out of here?"

I hadn't been looking forward to someone asking me that question.

"I don't know," I said, honestly. I put my hand up on the invisible barrier. "It's solid. It's physical, and she made it. I bet she can do it because she's got the Skulk stone. Maybe if we can get it back, we can get you out of here."

"Hurry," said Don. "Ben's not doing well."

I looked again at Ben. "Why, what happened?"

"She took him," Addie whispered. "She hurt him."

I shifted back around the barrier until I was a close to Ben as I can get, but he was sitting almost right in the middle and his head was down, leaning on his knees.

"Ben? Can you look at me?"

He raised his head, and I stifled a gasp. He had a black eye and a long, shallow tear right down his cheek. It wasn't bleeding, but it was weeping a horrid pale liquid. There were livid bruises coming up all over his chest and his arms.

"Why did she do this?"

"She knew," Ben said miserably. "This is all my fault."

"How could it be *your* fault?" Don asked.

Ben shook his head and his face flushed blotchily, on the verge of tears. "I'm sorry, I'm so sorry, I didn't think it was important, I didn't think you'd even notice it was gone..."

"Oh you total wanker," said Rand, but he kept his voice soft and his face twisted with sympathy. "*You* took the bloody stone!"

"What the hell for?" I demanded.

"I sold it. To pay for a – a holiday. That's why I haven't been around lately."

I glanced up at Don. His face was deep purple. He seemed too stunned to speak.

"But why did she hurt you?" Rand asked.

"He hasn't said," Don added.

"She said if I told you she'd have me thrown out of the window. I think she might actually do it," he moaned. "She shoved my face right up against the glass! Have you looked down recently?"

I had. I remembered the sound in my head like a swarm of bees and red clouds obscuring my vision.

"All right. I have to get the stones. That's all we can do right now," I said, looking over at James and Roxie.

"Oh, is that all," Roxie said.

I stood up, my knees weak underneath me. What were my chances of going snooping around Victoria's apartment looking for the stones without getting caught? Slim to none. Still...

Sssssssssssssss

I twisted on the spot, almost lost my balance, stared towards the corridor. I knew that chemical hiss.

Mo had both hands around the middle of a mad, pecking pigeon. It was coated in white spray paint and flapping madly, flicking paint into his eyes. He wrestled silently with it but his hands slipped on the paint-slick feathers.

I broke into a run, too late to stop the pigeon landing one, two, three hard blows on Mo's face with its beak, drawing blood. He dug his teeth into his lip to keep from screaming.

I grabbed the pigeon by the neck as its head bobbed viciously forwards to try to take out Mo's eye, and dragged it off him. Its wings beat around me and I smacked it into the wall, hard, just to try to stun it, to get it to stop before one of us broke and cried out loud enough for Victoria to hear.

I felt the delicate neck bones snap under my hand and the bird flapped for a horrible second longer before going limp and tumbling out of my fingers in a shower of feathers. Its wings spread white paint across the floor where it fell, a ghost impression of a bird.

Mo gathered me into a hug.

"Thank you," he whispered into my hair. Then he pulled away and gave my shoulder a reassuring squeeze. He edged down the corridor towards the lift, wiping the blood and paint from his eyes, listening for signs the struggle had been overheard.

I didn't take my eyes off the pigeon. Under the coating of paint, it was plump and brown. Its wings were strong and its feathers were messy. Bits of down still floated in the air around me.

I waited, tears searing down my cheeks, holding my sobs in my chest, trying not to make a sound. I waited for the pigeon to stretch and morph into the corpse of my father.

I couldn't think of anything worse, until I realised that it wasn't going to.

I fell back against the wall and slid to the ground, folding my arms around me and over my face as if

I could physically contain the wails that rose into my throat. I bit down hard on the neck of my hoodie and forced myself to choke them back.

Dad was dead. Mum was dead. They had been dead from the minute she changed them. My dad was never, ever coming back. Not even in death.

Mo came back and fell to his knees beside me, a horrified question forming on his lips, and all I could do was point to the corpse with a quivering hand and then fold up into myself. My throat and chest were burning up from holding in the sound of my breathing. If I'd allowed myself to make a sound I wouldn't have been able to do anything but scream.

I wished for this. I wished that they were dead, because it would be easier for me. *Easier.* I deserved to be carried off and fed to the fog, right now. Did I try to save him, really try? Did I do everything I could? His neck snapped in my hands. I wanted to cut them off at the wrist. I could have called all Victoria's minions to me, to finish the job, with one good scream... but Mo, but James, but Addie, but the Skulk and the Horde and Peter and all that was left of the Cluster.

I had to get them out of here.

I was going to get to those stones, and if I couldn't save them, I would destroy them.

Mo's arms slipped under mine. He lifted me to my feet. I swiped my arm through the air and pointed, furiously. He had to keep watch! The Skulk were already being careless with their voices, calling out to me, asking what was wrong.

Mo pulled away, but he was replaced at once. James' arms wrapped around me and he held on tight to the back of my head. I sucked in a breath, intending to gather myself, and only succeeded in letting out a tiny, hideous, strangled wail.

"Dad," I choked out. "He's gone."

James held me for a few minutes, my tears soaking into his shoulder.

I balled my fists in my sleeves and wiped at my eyes and nose, getting rid of the worst of the sticky, trying to clear my vision. More sobs rose out of the ground and hit me like the aftershocks from a terrible earthquake, but I managed to get to my knees, and then shakily to my feet.

"All right, darlings, listen up," James said very quietly, taking charge, not looking at me. "There's nothing more we can do here, we're going to find the stones and try to break whatever this is." He kicked the barrier. "Pay attention: if the box comes down, you all need to *run* – to the end of the corridor and turn left. There's a fire exit. Get out, go down the stairs and do not stop running."

"Anyone who gets out, meet at my mum's place," said Mo. "Peter, you can get them there, right?"

Peter nodded. "Yes, sir."

Roxie stood up. "I'm going with them," she said to Amanda.

"Good luck," said the Horde leader. "And if you see Ryan, kick his arse."

"Will do," said Roxie, with a little salute.

The four of us backed away into the corridor. Roxie

looked down at the body of the pigeon and then up at my red eyes, but didn't say anything.

"I think they're still upstairs," said James. "So let's search downstairs first."

I nodded silently.

James led the way, treading silently. Mo gave us a thumbs up as we passed and hung back to bring up the rear. Miraculously, I could still hear Victoria and Fran, talking upstairs. They hadn't heard the pigeon attack, or my sobs.

We passed the lift and came out into the airy sitting room. I glanced at the floor-to-ceiling glass and dearly wished I didn't know that Victoria was willing to use her wizard's tower as a blunt instrument. There was a glass and steel spiral staircase in one corner of the room, leading up to the second floor. With a single silent glance, we all agreed to go the other way.

I crept into the kitchen. It was similar in size and design to our industrial sized entertaining kitchen at home, though nothing here was padlocked. I guessed that meant she wasn't keeping the stones in her spoon drawer, but Mo and I hurried to silently open every drawer and cupboard, just in case.

Through the dining room, there was another corridor. An enormous, gleaming bathroom with a shower that would even put my mum's to shame. A library and media room with a TV screen the size of Texas, a plush and comfy-looking eggshell blue sofa, and crammed bookshelves.

It wasn't all specially purchased antique books that nobody had ever read, either – there were lots of well-thumbed paperbacks on philosophy, politics, history, sociology and psychiatry. I pulled a couple down, just in case I could find a lever that would reveal a secret passage… but nothing moved.

James crept past me. He paused to give a copy of *Mein Kampf* the serious side-eye, and then opened the door to the next room.

Tendrils of grey mist shot out and sucked him in. He let out a yell, and it was cut off as the fog closed over his head. I saw him lifted off his feet in the swirling current. He writhed and kicked and twitched in agony.

I drew out my spray paint, aimed and fired. A spatter of black spots hit the fog and whirled around James, boiling and pulsating, but nothing else came from the can except a weak hissing sound.

I get through Black so quickly. I should've brought the Pastel Rose.

"Meg!" Mo threw his can across the room and I snatched it out of the air, turned and fired. White paint burst from it, filling the fog cloud with crackling dots of ink. James vanished completely into the opaque cloud, and I heard him scream.

The cloud burst. White paint rained down, covering the room beyond, which was a closet full of Victoria's coats, her hats and her shoes. James knelt among them, panting and trembling and spitting out mouthfuls of paint.

Relief stole all the tension from my body and I sagged back. I allowed the paint can to be taken from my hand. Then someone seized one of my arms and pressed something hard and cold against my neck.

"Hello, Meg," said Fran. I tried to pull away. "Ah, I wouldn't. If you don't care for your own throat, how about the butterfly's?" She pressed the knife tight against my skin and turned me so we could see a young man holding Mo with another knife under his chin.

"I'll cut his throat," he said, "if you don't do exactly what we say."

I turned my head, very carefully, and looked up into Fran's eyes.

"You'd better take me to Victoria," I said. "I want a word."

Chapter Twenty-Seven

I saw Roxie and James exchange assessing looks as we were marched along another bright, panelled corridor. We outnumbered them, four to two…

A searing pain sliced across my throat and I stumbled to a halt. For a second, I thought I was going to die. The sensation drew me in, until I was nowhere but the skin on my neck, seeing nothing but pink mist. I could've fainted... but I wasn't dying. A red ache throbbed under my skin. Blood trickled down my neck and soaked into my clothes and I wanted to raise a hand to it, to feel how bad the cut was, but Fran held me tight against her and pressed the sticky blade to my face.

"It would be inconvenient for me to kill any of you right now, but I'll take one of her eyes," Francesca warned.

Fran held on tight to my arm, and dragged me up the spiral staircase to the second floor.

Four pigeons, red-eyed and sharp-beaked, shot along the corridor and battered around our heads. One of them had the skinny, slick body and dark grey feathers – but it wasn't my mother. My mum had been dead since the moment Victoria and her pigeons had tapped out that horrid rhythm on my drawing room window.

I tried to get my bearings. One big room dominated most of the second floor. Apart from a few load-bearing girders, it was open and almost completely empty. London surrounded us on three sides – the windows were as huge and clear as the ones on the viewing level. On the fourth side, behind us, there was a wall with a doorway that led into the gallery over the dining room.

I almost hadn't been far off when I'd guessed it might be a ballroom. The floor was made of wood, inlaid with spiralling patterns of light and dark, like the rays of the sun bursting out from a five-pointed star at the centre.

Fran released me and took up a position between us and the staircase, with her knife held to gut anyone who tried to make a run for it. There was no other way to escape the circle. Ryan released Mo, and he stepped over to press his hand into mine. I clutched onto it and glared at Fran.

Is this the knife you killed Blackwell with?

I wanted to grab it from her and throw it from the top of the Shard.

He tried to help me, and he didn't deserve to be gutted by a traitor. Another thought followed that one, panting at its heels like a faithful dog. *He may have known more than he let on, more than I know even now. And now he'll never be able to tell me the rest of it.*

At one edge of the circle, Victoria stood by a small table full of... *things*. There were a lot of blades and edges, some vials of clear liquid, screws, wide and glistening metal harnesses. There was a roll of wire, a silvery hammer, and a small blowtorch.

I wondered if you were supposed to be able to tell the difference between magic and torture.

Victoria turned, gave a little smile and waved Fran over.

She was wearing three of the stones. They'd been set into gold and she was wearing them around her neck. There were two empty settings too. She really was after the set. Three stars sparked out at me from the three stones: red, blue and... white.

Wait, a white stone?

The Rabble stone was yellow.

She had the Conspiracy stone. The power of the mind.

I ground my teeth with annoyance and felt the flap of skin slide, opening and closing, dribbling blood down the other side of my neck.

The Conspiracy. In their smart uniforms, in their supposedly impenetrable tower. It was their stone Victoria had stolen first – of course it was.

I wondered if Blackwell knew, or if he suspected, but he just didn't want to let on that he knew, not even to me. Or maybe he believed it was safe.

Victoria pressed her hands to her chest and shut her eyes. The stones glowed. The red Skulk stone gave off a heat haze and the floor beneath my feet shuddered. One of the dark inlaid lines buckled and rose up like a snake, curled around and between my legs, and then turned back to solid wood, trapping me in place before

I knew what was happening. Another pinned Mo's feet, and the next got Roxie around the waist. James almost moved in time, but the wood leapt up and smacked the backs of his legs so hard he buckled to his knees and was trapped there.

I tried to move my legs, to press against the wood, but it had gone completely solid; strong and dark as mahogany roots. It would be easier to break my own legs than break their bonds.

Well, at least I knew what my absolute last resort move was going to be.

Victoria picked up a gleaming silver implement with a black handle, and walked towards us.

"Welcome to my home," she said. "I hope you're enjoying the view."

I glared at her. Her dress was pale, creamy yellow silk and white lace. She should've been dressed like a sorceress, all black and pointy. Instead, she looked like she was going to a summer cocktail party right after she'd finished with all the kidnap and murder.

She stood in front of the four of us and turned the silver thing in her hands. It was a pair of heavy, sharp-toothed pliers.

"I have a question," she said. "I'm just trying to think who would answer it best."

"What is it?" I asked. "Why did you hurt Ben?"

"I thought I could get him to confess," said Victoria. "It was a stab in the dark. I'm very glad you're here, Meg. I think you're the one that's going to be able to help me now."

"You've got our stone," I said through my teeth. "I can't help you with anything."

"We'll see," said Victoria. "Tell me, which one of the Skulk is the leodweard?"

"Oh..." So she knew. Of course she did – there were seven of us and we were all here. Something rebellious sparked inside me and I scowled. "So Fran's stupid mix-and-match plan didn't work after all?" I glanced at Fran. Her face was like thunder.

"It was a slightly stupid plan," Victoria agreed. "But you should be polite to your betters. You can hurt her," she said to Fran. "But just a little."

I twitched in my wooden leg clamps and wobbled as Fran walked up to me. "Fran, don't." My voice sounded pathetic and childish. She raised her knife, as if weighing where best to stick me. Then she touched the tip to my forehead.

"Keep still if you don't want an unscheduled lobotomy," she grinned.

The pain was intense, deep in my skull. I let out a wail as she ran her knife right down the middle of my forehead, all the way to my nose. Blood streamed down my cheeks, mingling with my tears.

"All right, that's enough."

Fran stepped back at once.

"I want the metashifter," said Victoria, "And now I know I already have them. I just don't know which of you it is. So I'll give you one more chance." She pointed her pliers at me, and then at James. "Give the metashifter up to me and you'll die quickly and painlessly. Final offer."

"I don't know," I said quickly. "I really don't. Could be anyone."

"Don't look at me, darling," James muttered. I glanced at him, blinking the blood out of my eyes. Could I believe him? Would he believe me, for that matter? I didn't know who the metashifter was, but he didn't know that.

Victoria sighed. "All right, well, I apologise if this is unnecessary, but I have to be sure." Her hand snaked out and pointed at Mo.

"Fran, bring the boy."

"No!" I yelled. "He's not it, he's from the Rabble, it's a Skulk shifter you want!"

"Yes, I know," said Victoria. She grabbed my elbow. The wood holding me up suddenly gave way and I staggered forwards, barely keeping my feet as she dragged me across the floor to the window. She thrust me up against it, my face right beside the thin layer of basically nothing between me and a sixty-five storey drop. Then she spun me around and yanked my wrists together, binding them in front of me with some kind of silver wire.

Fran had walked Mo over to us, with her knife digging into his back. I saw him wince and a trickle of blood stain the edge of his T-shirt. She positioned him in front of the table of horrible silver implements.

The wood where he was standing snaked up again, more of it this time. It twisted and snaked around him until he was lying at forty-five degrees, his arms pinned.

"Feel free to try to run," said Victoria, when I looked down at my own unbound hands. "If you want to hurt him very, very badly."

I met Mo's eyes. His lips twisted in horror and he gave a tiny shake of his head. But I don't think he was telling me *run,* or *don't run*. Just, *No, all of this is wrong*.

"I don't know who it is," I said weakly. "I swear I don't. If you hurt him I'll just start blurting names; that won't actually help you, will it?"

I glanced back at Mo. He was shaking. I looked away again, my chest tightening painfully.

"Come here," said Victoria, crossing to the little table of horrid implements and beckoning me over, with a smile, as if I had a choice. Panic struck and I tried to dig in my heels, but Fran picked up a pair of scissors and raised them to Mo's ear, and I staggered forwards.

"I'm going, don't, I'm going."

"Meg," Victoria said, putting the silver pliers down on the table and not, for the moment, picking up anything else. "I really don't *want* to have to torture anyone, it's always such a waste of time in the end."

"Why don't you just use the fog?" I said, exhausted and confused and unable to look at Mo. "Summon some more of it and use it on me, then you'll know for sure everything I know."

Victoria didn't answer.

That was weird.

I looked down. The cloud parted and I saw the Thames glistening grey and cold, bending around the Southbank and Waterloo as it flowed towards us out of the east. I could make out the Eye, Parliament, the green vastness of Hyde Park.

A burst of homesickness hit me and I swallowed hard. I never knew you could miss a place so much while you were standing in the heart of it.

And then I looked up from the swirling cloud. "You can't use the fog because that would kill me," I muttered, my voice harsh and whispery. "You can't just kill us off until you find the right one, because our shift would go to the closest human, and that's *you*."

I half expected Victoria to lash out at me or give Fran the order to hurt Mo – but she smiled. "There you go!" she said, as if she was genuinely pleased with the fact that I'd come to this conclusion. "Hence, I'm afraid, the torture. I have to find out who has it without killing any of you. I wouldn't get too happy about that, if I were you, there are significantly worse things than death."

"And you want the metashift for yourself. So if you kill the wrong one of us first, you'll be stuck with the Skulk shift."

"And that would really ruin my day," she said.

I looked down at the table of implements, and then up at Mo.

I could ruin her day right now. I could kill myself, slice open a vein with any one of those and force her to take my shift. It wouldn't get the stones back, but it would put something in her way. She wouldn't be able to take *everything*.

The only problem was that I really, really didn't want to die.

But if it saves Mo… if it saves James and Addie and Susanne…

But would it? Or would it just make you feel you were actually doing something?

"Why do you want to be the metashifter?" I said, buying time while I climbed down from that particular ledge.

"You see these?" She ran a hand over the stones at her neck. The air crackled with static and my hair prickled, frizzing up almost as if I was in a cartoon. "The metashifter can do anything they want, go anywhere they want, take any stone they want, even if the other shifters have protected it. The leodweard is like a wild card, or a failsafe against corruption."

"Blackwell said it was their responsibility to keep the stones safe. Keep them apart," I said.

Victoria draped an arm around my shoulders and tapped my nose with one finger, like you'd do to a small child. Did she think I'd giggle? I thought seriously about biting her finger off.

"It's all about perspective. The metashifter could keep them apart, or bring them together. Obviously, I'm going for the latter."

I glanced out over London again. "I don't understand," I said. "Why do you want this ultimate weapon thing anyway? Are you really going to destroy it all?"

"Destroy? God, no. Rule." Victoria smiled down at the view, and then up at me. "All I want is all the power available to me. You can understand that, I'm sure."

She gave my shoulders a squeeze. I wanted to punch her in the face but could only twitch my hands against the wire.

"We actually have a lot in common, Meg."

I racked my brains. She seemed to think I'd know what she meant, but nothing came to mind.

"We both have excellent reasons to hate our parents," she said.

"I didn't hate my dad," I snarled. "He was... he was..."

"He never helped you. Did he?" Victoria said. "He never stood up to your mother. He let her hurt you and belittle you and never once considered that you were an innocent girl whose only crime was not being exactly what they wanted."

I sniffed back tears again, just like she wanted me to, but I frowned up at her through them. That was all a little too specific to just be about me.

"Why, what did your dad do to you?" I asked, not really wanting to know the answer – but every moment she wasn't torturing or killing anyone was a good moment right now.

"He treated me like I was less than human," she said. "Victoria Martin is my married name, my maiden name was Olaye."

I stared at her, my jaw dropping. "Oh, what the–"

"Donny is my little brother. He doesn't even know it's me who's captured him and his little gang, yet. I'm saving that particular pleasure for later."

"But – but–"

"The Skulk runs in my family. It runs from father to son." Victoria's pleasant psychopath façade fell away and her face turned stony. "My father was king of all he surveyed. From his little suburban castle. He led the

Skulk, and my mother and my aunts all served him, whatever he wanted, he got."

I glanced at Mo, while Victoria went on talking. He had his eyes firmly closed. Fran was trimming her fingernails with the silver scissors and dropping the trimmings onto his face.

"I was born wrong, born female, so I became a servant too. Little Prince Don got everything. Dad died when I was twelve and Don was six. Don got the shift, and I was expected to just let him lord it over me for the rest of his life." She shook her head. "I got out of there as soon as I could hold down a job. I improved myself. I did my research. And then I took the only thing more powerful than what my father had." Her fingers strayed over the three stones around her neck and hooked through the two empty settings. "It's a work in progress, obviously." She smiled again suddenly. "And look where I am, Meg." She swept her arm around, taking in the whole of London and the Shard. "Look what I *have*. I'm not like you. I didn't get given a solitary penny by my parents. I had nothing. Now I have everything, or I will do, very soon."

I stared at her, stunned, and for a moment I felt a deep well of sympathy for her. I wanted to root for her. I wanted her to have everything her heart desired.

Except that the deep well of sympathy ran bone dry right around the point where she killed my parents and my best friend and kidnapped Addie and tortured Mo to get it.

"That's it?" I asked. "Really? You're doing all this to get one up on *Don*?"

"Oh, well, no. Now I have slightly bigger fish to fry than Donny. You know, when I offered to buy this stone from the Conspiracy, there was only one of them who even objected? Stupid, old, white men surrounded by history and arrogance – I don't know why I'd expected them not to be corrupt as well. This whole world is so broken. There's no justice, Meg, none at all. I know you know that. My mother died living like a serf in her own house because Don never worked out there was any other way to treat her. Wouldn't it be a better world if injustice was punished?"

"Yes, it would, you *total hypocrite*," I said.

She shrugged. "We could stand here and debate ends and means all day. It doesn't change the fact that when people have a choice, they choose to be terrible." She looked up, and I followed her gaze. A flock of pigeons were settling on the girders. The one that had been my mum hopped closer and tilted her head to the side, one beady red eye glaring at me. I wondered again who all those other people used to be.

"Do you want to know all the sordid little things I found out about your parents, over the last few years?" Victoria asked.

"No," I managed.

"Not about your mother's corruption? About the blackmail? The backhanders? The threats? What about your father? I liked him much more than your mother, but even I could see he was a liar, and a coward, up to his elbows in fraud and exploitation."

I gazed out over the misty sprawl of London, tears pricking my eyes.

I wasn't shocked. She was trying to shock me, but I knew my parents had it in them.

What made me blink back tears was the fact that I would never know. I'd never be able to confront them myself. Because *she* had taken that away from me.

"Parents are people, and people are bastards," I said.

"Well put," Victoria smiled. "Still, your father did build me this wonderful place. You know, magic and towers are linked, right down in the deep bones of the world. The old wizards fought like *animals* over them." She gestured to the spread of the city below us. "Don't you just love it here? Far above the world. Above it all. No more family. No more stupid expectations."

No more family?

How dare you. Seriously, how dare you?

Victoria's voice softened again and she gave my shoulders another squeeze. "Listen, I understand the bird is dead," she murmured. "But don't worry, you didn't kill your father. He was already gone."

"I know," I said, through gritted teeth.

"It's actually for the best. There will always be casualties, when power has to be taken from the establishment by force. Damage will be done. If you help me now, perhaps fewer people will die," Victoria said, leaning in close. "I'll happily spare the Rabble boy and the little Skulk girl, but you'll have to help me do it."

"How can I?" I said, my breath coming in a hysterical half-laugh. "I don't know who it is, Victoria. I really don't."

"I don't believe that." She turned. "Fran," she said.

"No, don't!" I tried to run over to Mo, to put myself between him and Fran, but Victoria grabbed my arms, and then Fran had raised the scissors to his ear and...

I hated myself for it, but I looked away when he screamed.

Chapter Twenty-Eight

Blood poured down Mo's neck in rivulets. It soaked his T-shirt and dripped down the twisted wooden support and onto the floor.

Fran handed Victoria his earlobe, with the earring still in it. Victoria held it up in front of me and gripped my chin, forcing me to look. It was fleshy and red.

"There are so many, many parts of the body that are nonessential," she said. "We are really at the tip of the iceberg here."

"I don't know, I don't know, I actually don't know," I whimpered.

"I think you do. Let me jog your memory."

I flinched hard and bit my lip – but Fran hadn't moved. Mo was breathing hard and there were tear tracks on his face.

"I've done my research. The last metashifter pretended to be one of the Cluster for years. The two spiders I have downstairs knew him. He became friends with a boy named Angel Dalston."

I blinked. Angel knew him?

"He vanished from the Cluster and took the stone with him," said Victoria. "I looked high and low for that stone, but for a year, there was nothing. And then I heard from Ryan. He said that he'd fought a Skulk shifter who had the Cluster stone but lost them before he could finish the job. I had my fog have a look around, and what should I find, but a spider shifter who's been searching for their stone and found it in a school in Kensington? Next thing I know, there you are. Not the fox who fought Ryan. A new one. Do you see, Meg, where I'm going with this?"

I did see, and it was absurd. There was no way I was the metashifter. I'd know!

Wouldn't I?

Angel had known the metashifter. What if he'd kept track of him, or tried to find him again?

What if he'd succeeded, that night, but it was too late and Ryan had already mortally wounded him?

Wait a minute...

Chandran had said that the Skulk wouldn't have been able to hide the Cluster stone. It doesn't work like that.

But it did work. I felt it. I didn't make it up, I actually felt something when I touched the Cluster stone.

What, exactly, did that make me?

Holy shit...

"I think it's you, Meg," she said softly, smiling at me.

I think you're right.

And if I let you know that, you'll kill me on the spot.

And so right now, the best thing I can do for Mo and Addie and James is not die.

I forced a smile to cross my face, then looked up, caught Victoria looking at me, and frowned. "I can't do this anymore." I looked down out of the window and then cringed away again. "You've got me. It's me, I'm the metashifter. I've known for days. But I haven't changed because... because I knew you were watching me and I didn't want to give it away," I said, the fact that I was actually improvising helping a lot with pretending to improvise.

Victoria stared at me hard. "I'm sure it's you," she said.

But she couldn't be sure, or she would have done it already.

I took a deep sniff and gave the window another apprehensive glance. "Please, I can't bear it any more. Let him go. You can have the metashift."

"You're lying to me," Victoria snarled. "Why? Why would you tell me to take it?"

"I... I..." I raised my hands to my face and rubbed the bridge of my nose, as if lost in a terrible, hard decision. Then I brought my hands down hard towards Victoria's chest, caught my fingers in the chain of the necklace that held the stones, and tore it off her.

Sadly, that was the full extent of my plan. Victoria lashed out, her hand smacking into my cheek, reopening the cut on my jaw and sending me spinning to the floor in a burst of pain and drops of blood. I kicked out, catching her on the shin and making her stumble. I still had the necklace and I twisted my fingers in the empty settings and curled up around it. I had the stones and she'd have to prise them from my cold dead fingers.

Victoria kicked me in the stomach and I crumpled up, choking. She bent down and took hold of the necklace. No way. I locked my fingers and held on for dear, potentially very short life. She actually lifted me off the floor in her attempts to get it out of my fingers.

"Let *go*," Victoria snapped. She turned back to the table and picked up the silver hammer. It glistened as she turned it over and over in her hands.

"No!" Mo screamed.

Victoria raised the hammer.

I've never been particularly athletic, and I was especially bad at gymnastics. But then, I've never been about to have my fingers broken by a sorceress wielding a silver hammer before.

I waited for her to bring the hammer down and threw everything I had into rolling backwards and bringing my feet up to kick her in the stomach. She curled up, winded, and dropped the hammer.

I had seconds. Victoria was still doubled up and gasping. I writhed up to a sitting position, dropped the necklace, snatched up the hammer in my bound hands and brought it down as hard as I could on the white stone. It ricocheted with such force I thought I might tip over. There wasn't even a scratch on the smooth white surface. I growled with frustration.

Who the hell makes a hammer out of silver, anyway? It's hardly the strongest metal in the world!

But what's softer than silver? What's softer than just about anything?

Gold.

I brought the sharp end of the hammer down with all my might on the gold setting between the stones. It bent, and on the second blow, it snapped. There was a rush of air from nowhere, carrying a strange scent of salt and freshly cut grass. It blew Victoria onto her back. I tugged and bashed until the stones came apart in my hands.

Mo crashed to the ground and I saw Roxie and James shake off their restraints on the other side of the room. There was a cry of triumph from somewhere below us – the barrier must have gone down. I saw Ryan try to grab Roxie, and then felt a bubbling rush of laughter in my throat when she ducked under his swipe and head-butted him. He dropped like a stone.

Run, all of you, get out of here!

Then something else happened. The pigeons changed. They slid from their perches on the girders, wings flailing as the feathers shrank back and wing-bones turned into fleshy fingers, beaks into soft mouths.

I found her – Mum, flapping and shrieking, her long neck growing longer and her thin ribs widening. She clawed for a talonhold on the girder for longer than the rest, then her legs lengthened and became pink and skinny and she slid to the floor. One by one the pigeons transformed back into people. They flopped onto the ground and lay there. I stared at Mum. Her eyes were blank. She was breathing… but not *there*. Like someone in a coma.

"You little bitch." Victoria staggered over to me and kicked out. I flinched away and shielded my face with my hands and her shoe connected hard with my wrists. The pain made my head spin. She sank to her knees and made a grab for the stones. I elbowed them away, tried to get them underneath me, but her fingers closed on the white stone and she reared back with it clutched in a death grip, her knuckles standing out hard and bony.

Her eyelids flickered. The pigeon-people stirred. They got to their feet, slowly, and looked around. I felt my jaw drop in horror as I saw one of them make a pecking motion with his head. Another one flapped one arm, experimentally. Mum's eyes were full again – bright red, and full of birdlike rage.

I curled up over the other two stones, shielding my face and head, and she fell on me, scratching at my back, pulling at the wool of my hoodie and my hair. But I couldn't protect my neck. I felt the skin tearing, agonising shafts of pain opening up my nerve endings. Tears poured across my cheeks and splattered on the floor. One of the tendons in my neck gave a huge involuntary twitch.

I could smell smoke. Scent hallucinations? Didn't those come with nerve damage? Was this really it?

"What the – leave the girl, stop him!"

The weight lifted off my shoulders and I risked turning my head. There really was smoke. Mum and the other pigeon-people lurched towards it, running with tiny steps and their jaws thrust out. James was on the move, with a flaming torch in his hand. He got to Mo just before Mum got to him and swiped at Fran with the torch. I realised it was his own tracksuit top, tied around a pole broken off from the balcony and lit on fire. He helped Mo up and whirled the torch between him and the pigeons.

A warm feeling of relief and pride washed over me. Although it could've been the trickles of warm blood running through my hair.

"Stupid vermin," Victoria muttered. I tumbled onto my side and looked up to see her clutching all three stones. I wasn't sure when she'd got them back. I prayed the others had got out, far enough away that she couldn't just use the Skulk stone to reach out and grab them.

I sat up. I was right next to the table full of edges. I kept my eyes on Victoria as I shuffled over to it, but her eyes were trained on the pigeons and James' flaming trackie top, concentrating. Some kind of spell? I couldn't stop to watch. I grabbed a pair of silver shears with serrated edges that looked like they would cut through flesh and bone with ease, and contorted my hands until I could snap the wires binding my hands.

I was free!

I clambered to my feet and hurled myself at Victoria, knocking her to the ground. The Skulk stone slipped out of her hands and I seized it and drew my arm back. I yelled for James as I threw it across the room. Victoria recovered, elbowed me hard in the chest, and my throw went wide. The stone skittered across the floor as I doubled up and fell onto my back, seeing stars.

"Got it!"

James. James. Thank you. "Run!" I screamed. "Take it and –" Victoria's arm came down on my throat, choking off the sentence. Fury etched deep lines into her face as she looked down at me. My vision clouded, pink-grey afterimages pulsating where her eyes should be. I tried to kick her away, but my whole body tensed up, my breath hitching and aching in my chest, my lungs feeling as though they were about to burst.

Victoria reared back with a yell. The next thing I knew the pigeon people were on us, pecking at the air with their mouths and beating their arms around our heads. Victoria was in the middle of them, writhing and screaming. I felt hands around me and clung on to Mo as he dragged me to my feet. He was still dripping blood from his ear and one arm was red from a long patch of torn skin, but he was alive, and still moving. I glanced over his shoulder. James had gone. He'd gone! He'd taken the stone! I almost fainted with relief as Mo started to drag me away.

"Come on, Addie!" he yelled. It was only then that I saw her. The birds hadn't attacked Victoria – Addie, in fox form, was shooting in and out of the folds of her skirt, confusing them into clawing at their own master. Addie had the Cluster stone clamped in her jaws. She burst out and was gone across the wooden floor like a rocket. The bird people hobbled after her, but she was too fast for them. She vanished down the spiral stairs.

Victoria picked herself up off the floor, pressing a hand to her head. She still had the Conspiracy stone. Its white surface was streaked with her blood.

If I could get it away from her, would the pigeon-people turn back into real people?

Maybe not – but they could die in peace, without pigeons in their heads, without doing Victoria's dirty work.

Mo was trying to drag me away. We were halfway to the stairs, and Victoria was still reeling, wiping away blood from a long cut on her face. We could make it.

But I can still stop her doing this to my mum.

I wriggled out of Mo's grasp and launched myself across the room at Victoria, tugging the black spray paint out of my pocket, spraying it into her face. The compressed, chemical air still carried a few drops of paint, and it was enough to make her cough and recoil. I snatched at the white stone, but her fingers were tight on it and she wouldn't let it go.

"Never!" she shrieked, and spat into my eye. As I cringed away, she kicked my legs out from under me and I fell hard on my back. "This is *mine*."

I heard Mo gasp just a split second before a violent burst of heat seared across the back of my head. Fran had picked up James' torch and she was waving it at Mo, laughing hysterically.

"Run!" I yelled.

"Yes, run while you can, Rabble scum," Victoria snarled. "I'll come for you soon enough."

"I won't leave you!" Mo choked, but the flames seared past his face and he cringed back.

Victoria smoothed down her clothes. Her hands were shaking but her back was straight and she moved slowly and deliberately as she walked over to the table with its impressive range of ways to kill me. I got to my feet, tried to flex my aching shoulders. I looked at the window, and then over at Mo.

"I mean it. Go, before she fries you!" I looked him right in the eye. "Thatch is going to need you later."

He blinked at me. I nodded once.

Come on. Listen to what I'm saying.

He hesitated for one more second. "All right." It was more of a sob than a shout. "All right. I'll... I'll put the kettle on."

I swiped my sleeves across my eyes. "Thatch'll like that!" I choked, a broad smile reopening the cuts on my face.

He shrank in on himself and I saw something yellow and black flutter away and vanish.

Victoria walked up to me, a long blade in her hand.

"Fran, go put that out for God's sake, and drag Ryan somewhere out of the way," she said. "That was touching," she said to me. "Is that what you call that rat of a homeless kid?"

I feinted to the left and then threw myself right, but there was nowhere I could go. I pressed my back against the windows.

"Go on, kill me," I yelled. "You'll get the Skulk shift and you'll never be the leodweard!"

"It would be my pleasure," Victoria growled. "Give my regards to the pavement."

She stepped to one side and touched a control in the window frame. The window behind me flew open with a crack like the earth breaking in two.

Nothingness opened up behind me. Freezing air turned my blood to ice and the wind screamed in my ears. My hands grasped at empty air.

And then I fell.

My shoulder hit the slanted windows of the floor below and I yowled and bounced off into the blue, my whole world turning over and over. The Shard shot up and away like a rocket taking off, and the street below growled up at me, a mouth full of hard and jagged teeth. Sixty-five storeys down, and counting. My insides coiled and twisted. My arms waved like I was drowning. I felt the blood on my cheeks freeze and flake away. Tears tore out of my eyes and flew away into the clouds.

Be right. Be right. Let Victoria be right.

I curled in on myself. I twisted, shifted, fur bursting out of my skin. The wind took my clothes, stole them away, and I tumbled as a fox, without sight, without scent of anything but the cold air and the city rushing up to meet me.

Not helpful! Be something else…

I tried to twist again and felt the cut on my forehead stinging as I shrank into myself. Feelings pressed in on me, stretching in my back, in my head, at my sides. The air felt thicker, almost buoyant like water.

I'd done it. I'd changed. I was the leodweard. I was the metashifter.

I was the person I'd been looking for all this time.

Right now, I was a butterfly. All the way to the furthest reaches of my vision, there was nothing but empty space and shifting clouds of colours like I'd never ever seen before. What *were* those colours? There was a pink that was green and a brown that was purple…

I was falling *up* now, fluttering blind through a swirling tornado of colours and scents that were sort of also feelings. I reached out my antennae into a stream of orange air that had come a long way, sea air mixed with the scent of coal, oil, fishing nets. I spiralled through a swirl of hot steam that was perfumed and chemical and smelled of perfectly folded towels, and was caught up in a freezing blast that rose up from the streets, carrying the ancient dead, copper coins, horse shit, blood, history.

It was too cold, far too cold, and I felt like the wind might tear my wings right off my back. No matter how hard I beat them I couldn't get a purchase on the air. Instinct told me I was too far up, much too far, and I folded my wings back and tried to stretch into another shape.

I was going for raven, but I got rat.

No, anything but rat right now!

I dropped like a stone. I writhed and wriggled helplessly, unsure which way was up and which was down. Fur prickled out all along my face and my whiskers stung, as if the rushing wind was grabbing and pulling at them. My rat nose wriggled in front of me but after the crazy insect senses the air only felt cold. I lashed out, my tail whip-like and strong but grasping and curling in nothingness.

The spider came to me next. Eight legs, eight eyes. Mandibles. I floated on the air, not flying, not falling, just existing in this vast and terrifying place. I could feel the shape of the world below in the currents of the air on the billion miniscule hairs all over me, subtle vibrations that ran up my legs and filled my entire body.

And then my body filled out, changed, shifted one more time. I was numb with cold, aching, bloodied, hardly breathing. But when my feathers caught the air, I soared.

My sight flooded back, so far beyond what I'd had as a human that I tumbled and dived, distracted by the glinting windows of buildings, the cars, the people, the shimmering beautiful grey of the Thames.

I found the air again, beat my great black wings and swept up and over London Bridge, following the air currents wherever they wanted to take me, coasting with ease over rooftops and around spires and down between the valleys of buildings.

I twirled over the river, tipping this way and that, so fast it almost took my breath away.

I ached all over. I could feel and smell blood in my beak and in my feathers. And I wasn't exactly a hundred per cent triumphant. Victoria still had the Conspiracy stone.

Something bubbled up inside me and I laughed; a loud, throaty, slightly hysterical *cawww!*

Everything made sense. I don't know if I believe in destiny, but I'd taken responsibility for the stones, and as it turned out, it was my responsibility to take. I had the fate of all my friends to worry about, maybe the fate of the world – but I *wanted* that worry. I held it to my heart and loved it for what it was. A life. A purpose. *Mine.*

I spiralled away over the glinting grey tide of the Thames with a few strong beats of my aching wings.

Mo was waiting for me, back in Acton, with Addie. I pointed my beak to the West – easy, instinctive, even if I hadn't had London spread out below me like a map.

I soared. I was no longer earthbound. I was free.

Chapter Twenty-Nine

I landed on Susanne's front garden fence and shifted my weight back and forth for a minute, flexing my tail feathers and looking around, still amazed by the clarity of my vision. I could see every insect on every leaf. There were more greens and browns and blues than I'd ever seen before.

I was going to enjoy being a raven.

I flapped over to the window and looked inside. Susanne's sitting room was crowded with people and animals. I let out a soft *caw* of relief when I saw that Mo was there, human and cleaned up. He looked a little green, and he kept picking up his mug of tea, blowing on it and putting it down again with shaking hands. But he was alive. He had a big bandage around his ear, and it wasn't even too soaked with blood.

James, Don, Ben and Randhir were in human form as well, arranged around the room perched on the edges of sofas and tables. Rand had even got his jeans back, though Don was still missing his shirt. Roxie was human too, and treating Ben's cuts and bruises with Susanne's first aid kit. There were four rats on the coffee table. Addie trotted up and laid her head on the table beside them, swishing her brush, and none of them seemed to try to shoo her away.

I didn't see Peter anywhere. But I did see Marcus, and someone I didn't recognise. She was a white lady with very red hair and thick-rimmed black glasses. She was taking in the scene around her with an expression of pure bewilderment, which turned to shock and revulsion when two spiders crawled up the arm of the sofa beside her, one clinging on to the other's back.

Susanne walked into the room and handed the woman a teacup with a kindly, but rather stressed smile.

Was that everyone? I tried to count off on my fingers, but I didn't have fingers, or even paw pads – just three sharp toes on each foot and a bunch of wing feathers.

I took a deep breath, ruffled myself up and tapped on the window with my beak.

Mo leapt out of his chair and almost tripped over Addie.

"It's a raven!" he shouted, pointing. The humans got to their feet and the rats all froze. The poor woman with the red hair just looked confused. I hopped down from the window onto the garden path. A second later, Mo tore the front door open.

"Who are you? What do you want?" he gasped. "What has she done with Meg?"

I hesitated, and then threw out my wings and put my head down. My beak softened and lengthened and I fell, clumsily onto my front as my talons shifted into back legs and my feathers turned into fur. For a second I was half-fox, half-raven, and then I was all fox.

Mo stared at me. I looked up at him. His eyes filled with tears. “Meg,” he gasped.

Then a fuzzy orange bullet shot out from between his legs and cannoned into me.

“Ow, Addie, ow,” I said, as she licked me all over.

“I told them! I said you wouldn’t just die like that.”

“Come on Addie, let her come inside,” said Susanne, steering Mo out of the way. I went in, with Addie trotting at my heels and panting.

I went upstairs to turn human and get dressed. Peter was asleep in Mo’s room, so I put on a skirt of Susanne’s and a T-shirt of Mo’s from the laundry pile in the bathroom. It smelled like him. I felt a bit stupid for enjoying it.

“Meg? Are you decent? And human?” Mo’s voice came softly up the stairs.

“Yes, both,” I said, quickly smoothing the T-shirt down. “At least... somewhat both.” I smiled at him as he emerged from the stairwell.

He stood on the landing, smiling weakly at me. “Thatch,” he said. “There’s a cup of tea for you downstairs.”

“Yeah. It was all I could think of,” I said. My eyes strayed to his bandage. “Are you all right? Is it...”

“Well, it’s... gone. But I’m OK. I am now, anyway.” His eyes were dark and watery. I blushed. “Meg,” he said. “Um.” He took a step toward me, and then a sort of sidestep, as if he wasn’t sure whether to change his mind.

"We should go downstairs," he said. "We've got a lot to talk about."

I nodded. "We've got two stones, and no full groups to protect them."

"Fran's still out there, and so's Ryan."

"Victoria knows our hiding places. She knows where we live."

"She's still got the Conspiracy stone, *and* the actual Conspiracy."

We nodded at each other some more.

"I was so scared," he said. "I didn't want to die without... without telling you that I... think you're a great artist."

I felt a laugh bubble up inside me. *Mo, you are secretly a coward. Well, fine. If you're not going to do it, I bloody will.*

"She picked you to torture because she knew I had feelings for you." I opened my hands, offering up my statement of surprisingly obvious fact.

He smiled.

It's quite hard to kiss and smile at the same time. Your teeth tend to get in the way, and they did, a little. It didn't seem to matter. Mo tasted of warmth and spices and blood and someone else's tongue, which isn't really a taste but more of an experience. His knees tangled with mine and my hands went wandering over the back of his shirt.

We pulled away and he planted another kiss, soft and sweet, on my left temple.

"All of this has been a shit first date, let's have a better second one, OK?" He straightened his T-shirt, and then mine, apparently just for something to do with his hands. I nodded, because if I opened my mouth my heart might have fallen out and gone splat at his feet and that's just not attractive at all.

Susanne met us at the bottom of the stairs with Thatch's cup of tea. I sipped it gratefully.

"I think they're all hoping you have a plan," she warned me, with a glance back at the crowded sitting room.

"I don't," I said. "But that's OK. We can make one together." I smiled up at Mo and he put his hand on my shoulder. "Although," I added thoughtfully, "There is one thing I definitely want to do."

My wings sliced the night air and I circled the Tower of London in a wide arc, riding the current of warmer air that rose from the buildings, my feathers fluttering as I turned my whole body to steer myself in closer. The stones rushed past in a blur and I veered away again, chickening out from attempting to land.

This sounded like such a good idea when I was telling the assembled shifters in Susanne's house – or maybe it was just that they knew they didn't have to come so they were all for it. The top of the White Tower wasn't exactly a small target, but perhaps I should've done a bit more flying practice first.

No, I could do this. I circled the Tower a couple more times, and then let myself gently float down to land on the roof. I stumbled and fell at the last minute, tumbling over and over in a confused mess of black feathers. But nobody had seen me, so at least I my dignity was intact, if not all of my plumage. I hopped to my talons and settled in to wait.

I didn't have to wait long. A cawing started up down below. The ravens were sounding the alarm. They knew I was here. Only another minute or so passed before the first black shapes zipped past the edges of my vision. A raven shot past me with a tearing sound, and then I was surrounded. Five Yeoman Warders in the shape of birds. I twitched my tail feathers. Maybe that meant they hadn't found the sixth yet – the security guard who discovered Blackwell's body. Maybe I could still get to him first. But that was a task for another day.

"Who are you?" demanded one of the ravens. "What are you doing here?"

I tilted my head to one side in amusement.

Thanks for the perfect lead-in, Chief Yeoman Warder Phillips.

"My name is Meg, and I'm here because you're all traitors and thieves," I cawed, holding my head high and hopping around so that I could look at each of the corrupt Warders in turn. "I'm here to tell you that we know what you did. We know you sold your stone to Victoria. We also know that she doesn't care about you, or your Tower, or your traditions. I came to tell you that no matter what she does, we're still here, and we're still fighting. I came to say: we're going to win this fight. You need to make sure you know which side you're on."

And then I took off, wheeling up into the sky and away over the glittering river.

Acknowledgments

Some very heartfelt thanks:

To Catherine Pellegrino, the greatest agent, for believing in me and *Skulk* and for being patient and kind and generally wonderful throughout the whole agent-finding and submissions process.

To my brilliant editor Amanda, for saying all the things I knew deep down and helping me figure out how to make the book so much better. And to the Strange Chemistry team and all the other writers for being incredibly welcoming and helpful. (And for the *Skulk* symbol – I'm still not over how much I love that thing.)

To my Mum and Dad and Lizzie, thank you all for not really minding that I spent my teenage years shut up in my room writing on a very loud keyboard at all hours of the night. Thanks Mum for Wodehouse and Discworld, Lizzie for *Sandman* and *Hellblazer*, and Dad for everything.

To the entire Working Partners crew, for the support and the opportunities to write and improve, and for all the drinks. Thanks for still being interested even when my answer to "how's the book going?" was just "aaaaaaaaaaaaargh". You are all the actual best.

To the Scoobies and the Undiscovered Voices team, especially Sara O Connor and Sara Grant for giving me and so many others the biggest and best career boost ever. I probably wouldn't have ever actually finished *Skulk* if it hadn't been for UV2012, and I would definitely not be where I am now if it wasn't for Sara G's incredible talent for cheerleading and being wonderful.

To Imogen, who is the best audience, for fifteen years of nerd joy and unconditional writing love. You should write things. It's in a book so it must be true.

And obviously to Jessie, who was always there when I needed her and away when I needed to be alone, who read and helped with so many things, who had to live with me while I was writing and rewriting this book and still loved me even when I was stressed and horrible and didn't do the washing up. Thank you. (And Goph.)

EXPERIMENTING WITH YOUR IMAGINATION

"Exciting, funny, clever, scary, captivating, and – most importantly – really, really awesome."
James Smythe, author of The Testimony